BLOOD THREAT & FEARS

*Thirty-Three Great Tales
of Psychological Suspense*

Edited by

CYNTHIA MANSON

BARNES
&NOBLE
BOOKS
NEW YORK

This edition published by Barnes & Noble, Inc.,
by arrangement with Dell Magazines,
a division of Bantam Doubleday Dell Publishing Group, Inc.

1993 Barnes & Noble Books

Book design by Jim Sarfati

ISBN 1-56619-134-3

Printed and bound in the United States of America

M   9   8   7   6   5   4   3   2   1

ACKNOWLEDGMENTS

We are grateful to the following for permission to use their copyrighted material:
"Night Watch Hero" by Paul Amedick, copyright © 1982 by Davis Publications, Inc., reprinted by permission of the author; "When This Man Dies" by Lawrence Block, copyright © 1964 by H.S.D. Publications, Inc., © renewed 1991 by Davis Publications, Inc., reprinted by permission of Knox Burger Associates; "Dead Man's Switch" by Bill Crenshaw, copyright © 1984 by Davis Publications, Inc., reprinted by permission of the author; "The Letter Carrier" by Kathryn Gottlieb, copyright © 1979 by Davis Publications, Inc., reprinted by permission of Elizabeth Gottlieb; "Babysitter" by Dion Henderson, copyright © 1961 by H.S.D. Publications, Inc., © renewed 1988 by Davis Publications, Inc., reprinted by permission of the Larry Sternig Literary Agency; "Going to Meet Terry" by Rick Hills, copyright © 1982 by Davis Publications, Inc., reprinted by permission of the author; "Minutes of Terror" by Donald Honig, copyright © 1974 by Donald Honig, reprinted by permission of Raines & Raines; "The Ghost of Monday" by Andrew Klavan, copyright © 1987 by Davis Publications, Inc., reprinted by permission of the author; "The Innocence of Rachel Crewe" by Virginia Moriconi, copyright © 1982 by Davis Publications, Inc., reprinted by permission of the JCA Literary Agency; "Killer in the House" Jas. R. Petrin, copyright © 1988 by Davis Publications, Inc., reprinted by permission of the author; "A Summer Night's Visitor" by Gordon A. Reims, copyright © 1987 by Davis Publications, Inc., reprinted by permission of the author; "A Good Head for Murder" by Charles W. Runyon, copyright © 1974 by H.S.D. Publications, Inc., reprinted by permission of Scott Meredith Literary Agency; "The Wide and Starry Sky" by Michael Shaara, copyright © 1958 by H.S.D. Publications, Inc., © renewed 1985 by Davis Publications, Inc., reprinted by permission of the Estate of Michael Shaara; "The Man on the Stair" by Bryce Walton, copyright © 1973 by H.S.D. Publications, Inc., reprinted by permission of Scott Meredith Literary Agency; all stories have previously appeared in ALFRED HITCHCOCK MYSTERY MAGAZINE, published by Bantam Doubleday Dell Magazines.

"Dr. Temple is Dead" by William Bankier, copyright © 1979 by Davis Publications, Inc., reprinted by permission of Curtis Brown Ltd.; "My Son, My Son" by Robert Barnard, copyright © 1992 by Bantam Doubleday Dell Magazines, reprinted by permission of Sterling Lord Literistic, Ltd.; "See How They Run" by Robert Bloch, copyright © 1973 by Davis Publications, Inc., reprinted by permission of the author; "From the Balcony" by Christianna Brand, copyright © 1981 by Christianna Brand, reprinted by permission of Brandt & Brandt Literary Agents, Inc.; "The Anderson Boy" by Joseph Hansen, copyright © 1983 by Davis Publications, Inc., reprinted by permission of Curtis Brown Ltd.; "East Wind" by Daphne du Maurier from THE REBECCA NOTEBOOK AND OTHER MEMORIES by Daphne du Maurier, copyright © 1980 by Daphne du Maurier, reprinted by permission of Doubleday, a division of Bantam Doubleday Dell Publishing Group, Inc.; "The Other Side of the Wall" by Stanley Ellin, copyright © 1972 by Stanley Ellin, reprinted by permission of Curtis Brown Ltd.; "The Marked Man" by David Ely, copyright © 1979 by Davis Publications, Inc., reprinted by permission of Roberta Pryor, Inc.; "The Moon was To Blame" by Antonia Fraser, copyright © 1989 by Antonia Fraser, reprinted by permission of Curtis Brown, Ltd., "Golden Tuesday" by Celia Fremlin, copyright © 1972 by Davis Publications, Inc., reprinted by permission of Gregory & Radice Authors' Agents; "Ted Bundy's Father" by Ruth Graviros, copyright © 1989 by Davis Publications, Inc., reprinted by permission of the author; "A Place of her Own" by Joyce Harrington, copyright © 1979 by Davis Publications, Inc., reprinted by permission of Scott Meredith Literary Agency; "Things Had Gone Badly" by Patricia Highsmith, copyright © 1980 by Davis Publications, Inc., reprinted by permission of McIntosh & Otis, Inc.; "In the Clear" by Patricia

McGerr, copyright © 1978 by Davis Publications, Inc., reprinted by permission of Curtis Brown Ltd.; "The New Girl Friend" by Ruth Rendell, copyright © 1983 by Davis Publications, Inc., reprinted by permission of Sterling Lord Literistic, Ltd.; "At a Rest Stop South of Portland" by Robert Twohy, copyright © 1989 by Davis Publications, Inc., reprinted by permission of the author; "Placebo" by Andrew Vachss, copyright © 1989 by Davis Publications, Inc., reprinted by permission of Cohn, Glickstein & Lurie; "The Girl of my Dreams" by Donald E. Westlake, copyright © 1979 by Davis Publications, Inc., reprinted by permission of the author; "Meet Me by the Mannequin" by Cornell Woolrich, copyright © 1940 by Cornell Woolrich, © renewed, reprinted by permission of Scott Meredith Literary Agency; all stories have previously appeared in ELLERY QUEEN'S MYSTERY MAGAZINE, published by Bantam Doubleday Dell Magazines.

CONTENTS

INTRODUCTION

*B*lood, Threat & Fears presents thirty-three stories of psychological suspense selected from *Ellery Queen's Mystery Magazine* and *Alfred Hitchcock Mystery Magazine*. This anthology includes an impressive lineup of authors who probe the darkest depths of the human psyche on terrifying journeys into madness. Many of these thought-provoking tales concern twisted affairs of the heart, the kind that can drive a person to the edge, and over it to commit heinous acts.

The masters of suspense represented here include Cornell Woolrich, Celia Fremlin, Christianna Brand, Daphne Du Maurier, Patricia Highsmith, and Stanley Ellin, all of whom draw us into the warped minds of their central characters in a way that allows us a clearer understanding of the motivations for their irrational behavior.

Among the stories not to be missed is Robert Bloch's amusing yet dark tale of an unemployed and depressed television writer who keeps a journal of his therapy sessions as he sinks from bad to worse. In Patricia McGerr's brilliantly crafted story "In the Clear," a bizarre twist of fate finds a murderer caught between guilt and innocence because of his all too clever plan for a perfect crime. Robert Twohy's story "At a Rest Stop South of Portland," profiles a female protagonist as a killer who is deeply psychologically damaged. She battles her demons from the past in the present, rechristening herself "Park Warrior." "My Son, My Son," is a poignant story by Robert Barnard in which a father invents an imaginary son who becomes real (to him). Ruth Rendell takes a different angle on sexual identity which leads to betrayal and murder in "The New Girl Friend."

Psychological suspense is a subject of keen interest to both mystery writers and readers: we hope you will have your fair share's worth in this anthology. For fear of keeping you in suspense any longer, read on and enter a landscape of distorted but fascinating thought and emotion. And that's no idle threat!

—Cynthia Manson

In the Clear

PATRICIA McGERR

Frank Crawford was a careful man. Before taking any important action he figured the odds, balanced the gains against the costs, and made detailed plans. Although a moderate gambler, he did not bet more than he could afford to lose, seldom backed a longshot, and never drew to an inside straight. When his marriage at last became intolerable, he studied his alternatives with the same cautious deliberation that he gave a sales campaign for his appliance company.

After nearly 20 years of marriage the only feeling he had for Doris was a kind of mild contempt. The pleasing plumpness of girlhood had become middle-aged obesity. They had few common interests and her striving for intellectual improvement made her, in his eyes, an even greater bore. But she was an adequate housekeeper and put good meals on the table whenever he chose to come home to eat them.

For other satisfactions he looked elsewhere and had a long-standing arrangement with the manicurist in a shop near his office. Inge, though attractive and compliant, was not irreplaceable and he had no wish to make their relationship legal. Doris, on her side, was willing to ignore his infidelity as long as it did not disturb her comfortable existence. Thus there evolved a pattern that made it convenient for them to stay together while leading mainly separate lives. Neither had any reason to seek a change until Julie Casement came to work for the agency that handled Frank's advertising.

Julie was small and slim with shaggily clipped black hair and large trusting brown eyes. Frank took her to dinner and when the evening ended he tried to analyze his odd sense of exaltation. The feelings she stirred in him were different from any he had ever known. Desire was softened by tenderness. He wanted to protect her from all the hurts of the world, even from himself. I'm in love, he decided with astonishment, in love for the first time in my life.

But she turned down his next invitation after one of her co-workers told her he was married. The regret in her tone encouraged him to argue, but it was no use.

"I suppose I sound dreadfully old-fashioned," she admitted, "but it's the way I was raised. I can't go out with you again."

"You must know there's more between us than a casual encounter," Frank persisted. "I care for you, Julie. Last night I thought you felt the same way."

"I do. But there's no point in talking about it. Please don't make it any more painful for me."

"I never want to cause you pain."

"Then say goodbye now. That's all there is to say."

He heard the click of her phone and put his own down more slowly. She was so dear, so good, so defenseless. She needed him to look after her. That evening at dinner he raised for the first time the question of divorce.

"You got some girl in trouble?" Doris asked harshly.

"Of course not."

"Then why the sudden rush to break up our marriage?"

"It's not sudden. Our marriage has been unsatisfactory for many years."

"You may not be satisfied," she countered, "but I am. I don't intend to change my whole way of life just because some bit of fluff has caught your eye."

Leaving the table, he drove across town to Inge's apartment. Responding curtly to her greeting, he strode to the kitchen and poured a generous measure of Scotch.

"What's bugging you?" she asked. "Your old lady giving you a hard time?"

"What's that to you?"

"My, we are in a foul mood. If you don't want to talk to me, why did you come?"

In answer he pulled her toward him and pressed his mouth on hers with a roughness that made her wince. Later, when he left her, his tension was somewhat eased but his spirits were still low. I've got two women, he thought morosely. Two bad bargains. Doris, fat and silly. Inge, hard and greedy. Then there's Julie. Gentle and sweet and unattainable.

Lying awake, he thought about divorce. Doris' opposition might wilt under pressure, but the price would be prohibitive. Living in a community property state, she'd take half of his savings, plus high alimony. He wanted Julie to have a life of luxury, not to scrimp on Doris' leavings. Nor should he make Julie, with her high standards, the cause of a messy divorce. But if Doris should die . . .

In the dark he let his mind play with the picture of himself as widower. Lonely, bereft, turning to Julie for comfort. Ah, yes, that would bring her to him. If only Doris were dead!

It was a concept to which his mind returned again and again in the days that followed. He began to look at his wife with eyes that saw her not as a woman but as a victim. His fantasies showed him a variety of methods—knife and gun, rope and poison. But he knew that when a woman is murdered, her husband is the Number One suspect. And if the investigation shows that the marriage was unhappy and the man had a younger mistress, the police will look no further. Yet if he ruled out both divorce and death, what was left? A long arid stretch of life without Julie.

What he needed was an undetectable poison or a weight that would drop on her head when he was far away. But those were, he knew, impossible dreams. If he killed Doris, he'd go to prison. If he divorced her, he'd be impoverished. He was in a trap with no exit. As a realist, he was learning to live with that fact until one afternoon he saw Julie. She was walking beside a well-dressed young man, her faced raised to look up at him, absorbed in their conversation. The sight of her with someone else, the thought that he might lose her, was like a stab of physical pain. That was when he thought of Gregor.

Gregor operated a newsstand on a downtown street corner. In addition to papers and magazines, he sold candy, gum, cigarettes, and postcards. He also took bets on numbers and on a variety of sporting events. Through him, according to rumor, one could obtain loans at usurious interest. It was assumed, though no one said it out loud, that he had underworld connections.

Frank waited until evening, after the brisk rush-hour business, then approached to put $20 on a favorite in the next day's races. The transaction completed, he said with careful casualness, "By the way, a friend of mine has a problem. There's a guy who's—well, in his way, if you know what I mean. You know anybody who might—uh—have him taken care of?"

"Maybe." Without changing expression, Gregor scribbled numbers on a scrap of paper and handed it to Frank. "Ask for Dr. Brill."

"Doctor?"

"If he's looking for a permanent cure."

"Can you tell me what the—uh—doctor charges?"

"Two grand for a routine job with no complications."

"How does—"

"Look, you got the number. Tear it up, give it to your friend, do what you want. But don't tell me any more, don't ask me. You walk away and I forget we ever had this talk. Okay?"

"Right, Gregor."

He was trembling when he left him, the hand that held the phone number thrust deep in his pocket. I can't do it, he told himself. To put out a—what's the word?—a contract on Doris. To hire someone to kill her. It's a crazy notion. But he memorized the number before he burned the paper and he knew, deep within himself, that some day he'd make the call.

For the rest of the week he thought of little else. He must not be rash or hasty. Before he took an irrevocable action, he must study all the angles, make careful preparations. First, there was the money. If Doris died violently, recent large cash withdrawals from his account would be a signal to investigators. Instead he began to squirrel small sums away in a metal box locked in the bottom drawer of his desk. A run of winning hands at his regular Friday-night poker session brought in over $300 which went into the box intact on Monday morning.

While the fund grew he also gave thought to eliminating, or at least obscuring, his motive. On Doris' birthday he invited another couple to dine with them at the city's best hotel. There he presented her with an expensive amber necklace and was, through the evening, ostentatiously kind and attentive.

"What are you up to?" she asked suspiciously when they were alone. "Buttering me up for something, I can see that."

"We're stuck with each other, old girl," he said with false jollity. "Why not make the best of it? It wasn't bad in the beginning, you know. If we both try a little, maybe we can get back to that."

"I guess it won't hurt to try," she conceded.

As his next move he brought home a packet of travel brochures with the suggestion that they celebrate their wedding anniversary on a Mediterranean cruise. He could count on her to display the folders to her bridge and luncheon partners who would become, if needed, witnesses to his concern for his wife's happiness. If needed. That remained the operative phrase. Several times he came close to calling the number given him by Gregor. Each time he drew back.

What finally decided him was a story in the Monday morning paper linking a series of robberies that had taken place throughout the city and its suburbs during the past few months. The method of operation was, according to police, similar enough to point to a single perpetrator, nicknamed the Bike Bandit because a motorcycle had, in several instances, been heard or seen near the scene of the crime. Seven residents had returned from an evening out to find their homes stripped of money, jewelry, and other small valuable objects. An eighth, surprising the thief in the act, had been struck with a heavy candlestick and left unconscious. She was recovering in a local hospital.

Frank, reading the story a second time, knew that if he was ever going to act, it had to be now. He left his office shortly before noon to make the call from an outdoor booth in an isolated area. When a voice said, "Answering Service," he asked for Dr. Brill.

"Leave your name and number and the doctor will call back."

"This is Mr. Smith," Frank said, and read off the number from the dial. He had about a ten-minute wait.

"Dr. Brill here." The new voice was clear and authoritative. "To whom am I speaking?"

"Mr. Smith. Gregor said you can help me with a—a permanent cure."

"You know the terms?"

"He told me two thousand."

"Right, if it's a standard operation."

"I thought it might be made to look like the Bike Bandit."

"That can be arranged. What's the patient's name and address?"

"Mrs. Frank Crawford, 4100 Ringold Road."

"Have you set a date?"

"She'll attend a lecture from eight to nine thirty on Friday evening and get home about ten. If someone can be waiting in the house—"

"We'll handle the details. What about the husband? Will he be with her?"

"No, he has other plans for the evening."

"I assume you have the money ready."

"Yes."

"Then follow these instructions. Put the two grand in a plain brown envelope and leave it in locker number twenty-three at the airport before five p.m. on Wednesday. Got that?"

"Yes. Locker twenty-three on Wednesday. What about the key?"

"We don't need it. Just be sure the case is there on time."

"If you get full payment in advance, how do I know you'll carry out your end of the bargain?"

"How do you know a mechanic puts the parts he charges for in your car? You have to trust us, Mr. Smith. If you don't—well, it's your decision. If the money's in the box on Wednesday, the operation will take place Friday night. If not, the deal is off. No hard feelings either way."

Dr. Brill broke the connection but it was almost a minute before Frank hung up and walked out of the booth. I've done it, he thought. I've hired a killer. His mind veered away from the picture of Doris' dead body. He couldn't go through with it. He wasn't a murderer. He'd take the money from his desk, deposit it in the bank, and that would be the end of it. It would be as if the phone call had never been made.

But on Wednesday, Julie brought over an ad layout for his approval, and seeing her rekindled his desire. As soon as she left he sealed the money in an envelope and drove to the airport. On the way back he dropped the locker key into a roadside trashcan. His decision was irreversible.

On Thursday he stopped at the travel agency to make reservations on the cruise ship Doris had chosen. She was almost childishly pleased when he told her about it that evening. Everything was done. In one more day he'd be free. Then, on Friday morning, there was an unexpected snag. The man at whose house that night's poker session was scheduled came down with flu. Another player phoned to say the game was canceled.

"Oh, no!" Frank exclaimed. "We can't call it off now. We'll get a substitute."

"The problem is a place to play. Can you take us in?"

"No, that's not possible. How about Jim?"

"He's having his place painted. What's so bad about missing one week's game? You feeling lucky?"

"No, I just—" He paused, his mind working quickly. He'd overreacted. Mustn't leave the impression that the cancellation was important. "The thing is, my wife's going to an art lecture and if I tell her there's no game, she'll try to drag me along."

"I see your problem, pal." The other man chuckled. "My advice is, don't tell her. See you next week."

Frank sat looking at the silent phone. Damn. Damn. Damn! It was too perfect. I should have known something would go wrong. What do I do now? Call off the operation or postpone it? But the groundwork is all laid. It may be weeks before Doris and I have separate engagements for the same evening. And I'm sure Brill doesn't give refunds.

All right, calm down, think it through. All you've lost is an alibi. You've the rest of the day to set up another. Yet each idea was quickly discarded. Whatever he did must look natural. Any uncharacteristic activity would seem just what it was, an attempt to establish an alibi. He wasn't a moviegoer. He didn't bowl or shoot pool. He met his friends and customers for lunch not dinner. There was no one with whom he could, without strangeness, arrange to spend the evening. Except Inge.

His lips twisted wryly at the thought. She'd be a natural enough companion. And useless as an alibi. Who would believe a man's mistress if she said he was with her at the time his wife was murdered? And yet—He held onto her name a little longer. To call Inge when his poker game fell through was completely in character. If he took her to a public place and made sure they were visible and identifiable during the crucial time period, he'd be home free. With a lifting of spirits he reached for the phone.

Having made the date, he began to see ways it might serve as more than a simple alibi. Tonight he'd end the relationship, tell her he didn't intend to call her again. Then he could start fresh with Julie, with no old entanglements, no loose ends. More important, it would be one more piece in the mosaic he was building of an improved marriage.

Through the day he pondered his plans until every detail was perfect. He even rehearsed in the washroom the expression of stunned bereavement he would show the police. By the time he left his office he had begun to believe that the game cancellation was, in fact, a stroke of good luck.

He timed his arrival home for a few minutes before the friend with whom Doris was attending the lecture came by to pick her up. He walked with her to the car and helped her in.

"Have a good time," he told them both, "and soak up lots of culture. It will stand us in good stead in those foreign galleries. Did Doris tell you we're planning a cruise?"

"Yes, it sounds wonderful."

"See you later, hon." He patted her hand before closing the door, then watched with satisfaction as the car drove off. A touching farewell for Sue Farrell to describe when the police questioned her.

A short time later he was on his way to Inge's. Parking in an alley, he locked the car doors but left the lights on. Inge lived on the ground floor of an old remodeled house and he was about to knock on her kitchen door when he realized that if she noticed the car headlights on, he'd have to turn them off. Shaken a little by the near error, he walked around to the front.

Over drinks he told her that he'd reserved a table at a restaurant two blocks away.

"That Spanish place?" she protested. "I want to go some place fancy. You trying to cut expenses?"

"Somebody told me the guitarist is good. I'd like to hear him."

"Yeah? I didn't put on my Sunday best to eat rice and beans at a neighborhood joint."

"It's not that cheap." He cut short the argument. "Anyway, the reservation's made and I'm hungry. If you don't want to go—"

"Oh, all right." Sullenly she gave in. "Some great evening this is going to be."

Inge's shoes were not made for walking and her temper was not improved by Frank's insistence that the restaurant was too close to take his car. Her bad humor too, Frank congratulated himself, is in my favor. When the waiter tells the police we quarreled all through dinner, it will shore up my story of our split. He made no effort to be conciliatory but let her ramble on with her complaints. When the waiter put platters of paella in front of them he said loudly and harshly, "Shut up and eat. I'm sick of your bellyaching."

It was a silent meal. Inge sulked and Frank, secretly rejoicing, maintained an expression of grim displeasure. A mediocre flamenco dancer opened the 9:30 floor show. The guitarist wasn't much better, but Frank applauded with enthusiasm and sent the waiter to request "Adios, muchachas." The guitarist came to their table to lean soulfully over Inge as he sang. Frank thanked him with a five-dollar bill.

"What was that all about?" Inge challenged. "After being so mean all evening, do you think you can get round me with sentimental music?"

"No," he answered. "It's my way of saying goodbye. I won't be seeing you again." He signaled for the check.

"You what?" Smoldering resentment burst into flame. "You think you can brush me off like—like a squeezed lemon? You listen to me, Frank Crawford—"

"There's no need to shout."

"Oh, yes, there is." As expected, her voice rose higher. "You think you can pick me up and throw me away whenever you feel like it. Just let me tell you—"

"Hush, everybody's looking at us." He produced a credit card. The waiter took it and went away.

"I've got feelings too, you know." She pushed away the table and stood up. They were a center of attention for all the nearby diners.

"What do you want?" he asked with deliberate insult. "Severance pay?"

"You'll find out what I want," she said wildly. "You can't treat me like dirt and get away with it."

He signed the check, accepted his card and receipt, and stood. A glance at his watch showed it was 10:10. Right on schedule.

"Come on, let's get out of here." He took her arm. She jerked away and half ran to the door. Passing the matire d' he mumbled in half apology, "The lady's a little upset."

Following her to the street, he let her stay a few paces ahead of him until she reached her apartment. She darted inside and slammed the door. And that suited him just fine. Inge's part in the program was finished and she had, unwittingly, played it superbly.

He returned to the alley. His car was dark, the headlights no longer burning. He got behind the wheel, turned the key in the ignition, but the engine did not respond. As planned, the battery was dead. He walked through the alley to the next block where there was an all-night drugstore.

"Car trouble," he told the man on duty as he headed for the phone booth at the back.

"You'll have a hard time getting someone to fix it this time of night."

"I'm not going to try. It can stay where it is until morning. I just want to use your phone to call a cab."

In the booth he could not resist dialing his own number. It should be all over by now. He listened, hardly breathing, as the phone began to ring in his house. He counted up to ten. There was no answer. Satisfied, he called the cab company and gave the address of the drugstore. When he stepped out of the booth he was surprised to discover that he was drenched in perspiration. He mopped his face with his handkerchief as he moved to the counter and ordered coffee. When it came his hand was shaking so that half of it slopped over the counter as he tried to raise the cup to his lips.

The cab arrived quickly. Riding home he responded in monosyllables to the driver, discouraging conversation. He had to get his nerves under control, examine the plan for any last-minute flaws. He had left the restaurant at 10:15, entered the drugstore at 10:30. Even with wings he could not have got across town and back in that period.

The house, when the cab pulled up, was dark. The meter registered $2.45. Frank affected embarrassment.

"I'm afraid the smallest I have is a fifty," he said. "Can you change it?"

"You kidding, buddy? I don't carry that kind of cash on late night calls. Why didn't you break it in the drugstore?"

"I just wasn't thinking. If you'll come to the house with me, I'll get it from my wife."

"Okay, if that's how it's got to be." Grumbling, he accompanied Frank up the sidewalk. "Looks like your old lady's in bed. She won't like being routed out to pay your fare."

"She'll understand."

"Lucky you. Mine'd raise hell."

The driver waited on the porch while Frank unlocked the door and went inside. He took a quick breath, bracing himself, then flipped the switch that lighted the living room. Doris lay in the middle of the rug, arms outflung, eyes staring, mouth twisted in a grimace. Although the sight was expected, his sense of shock was genuine.

"My God! Doris—oh no!" He turned back to the cabman. "Something terrible has happened."

"What's going on, buddy?" The other man followed him in. "Oh, hey! Look at that! Is she dead?"

"I don't know." He dropped to his knees beside her, took her hand. It was cold, lifeless. "Call a doctor. Tell him to hurry."

"What you want is the police."

"Yes, I—you're right. Will you call them? The phone's in the hall."

"Sure thing." He went out.

Frank moved away from the body to a chair at the far end of the room and listened to the driver tell someone, "A lady's been killed." That's no lady, his mind appended with sick humor, that's my wife. All I have to do now is act dazed, broken, and tell the truth about how I spent the evening. When the driver came back he was slumped in the chair, his face buried in his hands.

"They'll be right over," the cabman reported. "He said for me to stay here and nobody should touch anything."

"Yes, fine. Thank you."

"Sorry about your wife, mister." He offered awkward sympathy. "Must be the guy they call the Bike Bandit. If the cops worked as hard chasing crooks as they do handing out tickets, he'd been in jail weeks ago."

His words rolled on but Frank stopped listening. He kept his face covered, his eyes closed, and his thoughts turned inward. At last the door bell rang, the cabman went to answer it, and the room was suddenly full of men. One of them squatted beside the body. Another crossed the room to Frank who rose to meet him.

"Lieutenant Hamill, Homicide," he identified himself. "This your house?"

"Yes, I—I'm Frank Crawford. And that—" He forced himself to look again at Doris. "That's my wife."

"How about it, Doc?" Hamill asked the man on the floor. "She dead?"

"No doubt of that." He was matter-of-fact. "Offhand, I'd say a blow on the head with a heavy object."

"Okay, boys, you know what to do," Hamill told the others. "Is there some place we can talk, Mr. Crawford?"

"There's a den."

"What about me?" the driver protested. "I've got to get back on the street. I'm losing a night's work."

"Yeah? What's your part in this?"

"I brought the man home. I was with him when he found the body. I'm the one who called to report the crime."

"I haven't paid your fare," Frank remembered. "I was going to get it from—" He looked at the handbag that lay a few feet from Doris' hand and his voice died away.

"Send a bill," Hamill snapped. "Clancy, get the cabbie's story and let him go. All right, Mr. Crawford, take me to the den."

The smaller room showed signs of disarray. Desk drawers were partly open, a cabinet door swung loose. Nothing obvious, just enough to suggest that a search had been made.

"You keep any cash or valuables in here?" Hamill asked.

"No, I—oh!" A delayed memory struck him.

"Yeah? You notice something missing?"

"Not in here. But I just realized, when I found my wife, I—I took her hand—her left hand—and it was bare."

"Bare?"

"No rings. She always wore a big diamond. Almost a carat." Brill's man, he thought, had helped himself to a nice bonus. It was worth it, though, to add credibility.

"I see. Later I'd like you to go through the house and make an inventory of your losses. But first I want to get a sequence of events. When did you last see your wife?"

"About seven thirty this evening." He sat down, clasped his hands to stop their trembling. "A friend of hers picked her up to take her to a lecture."

"You know the friend's name and address?"

As he asked the question, the man he'd called Clancy entered unobtrusively and flipped open a small notebook.

"Mrs. George Farrell." Frank watched Clancy write it down. "She lives on Maple Drive. I'm not sure of the number."

"We can find her. After they left what did you do?"

"I had dinner with a friend."

"His name and address?"

"Actually, it was a woman."

"Oh?"

"Inge Ericson. 1421 Grant Street."

Again Clancy's pen moved. He and Hamill exchanged glances.

"I might as well tell you the truth, Lieutenant." Frank did not try to hide his embarrassment. "Inge and I were more than just friends. We've been having—well, I guess you'd call it an affair. But it's over. That's why I went to see her tonight—to break it off."

"Yeah?" the lieutenant's tone was neutral, showing neither belief nor doubt. "How come?"

"To be honest, my wife and I have been through some bad times. I wasn't the best of husbands—you'll hear that from a lot of people. But lately we've made an effort and it was starting to work. We planned to go on a cruise, a sort of second honeymoon. Doris was really looking forward to that. And now—now she'll never—" He broke off, covered his eyes with his hand, and held the pose for several seconds. Then he straightened and made a brave attempt to smile. "Sorry," he said. "Anyway, that's what I had to tell Inge."

"I see." Skepticism broke through. "What you're telling me, Mr. Crawford, is that at the time of your wife's murder you were in your girl friend's apartment saying goodbye forever. I assume that Miss—Ericson, is it?—will tell the same story."

"We didn't stay in her apartment." Frank felt a secret pleasure at the way the detective had swallowed his bait. "Inge's got a temper, and I figured she'd take the news better if there were other people around. So we went to a restaurant near where she lives. La Paloma." Got that, Clancy? he wanted to add.

"And then?"

"We had something to eat, watched the floor show, and I told her what I'd come to say."

"How'd she react?"

"She blew up a little and I took her home."

"How long did you stay in her apartment?"

"I didn't go in. She was still sore and there was nothing more to talk about, so I came home."

"Don't you have a car, Mr. Crawford?"

"Lord, yes, I almost forgot that part. I drove to Inge's but La Paloma is in walking distance. Then when I tried to start my car, I found I had a dead battery. It's still parked there."

"How'd you get the cab?"

"I phoned from a drugstore at the corner of 15th and Stevens. When we got here all I had was a bill too big for him to change. That's why he came into the house with me. I was going to get some money from Doris, but instead—" Again he gave way to emotion, hiding his face.

"That jibe with the hacker's story?" Hamill asked Clancy.

"Yeah. His sheet shows a pickup at ten thirty-five and we got the call at eleven twenty-seven."

"That fits. Get somebody to interview Mrs. Farrell, find out when she brought Mrs. Crawford home, what she saw and heard. Also check the restaurant, the drugstore, and the Ericson girl."

"Will do."

Clancy left. Hamill waited for Frank to recover. When he looked up, the detective's eyes were more sympathetic.

"I know this is a bad time for you, Mr. Crawford, but you've given us a straight story. I'm sure you understand that in a murder case, everything has to be doublechecked."

"You have your job to do." He matched the other's courtesy. "I'll do anything I can to help catch my wife's killer."

"We'll get him," Hamill promised. "The routine's going on while I talk to you."

As if in proof one of his subordinates came to the door. "The doc's finished," he reported. "Okay to take the body away?"

"Got enough pictures?"

"From every angle."

"Okay, let the morgue have her. What else do you know?"

"There are signs of forced entry by the back door. A couple of the neighbors say they heard a sound like a motorcycle being gunned around 10 P.M."

Coincidence, Frank wondered, or part of the special Brill service?

The younger man left and Hamill turned back to Frank, his manner distinctly more friendly.

"We're getting a pattern," he said. "Maybe you've heard of a string of recent housebreakings?"

"The taxi driver said something about a—was it a Bike Bandit?"

"That's what the newspapers call him. He picks houses with no lights and no television playing and the occupants out for the evening. He steals small things, like money and jewelry, that he can carry on his motorcycle."

"Like my wife's ring."

"Exactly. Let's look around and see what else is missing."

With Hamill behind him Frank went upstairs and into Doris' bedroom. Like the den it gave the impression of a fast search. A jewel box lay open, its contents dumped in the middle of the bed.

"It's mostly costume jewelry," Frank said. "But she had a couple of good pieces—an amber necklace and a bracelet of heavy gold." He poked among the scattered articles. "They're not here."

"So he took the good stuff and left the junk. He knows values."

Continuing the inspection, Frank found that a pair of gold cufflinks had been taken from his bureau. That appeared to be the extent of the burglar's haul. They were in his bedroom when the phone rang. It was for Lieutenant Hamill. He listened for a long time, responding with grunts and short exclamations that apparently expressed satisfaction with what he heard.

"That about covers it," he concluded, "except for Ericson. Get her story and we'll have the whole package. I'll be here for another hour or so." He put down the phone "Your account is fully corroborated," he told Frank. "The restaurant owner, the waiter, even the guitar player—they all remember you. Your girl friend must have made quite a row."

"She was pretty mad," he agreed.

"The druggist remembers you too. And of course the cab company has a record of your call."

"Has someone talked to Mrs. Farrell?"

"Yes, she said the lecture ended about nine thirty and she drove your wife right home. The house was dark and everything looked normal."

"That's not much help."

"No, but at least the timing puts you in the clear. If you'll excuse me, I'll get on with my job. We have to go over the whole house for prints, et cetera. The fellow didn't leave any evidence in the other places, but sometimes they get careless and we get lucky. If you want to go to bed—"

"Thank you, no. I couldn't sleep. But I'll stay out of your way."

Frank remained upstairs while the lieutenant rejoined his associates. You're in the clear. In the clear. Hamill's words echoed soothingly in his brain. The tension that had carried him through the evening gave way to euphoria. His alibi was watertight and he was in the clear. Free of Doris. Free of suspicion. $2000 plus a diamond ring, an amber necklace, a gold bracelet, a pair of gold cuff links. He couldn't ask for a better bargain.

He was standing by the window gazing into the dark but contemplating a bright future when Hamill returned. Clancy was with him.

"You've found some evidence?" Frank asked them.

"Not here," Hamill answered. "But something else has come up. Tell me, Mr. Crawford, why did you go all the way to the drugstore to call a cab? Why didn't you use your girl-friend's phone?"

"We'd had a pretty heavy argument, you know about that. I didn't want to go back to her apartment."

"I'm sure you didn't. The druggist said you seemed very nervous, spilled coffee all over his counter."

"I suppose I was a little on edge. First the quarrel with Inge, then a dead battery."

"The cabdriver called you restless and fidgety."

"I may have been. What are you getting at, Lieutenant? What has all this to do with the murder of my wife?"

"With your wife? Not a thing. You know I sent a man to talk to Miss Ericson?"

"I heard you give the order."

"She didn't answer the doorbell and he couldn't get her on the phone. That worried him. Sometimes when a guy dumps a girl, she gets despondent, takes too many pills, or turns on the gas."

"Are you telling me that something's happened to Inge—"

"I think you know the answer to that as well as I do," Hamill snapped. "When they went in, they found her on the floor. The weapon, a heavy brass bookend, was lying by her side."

"Was she—is she—?"

"She's dead, Crawford."

"Oh, no! No, that can't be—"

"She yelled at you in the restaurant," Hamill said. "She made threats. A dozen or more people heard her. When you were back in her apartment, the fight got hotter. She wasn't willing to be dropped, maybe she had blackmail material. So you picked up the bookend, and crushed her skull. Is that how it happened?"

"No! No, you're wrong. I wasn't in her apartment. I only got as far as the door. She slammed it in my face." He paused, remembering how it had been. Himself on the outside, Inge going alone into the dark house. "He must have already been there. The Bike Bandit. He went in while we were at the restaurant. She caught him robbing the place and he—he killed her."

"That's what we were meant to think," Hamill agreed. "Somebody did a good job of imitating the Biker's m.o. It might even have worked if the Bike Bandit hadn't gone out on his own tonight. But we know he was here in your house at ten o'clock. And a man can't be in two places at once, can he, Mr. Crawford?"

Minutes of Terror

DONALD HONIG

*M*el Gifford's house was the last one on the dirt road, which ran nearly a mile in from the highway before becoming a dead end. There were only two other houses along the road and then Gifford's, and beyond that nothing but the pine forest, slowly elevating itself along the mountain slope, rising higher and higher, cresting at two thousand feet. There were ski trails on the other side of the mountain and when the Vermont winter drained the sky of color and spilled its snows, the area became a bustling ski resort.

Now it was November, one of the two transitional seasons (the other occurred in April); the fall foliage was gone and the snows had not yet come. Gifford called it the quiet season. There were no tourists on the roads or in the woods, and things were quieter in town too. Certainly there were fewer people coming into the bank. Many of the local businessmen took their vacations this time of year, just before the onset of the ski season.

"I wish my business were seasonal," Gifford said that morning after the alarm had brought him jarringly awake. He sat up in bed and with dull eyes faced the dim gray morning. Helen had barely moved. He looked at her inert bulk under the covers. No one ever looked graceful lying under covers.

"I said—" he began again.

"I heard you," she said, talking into her pillow.

"I wouldn't mind a month's vacation right now. Hadley left for Florida yesterday, for a month."

Hadley owned the next house down the road. The third house, the one nearest the road, had been rented as a ski lodge for the winter; the owners had already vacated and the new people had not arrived yet. So both houses were empty.

"A whole month," Gifford said, yawning. "He was in the bank the other day to say goodbye. Said he was going to turn off the gas, the electricity, the phone and pack up and go. The lucky stiff."

"You'd better get up," Helen said, "and wake the kids."

Gifford got out of bed and stood by the window. He gazed listlessly for a moment and then, as he turned away, he thought he saw something move among the pine trees. He turned back and stood at the window again, squinting.

"I think I saw a deer," he said.

"Must be a crazy one," Helen said drearily. "Doesn't know the hunting season's started, I guess."

He continued to peer out at the woods, hoping to catch sight of whatever it was that had moved, but all he saw was the extraordinary stillness of the pine in the windless gray light. After several minutes, he said, "I *think* I saw a deer."

"Mel," his wife said, still talking into her pillow, "please wake up the kids. You've got to take them to school."

"And open up the bank and sit behind my desk and smile at everybody. Look, I think I saw a deer and if I did, then it's the most exciting thing that's happened to me in six months."

"Don't be bitter, darling."

"Who's bitter?" he muttered leaving the window.

He put on his bathrobe and walked across the hall, first to Jennifer's room. He opened her door and paused, listening to the seven-year-old snoring lightly. Then he walked to the bed, gazed for a moment at the sleeping face, the dark hair sprawled over the pillow. Gently he put his hand on her shoulder and shook her. A querulous look crossed her sleeping face as she began to turn.

"Good morning, Jennifer," he said.

Her eyes opened, searched sleepily for a moment, then found him standing there by her bed.

"Get up, sweetheart," he whispered.

She stretched and yawned.

"Okay?" he asked.

"Okay."

Then he went to Billy's room. The towheaded eight-year-old was already up.

"I was dreaming, Dad," he said when Gifford walked in.

"Tell me about it later. First, get dressed."

Gifford returned to the bedroom window and peered out again, a puzzled frown on his face. Helen was fully awake now, lying in bed watching him.

"I thought I saw a deer," Gifford said, studying the pine forest with gravely thoughtful eyes. The night shadows seemed to be lingering among the poised, graceful trees. Nothing was moving.

"Maybe it was a hunter," Helen said.

"The woods are posted."

"Since when has that stopped them?"

"Well," Gifford said, "they'd better keep away from here."

After he had washed and shaved and dressed, he sat down to breakfast with his family. Billy and Jennifer yawned, and toyed uninterestedly with their food. Gifford noted it but said nothing; there was a general ennui in the house this morning which was catching.

While Helen helped the children into their coats, Gifford stood at the hall mirror, gazing at himself in a rather detached way. He was thirty-eight and he supposed he looked it. His brown hair had begun to thin. Soft, passive lines were appearing around his mouth. His brown eyes were cool, unreadable, good eyes for a banker to have; good eyes for listening. He thought he was getting a bit flabby, thought he did not really want to admit it. He'd ski again this winter, maybe do some hiking. Tone up those muscles.

He put on his topcoat, opened the door and went outside. He stood on the porch feeling the cool, fresh morning air on his face, then headed for the garage, hoping he wouldn't have any trouble starting the car this morning.

As he approached the garage—the door was open—he turned and looked over his shoulder one more time at the pine forest. Had he seen a deer or not? So he was not looking at the garage and did not see the man step from inside it and stand in the doorway. When Gifford finally did turn back and found himself being confronted by the stranger, they were about ten feet apart. He stopped dead in his tracks.

The man was much younger than Gifford, perhaps in his mid-twenties, but there was a lot of hard experience etched into his face, into the calculating steadiness of his gaze, and in the almost contemptuous nonchalance with which he stood. He was wearing a plaid jacket which was two-thirds unzipped, and one hand was concealed inside, at once calmly and menacingly.

"Who are you?" Gifford asked. "What are you doing in there?"

"Just relax, Mr. Gifford," the man said, the tone of his voice suggesting he was giving some very good advice. "You just keep your head and do as you're asked and nobody is going to get hurt."

"I want to know what you were doing in my garage."

"We were waiting for you."

"We?" Gifford said.

The second man appeared then, stepping out of the garage. This one was older, perhaps Gifford's age, with that same steady gaze that wasn't necessarily hostile or threatening, that was simply there to be observed, noted. He was wearing a trenchcoat and a small felt fedora and he looked almost European. He was holding a small revolver in his hand, pointed at Gifford.

"Get into the house," he ordered.

"Why?" Gifford asked, making a conscious effort not to look at the gun, as if refusing to acknowledge it, its primacy.

"Because I tell you to," the older man said impatiently.

"My family is in there."

"We know that. And the best way you can help them is to do exactly as we say, with a minimum of fuss and talk."

"There isn't much money in the house," Gifford said. "But whatever there is, you're welcome to."

"Just get in the house," the older one repeated, putting the gun in his coat pocket but keeping his hand on it. Gifford turned and, followed by the two men, walked back to the house. The door was still open. He could hear Helen talking to the children.

When she heard his footsteps on the porch, she said, "Don't tell me the car won't start."

When he walked inside, followed by the two men, Helen took one look and moved the children around behind her. She didn't have to be told that this was trouble. It was written on her husband's face.

"It's all right, Helen," Gifford said. "They haven't explained themselves yet, but it's all right."

Helen turned to the children and said, "These are friends of your Daddy's. Say hello to them."

Shyly, the children nodded to the men.

"Now take off your coats and go upstairs to your rooms," Helen told them. "We'll call you when it's time to go."

Slowly, uncertainly, with backward looks, the children went upstairs. The two men smiled pleasantly at them.

When the children were gone, the older one said, "Well, done, Mrs. Gifford. Now, if this kind of cooperation is maintained everything is going to be just fine."

"What do you want?" Helen asked.

"Sit down, both of you," the older one ordered. "It's very simple, really. All cut and dried, from point A to point Z."

The Giffords sat down on the living room sofa. While the younger man lounged in the doorway, his hand still inside his jacket, an expressionless, uncompromising look on his face, the older one stood before the Giffords.

"I'm going to drive into town with you, Mr. Gifford," he said. "My partner is going to remain here, to oversee your wife and children, as a sort of guarantee for your cooperation until our return."

"You mean you're going to hold them hostage," Gifford said angrily.

"Well, yes. I know you don't like it, but it's the best way, all around, believe me. Now, here's what's going to happen. Instead of opening your bank at nine o'clock, as you normally do, you're going to open a bit earlier today, before your staff gets in."

"And you're going to clean it out," Gifford said, "Well, you've overlooked one thing: there's a time lock on the vault. It doesn't open until nine o'clock and there's not a damn thing I can do about it."

The gunman stared sternly at Gifford for a moment, then began to laugh softly. "We know that, Mr. Gifford," he said. "Look, if it makes you feel any better, we're not amateurs. We know about these things. We've been studying you and your bank and the habits and procedures of all concerned. We've been here nearly a week, and the fact that you haven't noticed us tells you something about our expertise."

"You're not perfect," Gifford said. "I saw you in there yesterday at closing time."

The gunman laughed again, a short, mirthless chuckle. "So we're not perfect," he said, "but don't let that reduce your confidence in us. There's nothing like a smalltown bank. You're very trusting people here. You don't lock up all of your cash at night. Your tellers leave their cash drawers full. That's what we want."

Gifford looked at the floor. The man was right. It was not recommended practice, but out of old habits the tellers did leave their cash in their drawers overnight as crime was virtually nonexistent here. Bank robbers or other serious criminals all seemed so remote.

When Gifford looked up at the gunman there was resentment in his eyes, as if his trust had been betrayed.

"Now," the older man said, looking at his watch, "it's exactly seven thirty. The drive into town is forty minutes, which means we arrive at the bank at eight ten. It shouldn't take us more than fifteen minutes to do what we have to do. So it's then eight twenty-five. With the drive back, we should be returning here at a few minutes after nine."

"That's if he doesn't make trouble," the other gunman added.

"Don't worry, Alf," the older one said, smiling at Gifford. "He won't make any trouble. He knows what's at stake, don't you, Mr. Gifford?"

Gifford said nothing.

"Because," the gunman went on, "if we're not back here on time, and let's allow a few minutes for delays, then his family will be in deep trouble. If we're not back by, say, nine twenty, Alf will safely assume that someone tried to upset our plans."

"And then what?" Gifford asked. "What happens then?"

The gunman smiled, shrugged, and said, "Who can tell—with Alf's temper?"

The implied threat infuriated Gifford; the very idea that anyone would think of harming his family almost deranged his thinking for a moment and he had to suppress the impulse to leap at these men.

"All right," the older gunman said curtly, "let's get moving. For you and your family, Mr. Gifford, the clock has begun to tick."

Gifford did not, would not, get up until the revolver had reappeared. Gesturing with it, the gunman brought Gifford to his feet and followed him outside.

"We'll take your car, Mr. Gifford," the man said as they went down the porch steps.

So for the second time that morning, Gifford headed for his garage. This time he went in with his companion, got into his car, and backed out. As he turned to head down the driveway Gifford took a last, longing look back at his house. It suddenly had an aspect of closed, cold inaccessibility. It provoked in Gifford one single, driving resolve: to get this over as quickly as possible and get back to his family. He had no intention of trying to play the hero. They could take the money and be damned.

As he drove toward the highway he passed the two empty houses and for the first time realized how isolated he was back there. He passed the gunmen's car along the side of the road and knew that no one would see it, no one would pass who might be curious enough to question its presence.

When they got to the highway, Gifford pressed down hard on the accelerator and headed for town.

"Please observe the speed limit, Mr. Gifford," the gunman said. "We don't want to break the law," he added with a sardonic chuckle.

They drove in silence after that. Occasionally they exchanged glances and when they did, the gunman nodded politely and showed a faint, whimsical smile.

As they neared town, Gifford broke the silence. "Won't it look strange to people," he said, "you walking into the bank with me?"

"No, the people here don't have suspicious minds. No reason for them to."

"Suppose some of my staff show up early?"

"Have they ever?"

"No," Gifford said glumly. "But what happens when they arrive and the bank is closed?"

"I can tell you what will happen. They'll call your home, where your wife, with Alf standing right next to her, will tell them you overslept and are on your way in."

"But if someone has already seen me there, entering and leaving . . ."

"We'll let them puzzle it out, Mr. Gifford. By the time they begin to become overly-curious, it won't matter any more. Alf and I will be well on our way."

When they reached the bank, Gifford was told to park in the alley adjacent. They got out of the car and, without being seen by anyone, entered the bank. The blinds were drawn, concealing the bank's interior from the street.

"Eight ten on the button," the gunman said with a note of quiet satisfaction in his voice.

Gifford suddenly whirled and confronted him and, in an unnaturally loud voice, asked, "What happens to my family if we don't get back there on time?"

As if annoyed or perhaps alarmed by this sudden belligerence, the gunman drew his revolver.

"I'm asking you a question, damn you!" Gifford shouted, taking a step toward the other, and as he did the gunman lifted the revolver to eye level and pointed it coldly and directly at Gifford.

"Get on with it, Mr. Gifford," he said testily. "If you have your family's well-being at heart you won't tempt the fates by wasting time. Now, you have the keys to those cash drawers, so get on with it."

Gifford got his keys and began unlocking the drawers. The gunman went with him to the tellers' stations, holding a canvas bag which he had pulled from his pocket, and watched Gifford go from drawer to drawer filling it. The gunman had figured fifteen minutes in the bank; it took less than ten.

"All right, Mr. Gifford," the gunman said when all the drawers had been emptied, "now comes the delicate part—walking out of here carrying an obviously stuffed bag. I might add that with the money now in my possession my outlook on things becomes a bit obsessed. The idea of a large sum of money is one thing, the possession of it is another. If anyone challenges us I'm prepared to use this gun—on you or them. Do you understand?"

"I understand," Gifford said.

"So give me your car keys. In the event I have to shoot you dead I'll have to leave in your car."

Frightened now, Gifford handed him the keys. The gunman seemed tense, even angry, as if the mere thought of having to relinquish the money was intolerable.

They opened the door and walked outside. The sidewalk was empty, for which Gifford was grateful, for he had taken quite seriously the man's threats. They walked around to the alley and got into the car, Gifford in the driver's seat. The keys were returned to him.

"Now head back."

"What time is it?" Gifford asked, then looked at his watch. It was eight twenty.

"This is no problem, Mr. Gifford. Just get moving."

Gifford backed out of the alley. Several people passing on the sidewalk seemed to take no notice. In this small, insular New England town they were so conditioned to minding their business that they seemed to feel it was an intrusion even to glance at someone. Gifford damned their aloofness now. If any one of them had any brains they would notice that something was amiss here and call the police—except that the police in this town consisted of two middle-aged men who were totally inadequate to cope with a situation like this.

As they drove back along the highway, Gifford began having some disturbing thoughts. What would happen after they returned? Would the two gunmen simply take the money and leave? The more Gifford thought about it the more his doubts began to grow. At best, they would tie up the family, so as to have ample time in which to get away; and the worst—but Gifford didn't want to think about that.

Grimly silent, Gifford sped along the highway, anxious to get back, to be with his family, to face together whatever happened.

They passed few cars on the highway; there was only the constant passing on either side of the road of the endless evergreen. Between the monotony of the drive and the consuming depths of his thoughts, Gifford was paying only mechanical attention to what he was doing, to the extent that it was the gunman who had to point out that they were nearing the side road.

"The turnoff is coming up," he said, noting that there had been no deceleration to allow for the turn.

His voice barely penetrated Gifford's reverie and, with an uncomprehending expression, he turned his head to look at the man.

"The turn is coming," the gunman yelled, pointing ahead with his finger.

Instinctively, without thinking, without braking or even decompressing the accelerator, Gifford suddenly swung the wheel, but the car was going too fast, the angle too sharp. There was a shuddering and a skidding as the car bounded off the highway onto the dirt road; the trees seemed to be flashing through every window, swooping and abrupt, as if doing some wild dance around the car. Unable to make its turn, the car made a screeching sound and plunged off the dirt road. It bolted furiously through the roadside brush, ran over some scrub pine and came suddenly and barbarously to a stop with a sickening thud against an enormous boulder that had been cast from the mountaintop in another age.

Gifford remembered his head hitting against the window. He thought he had been knocked unconscious then, yet he remembered the car flattening the scrub pine and then the boulder looming up like something rising from the undersea. He also remembered the jolting and unceremonious stop to which they had come, but it was all vague and unreal, ill-recorded by memory.

He was lying against the door, aware of a dull aching in his head, his thoughts unable for the moment to emerge coherently from under the pain. He blinked several times before he was able to understand what it was he was seeing. The hood had been thrown into the air by the impact of the crash and hung now like the open jaw of some voracious bird of prey. He could not immediately remember where he was, what had happened. Then he turned and saw his companion, and he remembered.

The gunman looked as though he had been hurled against the door with great fury; he seemed crushed and crumpled. His face, in profile, wore an expression of shocked anger, made the more furious by a copious flow of blood. His hat was gone and his hair looked as though it had been about to leave his head and then stopped.

Gifford gazed at him with simple, uncomplicated curiosity, until the realization had set fully in—the man was dead.

Then Gifford remembered all the rest of it and a shock of terror rushed through him. He looked at his watch: it was ten minutes after nine. He turned around and stared with building panic at the road, then undid his seat belt and opened the door and got out. He walked around behind the smashed and seething car to the other door and opened it. The gunman, who had not been using his seat belt, tumbled softly to the ground. Gifford reached down and took the revolver out of the man's pocket.

He glanced again at his watch. There was still time. Alf was expecting them back at nine twenty and there would surely be allowed some margin for delay, but how much? He thought about the possibility of going back to the highway and hailing a car but that would consume time.

Another thought occurred: take the bag of money to the house, tell Alf what had happened, and perhaps he would go. The idea was appealing, except that Alf might suspect a trick, might suspect that Gifford was trying to trap him, and in that situation there was no telling what the man might do.

Then, under the pressure of elapsing time, with the determination to help his family, Gifford disdained all further thought and speculation and began to run toward his house, revolver in hand. He passed his neighbors' empty houses. A fleeting thought to break in and telephone the state police had to be rejected; the telephones in both houses had been disconnected.

What am I going to do? Gifford kept asking himself. He couldn't simply burst in there, gun or no gun. There was no telling what Alf's frame of mind was, nor what it would become. Doubtless an awful tension had been building in that house during the past hour. The young gunman had to be getting more and more concerned and nervous, and consequently unpredictable and dangerous.

Gifford stopped in the middle of the road, panting. He lifted his hand and covered his eyes for a moment. Get out of the road, he told himself. Alf would almost certainly be watching the road.

So he began approaching the house in a roundabout way, through the pine forest, moving slowly, cautiously. When the side of the house came into view he lay down on the pine needles, trying to formulate some plan, some kind of assault that held a reasonable chance of success. *Think*, he told himself. *Think. Think.*

He could enter through a basement window, carefully and quietly, and work his way upstairs and take Alf by surprise—but the least sound, with his wife and children sitting in front of a gun . . . He closed his eyes for a moment. Were the basement windows locked? He hadn't checked them in months; there was never reason to, in this "crime-free" environment. If they were locked, how could he get in without breaking one? There was no telling what the least sound might provoke in Alf's mind.

He should have gone back to the highway and summoned help, he realized now. This was foolhardy. He had no experience at this sort of thing. He was jeopardizing his family.

Then, as he lay there agonizing over his situation, a shot suddenly rang out, shattering the pristine silence of the pine forest. Gifford instinctively pressed himself tensely to the ground, his eyes glaring. He looked at his watch: ten minutes after nine.

Only ten minutes after nine?

With his eyes widening in terror he studied the face of the watch. The sweep hand was still. The watch had stopped, probably during the accident. But when? How long ago? How long had he been unconscious in the car?

Now the echo of the shot began to reverberate through him. What was happening in the house?

Without waiting to shape another thought, suddenly seized and impelled by an uncontrollable terror, he got to his feet and began running at breakneck speed for the house, pointing the gun out ahead of him. He crashed through the underbrush and out onto the road, running faster and faster, driven forward by the single, maniacal thought of getting the man who was inside the house, unmindful of his own safety, unencumbered by any idea of stealth or strategy. That was all gone now, replaced by the primitive urge to protect his family.

He ran across the front lawn, took the porch steps in two bounds and burst through the front door. He ran through the front door. He ran through the hallway—and was suddenly confronted by Alf. The gunman was in the act of running from the living room to the hallway, his gun swung out from his body.

Without stopping, Gifford fired, his finger suddenly frozen on the trigger. The revolver's recoil made him shudder and stagger as a fury of motion was enacted before him. The running Alf was struck several times in mid-flight and now his animation became spastic and grotesque as one after the other the bullets struck him. He slammed into the wall, then arched back, spun in a half circle and dropped to the floor.

Gifford raced into the living room where he found his startled wife standing, her clasped hands covering her mouth.

"Where are the children?" Gifford demanded.

Helen gasped, her fixed eyes upon the smoking revolver in her husband's hand.

"Where are they?" Gifford shouted.

"Upstairs," she said in a small, strained voice that sounded like a gasp.

"Are they all right? Are you all right?"

"Yes-yes-yes," Helen said, trembling.

Then she ran to him as Gifford let the gun fall to the floor and he threw his arms around her.

"I heard a shot . . ." he said, wracked by unspent tension.

"He was getting more and more restless and nervous," Helen said. "It was terrible."

"He didn't harm any of you, did he?"

"No."

"But what was he shooting at?" Gifford asked.

"He said he saw something moving in the trees. He thought it was the police. But I saw it. It was only a deer . . . but he didn't believe me."

She looked once at Alf's inert, bloody, bullet-torn body, then closed her eyes and pressed her forehead against Gifford's chest.

"A deer?" Gifford said softly. "That's what he shot at?"

"What happened?" Helen asked. "Are you all right? Are you all right?"

Gifford sighed and shook his head. "Not yet. Give me a little time," he said, closing his eyes as he heard his children calling from upstairs.

The New Girl Friend

RUTH RENDELL

*Y*ou know what we did last time?" he said.

She had waited for this for weeks. "Yes?"

"I wondered if you'd like to do it again."

She longed to but she didn't want to sound too keen. "Why not?"

"How about Friday afternoon then? I've got the day off and Angie always goes to her sister's on Friday."

"Not *always,* David." She giggled.

He also laughed a little. "She will this week. Do you think we could use your car? Angie'll take ours."

"Of course. I'll come for you about two, shall I?"

"I'll open the garage doors and you can drive straight in. Oh, and Chris, could you fix it to get back a bit later? I'd love it if we could have the whole evening together."

"I'll try," she said, and then, "I'm sure I can fix it. I'll tell Graham I'm going out with my new girl friend."

He said goodbye and that he would see her on Friday. Christine put the receiver back. She had almost given up expecting a call from him. But there must have been a grain of hope still, for she had never left the receiver off the way she used to.

The last time she had done that was on a Thursday three weeks before, the day she had gone round to Angie's and found David there alone. Christine had got into the habit of taking the phone off the hook during the middle part of the day to avoid getting calls for the Midland Bank. Her number and the Midland Bank's differed by only one digit. Most days she took the receiver off at nine-thirty and put it back at three-thirty. On Thursday afternoons she nearly always went round to see Angie and never bothered to phone first.

Christine knew Angie's husband quite well. If she stayed a bit later on Thursdays she saw him when he came home from work. Sometimes she and Graham and Angie and David went out together as a foursome. She knew that David, like Graham, was a salesman or sales executive, as Graham always described himself, and she guessed from her friend's lifestyle that David was rather more successful at it. She had never found him particularly attractive, for, although he was quite tall, he had something of a girlish look and very fair wavy hair.

Graham was a heavily built, very dark man with a swarthy skin. He had to shave twice a day. Christine had started going out with him when she was fifteen and they had got married on her eighteenth birthday. She had never really known any other man at all intimately and now if she ever found herself alone with a man she felt awkward and apprehensive. The truth was that she was afraid a man might make an advance to her and the thought of that frightened her very much. For a long while she carried a penknife in her handbag in case she should need to defend herself. One evening, after they had been out with a colleague of Graham's and had had a few drinks, she told Graham about this fear of hers.

He said she was silly but he seemed rather pleased.

"When you went off to talk to those people and I was left with John I felt like that. I felt terribly nervous. I didn't know how to talk to him."

Graham roared with laughter. "You don't mean you thought old John was going to make a pass at you in the middle of a crowded restaurant?"

"I don't know," Christine said. "I never know what they'll do."

"So long as you're not afraid of what I'll do," said Graham, beginning to kiss her, "that's all that matters."

There was no point in telling him now, ten years too late, that she was afraid of what he did and always had been. Of course she had got used to it, she wasn't actually terrified, she was resigned and sometimes even quite cheerful about it. David was the only man she had ever been alone with when it felt all right.

That first time, that Thursday when Angie had gone to her sister's and hadn't been able to get through on the phone and tell Christine not to come, that time it had been fine. And afterwards she had felt happy and carefree, though what had happened with David took on the coloring of a dream next day. It wasn't really believable. Early on he had said:

"Will you tell Angie?"

"Not if you don't want me to."

"I think it would upset her, Chris. It might even wreck our marriage. You see—" He had hesitated. "You see, that was the first time I—I mean, anyone ever—" And he had looked into her eyes. "Thank God it was you."

The following Thursday she had gone round to see Angie as usual. In the meantime there had been no word from David. She stayed late in order to see him, beginning to feel a little sick with apprehension, her heart beating hard when he came in.

He looked quite different from how he had when she had found him sitting at the table reading, the radio on. He was wearing a gray flannel suit and a gray striped tie. When Angie went out of the room and for a minute she was alone with him, she felt a flicker of that old wariness that was the forerunner of her fear. He was getting her a drink. She looked up and met his eyes and it was all right again. He gave her a conspiratorial smile, laying a finger on his lips.

"I'll give you a ring," he had whispered.

She had to wait two more weeks. During that time she went twice to Angie's and twice Angie came to her. She and Graham and Angie and David went out as a foursome and while Graham was fetching drinks and Angie was in the Ladies, David looked at her and smiled and lightly touched her foot with his foot under the table.

"I'll phone you. I haven't forgotten."

It was a Wednesday when he finally did phone. Next day Christine told Graham she had made a new friend, a girl she had met at work. She would be going out somewhere with this new friend on Friday and she wouldn't be back till eleven. She was desperately afraid he would want the car—it was *his* car or his firm's—but it so happened he would be in the office that day and would go by train. Telling him these lies didn't make her feel guilty. It wasn't as if this were some sordid affair, it was quite different.

When Friday came she dressed with great care. Normally, to go round to Angie's, she would have worn jeans and a T-shirt with a sweater over it. That was what she had on the first time she found herself alone with David. She put on a skirt and blouse and her black velvet jacket. She took the heated rollers out of her hair and brushed it into curls down on her shoulders. There was never much money to spend on clothes. The mortgage on the house took up a third of what Graham earned and half what she earned at her part-time job. But she could run to a pair of sheer black tights to go with the highest heeled shoes she'd got, her black pumps.

The doors of Angie and David's garage were wide open and their car was gone. Christine turned into their driveway, drove into the garage, and closed the doors behind her. A door at the back of the garage led into the yard and garden. The kitchen door was unlocked as it had been that Thursday three weeks before and always was on Thursday afternoons. She opened the door and walked in.

"Is that you, Chris?"

The voice sounded very male. She needed to be reassured by the sight of him. She went into the hall as he came down the stairs.

"You look lovely," he said.

"So do you."

He was wearing a suit. It was of navy silk with a pattern of pink-and-white flowers. The skirt was very short, the jacket clinched into his waist with a wide navy patent-leather belt. The long golden hair fell to his shoulders. He was heavily made-up and this time he had painted his fingernails. He looked far more beautiful than he had that first time.

Then, that first time, three weeks before, the sound of her entry drowned in loud music from the radio, she had come upon this girl sitting at the table reading *Vogue*. For a moment she had thought it must be David's sister. She had forgotten Angie had said David was an only child. The girl had long fair hair and was wearing a red summer dress with white spots on it, white sandals, and around her neck a string of white beads. When Christine saw that it was not a girl but David himself she didn't know what to do.

He stared at her in silence and without moving, and then he switched off the radio. Christine said the silliest and least relevant thing. "What are you doing home at this time?"

That made him smile. "I'd finished, so I took the rest of the day off. I should have locked the back door. Now you're here you may as well sit down."

She sat down. She couldn't take her eyes off him. He didn't look like a man dressed up as a girl, he looked like a girl—and a much prettier one than she or Angie. "Does Angie know?"

He shook his head.

"But why do you do it?" she burst out and she looked about the room, Angie's small, rather untidy living room, at the radio, the *Vogue* magazine. "What do you get out of it?" Something came back to her from an article she had read. "Did your mother dress you as a girl when you were little?"

"I don't know," he said. "Maybe. I don't remember. I don't want to *be* a girl. I just want to dress up as one sometimes."

The first shock of it was past and she began to feel easier with him. It wasn't as if there was anything grotesque about the way he looked. The very last thing he reminded her of was one of those female impersonators. A curious thought came into her head—that it was *nicer*, somehow more civilized, to be a woman and that if only all men were more like women—That was silly, of course, it couldn't be.

"And it's enough for you just to dress up and be here on your own?"

He was silent for a moment. "Since you ask, what I'd really like would be to go out like this and—" he paused, looking at her "—and be seen by lots of people, that's what I'd like. I've never had the nerve for that."

The bold idea expressed itself without her having to give it a moment's thought. She wanted to do it. She was beginning to tremble with excitement.

"Let's go out then, you and I. Let's go out now. I'll put my car in your garage and you can get into it so the people next door don't see and then we'll go somewhere. Let's do that, David, shall we?"

She wondered afterwards why she had enjoyed it so much. What had it been, after all, as far as anyone else knew but two girls walking on Hampstead Heath? If Angie had suggested that the two of them do it she would have thought it a poor way of spending the afternoon. But with David—She hadn't even minded that of the two of them he was infinitely the better dressed, taller, better-looking, more graceful. She didn't mind now as he came down the stairs and stood in front of her.

"Where shall we go?"

"Not the Heath this time," he said. "Let's go shopping."

He bought a blouse in one of the big stores. Christine went into the changing room with him when he tried it on. They walked about in

Hyde Park. Later on they had dinner and Christine noted that they were the only two women in the restaurant dining together.

"I'm grateful to you," David said. He put his hand over hers on the table.

"I enjoy it," she said. "It's so—crazy. I really love it. You'd better not do that, had you? There's a man over there giving a funny look."

"Women hold hands," he said.

"Only *those* sort of women. David, we could do this every Friday you don't have to work."

"Why not?" he said.

There was nothing to feel guilty about. She wasn't harming Angie and she wasn't being disloyal to Graham. All she was doing was going on innocent outings with another girl. Graham wasn't interested in her new friend, he didn't even ask her name. Christine came to long for Fridays, especially for the moment when she let herself into Angie's house and saw David coming down the stairs, and for the moment when they stepped out of the car in some public place and the first eyes were turned on him. They went to Holland Park, they went to the zoo, to Kew Gardens. They went to the cinema and a man sitting next to David put his hand on his knee. David loved that, it was a triumph for him, but Christine whispered they must change their seats and they did.

When they parted at the end of an evening he kissed her gently on the lips. He smelt of Alliage or Je Reviens or Opium. During the afternoon they usually went into one of the big stores and sprayed themselves out of the tester bottles.

Angie's mother lived in the north of England. When she had to convalesce after an operation Angie went up there to look after her. She expected to be away two weeks and the second weekend of her absence Graham had to go to Brussels with the sales manager.

"We could go away somewhere for the weekend," David said.

"Graham's sure to phone," Christine said.

"One night then. Just for the Saturday night. You can tell him you're going out with your new girl friend and you're going to be late."

"All right."

It worried her that she had no nice clothes to wear. David had a small but exquisite wardrobe of suits and dresses, shoes and scarves and beautiful underclothes. He kept them in a cupboard in his office to which only he had a key and he secreted items home and back again in his briefcase. Christine hated the idea of going away for the night in her gray-flannel skirt and white-silk blouse and that velvet jacket while David wore his Zandra Rhodes dress. In a burst of recklessness she spent all of two weeks' wages on a linen suit.

They went in David's car. He had made the arrangements and Christine had expected they would be going to a motel twenty miles outside London. She hadn't thought it would matter much to David where they went. But he surprised her by his choice of a hotel that was a three-hundred-year-old house on the Suffolk coast.

"If we're going to do it," he said, "we may as well do it in style."

She felt very comfortable with him, very happy. She tried to imagine what it would have felt like going to spend a night in a hotel with a man, a lover. If the person sitting next to her were dressed not in a black-and-white printed silk dress and scarlet jacket but in a man's suit with shirt and tie. If the face it gave her so much pleasure to look at were not powdered and rouged and mascara'd but rough and already showing beard growth. She couldn't imagine it. Or, rather, she could think only how in that case she would have jumped out of the car at the first red traffic lights.

They had single rooms next door to each other. The rooms were very small, but Christine could see that a double might have been awkward for David, who must at some point—though she didn't care to think of this—have to shave and strip down to being what he really was.

He came in and sat on her bed while she unpacked her nightdress and spare pair of shoes.

"This is fun, isn't it?"

She nodded, squinting into the mirror, working on her eyelids with a little brush. David always did his eyes beautifully. She turned round and smiled at him. "Let's go down and have a drink."

The dining room, the bar, the lounge were all low-ceilinged timbered rooms with carved wood on the walls David said was called linenfold paneling. There were old maps and pictures of men hunting in gilt frames and copper bowls full of roses. Long windows were thrown open onto a terrace. The sun was still high in the sky and it was very warm. While Christine sat on the terrace in the sunshine David went off to get their drinks. When he came back to their table he had a man with him, a thick-set paunchy man of about forty who was carrying a tray with four glasses on it.

"This is Ted," David said.

"Delighted to meet you," Ted said. "I've asked my friend to join us. I hope you don't mind."

She had to say she didn't. David looked at her and from his look she could tell he had deliberately picked Ted up.

"But why did you?" she said to him afterward. "Why did you want to? You told me you didn't really like it when that man put his hand on you in the cinema."

"That was so physical. This is just a laugh. You don't suppose I'd let them touch me, do you?"

Ted and Peter had the next table to theirs at dinner. Christine was silent and standoffish but David flirted with them. Ted kept leaning across and whispering to him and David giggled and smiled. You could see he was enjoying himself tremendously. Christine knew they would ask her and David to go out with them after dinner and she began to be afraid. Suppose David got carried away by the excitement of it, the "fun," and went off somewhere with Ted, leaving her and Peter alone together? Peter had a red face and a black moustache and beard and a wart with black hairs growing out of it on his left cheek. She and David were eating steak and the waiter had brought them sharp pointed steak knives. She hadn't used hers. The steak was very tender. When no one was looking she slipped the steak knife into her bag.

Ted and Peter were still drinking coffee and brandies when David got up quite abruptly and said, "Coming?" to Christine.

"I suppose you've arranged to meet them later?" Christine said as soon as they were out of the dining room.

David looked at her. His scarlet-painted lips parted into a wide smile. He laughed.

"I turned them down."

"Did you *really?*"

"I could tell you hated the idea. Besides, we want to be alone, don't we? I know I want to be alone with you."

She nearly shouted his name so that everyone could hear, the relief was so great. She controlled herself but she was trembling. "Of course I want to be alone with you," she said.

She put her arm in his. It wasn't uncommon, after all, for girls to walk along with linked arms. Men turned to look at David and one of them whistled. She knew it must be David the whistle was directed at because he looked so beautiful with his long golden hair and high-heeled red sandals. They walked along the sea front, along the little low promenade. It was too warm even at eight-thirty to wear a coat. There were a lot of people about but not crowds. The place was too select to attract crowds. They walked to the end of the pier. They had a drink in the Ship Inn and another in the Fishermen's Arms. A man tried to pick David up in the Fishermen's Arms but this time he was cold and distant.

"I'd like to put my arm round you," he said as they were walking back, "but I suppose that wouldn't do, though it is dark."

"Better not," said Christine. She said suddenly, "This has been the best evening of my life."

He looked at her. "You really mean that?"

She nodded. "Absolutely the best."

They came into the hotel. "I'm going to get them to send us up a couple of drinks. To my room. Is that okay?"

She sat on the bed. David went into the bathroom. To do his face, she thought, maybe to shave before he let the man with the drinks see him. There was a knock at the door and a waiter came in with a tray on which were two long glasses of something or other with fruit and leaves floating in it, two pink table napkins, two olives on sticks, and two peppermint creams wrapped up in green paper.

Christine tasted one of the drinks. She ate an olive. She opened her handbag and took out a mirror and a lipstick and painted her lips. David came out of the bathroom. He had taken off the golden wig and washed his face. He hadn't shaved. There was a pale stubble showing on his chin and cheeks. His legs and feet were bare and he was wearing a very masculine robe made of navy-blue toweling. She tried to hide her disappointment.

"You've changed," she said brightly.

He shrugged. "There are limits."

He raised his glass and she raised her glass and he said: "To us!"

The beginnings of a feeling of panic came over her. Suddenly he was so evidently a man. She edged a little way along the mattress.

"I wish we had the whole weekend."

She nodded nervously. She was aware her body had started a faint trembling. He had noticed it, too. Sometimes before he had noticed how emotion made her tremble.

"Chris," he said.

She sat passive and afraid.

"I'm not really like a woman, Chris. I just play at that sometimes for fun. You know that, don't you?" The hand that touched her smelt of nail-varnish remover. There were hairs on the wrist she had never noticed before. "I'm falling in love with you," he said. "And you feel the same, don't you?"

She couldn't speak. He took her by the shoulders. He brought his mouth up to hers and put his arms round her and began kissing her. His skin felt abrasive and a smell as male as Graham's came off his body. She shook and shuddered. He pushed her down on the bed and his hands began undressing her, his mouth still on hers and his body heavy on top of her.

She felt behind her, put her hand into the open handbag, and pulled out the knife. Because she could feel his heart beating steadily against her right breast she knew where to stab and she stabbed again and again. The bright red heart's blood spurted over her clothes and the bed and the two peppermint creams on the tray.

The Letter Carrier

KATHRYN GOTTLIEB

To celebrate his seventh anniversary Bill Lasker bought himself the biggest and best-looking Red Delicious he had ever invested in. He stuck an apple in his mail sack every day, but this apple was really something. It cost thirty-five cents.

It was not a family anniversary he was celebrating. Bill Lasker had no wife, no family, and, for that matter, no friends. For seven years to the day he had been delivering the mail along Route West in the little suburban town of Folsom, New Jersey, a day to be marked. The weather blessed him—a bright October sun, a cloudless sky, and, gliding past his ears, the many-colored autumn leaves.

He had been, as always, first man out, as soon as the sorted mail had come up in the truck to the Folsom substation. He wanted to put the little Main Street commercial section behind him before people began to arrive at the shops and offices along the way. Otherwise it was Good morning, How are you?, Nice day! (or How do you like this rotten weather?). Enough to drive a man crazy.

He kept a fast, steady pace through the crowded uphill residential streets beyond: a section of no particular interest. It was out beyond the end of Hightop Road that his own world began. There, in the narrow neck of woodland that slashed his route in two, lay his own private estate, and in the winding, pleasant streets beyond lived those he thought of as his family, although he had spoken not a word to any of them.

He covered the early part of his route in record time, pressing forward to reach his kingdom in the woods—a brook, rocks, solitude.

There he would rest, read, and eat that magnificent apple. Then, luck permitting, he would catch another glimpse of the young woman who had moved into 119 Folsom Road three weeks before.

One-nineteen Folsom was the only rental house in the neighborhood. It was painted a drab bluish gray and had the look of a place where people know they are not going to stay. No one had ever put in a garden there. She—he still didn't know her name—had moved into the dismal place alone. There was no man about the place when he passed by on Saturday mornings. On that day husbands were usually in evidence, putting up the storm sash or raking the leaves.

He had first glimpsed the new occupant of 119 as a dim figure moving across the rooms beyond the then uncurtained windows. A slender back, a drift of dark hair to her waist, a sense of quick and vital movement, and that was all. Beauty. He had been dropping a flyer from the local Shop-Mart into her box when he had caught that fleeting vision, and he had not seen her since. In three weeks she had received no mail. Plainly, she had left no forwarding address. He had concluded that she was, so to speak, on the run.

Marching down Hightop, he saw Mrs. Campbell and Mrs. Parker chatting away on the sidewalk in front of 93—waiting there to trap him with questions. It was meanness to begrudge them the brilliant day, but Mrs. Parker would say good morning and Mrs. Campbell would demand his opinion of the weather. His response, he knew, would be a jerky nod, flaming ears, and a burst of speed. And it was.

The old ladies watched his progress down to the cul-de-sac end of the road. Mrs. Parker spoke first. "What a handsome head of hair that young man has! My Joey had a mop of fair hair like that before he began to go gray."

"He's not what I'd call a young fellow," said Mrs. Campbell. "He must be close to forty."

"Half my age. I like to think that's young."

Mrs. Campbell grunted. "Have you ever seen him smile? Has he ever said good morning? When I say good morning I want good morning back!"

"Ah, well," said Mrs. Parker. "Maybe he has trouble at home."

Bill Lasker's path through the woods was leafstrewn and quiet. From time to time little animals scuttled across it, quaking at his thunderous approach. "Hey there," he called out to them softly. Chipmunks were easy to talk to. He thought, smiling, of the others, the night animals fast asleep in their burrows; garbage pail raiders. Under the trees grew clutching brambles and shrubs whose names he didn't know, and ferns in all the puddled spots. Through the neck of woods ran a curving brook in a stony bed—in the spring, and after rainstorms, a noisy torrent. The footpath crossed the brook by means of two planks laid side by side that tilted under his feet. Someday he'd go into the water—if any—mailbag and all!

Once across the makeshift bridge, he left the path and followed his own beaten track along the far side of the brook, deeper into the woods. There, out of sight of the path, he made himself comfortable on a kind of rocky sofa, where a boulder supported his back and a flat slab of stone made a seat at a convenient height above the ground. The autumn had been dry, and that morning there was no water running in the bed of the brook, which was filled instead with a river of yellow leaves. Bill Lasker stared down into it from his rocky perch. How pretty it was!

He reached into the depths of his mailbag, drew out his anniversary apple, and polished it on his sleeve. He then emptied the pouch and set the mail snugly down on the rock beside him; letters for Ramsay and Oak and Folsom Road, and Harrison to its junction with Main. His interest in the affairs of their recipients—on whom, when they met, he turned that unconsciously forbidding gaze—was benign and, until now, unflagging.

He picked up a handful of mail, took a bite of his apple, and read.

He scanned all postcards, picture and message; studied the return addresses on envelopes; and peered into those that were unsealed without disturbing their contents. And—lucky day!—slipped the Kolgers' *Playboy* carefully out of its wrapper, looked it over, and slid it carefully back. An overdue notice (purple) winked at him through its glassine-fronted envelope: the Second National wanted its money from the his-and-her Jaguars on Ramsay Place.

For the Wildes, next house after the spendthrift Jags, there was a nice postcard of Westminster Abbey from Jennifer Wilde, who was studying in England. Fabulous, she wrote. Good. She was a nice kid—always used to wave at him and never, never spoke. He was sorry for the Groleys, whose kid never sent them a line. Be fair, Bill told himself; maybe he calls up. But that wasn't what he called keeping in touch.

As he leafed through the mail he replaced it in neat order in the sack at his side.

The corner of Ramsay and Oak supported the Organization to Revive

Prohibition. He went on hastily past their monthly newsletter. (His beer!)

Mrs. Wiggram, on Oak, would lurk behind her draperies in vain, darting out to the box as soon as he reached the sidewalk. There was still no check from Mr. Wiggram, who lived in Tucson, Arizona. Short of money, poor lady. Which could not be said of her neighbors, into whose mailbasket he dropped little showers of dividend checks. It would be nice to play God sometime and do a little rearranging.

What would his own life be, he wondered, deprived of this route, these people, his place in the woods? How people stood to be shuttled around, like those families that whipped in and out of 119 Folsom, he simply couldn't imagine. What chance was there, in only a year or two, to get acquainted with a place? Here the bumpy tree roots and sidewalks and cobblestone curbing were as well known to him as the stairs in his house. He could have delivered the mail blindfolded. His route; his home. They'd never take it away from him. He was a steady and devoted worker; he showed up in the worst weather, ready to protect his mailbag with his life.

And so on that brilliant day he celebrated his anniversary. The apple was a treat, the *Playboy* another; but later, passing 119 Folsom, he caught no glimpse of its new occupant.

Three days later, he did.

He was walking past the orphaned-looking house, wondering if he would ever catch sight of her again, when she sprang to her feet on the far side of the hedge that bordered the sidewalk. She was clutching a garden trowel and her face was streaked with earth. She looked as pretty as a picture.

"Good morning!" she said.

The miracle shocked an answer out of him. "Good morning!"

"I've been putting tulip bulbs in," she said. "You don't think it's too late in the season, do you?"

"Of course not—they'll do fine." Her eyes were as blue as the sky; *today's* sky. "My mother never put bulbs in until the real cold weather. She—" But there he stopped. Long years ago she had told him, laughing, that she was punishing herself for her extravagance. Someday he might be able to tell that to this extraordinary young woman, who now shrugged her shoulders in a mock-guilty gesture and said, "I mustn't keep you from your appointed rounds, must I?"

Over so soon. "I guess not."

She gave him a little wave of the trowel and sank back to her knees. He marched down the street, his heart pounding. She was the prettiest woman he had ever seen, and the kindest. Had he not *spoken* to her?

And speak to her he did, day after day, as he plodded up and down the streets of that familiar route. True, he had yet to see her again, but the conversation, once begun, went on and on in his head. You know, he told her, there's nobody around here would believe the way you and I were talking about those tulip bulbs. And it's the God's truth, I'm not the local chatterbox. But I don't mean to be unfriendly—you know what I mean? She always knew what he meant, of course. Never any doubt of that.

And I'll tell you another fact—he was at the moment dropping Mrs. Wiggram's check into her box—nobody would believe what a talkative kid I was at one time. One door past the Wiggrams' he stopped still— the name of his mother's favorite tulips had just popped into his head. General de Wet! And the day they had planted those bulbs—it must have been November, cold enough to burn your ears off. Imagine re- membering General de Wet, bright orange, after all these years. That girl at 119 must have opened some magic door in his head.

A week passed and he caught no further glimpse of her. On Tuesday, and then again on Thursday, there was the sight of her car in the driveway to console him—she was *there*—but when the driveway stood empty his heart flapped in panic. Suppose she had gone away? Non- sense. She had to go down to the Shop-Mart sometimes, didn't she? Or the bank, or the library—or maybe she'd taken some kind of a job. People didn't just stay shut up in their houses day in and day out. Still—he frowned, thinking about it—she still hadn't gotten any mail. Nothing personal, that is. He had put a soap sample in her basket and more flyers from Shop-Mart, all addressed to Occupant.

Occupant. He still didn't know her name.

The conversation went on in his head, confiding. When I first started to get really quiet, he told her, was after my mother died and I got sent to live with my Aunt Ethel. You're probably wondering about my father. He wasn't dead or anything like that, he just wasn't around. I hardly remember him. Aunt Ethel was really my mother's aunt. She seemed like a hundred years old to me then and I'll tell you the truth, the poor old lady didn't know what hit her, getting this thirteen-year- old boy dumped in her lap. She was a real old maid, if you'll pardon the expression, and just the sound of my footsteps crashing around in her house must have been enough to drive her crazy, let alone the sound of my voice.

At that point he was climbing the steps to Mrs. Parker's porch, and he turned off the conversation until he was back on the sidewalk again. I have to admit it, there was no reason for that woman to love me. I was kind of a homely kid and I never could think of the right things to say. So after a while I just shut up. My mother and me, we used to talk about stuff and make jokes together, and I was *somebody* in our house. I could change a faucet washer before I was ten, and I mean so it didn't leak or shriek when you turned the water on. But with Aunt Ethel the talk just went out of me.

On the next day the fine weather broke, and the postcards began. Bill Lasker woke to an overcast sky—the exact color of the house at 119—and a smell of rain on its way. Seated on his rock in the woods, dampness beading his hair, he pulled the mail out of the sack, looking for 119 Folsom. His interest in all the others—on Ramsay, on Oak, all along—belonged to a time that no longer existed. And there, sand-wiched between bundles of mail for 117 and 121, he found a picture postcard of Los Angeles, view side up. Sorter's error. It was a nighttime view from someplace high up—a lot of black and little dots of lights. He stared at it like a man in a trance, and then he turned it over.

Mrs. Jean LaBarre. He repeated the syllables like a man reciting a poem. Jean. Jean. Jean LaBarre. He read the message, and read it again. "Found you!" it said. The writing was ugly; a triumphant scrawl that almost filled the message space. "Found you," he said aloud. What would be the proper tone of voice? *Found you!* The card had been mailed from Los Angeles. It was unsigned.

Her car was not in the driveway when he slipped the card into the box.

Two days later he found another postcard addressed to her. It had been mailed from Flagstaff, Arizona, and held a one-word message: "Closer." No signature.

Closer? It was a good thing, Bill Lasker told himself, that she was hearing from somebody after all this time; it was no kind of a good thing for her to be living alone and apart from people—*his* kind of life. But what kind of a friend wrote cards like this? He leaned back against his rock and closed his eyes. A picture came into his head clear as day:

a man driving a car with California plates, headed for Folsom, New Jersey, face a blank, character and intentions unknown.

The next card was postmarked Albuquerque. Bill Lasker read it and it slipped from his hands, like a leaf, onto the ground. "My darling." Damned fool! Damned fool! That let him out, didn't it? Mr. California Plates and Mrs. Jean LaBarre were none of his business. They had had a lover's quarrel. Lovers quarreled and made up. He picked up the card, replaced the mail, and got to his feet. The sack weighed a ton. He felt old and hollowed out. All the same, on his way home in the late afternoon he stopped at Pringle's Stationery and bought a road atlas of the U.S.A. He looked for Albuquerque and found it; east of Las Vegas. "Closer."

On Sunday he sat home and watched TV and drank beer and the day was a thousand years long. Monday there was nothing in the mail. On Tuesday a card arrived from Amarillo, and it was different from the others. The message was so long that, though the writing was very small, it reached the bottom of the card and then continued, curling up and around twice, crowding the address space illegally. "Oh my darling," he read. "Each day draws me nearer to you and my heart is renewed with gladness. Soon we will join hands and you will believe with me that we never should have parted. Oh my love, why did you leave me? Whom God hath joined together! Joined together! But I will not repeat it. I patiently explained to you His holy command and I know in my heart that you repent. It is that knowledge that draws me to you—I love you, I forgive you. Oh my Jean, never again—" At that point the message began its long tailcurl around its own body and Bill Lasker stopped reading and looked away from the card. Not three feet away a chipmunk sat at the farthest edge of the slab of stone and stared back at him. "I don't know," said Bill. The chipmunk ran away. He looked at the card again. The man was out of his mind. Or was he? Maybe he was just very religious. Bill shut his eyes. He could see the car bouncing down the dusty desert roads.

He would knock on her door, put the card in her hands, and say, "If you're in trouble, Mrs. LaBarre, I'll protect you from this man—" and he heard her voice, shocked, angry: "You've been reading my mail!" And then God knows what. They'd take him off the route—no, they'd fire him—and then he'd sit alone in his room day after day until he was as crazy as the man in Amarillo.

He jumped to his feet and threw his half-eaten apple in the direction of the chipmunk. He had time. Texas was far away. But of course the man was traveling ahead of the cards. Never mind. He'd work something out.

For three days there was no message, and then two cards arrived together, both posted from Colorado—some town named Trinidad. One card read "Jean"; the other, "Zigzag." That night, frowning over his atlas, he found Trinidad—small print, small town. "Zigzag" described it: the place was north and west of Amarillo. And then, for days, there was silence. Maybe California Plates had given up and was heading back to L.A.

On a day of pouring rain he delivered half a ton of shampoo samples, one in every box: to Mrs. Campbell, *no hair*; to the Prohibitions, "Drink it!" The very next day, Jean LaBarre was outside on her lawn, facing away from him, grubbing the leaves out from under the decrepit shrubs in front of the house. Today of all days there were no samples, no flyers, no postcard. Could he hand her somebody else's mail? He stared at the long slender back and the shining dark hair, then trudged on down the road. "I've been reading your mail." How could he say it? For the rest of that day he even stopped talking to her in his mind. The situation was impossible.

The week ended. Sunday passed. On Monday morning, under a sky as hard and gray as any November would bring, Bill found another card in his hands. The fellow was back in Amarillo, and he sounded just as ordinary as the guy next door. "Damn this car. Broke down again. Half the time I don't know where I am!" She wasn't home for him to put the card into her hands, and she wasn't home two days later when a card came from St. Louis. That tiny handwriting again, the message curling around and around. This one he read to the end. The ending was obscene. His hands shook when he put the card into her mailbox. If her car had been standing in the driveway he would have rung the bell and told her everything—that he'd read every word. Let the sky fall on his head! "You'd better get out of here," he'd say. "I'm telling you, you've got to get out!" And then a voice whispered in the back of his head. You do and she'll get out, all right—out of your life.

The next day, when he was just two doors past her house, she backed the car out of the driveway and shot off down the street, waving a friendly hand as she passed. He waved back vigorously and continued to confide in her, tramping down the sidewalk, everything that went on in his head. He complained in a good-humored way about the old ladies who sprang conversation traps on him. I deliver their mail, he said. Do I have to give weather reports, too? He smiled at her, and the Jean in his head smiled back. He told her the plots of the programs he watched every evening, and she agreed with his opinions, absolutely. "Dumb stuff!" "Isn't it though? Why on earth do we watch it?"

Two days after the ugly message from St. Louis a card arrived from someplace he couldn't make out in Kentucky. "I don't know what comes over me," wrote the man who never signed his name. "But don't be afraid of me ever again. *Please.* Don't run away from me. You are my only friend."

Oh, you're safe, he told the card. She's not running. Runners don't plant gardens. She'd be right there to face him when he came knocking on her door. But which man would stand on her doorstep—the pathetic pleader of Someplace, Kentucky, or the madman of St. Louis? Oh, God help me, thought Bill, what can I do? Talk to the guys at the post office? But he never talked to them. They'd think he was the crazy one.

For the first time in his life he wished a man dead.

He still went each day to his woodland place. The weather had turned cold, with the bite of winter in it, but he was sturdy, and indifferent to the change of season. He looked at no mail but hers. Out of habit he continued to carry an apple in his mail sack but, distracted, half the time he forgot to eat it. On a day of pallid sunshine he found the next message in his hands. "Soon." The postmark was Akron, Ohio. Akron! The man might *be* here!"

He stepped along Ramsay Place at a pace that left him gasping. The mail sack weighed at his shoulders and every damned house on the block had mail. The same on Oak, where he had to slow down; the pain cut right across his shoulders. When he reached the top of Folsom Road he stared in terror down the sloping street to her house. Peace and quiet. No one on the sidewalk, no strange cars.

He went on at a human pace and got his breath back. Her car was not in the driveway.

It wasn't until he had rounded the downhill corner and got halfway down Harrison to Main that he spotted the car parked in front of the empty lot past 168. Dark plates; out-of-state plates—Jersey is black on cream. It was a beat-up Chevy, he saw, coming abreast of it, and the plates were yellow on navy blue. California. The driver was sitting in the car. Passing, Bill glimpsed an oil-stained khaki sleeve. The man's hands rested on the wheel, holding something—some piece of paper, too small to be a map. Big hands, a long arm: more than that he couldn't have seen without stooping to peer into the window. He forced himself on, one foot in front of the other, up one walk and down the next. He wanted the strength to turn back but the habit of his route, of his perpetual silence, held him in its grip. What would he say? How could he say it? Jersey was full of out-of-state plates, and that empty lot was for sale. The man could be some stranger looking at the lot to buy it.

He finished his route and went home.

That night he slept badly. He dreamed of a man at the wheel of a car. The man had no face but spoke to him all the same. "You wanted me to drive into a ditch," he said. His voice was reproachful. "But you don't get what you want in this world. Don't you know that?"

The last postcard came the next day. A picture of the Folsom War Memorial, a Folsom postmark. It was addressed to Mrs. Jean LaBarre. There was no message.

He fled from his place in the woods, the mailbag jouncing against his hip. He delivered the mail on Ramsay and Oak at a run, groaning for breath, pushing at a task he hadn't the strength to abandon. He rounded the corner of Oak to the top of Folsom Road.

"No," he said aloud.

A knot of people had gathered out on the sidewalk in front of her house.

"No." All the way down the hill he delivered the mail. "No!" The word tolled in his head like a bell. When at last he stood in front of 119, Mrs. Parker from 93 Hightop looked at him and spoke. "That poor young woman." Her lips were trembling. "Poor child! She was beaten to death last night.

"A package came from United Parcel this morning and the driver found the door open and—" the old voice faltered "—they found blood just inside the door. She must have struggled to get away. Poor child! They say she was only twenty-five."

He was standing like a man turned to stone.

"Are you all right?" asked Mrs. Parker. "Are you feeling all right?" She was looking at him anxiously.

"Yes," he said. "Thank you." He moved to go on, and then he saw the stranger standing at the edge of the crowd, staring at the house. A tall man, young, with a deeply tanned and rather coarse complexion, and sun-bleached hair cut very short. He was wearing the khaki shirt with the oil stain on the sleeve. Bill Lasker moved on, stuffing mail into every box—*Time, Newsweek,* dunning letters, love letters, hate letters—he didn't know what was in his hands. What was the use of any of it? Why did anyone want it? Rubbish. Heartbreak. Trouble. Sorrow.

When he turned the corner into Harrison, he saw the Chevy with the California plates. It was parked in front of the empty lot, just as it had been yesterday; as though it were yesterday. He threw his mail sack to the ground and ran up the street. At the end, at Main, he thrust himself into a telephone booth and dialed the police; reported the watching stranger, the waiting car.

He had expected a reprimand for a task abandoned, a mailbag thrown God-knows-where, but instead he found himself congratulated for his quick thinking and fast response. The California driver, a man named Frank LaBarre, had been picked up at once for questioning. He had admitted readily to the murder of Jean LaBarre, who had once been his wife. It was something, he stated, that he had had to do.

The abandoned mailbag was retrieved, its contents apparently intact. The letter carrier received his commendation without response. He asked to be transferred to another route. The request was refused. He was the hero in the neighborhood.

Kept from his little kingdom in the woods by the deep snows of winter, he did not return to it in the beautiful days of spring. He took no apples with him in his mail sack, and never read the mail any more.

Late in April the tulips bloomed inside the hedge at 119. When he saw them he cried like a child.

At a Rest Stop South of Portland

ROBERT TWOHY

*C*op cruiser comes up behind me, maybe tails me a little. I get that
tingle—is the word out to flag down Cal. PKWDTOM?

Not yet. He zoops on by.

I send notes to PD's and Sheriff's Departments in various states signed
Park Warrior—Don't Tread On Me. Then I sketch a kind of teddy-bear
face, Cal. being the Bear State. Simple enough. Any word game is when
you know the answer.

I don't end all the notes that way. Some I put just *Park Warrior.*

My first glimpse of a cop on my tail, part of me says, Good. I don't
think I'd do time if Illinois didn't get connected, which there's no reason
it should, I didn't send a note that time. Or after San Francisco. Or
Mississippi. Those two don't worry me, they were clear cut and I'd just
tell what happened those places. Only Illinois is ambiguous and could
be a problem, maybe long-term. But I don't think they'd connect it. If
they did, I'd just say, "No, sir, not me," and they'd have to make a case,
which I doubt they could.

Most likely if arrested, I'd do a few months for leaving the scene,
maybe a lot of scenes. Which would be okay. I'd have time to rest up,
get my head organized, maybe do some writing.

I've had thrills, spills, pain, terror, that great sweeping rush that hits—
the agony and the ecstasy, life on the knife's edge. But at thirty-one
you're on the downgrade—though I don't feel it, I know it's so. And
there've been nights I had to be a hundred percent and still reach for
that extra something, which maybe one night won't be there.

But I won't turn myself in. The play ends when a cop flags me down or I get involved with someone I can't handle and he goes on to kill or cripple me. The word is fatalism, I guess—I started the play, but it's got its own life now and ends when it ends, not when I say.

I was in Mississippi on my way back from Montgomery, Alabama, where I'd been a month, nothing happening. So it goes. Most of my trips all I get is a view of the place, a stretch of anticipation, excitement—then fadeout, back home until next trip.

About twenty percent wind up with a note to the cops, along with whatever souvenirs I can send them—the guy's wallet, driver's license, weapon, ring, wristwatch, anything that might be helpful. When he's carrying nothing, I try for his photo with my minicamera and/or his prints on one of the 3×5 cards I carry. If he gets away clean, all I send is the note, describing the incident, time and place, him as good as I can, then the signoff—in full or part, depending on my mood or what happened.

Twenty percent might be a good average, but I have nothing to compare it to. There may be others doing what I'm doing, but I don't know of any and nobody knows me. I'm the complete loner. Which wasn't true my first twenty years—but that was a different person then, who I lost on purpose. Now I'm Park Warrior.

This is the first I've written in a long time. Why, I don't know, except long ago I wanted to be a writer and maybe that's suddenly coming back, the urge to string words.

At UCSB, the Creative Writing guy—Sprague? Sprott?—he said find your point and stick to it, move everything toward the finish. But what's the point? What's the finish? I don't know. I'm sitting here writing in this notebook about Park Warrior, whose finish might be in a park in a city I haven't been to yet, though parks aren't the only scenes I play. It might be on a beach, in the ocean, a slough, a gully in the wilds somewhere.

Or in jail, the play closed down, me resting up and preparing for the next stage I'll play. Maybe up in Canada where I've never been. I could rent a house in a quiet, slow-lane town, write stories, get known and have friends.

For seven years I've been in a play with no script, and if there's a plot-line only the Great Writer knows. But maybe He, She, or It is just an off-scene player in the no-script play with scenes just happening—Theater of the Now, of the Knife.

I started to tell about Mississippi—why? Spogue—Sprain?—said catch the attention early with a specific scene. Whose attention? Who am I writing this for, and why? Those are questions whose answer I don't rightly know, but it could be the play is almost played and what's left now is summary.

I'm pulled up at a rest stop on a hillside in Oregon—47 miles to Portland, the last sign said. It's just on the soft edge of dark. I started from L.A. early yesterday, stopped last night at a Travelodge, started out again at dawn, and here I am. In Portland I'll be as long as it takes to play a scene, or not play one, then back to L.A. Or maybe not. Maybe I'll get flagged down.

I'm hungry and there's no food in the van. But I'll go on with this whatever-it-is—essay? diary? confession? Then I'll find a restaurant, then park somewhere and go into Portland tomorrow early and poke around, read the papers, get a map, and stroll some parks and see if the feeling hits that says, *yeah yeah, start here.*

Thirty-one is young for a writer, or young enough, and I'll go to Canada and write good stories and make friends in that quiet town I'll find, go on dates, have laughs and fun that isn't on the edge of the knife, and maybe closeness developing with someone.

Park Warrior has been my passion for nearly seven years and I have the feeling more and more that the play is winding down.

Okay. Summary: overall I've done good and a few women, maybe more than a few, are better off for me.

Not the guy's wife in Illinois, or his daughter or two granddaughters. Not them, but—but what? But nothing. They got hurt probably wrongly and that's how it was.

I never wrote them. What was there to say? *I'm sorry about your man, who was probably all right but maybe not—maybe that's my own fiction that he was. Maybe I read his eyes wrong.* I never wrote them or the cops there.

I don't know the reality of that scene in Illinois and never will.

Okay. Lay it out flat and cold how Park Warrior began. I was a young bride living with Tim in a rented cottage near UCSB. He was going to be a doctor and I was going to be a writer, and one evening we rode to a lake in the hills and strolled, and it was lovely and right and then it was over, that life of innocence and trust and closeness. I was a young widow being raped by the first of three men who were the first to know me in the biblical sense but Tim—after which they left me with internal damage and skull fractures. I was in the hospital, then out, raving at cops why they didn't catch the killers. Then it was the nuthouse for two years. The killers weren't caught.

Then I was home with my parents, an outpatient for two years. Then Mother was killed in a car crash and Dad lingered a few weeks, during which we got close for the first time since early girlhood, when I got all wrapped up in my emerging wonderfulness as young girls do. My grief for Tim got mixed up with the sorrow for Mother and Dad when he went.

I was twenty-four and inherited, sold the house, and moved into a triplex rental in a quiet part of L.A., which is still my address—though half the time I'm on the road in my van, which inside is fixed like a little paneled room with an oil lamp on now as I write. I've got framed prints on the paneling—Cezanne, Klee, Monet—and a narrow flat mattress and blankets and throw-pillows and a little low desk and books and shades on the windows and a good lock on the side door. It's Park Warrior's traveling camp and always in A-one operating shape.

I realized the cops would never find Tim's murderers and stopped bugging them—I was one young widow among many they had to deal with, along with doing their best to find the killers without any leads, so why plague them? It was my problem to work out myself, or work myself out of.

How?

One night came lunging into my head from nowhere a still from that great old Mel Gibson movie, *Road Warrior*, him standing hand on hip with his gun and that wonderful I'm-ready-for-all-you-got look—and it wasn't *his* face but mine. And came that sweep of joy that comes when you know an answer is without any doubt the only and true answer. I whispered, "Park Warrior," and had a point to my life for the first time since Tim.

First I got fit with aerobics and weights, and also a Chinese philosophy-of-movement course I'd heard of in college—you get aware of every part of your body and how moves relate and how to get your mind in tune with the moves. Harmony of mind and body with nature is the goal—harmony is the ultimate power. I was dedicated. I got good. I've stayed good. But I'm thirty-one. Thirty-one or fifty or older don't matter if you're completely into that philosophy, but I'm not completely into it, part of my mind is apart. And that's the part that getting older affects, that can screw up the whole. One move or thought a hair out of sync could be my last, as was almost true in Mississippi.

Maybe I just wrote that to make clear to myself that it's time to wind down the play. Which I said earlier I couldn't do on my own. But that thought could be changing. I could be working into a new thought as I write. Maybe that's why I'm writing.

I bought the van—with regular plates then. PKWDTOM came later.

Road Warrior had a gun but Park Warrior didn't want a gun. Something sudden happens and BOOM, that's it, and maybe you weren't sure of the situation or read it wrong. Or the gun jams and there's no boom. Or BOOM and you miss, and in her apartment a block away a young bride is fixing dinner for her love and your bullet comes strolling in the window and she's dead. So no gun. I wanted clear confrontals, encounters of the closest kind, me and whoever, no bystanders or witnesses—just me and him, no boom.

Confrontals. I meant *confrontations*. But confrontals, I like it. Shorter and suddener.

Sparkman—that was his name, the Creative Writing guy. So what? So he said, "Don't put in something and just leave it hanging." Okay, man, I hear you—now you're not hanging.

I got some tough clothes and hung around some low-grade places in L.A. I knew what I wanted. I got tangled up with some guys best forgotten, lay it to making myself into a girl I'd never been and decided I'd better be. Anything that happened those nights was my own doing and nothing too dire happened. I got beat up a few times and a girl went for me with a knife and meant it, but I slipped clear and next time I saw her we were friends again. She said it wasn't me but another girl trying to take Earl from her. It *was* me, but he and I were careful after that.

He was what I'd been looking for—a real switchblade ace. I had him get me one and he taught me a lot, and after a while I knew all he knew and was better. He said I was a natural and I wasn't, it was the fitness classes and the Chinese mind-body harmony and the hunger to be good that made me good. I left that scene feeling the time had come.

I knew I'd never find the guys who had murdered Tim and the me I'd been then, but they had stopped being primely important. They were just three among a horde of men with such a lousy view of themselves that they can rise out of it only at the moment of dominance of a terrified, helpless woman—which for some is only foreplay for the ultimate ecstasy: ripping her apart and throwing her away.

Every man has a beast in him. That's from Freud, sort of—most men control it, some don't. When they don't, you can say it's not their fault, they just lack good control equipment. It doesn't matter to me—my thing is to confront the beast, whoever he's using that night, and get him down with my knife at his throat. That's the big rush I spoke of—turning the terror back on him, seeing it shine in his eyes.

I walked alone in still places, in parks, on beaches, down mangy streets. I didn't flaunt, but dressed quiet—jacket, bandana over most of my hair, walking like a woman bound somewhere, didn't linger. I wanted no ambiguities but clear definition as to who started the waltz, who was the aggressor.

After a confrontal, I'd send the cops there a note with whatever I got from the guy—if nothing, his photo and/or fingerprints if I could. Sometimes I couldn't, he got away. Those times I'd describe him as clearly as I could, including wounds I might have given him.

I knew they couldn't charge him without me in person, but they could check on him, maybe connect him with some unsolved crimes against women in their files. Or if not, let him know they had their eye on him. I'd tell the guy I was sending the note, just to make his rotten night a little worse.

The personal plates as clue to the signoff line came after the seventh or eighth confrontal. I thought I was giving cops a sporting crack at me, like Zorro with his Z, but that was kidding myself somewhat. I know now those early notes were my first whisper: *This is a dangerous play I'm in, and it could end hard and bloody for me. So work out the clue and find me, okay?* Part of me back then wanted out of the play and does now.

Mississippi I mentioned. Tell about it.

I was passing a third-rate camp place, coming back from a nothing trip to Montgomery, and got the feeling I should pull in—a feeling I respond to as it signals a confrontal often enough so that when it hits me I respond.

Within an hour there, I knew a lunkish man had his eye on me.

The rest of that day I spent mostly in my van, completely so after dark. I gave him that time to pull out, if he was going to, next day. I don't push things—we'd meet if my feeling was right and we had a scene to play.

Next day I browsed in the near town and saw him there.

A depressing kind of woods was behind the camp and I took a walk there and saw him. Others were walking. He looked at me.

About ten that night, it was quiet and dark in the trailers, campers, and the few cabins. I came out of my van and strolled to the far edge of the grounds. I wore a neat red shirt and trim gray denims and, resting my arms on the fence, gazed at the pale Mississippi moon.

I wrote earlier that I don't linger or flaunt. Was I flaunting that night? Oh, yes, sir. Oh, you bet. Shirt, pants, the way I stood were flaunts. I should have written, *rarely* do I flaunt. That night I did.

I knew he was close—faint beast smell? Close and coming closer, me at the fence gazing moonward.

His lunge was with a grunt and I jumped to the left, spinning, and saw a gun in his left paw still on the way to where my head had been. He'd meant to knock me cold, get me over or through the fence and into the woods, and, after using me, throw me away.

He was on his right front foot, his arm raised, freeze-frame. I slashed the gun hand, reached my left hand, and jumped back with the gun.

His eyes had that shine of fear and I got the rush. "Get over the fence," I ordered, and if he hadn't twisted to the fence he'd have been stuck good. I jabbed again and he got over, with me alongside, keeping the gun pointing at him, sure by the way he eyed it that it had at least one bullet.

We walked into the woods, me off to his left, he gripping his slashed hand. "Give me your wallet," I said. He said no. I stopped him with the point of the blade on his neck and the gunhole a foot from his face. His eyes were slick-sick and he mumbled, loose-lipped, "I don't have it on me. It's back in my truck. Honest."

Maybe true, maybe not. I wasn't going to parade him back through the campgrounds. Before I left him I'd make him pull out his pockets. I'd walk him deep into the woods and take his shoes, and before he limped back I'd be gone in my van. Tomorrow I'd mail the cops in the near town a note with his gun and whatever he had in his pockets, or a snapshot and prints—and his shoes. Why not? Often they can be a clue to a crime.

That was thinking ahead which, I see as I write about it, tips off that I wasn't a hundred percent that night. Thinking ahead is dumb. The mind should be full on the now, as things can happen sudden.

I walked him a way farther, then sat him down, made him stretch his legs out all the way and lean his weight back on his hands. A tree was a foot or so behind him, too close—make mistakes and learn from them. I wasn't a hundred percent. The moon came down on us through the tops of the trees. I was in a crouch two feet from his shoe soles, gun on him, switchblade back in my shirt. "You were going to rape me."

"No."

"Going to kill me after?"

"No."

"You've raped a lot of women?"

"No."

"Killed any?"

"No." Four lies in a row, each showing clear in his eyes, which slid down to his slashed hand, oozing not much now. "You cut me bad. You didn't have to do that."

"Are you wanted?"

"For what?" He was wanted.

"Where'd you kill the woman? Or is it more than one?"

"Are you a cop?"

"Park Warrior. Don't tread on me."

"What are you gonna do?"

"Shoot you if you act smart." I'd partly come out of the crouch to pull the camera from my left hip pocket, and that was, as I mentioned, getting out of sync. Pulling in his feet, he heaved up and back into the tree and off it on his toes, diving, looming over me and coming down arms wide. I had one move, my finger on the trigger—BOOM, bullet into his wide-open-mouth taking out the back of his head as he came on down with his brains floating behind. His stretched right arm clubbed me down.

In the light of the Mississippi moon.

I walked to the fence and looked over the campground. No lights were on. I saw no flashlights and heard no questioning shouts. Those who heard the BOOM, as some must have, figured it was none of their business if they didn't make it so and they were right.

I walked back to him, wiped the gun on my shirt, put it in his left hand, and walked back to my van.

If anyone wandered into the woods the next morning and found him, I didn't know it, being long gone.

I'm forty-seven miles or a little less from Portland. I'm hungry and tired. I'll stop this, drive on, and find a restaurant. But I'm near the end—of what? I'd be days writing about the last seven years, if that's what I'm doing. What am I doing? I don't know. All I know is I'm still writing and can't stop yet—I don't know why, but have to go on a while.

I didn't send the cops a note. They'd find him or hear about him in time or not, tie him to rapes and a murder or not. I never knew who he was, where he'd killed the woman or women, never tried to check. He didn't interest me dead. The beast had lost a stooge was all, and a few Mississippi women were better off, if he was a Mississippian.

The beast is without brains or memory and has never learned that with my blade I'm better than most he sends against me.

But not all. I'm not Bionic Woman. I run when I have to, when I can. Sometimes I can't—I've had two switchblades taken. After the first one, I went to Earl but learned he was dead. He was a good teacher. So was Sparkman, whether I learned anything from him or not. I scouted elsewhere and got one, then later from that source the one I have now.

The times I ran or got put on my back I've written the cops as to when and where, described the guy as I could, signing off just *Park Warrior* without the brag or the bear. If flagged down and arrested, I'll have my lawyer try to turn up some of those loser's notes, which would be in my favor, showing I'm not some kind of grotesque who never gets hurt but only hurts others. I get hurt. When pricked, I bleed. I don't think I'm some kind of grotesque.

At a library near my place in L.A., where nobody knows me and I know nobody, I browse out-of-town papers, looking for stories of crimes against women. I study details, and maybe one case in twenty I get the feeling I should go there. If it stays strong, next day I pack the van and head there.

It's a shot in about 10,000 that that killer or rapist or rapist-killer will pick up on me—but he's not the point. The beast is the point, whoever he's using. Two trips in ten I confront him, if not in the particular place then on my way there or coming back—as coming back from Montgomery that night of brains in the moonlight.

In Denver a man sobbed that it was his first attack on a woman, and his eyes and tone were true. He said he didn't know what had come over him and he'd get therapy. He was a junior exec, I found out from cards in his wallet, young talent on his way up—photos showed a nice house, a nice wife, a young son. He begged for a break—he'd give me $800.00, all he had, as his bankbook showed—and tomorrow he'd meet me anywhere I said with the cash. I didn't doubt him, he meant it. He swore that tonight he'd learned a lesson he'd never forget. He'd get therapy.

I said, "Good," gave him back his wallet, and told him I was going to send his driver's license to the Denver cops with a note describing the night's action and he could go to them for his license or they'd come to him. I left him in a heap, pounding his fists in the grass.

His little boy maybe loved him a lot. Maybe he was a wonderful husband and father. Maybe sending a note and his license to the cops was the best thing I could have done for the three of them. Maybe it was the worst. I do what I do.

I killed a man in Illinois and one in San Francisco. But my object isn't to kill. I could have many times. Anyone good with a blade can kill when she's disarmed the man, if he was armed, and has him down with the blade at his throat. I've written about how seeing the terror in his eyes is the great rush—the ecstasy? Yes.

Park Warrior will be in the past and I'll be a writer. I know that more and more as I write this, that I can close the play down and move on to the life ahead, a writer's life in Canada, finding closeness with someone there.

I was in a town in Illinois, a nice town, coming back from Chicago, where nothing happened. In this town was a park, clean and trim, with trees in rows and well kept bushes and flowerplots. I walked there because it was cool and pretty and that's a lie because I don't walk in parks at midnight in a town I've come to on a trip except for the one purpose.

A thin gray man came at me onto the path from my right, with an arm out to take me around the waist. I spun clear and he pulled up, teetered on his toes, and gave me an odd look of yearning, then fell forward.

His chin was up and his throat was bare and stretched, and I held my wrist stiff and the knife slid in.

I'd never stabbed a man in the throat and didn't that night. His throat went for the point, which I held there for that half second, and he kept falling and the handle dug into the sod and all the blade was in his throat.

He lay there and died without another move. Blood, not a lot, was around him in the grass. Reaching under, I worked the knife out, wiped it and my fingers with grass, tucked it in my shirt, and left the park running. What the look he gave me meant hit me as I was running.

And that's a lie that I've told myself until right this moment—that not until I was running away did I get what the look meant. I knew right away as he teetered, what it meant—that he didn't have the beast in him, that he wasn't out to hurt me.

In another town the next day I got the paper from that nice town and it was the big story, half the front page and two inside pages with photos. He ran a department store and was on the city council. The photos were close up, as in life, of a pleasant face with good quiet eyes, and of him with his family—widow, daughter, two granddaughters. Nice family, good people.

The townspeople couldn't believe it—"Who would murder Tom?" Everyone agreed it had to be a madman from elsewhere, killing from madness as Tom hadn't been robbed.

Tom was found within a half hour of the killing. If I'd lingered to go through his pockets to find who he was or, if he had a weapon, I'd have been spotted and taken—with my knife—and who would have believed that that man of fine reputation had rushed me and I'd defended myself?

I hadn't defended myself. He was falling with that look of yearning and I'd held my wrist stiff, knowing he wasn't the beast.

You can know nothing about yourself for a long time and everything in the second that you strip away the lie you've hid behind.

I wrote that scene because I had to. It's the scene that has troubled me, and no other has. I had to find the truth of it. He wasn't the beast, which I saw clear he wasn't and would not accept. I had tripped to Chicago and not found him and had gone to that park for him and wanted him. As Tom teetered and I saw he wasn't him, I called for him—didn't call but sent the signal, and he came and we killed Tom.

Why did he rush me? The paper said he was a Viet combat vet with ribbons and honors. Did he get a split in his head that night? Did he often get a split in the head and his wife and daughter never let it be known? Was he peacefully walking home from a meeting across the park and was it suddenly not the park but someplace in Vietnam, shells coming in—and did he spot not me but a Vietnamese girl he loved, and did he rush from another path to sweep me clear of shells coming in?

That's fiction, of course. I don't know why he rushed me, but somehow I know it wasn't to overpower and dominate me. I think he wanted to catch me and carry me clear of danger that thundered in his head, or die with the girl he loved.

If I'd pulled back the knife, he'd have gone on his knees and I'd have kicked him over on his back and put the knife to his throat and asked questions as I watched his eyes and learned why he rushed me or if he was lying. As it is, I know nothing except that I had a split-second to pull the knife back and instead held it stiff so the beast and I could share my gift to him of blood.

Hate and love—two sides of the same coin? I suppose. Did I hate the beast because I dared not admit I wanted to be loved and possessed by him? Did I want him in me? Has that been the point of the play, which wasn't the point at the start but somewhere along did it become the point—to prove my love, as I did that night, to take him into me and be one with him?

Thoughts I've never had before, or, if so, have pushed away. That's what this compulsion to write has brought me—a view of myself I've never had. You know when a perception is right and true.

I read the words that come out from under my ballpoint like this is a story I'm reading. I've heard of automatic writing and I guess this is it, the writing doing itself as I hold the pen and turn pages in the notebook. The finish will be when the writing stops itself, when I'll put down the pen.

I've killed three men. Now the third death will get told. Why, though? Wasn't the Illinois murder the point?

A mean street in San Francisco. That's Chandler's term, mean streets. He never wrote of San Francisco that I know. His mean streets were in L.A. and environs. What do I care, what does he care? The words just come. But you should stay in the place you know and feel. As a new young writer, I'll go to Canada and find a slow town and learn it and become at home there and write about it, and have friends and closeness with a man there. Right now I'm at home anywhere if it's a park and dark and still. Though only in Illinois was the killing in a park.

In San Francisco it was in the Mission, the district that evolves around Mission Dolores there. I was on my way to a park at 1:30 A.M. and a man came behind me and looped his right arm around my neck, not tight enough. I dropped through, spun to my left, and came up with the knife—and a second man was there and the blade drove into his groin. He screamed and fell into me, knocking me into an iron stairrail, and the first guy had a flat rock in his right palm and went for my head while the groined guy went down to the sidewalk and rolled away, holding himself and screaming, blood leaking through his fingers.

I was ducking and slipping the rock and betweentimes reaching and slashing. He was lean and quick, and his friend twisted and arched in the gutter and screamed. I suppose lights had gone on and people were at windows, but I had no time or interest to check that. The man wanted to brain me and what would come of that afterward didn't matter to him right then—he was into the kill, a lean and avid beast with a rock. I was a beast with a knife and quicker, he was stronger—and the beast owned us both, I see now, and loved us for the gift the three of us would share.

I cut his arm. He was making quick pokes with the rock, to stun me so he could measure and brain me. I was up and down and to the sides, mostly avoiding the pokes but taking a few, mostly on the left arm I was using to block. A backhand slash sliced deep into his wrist. Blood spurted and he yelled and dropped the rock. To my left in the gutter, the man twisted and screamed.

If the man had stepped back from me, I'd have been gone from that scene. Maybe eight or ten seconds we'd fought. But the beast roared in his head that he must fall on me, and he did. I was flat on the sidewalk and his left hand was under my jaw, pushing as he groped for the rock, and that was wrong, the beast is not bright. His weight on my right hip had been pinning the knife under me. Stretching for the rock took the pressure off my hip and chin and I slipped my head to the side and raised my hip, freeing the knife. His throat was stretched right over me and I slashed, and kept slashing. As his blood rained on my face, my head rang the beast's scream of delight and I screamed with him until his head fell on my shoulder and his body was dead weight and the fight was over.

I pushed and wriggled out from under. His head was on the sidewalk, left profile up, and the brown eye closed, then popped open like a wink.

Muscle reflex, I suppose. Or I imagined it. But for some reason, probably perverse, I think he gave me a goodbye wink.

What's real? Real is the moment and not the remembrance in words. Words are symbols we use to make order and reason where none was. Words are to verify that life makes sense and death, too. Which may be the great myth. But it's a myth we want to believe and are fools if we give up, because if so what's left? Only the beast in all of us.

After the wink he gave me, or didn't, his eye was clear for a second, then went to gray glass. I was up. Where the wounded one was I didn't know and didn't hear him.

How long was the fight—twenty seconds? half an hour? Time's a myth, too. A woman with blood all over her clothes, face, hair, and hands ran south up that mean street.

Nobody rose in front of me and nobody shouted to stop me, and a couple of sets of headlights came up but kept going. I ran to the next corner, cut left, and ran another block south. I piled into my van and heard sirens—and stayed low until they went by on Mission Street. One turned up my street and went past. Later I wended side streets and eventually got on 101 southbound, not slowing until just north of San Luis, halfway point to L.A.

Pulling up a farm road, I parked under trees, got in back, and peeled my bloody clothes off and into a plastic sack, then huddled in blankets and went to sleep.

If the farmer had come around and called the cops, the play would have ended that morning.

I was up early and rubbed and picked blood off my face and hands and out of my hair, wrapped a fresh bandana around my head, and got into clean clothes. I wiped and picked the cockpit and wheel more or less clean, drove to an early-open service station, filled up, and drove home to L.A. There I burned the clothes in the fireplace. After that, I took a complete bath and slept until the next day.

At the library, the San Francisco paper said the man died on the way to the hospital of loss of blood and the other was seriously but not fatally slashed. He said they had walked past a woman, who for no reason ran back in front of them and started slashing. He had no view of her, as it was so quick, and witnesses at windows couldn't describe her as she was all over blood. Nobody said anything about the van.

I didn't send the SFPD a note.

*   *   *

The play is over. That's why I wrote this summary of my three killings, which are now in the past, with nothing more to say or think about them.

I've found out that I hate the beast and love him, and those killings were acts of love, as he knew all the time and I know now.

Words make the myths we live by and die for. The beast is reality, the white-hot core of humankind, so somebody said. And so what? Rise above reality into myth. If love is a myth, give me love. If beauty if a myth, like an evening by a lake, strolling with the one you mythically love, I'll take it and believe in it—not the reality that intruded on us there.

Love, honor, decency, loyalty, compassion for others—are they myths? Why not? Guard and treasure them.

The play is over. I can't handle the beast any more—he's taking me over and I know my love for him has become too much. I can't stand him any more because I can't withstand him any more. I know that, having seen myself—in this essay or analysis or whatever it has turned into, as I was in that park in that nice town in Illinois that night.

I'm at this rest stop south of Portland because I read in the library of a man savaging women there. He's killed three. The last was a month ago—which seems his pattern, a month or so in between.

Here's a question many men ask—why do women walk or jog alone in dark places? And then ask it to set up the answer, which can be put as a question. Are they looking for trouble, is that what they want? Which sets up the conclusion, also as a question. If so, when a bad thing happens, isn't it at least partly their fault?

I've never had that 1–2–3 set of questions put to me, but I've heard them put man-to-man in a bar or restaurant following some horrible crime in the news. I never cut in, being the cat that walks by herself. But once or twice I've been tempted to say, "Are you asking me specifically? Okay, I'll answer specifically—you're dead right and right on. That's why I walk alone in dark places, looking for trouble. Send me a rapist-killer and see how I do with my switchblade. Send me the beast, send me my love."

And I'd go on, in this monologue that'll never happen. "Other women I can't speak for. Each is herself. She may walk or jog alone in dark parks because she feels she owes it to life not to be afraid. Fear that would keep her behind locked doors at night may be anti-life for her, and she'll give it no room. She'll stroll or jog in parks and be free and alive while she's alive. Afterward is too late. She'll honor life now, and when death comes know she lived."

Here I am at the end of this that's turned into a discovery trip of myself and I'm hungry and tired and it's 12:38.

I hate and love him and have that strong feeling he'll be in a park in Portland.

I'm good. Maybe not as good as five years ago, but a lot better than most twenty-fives or twenties. I'm good, and you don't stop while you're good.

One more scene, one more waltz, one more ecstasy—*then* Canada? Maybe. Wrong to look too far ahead. The living is now.

I went away from the thought I had at the beginning of this, which was the right thought and I know it and am back to it: the play ends when it ends, not when I say.

On a night in March, a young woman in old jeans and a scruffy shirt, blanket wrapped around her, wrote all that over about six hours without pause, except once to get a fresh ballpoint from the desk drawer. Then she closed the spiral notebook and put it and the pen in the drawer and, tossing aside the blanket, got up, stretched her whole body for a few seconds, then stepped around, letting up the shades on the windows. She slid her feet into sandals, put on a jacket, tied a green bandana around her hair, turned off the lamp, and, shoving back the front curtain, got in the cockpit. In a couple of minutes, she had backed the van clear and was on the highway toward Portland.

Her taillights proceeded straight about a half mile, then veered around a curve just as a highway cruiser passed the rest stop northbound. In a few seconds its taillights veered around the curve.

A play ends when it ends.

The Moon was to Blame

ANTONIA FRASER

*I*sabel said afterward that we were really getting too old for that sort of thing: which remains perhaps the best verdict on the whole sad affair. Unless you take the line—as my wife did—that the moon was to blame.

They've never found out who did it: just some ugly little incident among a lot of drunken campers. Since clearly none of us was involved, they let us all go and back we all came to England. Not immediately— that would have looked odd since we'd rented an expensive villa—but a little sooner than planned. You could hardly blame us for cutting short our holiday by a few days. A death on the beach below, police crawling all over the place, *Greek* police what's more: not that we put it like that to the charming young woman in the villa rental office, given that she was a Greek. In any case, she was most understanding. Especially as we showed no signs of asking for a reduction in the rent.

Obviously none of us four were involved—how could we be involved, up in that great big villa on the rock? How could a smart villa party of well-off married people from London be involved with some little scrubber camping down below? Different worlds. Utterly different worlds. Quite soon, the police took that line, too.

The world of the campers below was not only a different world, but a pretty horrible one to boot. Crowds—there must have been nearly fifty campers down there—and squalor, naturally, since there was no sanitation beyond the natural shade of the olive trees, those graceful trees whose leaves had flickered so exquisitely in the sunlight on the day we arrived, when the beach was still empty.

"Do you realize that apart from anything else—apart from the noise, ye Gods, the noise, we hardly slept a wink last night, did we, Isabel?— do you realize that it's *illegal?*" That was Nick. Isabel nodded vigorously, as she always agreed strongly with everything that Nick said in public. (In private, since the villa walls were not entirely soundproof, we were aware that matters were somewhat different.) But my wife, Dinah, did murmur to me afterward in that light voice of hers—the one she uses for her really snaky remarks—that it was wonderful to have Nick standing up for the law here on the tiny island of Bexi, it really must be the effect of the sun, since back on the great big island of Britain Nick sometimes took rather a different line about the law.

But I had better begin at the beginning. No, not at the very beginning, not from our very first business enterprise; suffice it to say that the four of us, Dinah and myself, Nick and Isabel, had become close enough over the years to take villas together in sunny foreign parts over a considerable span of time. The Algarve, Italy, Greece (Corfu followed by Paxos), all these have produced comfortable villas, more or less, and happy holidays, of which the same could probably be said. And frankly, a holiday which is more or less happy is way above most holidays you take: which is, I think, why we all persevered with the arrangement.

Did I mention that something else unites us—beyond the same line of work and living nowadays in the same part of London? We're all childless, or effectively childless. Nick did have a son by his first marriage, I believe, but either the mother kept him to herself or Isabel dumped him—the story varies. At all events, he never figures in our lives. As for ourselves, we've certainly never wanted children. We're enough for each other, always have been. I look after Dinah, she looks after me, as we're fond of saying, so that at the age when our contemporaries are spending all their time worrying over their ungrateful twenty-year-olds and a good deal of their money rescuing them from this, that, and the other, also without getting much thanks, we four have the luxury of our time to ourselves. And our money, too, come to think of it.

Douceur de vivre: that's our motto (and, yes, it does sound much better in French, but then we four are, I fancy, rather more enlightened in our enjoyment of luxury than the average couples who toast "the sweet life").

This year we decided to experiment with a lesser island and go to

Bexi. An island paradise, said the brochure. And so I suppose it was—in a way. Much less spoilt than Corfu and much nearer to a decent airport than Paxos. Villa Aglaia was pretty near paradise, too. At first. Even my wife, who generally finds something to say about the washing arrangements or lack of them, approved the separate showers for each double bedroom, to say nothing of a water supply which actually did not run out. (Remembering that time outside Portofino!) And the view was so extraordinary, right there on the cliffs; we would look toward Albania at night and watch the moon rise. A thin crescent the night we arrived—amusing to be drinking retsina again, once the duty-free champagne ran out—but rapidly growing.

The moon: yes. Perhaps, after all, Dinah was right and the moon was to blame. Insofar as anyone else was to blame. Certainly the moon appears to have been to blame for what started to happen on the beach. When the first campers appeared—one large gray tent under the olives and one girl who slept under an old boat—we even thought them quite picturesque. The girl, anyway. "The local Samantha Fox," my wife dubbed her on one occasion, since she certainly had the most fantastic figure—the sort you could photograph for Page Three, as we couldn't help noticing since she seldom wore anything but a bikini bottom.

But Samantha Fox wasn't quite right since Brigitte—that was actually her name—happened to be brown all over, having an amazing tan apart from having an amazing figure. As a matter of fact, I chatted to her quite a bit in early mornings when no one else was around, and she was really very polite and friendly—just a kid working her way around Europe as a waitress, taking a holiday on this beach in between. German probably—or was she Swedish? She had this special feeling about St. Peter's, Rome, I remember, the square at St. Peter's; she was absolutely determined to see the square. We had quite long talks about it.

Not when the others were around, however. Then, I have to say, the conversation was on a very different level. Well, we were on holiday. There was one famous occasion when Brigitte, topless, wobbled so perilously near Nick, sunbathing on the stones, on her way to the sea that my wife and I both involuntarily looked toward Isabel.

The fact is that Isabel, who does sometimes bathe topless (but always discreetly up at the villa), does have the most lovely slim figure, everyone agrees about that. But if Isabel has a fault, it's the fact that, good-looking woman as she is, she is totally flat-chested. Perhaps that explains why I've never really fancied her, and perhaps that explains again why we've all holidayed so happily together. Be that as it may, on this occasion Isabel merely smiled in her most tranquil manner and murmured something like, "I should be so lucky." Later in their bedroom, however, it was rather a less tranquil story. What a tigress! That serene, smiling woman. Still, the end of it sounded rather satisfactory—at least from Nick's point of view, and I assume Isabel's as well.

All the time, the moon was getting stronger at night—I should say bigger, but was it the increasing strength of the moonlight rather than the size of the moon itself which was so unsettling? Could you believe moonlight could be so white? Even when the moon was only half full. That strange, cold, ancient light illuminating the sea which washed the rocks beneath us, the sea stretching out to the Albanian coast in a vast series of black-and-silver eddies with that broad flare path in their center.

We took to sitting later and later on the terrace with our wine—a light Greek wine, for after dinner. "So light, it's like drinking water," Nick had said jovially on our second night. But of course it wasn't quite like drinking water, particularly not in the quantities in which we consumed it. Perhaps it was all that wine late at night which made us so unsettled. They were odd, quirky, even slightly sinister, those sessions we had on the terrace. Yet hadn't we drunk wine in the Algarve and Italy and Paxos only the year before, the result being mere pleasure, relaxation?

Most unsettling of all, after we finally left the terrace, my wife and I had to lie, silent and sleepless, in our bedroom hot behind the shutters and listen to Isabel, the tigress of the night, who was growing more and more ferocious in the room alongside ours. Was *that* the wine? The wine coupled with the moonlight (I noticed they did not close their shutters)? Or was it the noises coming from the beach?

For the waxing moon brought campers, more and more campers. And given its provocative light, bathing the beach in its brightness like a too-well-lit stage where there had been nothing but discreet blackness before, we could hardly ignore their presence. There was—I can see it now, and my wife can see it, too—a feeling of working toward some kind of climax long before we heard the news about the party.

Besides, one or two fires began to flicker down below: those fires so dangerous to a wooded island depending on its olive groves, which was in fact the official reason for the banning of campers on Bexi. When we went down to swim in the early morning, we would find the black shells of night fires among the stones. There would also be cans of coke, beer, and bottles abandoned. And other even more distasteful signs of what had taken place on the beach the night before. Signs of "safe sex" perhaps, but as my wife observed, wrinkling her nose (I hastily removed one of these signs from her favorite path into the water, burying it under a big cairn of pebbles), "Safe sex is all very well, but what about a beautiful beach?"

Oddly enough, Brigitte very much kept to herself, apart from it all. She was friendly enough with the campers—she was a friendly girl, as I've said—but she never joined in with them at their various unpleasant goings-on. I know that, because I used to watch her sometimes from the lookout up above, watch her gazing out to sea, smoking the odd cigarette. What was she thinking about? St. Peter's square in Rome, perhaps, something like that. But I kept all that to myself, just as I never mentioned our morning conversations before the campers came.

At least the Villa Aglaia remained airy and remote from the squalor. In the daytime, when the campers were asleep or away in the little town of Bexi, so long as you didn't go down to the beach or visit the lookout you could cut yourself off from the squalor altogether. My wife cut branches of myrtle from the bushes which lined the steep but short path from the villa to the beach and put them everywhere in vases in the big rooms. But as the noise grew in proportion to the number of campers, I asked her not to cut back any more of the myrtle, for the bushes did at least conceal the path to the villa. What if the campers, drunk—or drugged, I put nothing past them—all decided to surge up the path in the small hours?

"Then you, darling, will have to be a big he-man and protect me," Dinah said in her snaky voice. "I somehow don't think Nick and Isabel would notice."

It was Nick who brought back the news of the party which was going to be held on the beach on the night of the full moon. He had been into the little port in the Landrover just before dinner, while Isabel was washing her hair, to cash some traveler's checks. He came back looking white, or as near white as anyone as perfectly cared for and turned out (which means tanned) as Nick can ever look.

"A bloody great notice!" he exploded. "In English, what's more. Full Moon Party. On Aglaia Beach—our beach. Everyone invited. Bonfires, dancing, naked bathing. Come by boat! Come by moped! On the night of the full moon. All this on a notice fixed to a tree just outside the town." He repeated: "And in English, too."

"If it hadn't been in English, Nick," my wife pointed out reasonably enough, "you wouldn't have understood it." But Isabel, short, carefully streaked hair in a shining halo, was busy giving Nick a rewarding pat.

"Well done, Nick. At least you've warned us."

"Warned us! I damn well have. Look, I'm going to have a whiskey. Have we got any left? It's a disgrace. Tomorrow I'm going to tell that little Greek girl in the office that I want it stopped, stopped without question."

"But tomorrow will be too late, Nick," Dinah continued in that same reasonable voice. "Tonight is the night of the full moon. Didn't you notice last night? It was very, very nearly full—only one tiny sliver missing."

I must say that I was surprised at the time that my wife had that kind of information at her fingertips, but then I read in one of the magazines you only read in airplanes that retaining the capacity to surprise your spouse is the secret of a happy marriage. I daresay it's Dinah's remarkable sense of order which made her interested in something equally regulated like the phases of the moon.

So we come to the party. I have to admit a certain reluctance in thinking about it all, even now, back in London W.11 in our beautiful house, the house which some people laughingly suggest is too big for us—"too luxurious even for you two"—but is actually a wonderful monument to my wife's exquisite, cool, and above all fastidious taste. A showcase for a sense of order, somebody else said.

If that's true about our house, and it probably is, then you can just imagine how poor Dinah suffered during that nightmare buildup to the Full Moon Party on Aglaia Beach. The utter chaos, the noise, of course—the noise was indescribable—and let me not leave out the fear. The four of us, four sophisticated people, crouching there—I'm afraid after a while we were definitely crouching—as the car lights came toward the beach along the edge of the cliff, an army advancing on us, and the full moonlight lit up what went on below. In a way it reminded me of some medieval picture of Hell—all the couples writhing as though in torment, their white limbs gyrating. In fact, they were of course dancing and copulating. You would feel like using that word if you had seen what we saw.

"Supposing they do decide to come up here?" Nick said that, I know he did. "Just supposing?" Nick is a big man, very heavily built in spite of all the exercise he takes. We're both of us big men, come to that, two big men with two fragile wives—that was another thing we had in common. Dinah, like Isabel, is wonderfully slender—well preserved or whatever you call it. Naturally she takes marvelous care of herself. But even Nick sounded frightened. And I was frightened, too.

It was some time after that that it happened.

"Supposing you went down there? Just supposing." Who said that? Who spoke those words? It must have been my wife, for who else was present when those words were spoken? Nick and Isabel had gone off to bed at last, their shutters open to the noises of the hot inflaming night, and the light of the coldly lustful moon. We could hear that the tigress was already devouring her huge submissive prey when those words were spoken.

The excitement comes back to me now, the secret, thrilling fear of it all, and the whispered words which went on: "Take her—you want her. She's down there. Find her and take her. You want her, don't you? Take her, you want her. Take her, you want her."

Take her, you want her, wanton and naked, wanton and naked, the words became like a rhythm beating in my brain. Wanton and naked: but no, these last words were never spoken, even by my wife, but they, too, became like a rhythm in my brain.

Those were the words which continued to turn and tumble in my mind as I went down alone, down the myrtle path to the Aglaia Beach.

It wasn't difficult to find her—Brigitte, the brown goddess of the beach. She wasn't even dancing with the others round the fire; she was sitting by the upturned boat, alone in the dark shadow cast by the boat. She was smoking one of her cigarettes and looking out to sea. Perhaps she was thinking about Rome and St. Peter's. I rather hope so. I really rather hope she was thinking about something nice. Even by the boat, the noise of all the others was incredible, confusing, and they had transistors now, belting out their dance music across the moonlit sea, desecrating the moonlight, desecrating the whole beach.

I took her quite easily. I grabbed her, grabbed that round brown wobbly body. She was quite little in my arms, in spite of her fullness—much smaller than I thought she would be. So I took her and held her tight. She couldn't shout, either—not that it would have mattered much if she had, the noise was so loud, the other people so busy round the bonfire. All the same, I put my hand across her mouth.

"Now show me you're a man, after all—a real man. Take her!" But she didn't say "take" this time—she used something far rougher, cruder. That was my wife's voice again, she must have followed me down the myrtle path, but it was a voice so avid, so ferocious, that for a moment it even might have been the tigress, Isabel. And besides, I'd never heard my wife use a word like that in all our married life.

And I did take her. Didn't I? I would have taken her. If only she'd cooperated just a little, practiced a little of that love and friendship she talked about to me on the beach.

Instead, she struggled—struggled rather a lot. I mean, why flaunt yourself like that, half naked, sometimes wholly naked, if you're not prepared to cooperate just a little?

As to what happened after that, there's really no point in recounting it all. Sad and rather squalid, really, but a complete accident. Even a misunderstanding, you could say. If it hadn't happened with me, it would have happened sooner or later with any of the other men she led on and didn't satisfy.

Afterward I hardly remembered the details of it all, isn't that odd? Just coming back so carefully and silently up the myrtle path, my wife's eyes gleaming like a cat's as we felt our way. Afterward holding her in bed, and my wife, usually so fastidious, holding me, too. Nick and Isabel were silent by then. That night, very late, it was my wife who was the tigress at the Villa Aglaia . . .

There's so much more to tell. As I said, the police didn't really bother us much, just a great many questions and all that, naturally, but mostly the obvious questions about the party and the noise and then the tragedy—had we heard anything, seen anything, that sort of thing. It went on for hours.

Heard anything! Nick really snorted at that one, I can tell you. For a moment I thought he was going to start up all over again about the noise and the camping being illegal and why didn't the police stop it? Which under the circumstances wouldn't have been quite appropriate. But as a matter of fact, Nick's pretty good with the police, officials generally, knows the value of politeness and all that. He also cut quite an impressive figure, all washed and shaved and tidy.

We all were—washed and shaved and tidy. And the Villa looked immaculate. As anyplace with my cool, collected wife at the helm invariably does.

As to Nick being so good with the police and officials generally, my wife did murmur afterward: "Well, he's had a certain amount of practice, hasn't he?" But then, as I already mentioned, my wife has always been a little tart—one can't say more than that—about Nick's sharp business practices. As usual, there's a good deal to be said for her point of view.

The conversation with Nick and Isabel after the police left really rather proved her point.

First of all, Isabel said, yawning slightly: "Listen, folks, we've been thinking it over. We're really getting a little old for this sort of thing— holidays à quatre, I mean. It's been great, of course, no need to say that, but it's a hotel for us next year. Villas on the sea can be noisy. You can hear everything. That's a fact. The most peculiar things. The later at night, the more peculiar. So it's a luxury hotel à deux for us, in future."

She didn't seem to expect an answer to what she had just announced and I suppose there wasn't much we could say. She didn't look at either of us as she spoke, I do remember that.

Then Nick chimed in. He'd been thinking overnight as well, it seemed. And what Nick had been thinking about was the next big deal—the one where there'd been a bit of an argument, seeing as I had done all the work from start to finish and couldn't see that he should have more than a very small cut. Well, on this particular deal, he simply stated that the split would be fifty-fifty. With no argument. He didn't seem to expect an answer to that one, either . . .

As a matter of fact, I don't miss our joint holidays with Nick and Isabel. She was right, we really had grown out of all that. It's that fifty percent which still rankles. But whenever I say so to my Dinah—I groan and ask, "Why did I agree?"—she replies in here snaky voice (which, generally speaking, she uses a great deal less nowadays):

"You lost your head in Bexi, that's why." Then she adds more softly, "It was the moon that was to blame." There's even a voluptuous note in her voice when she asks in her turn: "Wasn't it all worth it?"

Night Watch Hero

PAUL AMEDICK

A drop of perspiration streaked down his throat and chest, down behind the little fox on his light blue pullover shirt. Harvey Nimmons steered his Pinto into yet another cul-de-sac and thought that it was too hot for this late in the summer. And much too hot to be wasting his Saturday night driving all over the neighborhood like a fool.

His hand fondled the portable citizen's band radio on the seat beside him, then pulled back as if it had burned. I won't make that mistake again.

Harvey leaned forward and held his wrist up to the dashboard lights. Nearly midnight. Only two hours to go on his shift.

His car lights lapped gently over the cracks in the winding concrete road and illuminated asphalt driveways leading up to redwood carports. Harvey peered through the windshield at the half-moon shadows cast by trees scattered over neatly trimmed lawns. Could be someone lurking behind any one of them, he thought. Ridiculous.

He tried to refocus his mind on more pleasant things, like tomorrow's regular Sunday afternoon softball game with the guys from the office. Nice to escape from the house for a while, even with a bunch of other middle-aged architectural draftsmen who thought they were Pete Rose or Reggie Jackson.

The heat trapped during the day seemed to rise up from the road and enter the cramped car. Harvey shifted his slight frame and pushed his thinning hair back from his forehead, hesitating for a moment on the balding spot in the back. He gripped the steering wheel and willed

his mind to concentrate on watching, but the heat and the sweat running down his neck kept reminding him of the early summer evening
that had gotten him into this.

The school auditorium that Sunday evening had been crowded with
angry citizens shouting their concern over the rash of burglaries that
had invaded the quiet South Jersey suburb of Chestnut Run Township.
Harvey slouched in his front-row seat, holding himself midway between
his wife, Norah, on his left and an old man dozing on his right, trying
to keep his sweat-soaked shirt from touching anything. And trying not
to be noticed by the three town leaders seated on folding chairs on
the platform. The honorable councilmen—Harris, Wiley, and Steinberg.
Sounds like a law firm, Harvey thought.

He stared at his mud-encrusted sneakers and tried to block out the
overpowering sounds of the voices raised around him.

Norah elbowed his ribs. "Sit up straight, Harvey. And for God's sake,
pay attention." And then she was on her feet, waving her pudgy arm
at the council chairman. "Ralph! Ralph Harris! We've debated this long
enough. We need this program. I know it and you know it and I call
for a vote right now."

The Chestnut Run Neighborhood Watch program was born that
night.

"Norah, I really don't think this is for me."

"Harvey, you have to do your part too. What's the big deal? You'll
put in your time like everyone else."

The time! Past time to check in. Harvey stretched out his hand and
searched in the dark seat beside him for the portable radio. "This is
unit fifteen, unit one-five calling base. Come in."

The high-pitched voice of Edna Hopkins, the town clerk who was
on as "dispatcher" that night, crackled over the speaker.

"That you, Nimmons? Everything all right out there?"

"Yes, Edna. Everything is quiet here. No problems."

"That's good. Sure hope you don't have any more trouble, like you
did last month."

Harvey felt himself flush as he heard her giggle come over the radio,
and quickly snapped the set off. There was no need for that. Not with
everyone else on the network listening in. And laughing now. One little
mistake. It was only his second night out, and who could blame him
for calling out the police backup unit? Lights shouldn't go on in someone's house when they're on vacation. Unless they have automatic tim-

ers, he thought bitterly. One little false alarm and everyone thought it was so darn funny. Particularly Norah.

Harvey jammed the radio down between the seats and tried to push the memory from his mind. Concentrate on the road, he told himself.

The cry of a mockingbird filtered through the open window, carried on the still air, and Harvey thought of the squawking of gulls fighting over scraps of bait as he fished alone in a small boat. Norah didn't like fishing. He smiled.

Harvey turned right onto Walnut Lane, the last of the streets in his assigned area.

Manicured lawns and trimmed shrubs protected each two-story house from the intrusion of its neighbors. No raucous parties here on celebrity row, Harvey thought.

He hunched forward with his forearms on the steering wheel and glared into the shadowed porches and darkened windows drifting slowly by.

The tiny explosion of breaking glass echoed through the stillness, and Harvey bumped his head lightly on the windshield as he jerked the car to a stop. He cut the engine and turned off the lights. Silence.

And then he heard it. The tinkling of glass falling on a hard surface. Over there, across the street, somewhere behind the sprawling house directly opposite him.

Harvey reached down and pulled the CB radio from its nest between the seats and flicked it on. He hesitated. Another false alarm? They'd never let him forget it. "Nervous Nimmons" they'd call him. And Norah. What would she have to say? "What, again, Harvey?" He didn't want to think about that.

He turned the radio off. Maybe he could just ignore it, he thought. Who would know he was even here? But if someone did break into a house in his patrol area, that would be a big joke too. Some neighborhood watcher! Steal you blind right under old Harvey's nose. He'd have to check it out, just in case.

Harvey eased the door open, cursing under his breath as the dome light flooded the car. He hopped out and shut the door quickly, careful not to make any sound.

After two tentative steps across the road, he stopped. He didn't like the idea of sneaking around in the dark empty handed. Keeping his eyes on the corner of the large house, Harvey backed up to the rear of the car, fumbled for his car keys, and opened the hatchback. There, under the disarray of old Municipal Building drawings, was his Mike Schmidt-autographed softball bat. That would do. But what if he has a gun? Harvey shook his head to clear his thoughts, and push aside the fear. Don't be ridiculous. It's probably nothing at all.

As he pressed himself against the front corner of the house, Harvey again heard the muted tinkle of glass from the rear, followed by a grunt and a murmured curse.

He took a deep breath and edged down the side of the house, his back rubbing against the warm roughness of the stone siding. At the back corner, he gripped the softball bat tightly and froze. His heart pounded inside his chest, and he thought that surely the thumping could be heard a block away. He held his breath and peered with one eye around the corner. No false alarm this time. The dark figure silhouetted by the moonlight was hunched against the house, intent on prying jagged pieces of glass from the window frame.

Harvey pulled back from the corner and flattened quickly against the house. Have to call in, get the cops here. The sweat ran down his forehead and into his eyes, burning. As he shifted the bat to his left hand and reached up with his right to wipe his eyes on his sleeve he felt his grip loosening on the bat, slipping down. He grabbed for it.

The sound of the hard wood striking the stone wall was like a gunshot in his ears, ringing out clearly in the stillness.

"Who the hell's that?" A gravelly voice, full of anger and menace.

Harvey gripped the bat in both hands, raised it straight in the air in front of him, and whirled around the corner. "Don't move!" he shouted.

The black figure in front of him hesitated, then raised his arm and took a step forward. Moonlight glinted on a shiny surface. "I'll 'Don't move you!' "

The man took another step forward, and Harvey swung, feeling the soft crunch of the bat as it struck. The man collapsed face down at Harvey's feet.

Harvey stood paralyzed, his breath coming in gasps, his hands shaking. The bat slipped from his fingers and slid to the ground beside him, echoing hollowly on the paving stones and rolling up against the still figure.

Harvey slumped to his knees and gingerly touched the shoulder of the man on the ground. He prodded him gently, then more firmly. No movement. No sound. He placed his fingers on the man's neck, to feel for a pulse the way they did on television, but jerked his hand back as he felt the warm stickiness.

Standing on trembling legs Harvey stooped over the figure, gripped one shoulder with both hands, and slowly pulled the weight toward him. The moonlight reflected on the whiteness of the man's face, and cast a shadow on half his features. A dark smear spread across his forehead. The man rolled fully onto his back, one arm flapping to the side and striking Harvey's leg.

Harvey jumped back, stared at the man's face, and gasped. Councilman Wiley! As the realization hit him, Harvey clutched his stomach, staggered to a tree, fell to his knees, and retched. Nausea swept over him and acid bile burned his throat.

When he could breathe again, Harvey wiped his eyes with his sleeve and slumped to the ground with his back against the tree. Why the hell was he trying to break into a house? He's no burglar. And then Harvey knew, and the waves of nausea washed over him again.

As his head cleared, he stared at the still form lying by the house, then forced himself to his feet using the tree for support. He had to get help. No help for the dead, he thought. He had to tell the police, tell them Councilman Wiley had been killed breaking into his own house.

Harvey bent over the body and saw the long, thick screwdriver on the ground by the dead man's shoulder. Almost in a trance, Harvey picked up the softball bat which stuck out from under the body, and turned the corner of the house.

When he saw his car parked on the opposite side of the road, he broke into a run. Flopping into the front seat, he pulled the door closed and put his face in his hands. Sobs shook his body and hot tears joined the sweat running down his cheeks.

Finally he leaned back in the seat, his neck arched back, gasping in the still night air. He took a deep breath and fumbled for the radio. He clutched it in his sweaty hand, turned it on, and pushed the talk button.

What am I going to say? That I just killed Councilman Wiley? Blurred images flew through his mind. The thundering voice of the public prosecutor. A steel door slamming closed behind him. Striped uniforms. Stinking toilets. Rats. Disgrace. Norah's shrill voice. "You damn fool."

He dropped the radio and rested his head against the car seat, consciously controlling his breathing. In. Out. Think. His head jerked forward and his hands gripped the steering wheel. Quickly he snapped the car door open and hopped out. Nothing either way. No cars. No late night dog walkers. The mockingbird was still singing in a far off tree, as if nothing had happened in the past ten minutes. Harvey turned in a circle. No lights on in any of the houses on the block. He wiped his forehead and eyes with a handkerchief.

The voice inside his head screamed at him. Run! Get away! Harvey pinched the bridge of his nose and rubbed his eyes. But what if someone saw the car here, while I was . . . back there? No answer to that. Run! Too late.

Harvey reached in the open car door and pulled out the softball bat. Raising the hatchback he removed several large blueprint drawings and carefully wrapped the bat in them, then placed it underneath the rest of the scattered papers.

He sat in the front seat and took a deep breath, then started panting heavily. After a few moments he picked up the two-way radio and spoke breathlessly. "Base, this is Harvey. Come in. Hurry." He waited a few seconds and called again. "C'mon, Edna, this is an emergency."

The radio crackled and Edna's voice came over. "This is base, Harvey. What's the matter with you?"

"Edna, get a patrol car over here fast. There's been a killing."

"What?"

"I said there's been a killing. Get the cops here fast."

"Okay, Harvey, now calm down. Just where are you?"

"Wiley's. Councilman Wiley's place on Walnut Lane. I'm right across the street."

"Stay right there, Harv, and don't worry. I'll have the police there quick."

Harvey dropped the radio and slumped back in the seat. "You see, officer, I was patrolling and I saw this guy running from behind the councilman's house. It was just past twelve thirty. . . ."

"C'mon, Norah, it's almost four. I need some sleep." The rays from the half moon streaked across the flowered sheet, and Harvey pulled the cover up over his chest and closed his eyes. He wanted to close out her voice too.

Norah propped her chin on one pudgy hand as she rolled toward Harvey. "How can you sleep? After all that excitement?"

"I'm really worn out. I've told you everything, so let's forget it for now and let me sleep."

Norah dropped back down on the bed on her back and stared at the ceiling. She sighed. "Who would have thought it? You know, Harvey, you're almost a hero. Being that close to a real murderer. And actually chasing him."

"I didn't really chase him that far. I told you I got out of the car and started after him, but he was too fast so I went back to check the house. That's when I found, you know, the body."

"Yes, but you tried and when they catch him, you'll be a real hero. People in this town will look up to you now."

"He's probably a hundred miles away by now. Took off like a bat. The police will never find him."

Norah rolled toward him and flopped her arm across his chest, pulling him toward her. "Oh, Harvey, I'm so proud of you." She walked her fingers slowly over his chest and down his stomach.

Harvey turned his head toward the open window beside him, staring at the curtains hanging limply in the damp heat and feeling the sweat on the back of his legs and the knot slowly tightening again in his stomach. "Not now, Norah. It's too hot, and I told you I'm exhausted." And Wiley's bloody fish eye keeps staring at me and I'm going to be sick.

"In the morning then, hon. After you've had some sleep and feel nice and rested." She giggled and snuggled her nose into his neck.

The phone rang.

Norah bumped Harvey's chin as she jumped off him, reached to her nightstand, and grabbed up the receiver. "Hello. Hello."

She cupped her hand over the mouthpiece and shook Harvey. "It's a Sergeant Cummings." Turning back to the phone she said, "What is it, sergeant?" She listened for a few seconds and nudged Harvey again, pointing to the receiver and mouthing words.

He couldn't understand. She listened for several minutes with an occasional "uh-huh" between silences. Finally, she said, "Yes, sergeant, we can do that. We'll be right there." She hung up, a grin spreading over her face.

"I told you you're going to be a hero, Harvey. They got him. They got the man who did it. Isn't that great?"

Harvey bolted upright in bed and stared at his wife. "You've got to be kidding. They couldn't have." His shaking hand rubbed his eyes, trying to wipe out the images that came flooding back. "It's impossible."

"No, it isn't, hon. They got him, and they want us to come down to the station, so you can identify him. Oh, Harvey, isn't it exciting?"

Harvey threw his feet over the side of the bed and started to get up, but sat back down, suddenly dizzy, his stomach churning. He turned to his wife, his voice almost a whisper. "Who is he?"

"No one from around here." Norah was pulling her cotton nightgown up over her head, being careful not to disturb the tiny rollers in her hair. "From somewhere in Massachusetts. Or was it Mississippi? I don't know. They said he's probably just a drifter. A no-good, obviously." She pushed her feet into slippers and flapped into the bathroom.

Harvey called after her. "But how did they find him? Did they put up roadblocks or what?"

Norah's voice was muffled by the water running in the bathroom sink. "I don't know. They found him in the Country Lane Diner, over on Route 206. Just sitting there as pretty as you please."

"Impossible," Harvey muttered, as his head dropped into his hands.

"He tried to run, but they got him." She stuck her head around the corner of the bathroom door. "C'mon, Harvey. Get a move on. Isn't it exciting? They need our hero down at the police station."

The pale green paint on the walls was chipped and peeling, and Harvey stared past the broad shoulder of the police sergeant sitting opposite him. He concentrated on one pattern in the flaking paint that looked to him like a sea gull, skimming the water.

"Really something, Mr. Nimmons. Mr. Nimmons?"

Harvey slowly refocused his eyes on Sergeant Cummings. "Huh?"

"I said it was really something the way we caught that guy." His voice seemed to fill the tiny room. "Can you imagine the nerve? Sitting right there in the diner, just drinking coffee. Until my boys came in, that is. Tried to bolt out the back, but they nailed him."

Harvey looked down at his hands in his lap, and fiddled with his shirttails. Self-consciously, he began to tuck them into his pants. "Didn't get dressed very well. My wife said you wanted us here right away."

"Oh, no hurry really. He'll be in that room in another minute, and then you can get a good look at him." The sergeant indicated a glass panel in the wall beside Harvey, a heavy curtain drawn across it. "Don't worry. He won't be able to see us. It's one-way."

Harvey squirmed in the metal seat. The heat seemed worse in here, and his pants were wet and sticking to his legs.

Harvey watched the sergeant rummage through a stack of papers on the desk, then pull out a neatly typed form. He looked up at Harvey. "I'd like to go over a few details while we're waiting. Won't take long."

Harvey nodded, and ran through the story once more in his mind. The story he'd told the first policeman who had come screeching to a stop beside his car on Walnut Lane. The story he'd repeated to this sergeant and another officer when they had arrived. The story he'd related to Norah when they finally let him go home.

The first time had been hard. But then as he added details, the story became clearer in his own mind. Perhaps if he told it enough times, it would become real, and blot out that other story, the one that was etched in his brain and kept running like a continuous movie behind his eyes.

"You say he had something in his hand, like a stick, but you couldn't tell what it was?"

Harvey jolted back to the present and replayed the sergeant's words in his mind before answering slowly. "Yes, that's right. I couldn't really tell what it was. But it was long."

"Well, that's not important right now. We'll find it. Now that we know which way he went, we'll search the route and find it, don't you worry."

The sudden buzz of the phone on the desk startled Harvey and he jumped in his chair. Sergeant Cummings lifted the receiver, listened, and hung up. "We're ready." He stood and pulled a cord hanging beside the curtained window.

Harvey kept his eyes on the desk in front of him, not wanting to see through the one-way mirror, not wanting to see at all. Finally, he pulled his eyes from the desk and turned in his chair to stare through the glass. At him. At the man they had caught. In the diner. As calm as you please. Tried to run.

The man slouched in a straight-backed chair in the center of the adjoining room, alone. He turned his head and his dark eyes stared toward the glass, seemed to look into Harvey's eyes, straight through him.

Harvey felt his breath catch in his throat, felt the blood thumping in the veins in his temples, felt his stomach knot into a lump and churn. He slumped forward in his chair.

"Hey, you okay?" The sergeant was beside him, gripping his shoulder. "Just stay still a minute. Keep your head down. I'll get some water. It's a shock to come face to face with a killer. Be right back."

Harvey covered his face in his hands.

As his heartbeat became more regular and his breathing eased, he forced himself to raise his head and look through the glass at the man in the opposite room.

Harvey saw that he was tall, and his arms muscular, stretching the material of his dirty white T-shirt. The man flicked his long black hair back from his forehead, crossed his arms across his chest and tilted the chair. He clumped one foot onto the table in front of him. A dirty black boot.

"He was tall, officer, several inches taller than me. And built, big, you know. He was wearing a T-shirt and jeans, not new ones, faded. And some kind of boots. I could tell by the way he was running. But he was fast, too fast for me. His hair was long, and not too clean-looking, straggly, you know."

Harvey stared at the man. But that could describe thousands of people, he thought. Why did he give them so much detail? So they'd believe him. It had to be real. And the details just kept coming out. But where did this guy come from? Just passing through. Stopped to have a cup at the all-night Country Lane Diner. Then he ran.

What else had he told them? Harvey rubbed his eyes and leaned back against the chair, remembering.

"Any distinguishing marks, Mr. Nimmons?"

"It happened pretty quick."

"Anything for us to go on. Any details? It's important."

"Well, I think he had some sort of a chain around his waist, as a sort of belt." A tattoo. No, too obvious.

In the next room, the tall man slammed his chair back down, slapped the table and stood up. He began to pace, his hands stuck into the back pockets of his jeans.

Harvey's eyes were riveted to the heavy rope wound through the man's belt loops, tied at the waist and hanging down in two strands.

Just sitting there in the diner, as pretty as you please. He tried to run, but we got him. Harvey stared at the pacing man. Just a drifter, a nobody.

As Harvey watched the man before him, he saw the black and white stripes of the baggy uniform, heard a steel door slam closed, smelled the toilets, heard the rats scuffling beneath the bunk.

Harvey jumped as the sergeant entered behind him, and his hand trembled as he took the cone-shaped paper cup. He gulped the luke-warm water in one swallow, pulled his eyes from the sergeant standing above him, and turned toward the glass.

Harvey closed his eyes, then opened them and swung his body slowly toward the blank wall. He wiped the wetness from his forehead, took a deep breath and focused on the chipped paint, at the gull flying above the cresting waves.

"That's him, sergeant. That's the man."

Sergeant Cummings reached over the desk and picked up the telephone receiver. "Okay, you can take him out now." He pulled the heavy curtain across the window. "Want another drink of water?"

Harvey shook his head and looked up at the policeman. On the floor below a heavy door slammed.

"An interesting thing, Mr. Nimmons. While I was out getting your drink of water I saw your wife. Norah is it?" He crossed his ankles and arms and leaned back against the desk.

Harvey nodded. The heat seemed to press down, on him and a small knot formed in his stomach and moved upward toward his chest, his heart.

The sergeant went on, his voice pouring over Harvey like waves. "She's really impressed with the efficiency of our local police department, the way we snagged that man. Says you were surprised that we caught him. Why is that, Mr. Nimmons?"

Harvey licked his lips, all the moisture suddenly gone from his mouth. "Well, I thought he'd be gone. Out of town."

"Yes, it was strange that he was hanging around the Country Lane like that. We thought so too, but then he did try to run. Funny, that."

Harvey nodded. "Yes, he did try to run, but you got him."

"Yes, we got him. And we checked. Got the word back just a couple minutes ago. He's wanted for assault over in Pennsylvania."

Harvey wiped his forehead and eyes with a now soggy handkerchief and stared at the wall.

"We did some more checking, Mr. Nimmons. You see, he says he was at the Red Ridge Tavern for a couple hours before going to the diner for coffee. We checked there too. Sent some boys out to talk with the bartender. Funny thing, how a man can be in two places at once."

Harvey felt the waves of nausea pass over him. His head spun. The voice boomed, the door slammed, the rats scuffled. Harvey's eyes blurred and the bird on the wall wasn't a gull anymore, wasn't anything but chipped paint.

A Summer Night's Visitor

GORDON A. REIMS

*T*he trees were motionless in the misty twilight, as still as though they were part of an indoor stage set. The path through the underbrush had become indistinct, and the growing darkness seemed heavy behind him—almost sinister. He paused. He had a feeling he'd left something back there in the woods in his haste. But whatever it was, it would have to wait until morning.

There was something else, too. He wondered if what he thought he'd seen was still there—that strong suggestion of something yellow, something living, moving slowly toward him, far back in the deepening shadows. Was it just an illusion? A trick of the fading light? There seemed nothing there now but silent darkness.

He stumbled twice as he moved hurriedly forward again on the dark path, and felt a sense of welcome relief when he came out onto the broad lawn, with the house silhouetted before him against the deepening amber of the western sky. He walked around the dark rectangle of his wife's rose garden to the back entrance, opened the screen door, reached inside, and flicked on both indoor and outdoor lights. A few insects circled about him as he paused at the threshold and looked again toward the darkening woods.

It was then that he was sure he saw it once again, just at the point where he had emerged from the woods—that bare flicker of dull yellow; that fleeting suggestion of movement. He suddenly felt the grip of an unaccustomed tightness in his stomach.

He lingered in the doorway and watched and waited. Yes, it was definitely there, closer, and moving. It was on the lawn. The door light and the fading light from the sky combined to dimly reveal a moving slither of deep gold, a small reptilian head, two glistening beads of eyes. Like some tawny living garden hose, he could see it silently undulating as it moved toward him—directly toward him, just as he thought it had in the woods.

Standing still, he watched its progress—sometimes clearly visible; at other times so blurred into the shadow that he was almost convinced he had imagined it. Then he was sure it had reached the rose garden. But it didn't go around the beds of roses and peonies as he had done. It moved straight on into the bed's leafy shadows, noiselessly curving and uncurving. Its course was still straight toward him.

He wished for his flashlight, and remembered that it was in the pickup truck, parked in the driveway little more than twenty yards away. He walked quickly to it and, after fumbling briefly at the cluttered shelf behind the seat, found the object he was seeking. Walking slowly back, he played the flashlight beam at the dark rose bed, and then over the short stretch of lawn between the bed and the door. There was no sign of any creature.

His beam next played along the windowsills of the house, danced up and down along the wisteria vines, and probed the dark places under the heavier shrubs. Somewhere off in the woods he could hear an owl's familiar cry.

He was a few feet from the back door when he discovered with startling suddenness why he had not yet seen the creature. There it was, entwined around the bracket which held the outdoor light above the back door. Its head was poised just over the entrance like a thick golden knot—and its eyes seemed to be looking straight at him. The entire pose was one of waiting.

He'd rather not walk back into the house—not at this door. He headed quickly for the dark area of the front entrance. Flashlight beam before him, he gained the steps and tried the knob. Locked. He slapped his hands against his pockets, but no, he had no keycase with him.

Back down the steps and completely around the house in a slow circle, playing the flashlight on lawn and shrubs as he went. When he again reached the back door the bracket was bare. There was no reptile in sight. Taking a deep breath, he opened the door and stepped quickly inside. Then he closed and latched both screen door and inner door behind him.

The house seemed unusually quiet. Because Clara was not there, of course. He found himself gaping at the pot that hung over the stove; the dish-drying towels on the wooden hanger; the calendar in the corner with its little notes in the margins. He walked into the adjoining study that had once been a dinette, then down three steps into the living room where Clara's array of photographs lined the mantelpiece of the fieldstone fireplace. Each room came to life in turn as his fingers flipped wall switches. Then he returned to the kitchen, opened the refrigerator door, and grasped a container of beer. This was what he needed; this was welcome normality. He opened the container, stepped into the study, and sank into the old leather easy chair.

Almost immediately he found his attention attracted to the little west window on the wall before him. Was he mistaken, or had he caught a sudden movement in the hemlock branches just outside? He set his beer on a lamp table, stepped to the window, and pulled the shade all the way down. Then he went to each window in all the downstairs rooms, closing those that were open, despite the warmth of the night and the protective presence of screens. When he returned to the study he was surprised to find that his hands shook slightly as he raised the container of beer.

He sat quietly for a few minutes, sipping, but the silence was almost tangible. Restlessly, he left the chair once again, and this time walked to the dark stairwell. Pushing a button to flood the upper hall with light, he began to ascend the stairs.

It was as he reached the top step that definite movement caught his eye at the window at the end of the short upper hall. A thin curving shadow, dark where it was farthest from the window; slightly golden where it caught the light close to the screen. The window was open about five inches.

He forced himself to walk forward. The curtain had been pushed aside to let in air, and as he approached he could see all of the snake's form. It seemed at first suspended in air with no visible support, like a ghost or an illusion, curled in half a hoop with the triangular head looking straight into the hall. Then he realized it was hanging from the support wire which stretched from the outside ledge to the narrow chimney.

He slammed the window shut and pulled the curtain across. Through these brief seconds the reptile had been motionless, the yellow, looping cords seeming enormous. He closed all the remaining upstairs windows.

The attic? No, he wouldn't worry there; he'd just make sure the attic door itself was firmly closed.

He walked into the square front bedroom, with its flower-patterned wallpaper. Here the stillness and Clara's absence seemed doubly noticeable. He decided then that he would sleep on the cot in the study.

Returning downstairs, he went to the kitchen and stuffed a dish towel into the floor opening around the drainpipe under the sink. He made sure the cellar door was closed. Then he spotted the telephone on its blue kitchen ledge, and a moment later was dialing a number from memory.

"Bart? This is Jess. Tell me, did you ever hear of snakes following people?"

"You mean like chasing them?"

"I've been followed by a snake, Bart, right out of the woods and across the yard. It came after me—all the way to the house! It's been looking in the windows at me. I think it's trying to get in!"

A brief silence at the other end. "I'll be damned, Jess—never heard of a snake following anybody. Maybe it has a nest in your foundation or is looking for mice. What kind of snake is it?"

"It's golden, Bart—pure gold in color. As long as a blacksnake, but pure smooth gold."

"Now, Jess, there's no such snake around here." Bart's voice was low and relaxed and somehow reassuring. "Blacks and garters, yes, but that's it. Haven't seen a copperhead or a rattler near here since I was a boy. Where'd you say you first saw it?"

"On the rocks back there in the woods. I wasn't too sure at first. It seemed to slide off the rocks and come toward me."

Bart chuckled. "Hell, it likes you, Jess; you've got a new pet. Anyway, I wouldn't really worry—it'll probably be gone in the morning. Is Clara worried?"

"Clara's visiting her sister in Springfield."

"So that's why you're scared!" Bart laughed again. "Being alone up there by the woods is getting to you."

"Don't be ridiculous. But it's damned eerie to have a snake follow you—to actually stalk you. I'm telling you, this one came right to the window and looked straight at me with its beady little eyes!"

He heard Bart chuckle. "If I didn't know you better, Jess, I'd think you were imagining things. I sure never heard of a snake chasing a man—they usually try to avoid you. Even a rattler will attack only if it thinks it's on the defensive. I wouldn't give it a worry, Jess—it'll be gone in the morning."

Replacing the telephone, Jess returned to the leather chair, leaned back, finished his beer, and reflected. His mind drifted to stories of the supernatural; to animals mysteriously guided by villainous minds; to hallucinatory snakes. Something he'd read long ago, perhaps in childhood, crept darkly into his thoughts—the story of a reptile whose mind had been controlled by a departed human spirit.

Annoyed at himself, he kicked off his shoes and stretched out tentatively atop the spread on the old cot. The stuffed toy dog from Clara's childhood peered comically down at him from a corner shelf; beside it the old broken cuckoo clock he'd long promised Clara he'd have repaired. He really didn't think he could go to sleep, but he'd give it a try.

Perhaps he did sleep briefly. He thought that he finally must have dozed off, for he suddenly awoke from a half-dream with a decided sense of time lapse—and of alarm. He'd heard a sound.

It was just a small sound, not alarming in itself, but unusual in the house at night. Because it was different it brought back all the deeply seated uneasiness. It was just a metallic "ping"—a muted, gentle, metallic contact of some kind. It came, or seemed to come, from the living room.

His mind raced over possibilities. A moth or large flying bug striking something metallic? A drop of water hitting a metal utensil? But that would have to be in the kitchen. He lay listening, alert, focusing his mind on the recollection of the sound, straining to hear if it might be repeated. And now there was something else—very faint; very slight. A loose cloth being pulled across a rough wood edge? No, that would likely be his imagination.

His thoughts went back to metallic objects. What was metallic in the living room or elsewhere close by? Should he investigate? And then came a familiar creak—much fainter than usual but familiar. It was the sound made when someone started up the three steps to the study from the living room. He sat up on the couch and stared at the stairway opening. He could feel a tingling at the base of his neck.

He knew suddenly what the metallic sound had been. It had been made by something striking the andirons that hung in their places at the fireplace. The fireplace! The one possibility he'd failed to foresee—the one opening through which a snake could enter. The creature had been on that chimney support wire outside the upstairs window, and had only to follow it to the chimney itself and slip down into the fireplace. Now it was undoubtedly mounting the three steps.

He groped frantically for the light beside the cot. If the snake had crossed that loose board those many seconds ago it might well be reaching the cot right now. He suddenly recalled reading that some snakes can "see" animals or people in the dark through heat-sensitive nodes in their foreheads. Flinging his arms out wildly he struck the lamp, almost knocking it over, but finally found the switch.

As light filled the room he heard car engines. Headlight beams flared across the window. He glanced around him just long enough to make sure there was no snake on the cot or on the immediately adjacent carpet. Then he leaped from the cot. In stockinged feet but still fully dressed otherwise, he raced into and across the kitchen. In a hasty fumble he opened inner door and screendoor, and ran out onto the cool damp grass into the glare of headlights.

"There's a snake inside!" he shouted.

Two vehicles were present. One was obviously a police car, with its rotating light on the roof and the loud squawk of radio voices. The other was merely represented by bright headlights glaring out of the dark.

"Mr. Sebring?" A heavy, brisk voice. A strong flashlight beam played quickly over him, up and down.

"Yes, yes. There's a snake in my house."

"A snake in your house?" The brisk voice seemed challenging.

"Yes, a yellow one. It was trying to get in and I closed all the windows, but it came down the chimney!"

"Just like Santa Claus?"

Off to one side, another flashlight beam focused briefly on the shrubbery and then moved to the back door of the house. The figure behind each flashlight was but a vague shadow.

"Mr. Sebring." The figure holding the first flashlight lowered it slightly. "I must remind you that you have the right to remain silent; you have the right—"

"What do you mean?" A confused and wary tone crept into Jess's voice. "I'm only being chased by a snake!"

"I'm afraid it's a little more than that, Mr. Sebring," the brisk voice responded. "Incidentally, I'm Sergeant Brusette, Lakeside Station, State Police."

Every bone and muscle in Jess's body seemed to sag at once.

A third figure, more recognizable, now appeared at Jess's side. "I went into the woods after our phone conversation," Bart Clary said in his low, easy voice. "I went up that path with my son. I was curious, and concerned. I live near the path, too, you know."

He took something from his pocket and held it in front of Jess. "Out there by the rocks I thought I saw a yellow snake, too. But it was just this, dangling across the rocks. Isn't it Clara's?" The object in his muscular hands was a slender yellow belt.

"You left your shovel out there, Mr. Sebring," Sergeant Brusette added in a flat voice. "That's what led us to dig."

Jess covered his face with his hands.

"Under the stones," Bart said, "we found Clara's dress—and then Clara."

"We understood that your wife was to have visited her sister in Springfield," said Sergeant Brusette, "but with Mr. Clary's assistance we contacted the sister and found this to be untrue."

Jess shook his head slowly in the loose grip of his hands. "I didn't mean to kill her," he murmured. "I didn't mean to."

The screen door slammed, and the carrier of the second flashlight emerged. "No snake in the house as far as I can see, sergeant." A few steps from the house he added, "Oh, and the fireplace flue was closed."

The Marked Man

DAVID ELY

*J*t was early evening when he entered the Park. He headed for the darkest part, away from the lamps that lighted the pathways. He didn't see any other strollers, but he hurried all the same, not wanting to take chances.

When he reached the shelter of the first trees, he stopped and looked back toward the drive, even though he knew the car was no longer there. They had driven off as soon as they'd let him out. He'd been clapped on the shoulder—like the jump sign in a plane—and one of them had said, "Good luck, Major," and then he'd stepped out, with the weight of his flying suit dragging on him.

Good luck, Major. If he did have luck, those would be the last words anyone would address to him for four weeks.

He pulled back, startled. Someone had run past him, right past him, no more than a yard away—a man or boy running hard but with light steps in the direction of Fifth Avenue.

The Major squatted; his breath came quick, his pulse beat high. That had shaken him, whatever it had been—some college kid training for track, or some fellow running for the hell of it, or maybe a purse snatcher, and in that case there might be police on the way. The police were the ones he feared the most. The Agency had cleared things with the Commissioner, and the captains of the nearest precincts had been informed, as a safeguard against publicity in the event he got caught, but of course the ordinary officer didn't know. Just one flash of a patrolman's torch could put an end to the project.

He had to avoid the lights. He'd had no idea there would be so

many, not only the lamps along the pathways but also the automobile
headlights on the drive that crossed the Park, and the big hotels and
apartment buildings along its boundaries.

He kept moving through the trees, trying to shore up his confidence
by physical activity. This first night would be the hard one. He knew
that. If he managed this one, and the day to come, he'd probably be
all right. He'd have to pick a hiding place that was far from where
people normally went—away from the zoo, the lake, and the playing
fields. He'd rather be caught by a policeman than by kids playing ball.
If one of them got a glimpse of him, they'd all come shouting and
pointing. He imagined a grotesque chase—a gang of boys pursuing a
man made clumsy by the pilot's suit. They'd be yelling: *His head, his
head. Look at his head.*

The head—that was the Agency's guarantee of his honesty. He
couldn't cheat, not with that head. When they'd told him about it, he
hadn't objected. He knew they were right. The project psychologist
had talked to him for a long time about it. The object was to measure
the psychological stress on a man hiding in the midst of a hostile
population. If they could do that, then they could build a rescue program that made sense for the one pilot in twenty who'd been shot
down but not captured, and had managed to hide somewhere—in a
field, a bomb-blasted ruin, an abandoned apartment, anywhere he could
find.

"You'll be that twentieth pilot, Major," the psychologist had told him.
"You'll make it to the Park. Then you'll have to hide until you're rescued.
But remember, you're a marked man. You're isolated from the people
around you by the one thing you can't change—you can't speak the
language. Well, for the purposes of this test, we can simulate almost
anything but that. Nothing would prevent you from hiding that flying
suit and swiping the pants off some Park tramp if you had to. Then
you could just stroll over to the nearest bench to spend a quiet day
reading the papers with nobody the wiser, and if some policeman came
up to you, you could pass the time of day with him just as nicely as
you pleased.

"Oh, we know you have no such intention, Major. We know you're
determined to play this thing straight. But we also know that when a
man is in a stress situation, even if it's a simulated situation, he may do
things he wouldn't normally do. So you understand that we've got to
protect the project. We've got to give you a handicap that's roughly

the equivalent of loss of language. We've got to make you conspicuous in a way that's beyond your control."

And so they'd shaved his head and stained it green, a clear fresh green, green as new-grown grass.

The Major found a crevice between two boulders at the base of a small ridge. It was just wide enough for him to squeeze his body through. He worked for several hours in there with his entrenching tool hollowing out a cavity in the earth. He had stripped off his pilot's suit and laid it on the ground to hold the dirt he dug out. When he had a load, he gathered up the suit in his arms and carried it off, shaking it, so that the dirt was distributed over a wide area. Then from one of his pockets he took a small can—dog-repellent—and sprayed his entrance carefully.

The spring night was chilly, but at least it wasn't raining. On a wet night he'd have left muddy prints and tracks all over. He was lucky, too, that it was mid-week, for there'd be fewer people in the Park during the day. It was the weekends that brought the crowds, and by the weekend he'd have his place improved or would have found a better one.

The night was ending. Dawn was on its way. He watched the sky lighten, and the trees and shrubs take shape. The cold mist was drifting where the ground was low. In the distance the skyscrapers blazed with red fire as the sun struck their crowns. He edged out of the crevice to examine the entrance one last time. There were no traces of his work. The grass was flattened where he had laid the flying suit, but it would rise again, and besides, the Park was full of places where kids had played and couples had spread blankets.

Then he saw his entrenching tool lying on open ground ten feet away. He crawled over and grabbed it, scuttled back, wedged himself through and inside, and lay there, breathing hard. That was worse than carelessness, he thought. The psychologist had warned him that he'd be his own worst enemy, that there'd be times when his fear would make traps for him, that there'd be a weakness in him that couldn't take the strain. He cursed himself, and spat in the dirt. Suppose he hadn't seen that tool and had left it there? Typical, he thought bitterly. He'd always forgotten something; he'd always fallen short. He'd tried to qualify for the space program, but he'd been rejected. He hadn't quite been up to the standards.

But the project psychologist hadn't made it either, had he? The psychologist had been nosed out by psychologists who had just a little bit more on the ball. Yes, the Major thought, he and the psychologist were leftovers. They hadn't made the space team. They weren't quite good enough.

And maybe the project wasn't any better than they were. He had wondered about it already. True, it didn't look bad on paper. But suppose a man could survive undetected in the middle of Manhattan for four weeks—would that really produce much useful information for survival-and-rescue planning? Or was it just a flashy stunt dreamed up by some Operations lieutenant bucking for promotion?

Well, it wasn't his job to criticize the project. He was supposed to make it work—and he wasn't starting off very well. He hadn't made that hole long enough. He couldn't stretch out full length. Already his legs were cramping. He began massaging them. Weariness came on him, and hunger. He hadn't eaten since afternoon. He opened a can of rations, and ate with his fingers, then buried the can in the earth beside him, and put the sleeping mask on his face—it covered the mouth to muffle snoring—and settled back to wait out the day.

By nightfall he was in agony. His legs tormented him. He felt stifled by the mask. He kept falling into a dangerous kind of sleep where he twisted like an animal trying to burrow deeper, or maybe to burrow out into the air and sunlight, his traitor hands trying to rip off the mask, his legs threatening at any moment to go into a full screaming cramp.

The entire population of New York came, it seemed, to climb on his boulders and sit on the ridge above him. He heard voices, footsteps, shouts, laughter. At times unseen feet sent dirt sifting down. He cursed those who came. He feared them, he hated them. Yes, it was a definite reaction. He ought to remember to tell the psychologist. He could imagine what these people were from their voices—stupid kids and nagging mothers, and old men full of nastiness, and younger ones who had no business lounging around parks during the day. He was their prisoner. The least of them might find him, and turn him out to sunlight, like a mole. He clasped his knees tighter, and rocked his body to and fro, grinding his teeth to keep from crying out in pain and rage.

When darkness came, he stretched out at last, his head and shoulders thrust out of the hole and into the narrow space between the boulders. He slept until midnight, and woke in panic when the moon sent its light slicing through the crevice to fall on his upturned face. Then he worked, digging to make his burrow longer. After that he crawled about the area outside picking up candy wrappers, cigarette butts, and sandwich bags—why, he didn't know. Perhaps to wipe out every trace of the people who had tormented him all day.

He forced himself to walk off through the trees. He needed to stay away from his refuge until dawn. The psychologist had warned him he'd be tempted to keep too close to it for the safety it offered, until finally he might surrender to a compulsion to remain in it night and day.

He knew he would have to be careful. He was under unusual pressure: a man alone, fearing every hint of human presence—every voice, every movement, every sound—fearing the light of day most of all. True, it was a simulated situation. He could end it any time he chose. But that would be humiliating to his pride, and hurtful to his career. And he was a volunteer. He'd asked for it.

From one of his pockets he took a radio no larger than a pack of cigarettes. He could transmit three simple signals. The first meant: *I am here.* He sat at the base of a tree, holding the radio, studying the shadows that stretched toward the glow of the lamps along the pathways. At five-minute intervals he repeated: *I am here, I am here.* Somewhere someone was listening. He was in contact with another human being. But then he reasoned that the Agency would be unlikely to pay a technician to sit up night after night simply to monitor his signals. They'd have a machine record them. And the machine would answer him—yes, there it was, a return signal, barely audible.

The return signal meant: *We hear you.* He was heard, then, but only by a machine, and it wouldn't be until morning that they'd check to be sure their man in the Park had called in.

He wondered if the green head had been talked about. Probably. It was too ludicrous for the Houston people to keep quiet about. "Remember that gung-ho major who didn't make the space program? Well, guess where he is now. And guess what color his head is . . . That's right, I said his *head.*"

He signaled again—*I am here*—just to hear the machine whisper back: *We hear you, we hear you.* Four weeks of this. They said they'd need that much time in a real situation, first to alert the nearest undercover agent that a flyer was down, and then to allow the agent to track down the signal, and finally, to work out a plan of escape.

He sent his second signal, a variation of the first. It meant: *I receive you.* And the machine dutifully replied: *We receive each other.* That was all. A few pulses through the ether, back and forth, meaningless to an enemy monitoring system, and then one day the *we hear you* would become more frequent, indicating that the agent was coming for him.

There was a third signal. *Emergency.* Which would mean he was sick or caught or couldn't stand it any more and was giving up.

I am here.

I receive you.

Emergency.

This was his vocabulary. This was all he had, he thought. He was just a green-headed man in a dirt-caked flying suit, sitting in a city park at night, talking without words to a machine he'd never see.

As the days went by, he deepened his burrow, made it more comfortable, more secure, better camouflaged. By night he explored the Park, studying each unknown reach of ground with care before venturing onto it. Whenever he passed the zoo, the animals sensed him, and stirred. It occurred to him that he was like them, in a way—a creature caged, and troubled by the scent of man.

Sometimes he saw others at night. He hid from them, drawing back in the deepest shadows. He had known he wouldn't be alone. The Agency people had told him he'd find himself among the scourings of New York—the weird ones, the oddballs, the misfits, the crazy men, all roaming the Park, hunting one another down. Well, he could take care of himself. He could handle two or three of them with judo and the knife. Besides, anybody who got a look at his head would run, for he was weirder than any of them, and more alone. Except that he would have just four weeks of it, and they were trapped for life. That was a difference; quite a difference.

They were frightened; so was he. They were hungry—and he'd be hungry, too. He didn't have enough rations for four weeks. The people at Houston had explained that they wanted him to live off the land—in part, anyway. That meant he would have to rummage through trash baskets looking for apple cores and sandwich leavings. If he had to, he could graze on grass, wild onions, daisies, and chew the bark of saplings. With care he might be able to stretch his rations. He had spent nine days in the Park already. There were nineteen to go, then. He could calculate how much he could allow himself to eat each day.

But of course a downed pilot wouldn't know how long he'd have to hold out. And therefore he, the Major, shouldn't know, either. Surely the Agency people had thought of that. Surely they had planned something to simulate the uncertainties of a real situation.

The Major thought about that. It worried him. He wondered if the Agency people intended to lengthen the test. That must be it. Nobody would come for him on that twenty-eighth night. They'd make him sweat for a few more days, maybe as long as a week.

Or they would trick him in another way. Perhaps they had filled some of the ration cans with water, or sand. It could be that. He would go along half starving himself to maintain food discipline—and then he'd find two or three useless cans.

He hefted each can, and shook it near his ear, but there was no way of telling what was inside. He'd have to wait. He couldn't open the cans early.

They would know that these doubts would occur to him. They would know he'd worry about them. They had planned it that way. It was part of the test. The tension, the strain. On top of the loneliness, on top of the fear. They had lied to him—lied for the good of the project, of course. But it was a dirty business, lying. You told the truth to your friends. That was the rule, wasn't it? It was the enemy you lied to.

The sounding of a siren deep in the city came echoing across the Park. He glanced uneasily around in the darkness, hearing something in that distant mechanical cry that made him want to speak out—to curse, to pray, anything—just to hear his own voice. But he was afraid to speak aloud; he was afraid.

He had premonitions of deep hunger. His limbs and eyes would ache. Sometimes he would drift in the delirium of fatigue. He worried about remembering things. When he filled his canteen at the lake, had he put in the purifier? Fear nagged at his senses, sharpening some, dulling others. He lost the exact count of his days—was it sixteen, seventeen?—but he had a greater awareness of the shape and touch of things.

He lived in the dark. He never saw the sun. By day he lay in his hole, sweating in the thick air, listening drowsily to the voices of people he could not see. He dreamed of capture, of death. When night came, he crept out, his body stiff, his bones aching, to face the dangers of the darkness.

One night he saw an old man shuffling along a path some thirty yards away, and he knew what would happen even before it occurred, as though it had taken place already in his dreams. Two figures rushed out of the dark; the old man fell at once to the ground beneath their blows. They tore at his clothing, searching for something of value. The Major crouched where he was, his knife open in his hand, but he was unable to intervene. He could not jeopardize the project.

Besides, the robbers moved with the swiftness of young men. He might not be equal to them, weakened as he was. They found nothing, and in their fury they kicked their victim, and stamped on his face before they ran off. The old man might be dead or dying, and yet the Major could do nothing, and so he turned away, in a rage that he had been the one to see that attack, impotent as he was, when those who might have helped were sleeping in comfort far away—the ones for whom the Park had been created, for whom it was patrolled and kept clean, and for whose amusement the zoo beasts were caged. The body would be found in the morning, and removed. They would not know about it. The incident was too common to warrant more than a line or two in the newspapers. At noon people would be walking over the very spot.

He saw other things on other nights—a dog stoned to death; a woman raped; a cripple beaten with his own crutch; a tramp sleeping in newspapers set afire and sent dancing, dressed in flames.

His anger left him. He watched as an animal might watch, ready at any moment to retreat and hide. The daytime people had lost the attributes of humankind. They were only voices, and footsteps. He could no longer imagine their faces. The ones who appeared at night were little more than shadows; still, they seemed more real to him. He thought about them often, wondering if any of these miserable, ferocious outcasts inhabited the Park as he did, hiding by day, prowling by night. He wasn't sure; he couldn't tell. But he wanted to believe there were at least a few. It made him feel less alone.

There were heavy rains for several days. His shelter was a morass. He himself was smeared with mud. His hands were blackened now. He thought that perhaps his face, too, had changed color, for the filth and dirt of the Park had been ground into his skin. He could feel his new-grown hair and beard stubble, and he wondered what he might look like, but he could not form a satisfactory picture in his mind.

He thought the full period had elapsed, but he wasn't sure. In any case, he had mastered the test; he had survived. But his achievement wasn't much. He had got through a few weeks. Those others—the night people of the Park—they had survived years. And in all that time no one had come to save them. No one had sought to arrange their escape.

He picked up his radio, and sent the signal. *I am here, I am here.* And the answer came back as always: *We hear you, we hear you.* But now he wondered—did they really hear him, were they listening?

For a time he was ill. He didn't know for how long. He lay in his burrow shivering with fever day and night. He had difficulty remembering why he was there, and pondered the matter, puzzled, until the answer came to him—oh, yes, the project. But it seemed to him that the project was not reason enough for him to be buried this way, alone and suffering and sick. There must be another, more important reason. He could not think what it might be.

His fever slackened, but he remained hidden. He did not care to leave his refuge. The project people might be searching for him, he realized. They would come at night with dogs and flares. But if they couldn't find him? If he'd hidden himself too well? Perhaps this time he had done that absolutely first-rate piece of work he had been struggling to do all his life—and it would be the end of him. How the Agency men would grumble. How annoyed with him they'd be. They might suspect that he had sabotaged the project on purpose, vanishing into the earth like that.

Or maybe they wouldn't come at all. Maybe they wouldn't search. They hadn't looked for the others—the other men who lived underground. They hadn't cared about them. Perhaps he, too, would be abandoned.

He crawled to the lake. He was too weak to stand. At the water's edge he plunged his head down and drank at the reflected lights of the buildings as though by drinking he could extinguish them. He drank the foulness of the water that had already put poison in him, but the lights remained on the surface, and when he roiled the water with his hand, the lights raced back and forth, dancing, shaking, as if quivering with laughter.

The days were hot now, the nights humid. There was the odor of decay everywhere. The rain slid down like grease. There was no grass to eat; it had been trodden away. The bark of the young trees was denied him, for somehow he had lost his knife. He scraped with his fingernails at the saplings, pulled weeds from the earth, leaves from the shrubs.

It was clear to him now that he had misinterpreted the meaning of the test. The object wasn't survival. A man who wants to survive doesn't hide in the earth, doesn't make himself sick with loneliness and fear— no, no, a man who does that has been betrayed into doing it. *Good luck, Major.* They had sent him off to get rid of him. He wasn't quite good enough for their needs, and so they shoved him out with a Judas touch to bury himself among the other outcasts for the sake of the project, which was death.

He was expected to die. He knew that now. They did not really believe, did they, that a man shot out of the sky could be rescued? The risks were too great. No agent—if there were any agents—could be asked to undertake them. Rather, their intention was to prevent a pilot from surrendering by persuading him that all he had to do was find a hiding place and wait for a rescue that had never even been considered. It would be death that came instead.

The radio was the cleverest part of the trick. A desperate man would believe its lies right up to the end, but there was no one listening, not even a machine, for surely it was the radio itself that produced those answering responses, as if they came from far away: *We hear you.* That was the ultimate betrayal, to kill a man with hope.

He was to die, like those others who lived underground, the hopeless ones, too weak to strike out at the enemies who had promised to save them but didn't come, who gave them short rations and told them to eat grass, who'd shorn their heads to humiliate them into hiding. And the poor crippled fools, they had accepted all that, just as he had. They had been eager to make the project work—and if the daytime laughter overhead sometimes drove them to violence, all they were capable of doing was to maim and to kill one another.

The project was death. They were all to die. Very well, he thought, but let them die in the sight of their executioners, let them die in the open air, beneath the sun.

He left his refuge at noon, when the Park was crowded. The sun was blinding. At first he could hardly see the people among whom he staggered, his arms outstretched, feeling his way. He gestured impatiently at trees, bushes, rocks; he shouted for the others to come out of hiding, too. He went tottering about looking for them, commanding them to appear.

The crowds gathered to follow him, warily and at some distance until they saw how weak he was. He fell sometimes, and crawled, rose again to his feet and lurched forward, crying out a summons that went unanswered.

People came nearer; they circled around him. Boys ran up close, hooting. Women held their babies high, so they, too, could see, the young men jogged over from the playing fields, anxious to look at the green-headed man crusted with dried mud, the madman in rags, the zany, the fool howling in their midst—yes, all were eager to have a good look at him before the police arrived to bundle him away.

The Other Side of the Wall

Stanley Ellin

So," Dr. Schwimmer said. "So. It comes to this at last. The inevitable. Confrontation, penetration, decision-making, action. Wait."
The office door was partly open. Through it could be heard the sound of a typewriter being pecked at slowly and uncertainly. The doctor rose from behind his desk, crossed the room, and closed and locked the door. He returned to the swivel chair behind the desk. The desk was long and wide, a polished slab of walnut mounted on stainless steel legs and without drawers. Arranged on it were a crystal ashtray; a cardboard box of straw-tipped Turkish cigarettes—("I don't even enjoy smoking," the doctor remarked, squaring the edge of the box with the edge of the ashtray, "but these help the image, you understand. The exotic, somewhat mysterious image I cultivate to impress the impressionable females in my clientele."); a razor-edged, needle-pointed letter opener of Turkish design—("Also part of the image, naturally. Again the exoticism of the Near East, with its suggestion of the menacingly virile."); a cigarette lighter; a small brass tube like a lipstick container, which did not contain lipstick but a breath deodorant that left the mouth reeking of peppermint; and a neat little tape recorder, an XJE-IV Memocord, not much larger than the box of Turkish cigarettes.

"So." The doctor leaned toward the tape recorder. He hesitated, then sat back in his chair. "No. No need to put any of this on tape, Albert."

"Why, Doctor? Is it too intensely personal to be recorded for posterity?"

"I am a psychotherapist, Albert. All the business transacted in this room is intensely personal."

"Never to this extent though, is it? And that name Albert. Must you continually address me by it? You know how I detest it."

"Too bad. But I will address you as Albert. This is necessary. It is a way of establishing identities and relationships. And consider the distinguished men who bore that name. Einstein. Schweitzer. They seemed to survive it reasonably well, didn't they?"

"I still detest it. There wasn't even a sensible reason for being saddled with it. No one in the family ever had it. Mother was enamored of the figure on the tins of tobacco father smoked, that's all. An incredible woman. Imagine naming one's first-born after a pipe tobacco. Or was she so viciously foresighted that she knew this was the perfect name for a child who was doomed to become a bald, potbellied, blobby-nosed little man with weak vision and a perpetually nagging sinus condition?"

"So. Suddenly we are faced with the ghost of the mother?"

"Why not, Doctor? I didn't manufacture my own ugliness, did I?"

"Albert, if I were a Freudian, we could have such a good time with this mother image. We could make it your sacrificial goat, stuff all your problems into it, and slaughter it. So. But luckily for us, I am not a Freudian. Your dead mother deserves better than to be declared guilty of your misfortunes. Consider how she made it her duty to bolster your shaky ego every day of her life. Your academic brilliance, your professional success, your devotion to her—it was like a catechism to her, the recitation of her admiration for you day after day."

"It was a trap. It was a pit I lived in like a captured tiger, feeding on those greasy chunks of admiration she flung to me."

"So. Very dramatic. Very colorful. But an evasion, Albert. Only an evasion."

"Is it? Then what about the father image? The big, handsome, loud-mouthed father. And the two handsome, muscular brothers. The overwhelming males in my home. And me the runt of the litter."

"You were, Albert. But never overwhelmed. Consider the facts. Your father died when you were a child. His absence may have affected you, but never his presence. And that pair of clods, Albert, those two handsome, muscular brothers, stood in awe of your intellect, were wary of your cold self-restraint, terrified of your unpredictable explosions of temper. They quickly learned not to step over the lines you drew. Do you remember how one earned a broken leg when he was tripped up by you at the head of the staircase for trying a little bullying? How the other found himself playing a game where he was locked in a trunk and almost smothered in payment for a small insult? Yes, yes, a few such episodes and they soon came to understand that one did not carelessly tread on the toes of this small, fat, pale older brother with the thick eyeglasses and the sniffle. They are still afraid of you, Albert. They are two of your very few triumphs. But it is your failure alone that concerns us. Let us get on with it."

"My failure? Am I the only one in this room stamped with failure? My dear Doctor, what about the way you've managed to destroy a splendid practice in a few short months? Eccentricity is one thing, Doctor. Patients like a little eccentricity in their therapists. But they also draw lines. A therapist who lives in a daze, who sits lost to the world when patients are trying to communicate with him, who angrily sends them packing when they resent this—what did you think was bound to happen to this practice in short order? And what course did you think your fellow professionals would take when they observed your grotesque behavior? Your inexplicable compulsions? Did you really expect them to continue to refer patients to you? No, Doctor, there is no need to rush through this consultation. No need to look at clocks and measure out your time in expensive little spoonfuls any longer. The clocks have stopped. We have all the time to ourselves now we can possibly use."

"Albert, listen to me. This room is not meant to be an arena where we turn our cruelty on each other. We are not antagonists. We will achieve nothing through antagonism."

"You're a coward, Doctor."

"We are both cowards about some things, Albert. Do you think I disparage you when I say you are essentially a creature of emotion? Believe me, I do not."

"I don't believe you. You're much too clever with words, Doctor, to be believed in that regard. Creature of emotion. What you mean is incorrigible romantic, don't you? An ugly little wretch stuffed to the bursting point with romantic visions. Made self-destructive by them. A fifty-year-old man flung back into adolescence and unable to claw his way out of it. Why shouldn't you disparage him?"

"Because, Albert, you are not play-acting your condition. You are not pretending you face a crisis. The condition is real. The crisis is real. One does not disparage a reality."

"A reality based on dreams? On sexual fantasies dredged up from my unconscious while I lie snoring in bed?"

"All these are realities, too. Are scientific laws and material objects the only reality? No, no, Albert. Your mistake from the start was in not recognizing the validity of those dreams. Of the situation they depicted."

"But the situation was all in my own mind."

"In your emotions. Your emotions, Albert. If tests were made while you were asleep and dreaming of this woman, they would clearly indicate physiological reactions. A quickened breathing, an increase in blood pressure, sexual excitation."

"Just as I told you. All the symptoms of delayed adolescence. The pimply high school boy's nightly dreams of his nubile girl friend. The only difference is that in the daylight he joins her in some noisy roost where they happily share a nauseous concoction of ice cream and syrup and hold hands under the table. While all I could do was turn night dreams into day dreams."

"Slowly, Albert. Confrontation, penetration, decision-making, action. Each in its turn. So far we have barely begun the penetration. We have merely put aside the clichés of the possessive mother and bullying siblings and turned to the image of the dream woman herself. We have a distance to go before the decision-making."

"Girl, Doctor. Maiden, if you will. Not woman."

"So? Is it important that she has not reached full womanhood?"

"Yes. I don't like women. Something happens to a girl the instant she becomes one. In that instant she becomes too knowing, too wise, too self-sufficient to provide happiness for any man."

"Not any man. Perhaps only men who are afraid they don't measure up. Tell me, Albert. What kind of man were you in your first dreams of this girl? Still the small, fat, fifty-year-old lump of self-hatred? Or heroic in dimensions?"

"I don't know. It's hard to remember."

"Think. Penetrate."

"I'm trying to. Not heroic. That much I'm sure of. Beyond that, I still don't know. I wasn't aware of my body, my appearance, my deficiencies. Only of my sensations when I saw her there. Ecstatic recognition. Passionate desire for her. And I remember my own astonishment that I should feel this. I hadn't ever known I was capable of such feelings. All

my life I've paid for my female companionship. Paid to satisfy my
physical needs. There was never a suggestion of emotional involvement
in the transactions. Now here I was, being drowned in emotionalism. I
woke up suffocating with it."

"So. And you knew on waking that this dream girl was based on an
actuality? That she had a flesh-and-blood counterpart?"

"Not then. Not the first time. Only later when I realized the dream
was recurrent. And then only when in one of the later dreams I realized
that I knew her name. Sophia. When I woke that morning it struck me
that of course she was the counterpart of a real Sophia. The inept child
I had recently hired as my receptionist."

"She resembled her?"

"More and more, once I knew her name. At first she was shadowy.
She was only the suggestion of a beautiful Greek maiden. After I knew
her name she took on clearer and clearer definition. Still shadowy,
because we always met at night in dim lighting, but now as if a veil
had been removed from her face. No more chiaroscuro, but every delicate curve of feature revealed. Sophia. I can even remember the idiotic
imagery, the coinage of every bad poet, that crossed my mind in that
dream when I stood there looking at her in full recognition for the first
time. Doe-eyed, raven-haired, swan-necked. My God, I didn't even
blush at my own puerile poeticizing of her. I rejoiced in it."

"You think this girl in the dream was aware of your feelings?"

"She must have been. How could she help it? I tell you, Doctor, I
yearned toward her with such intensity that she must have felt the
current surging from me. This was before I even recognized her identity.
I walked into this room, a bedroom lit by a small lamp somewhere, and
she stood silent and unmoving in the middle of the room dressed in a
white gown—the classically simple Greek gown—and with what seemed
like an almost transparent veil covering her hair and face. A tender,
living goddess. I was stricken by the sight of her. The emptiness in me,
my lifetime of emptiness, was suddenly filled with a white-hot lava of
emotion. You see? Again I am poeticizing like a fool, but what other
way is there to describe it? In psychologic jargon? In those deadly
words: *I fell in love?* Although, believe me, Doctor, coming from me,
those words mean infinitely more than they would coming from the
ordinary man."

"I do believe you, Albert. But are you sure you never knew such an
emotion before?"

"Never."

"Think, Albert. You were not born middle-aged. In your youth there must have been some woman—girl—who excited this emotion in you."

"Never. I never permitted myself to feel anything like this. I knew the response my size, my ugliness, my sweaty, tongue-tied ineptitude in conversation would draw from any girl I thought desirable. Why invite disaster? Better to freeze the heart into a block of ice than have it torn to pieces."

"And you did not experience any of this when you confronted the dream Sophia? When you let her feel the current of emotion surging from you?"

"No. I seemed to have no room in me for anything but that aching desire."

"Sexual desire?"

"That would have been later. In the early dream, all I wanted to do was touch her. Just touch her shoulder gently with my fingertips. To reassure her, perhaps. Or myself. I moved toward her with my hand outstretched, and she moved away a little, barely out of my reach. Then suddenly we were someplace else. I recognized where at once. The hallway outside the room. The hallway of my brownstone house."

"Yes?"

"The old brownstone. My living tomb. My office downstairs, the bedrooms on the second floor where we stood. All those empty bedrooms. I was jubilant. This lovely, veiled creature was with me in my domain, I was not trespassing on hers. I looked and saw her standing now in the middle of that long gloomy hallway. While I watched she held out a hand as if inviting me to clasp it in mine. She pressed her other hand against the wall there, the blank, wallpapered expanse between two doors, and an opening showed in it. She moved through the opening, it closed behind her, and she was gone. I was frantic. Wild with despair. I ran to the wall and searched for some clue to the opening, but there was none. I struck my fist against the wall, but my fist had no substantiality, no strength. It moved in slow motion against the wall, it met it with hardly the impact of a feather brushing against it. That was all. I woke up drenched with sweat, weak with a sense of futility.

"I knew at once it had been a dream. I knew that the logical thing to do was either lie there and dispassionately analyze it or to clear it completely from my mind. But I knew that either way would purge me of the glorious new emotions I had discovered in the girl's presence. I was in love. For the first time in my life—at the age of fifty, mind you—I was willingly and hopelessly in love. I had the sense of it in my every nerve.

"It was dawn now. Incredibly, I got out of bed in that gray light and went out into the hallway, searching along its wall for the mysterious opening in it, desperately running my hands over its smooth surface. I went into the room on the other side of the wall there, my youngest brother's room, empty of all its furniture since his marriage, and it was as empty as ever, a fine dust on its floor and that was all. I knew then that the only thing left to me was the recurrence of the dream, a re-entry into the shadowy world where the girl might be waiting for me. Would surely be waiting for me."

"So." Dr. Schwimmer rested his head against the back of his swivel chair and closed his eyes. "Then from the very start, Albert, you surrendered to this girl completely."

"Completely."

"You asked nothing in return. You expected nothing in return."

"At the start, nothing. Only her presence."

"And later?"

"Later, as the dream recurred again and again, I wanted her response. Her acknowledgment that she felt for me at least a part—a little—of what I felt for her. I wanted her not to retreat from me every time I reached toward her. But I forgave her for it each time she did. I knew it was because this experience was as strange and novel for her as it was for me. She was very young. Untouched. Timid. She was to be wooed gently, not taken by force. And I was willing to be patient, because my fingertips came infinitesimally closer to her each time. I settled for that."

"So. And when you realized that this girl of the dreams was, in reality, the pretty little receptionist who sat in your outer office every working day of the week it did not break the spell?"

"No, because it didn't end the dreams. At night I had the Sophia of the dreams; in daylight I had the Sophia of reality nearby where, whenever I chose, I could look at her, speak to her.

"And the living reality, as it turned out, made the dreams that much more exciting. Every detail of the flesh-and-blood Sophia was transmitted to the dream image I loved. Now that image removed its veil and showed me the glowing eyes and parted lips and curve of cheek of the enchanting child I employed in my office. The length of leg, swell of breast, everything became substantial in the dreams."

"But you did not transfer your emotions to this flesh-and-blood girl? Then or ever?"

"No."

"Are you sure of that, Albert? Consider this very carefully. It is important."

"I still say no. I didn't want to risk it. I didn't have to. It was more than enough that I had the dream Sophia to woo and win. In the daylight there were mirrors in the house where I would catch sight of myself at unexpected moments. A self that invited rejection. In the dimly lit room and hallway of the dreams there were no mirrors. I had no view of myself then. I never gave thought to what I looked like. Above all, somehow I knew that the brownstone house stood all alone in the dream world and that there was no one else in it besides the girl and me. I was the only man in her existence, she had no freedom of choice. Ultimately she would have to give herself to me."

"A quaint way to phrase it, Albert. Almost Victorian. And what does it connote? She allows you to touch her at last? To press your lips to her blushing cheek? Or more?"

"More. Much more."

"Yes?"

"She would be my slave. My willing slave. Grateful that she could be possessed by me. She would not so much love me as worship me."

"So. And all this, Albert, in the light of your futile pursuit of her through dream after dream? The nightly confrontation in the bedroom, the scene in the shadowy hallway where, at the crucial moment, she disappears through that blank wall? Now tell me. Did you never wonder what lay on the other side of that wall?"

"I didn't have to. I was sure I knew what was there. Her room. The small room with carpeted walls and floor where she lay on a bed under some diaphanous covering breathlessly waiting for me to find my way to her. Afraid of the moment when I would, but eagerly anticipating it. Her room. Her solitary, sweetly scented refuge."

"So there it is, Albert. That preconception was your great mistake. Your tragic misjudgment."

"The room was there. I entered it. I found it exactly as I had imagined it."

"No, you did not. Otherwise, would there be this crisis? This anguish? You should have been prepared, Albert, for more than you bargained for. You should have known yesterday when you first saw your real Sophia's young man in her office, when she proudly introduced him to you, that there was a crisis brewing. Admit it. Didn't your hackles rise when you met that young man? When you took his measure?"

"All right, yes. Yes. But I didn't make anything of it then. Why should I? All my life I've hated these hulking Adonises, these huge, handsome, brute images of masculinity. My hatred for this specimen was innate. Why should I think it had anything to do with the adoration my infatuated, flesh-and-blood Sophia aimed at him?"

"Hard words, Albert. But the dream Sophia is cast in the image of the flesh-and-blood Sophia. There was one danger signal. The other was at the instant in your dream last night when you pressed a hand against that wall, that barrier to her hidden room, and at last it opened to you. Didn't you wonder why, at long last, it should suddenly open? Didn't it enter your mind that it might be a means of providing you, not with the ultimate experience, but with the ultimate truth?"

"No. And you yourself know this only through hindsight. When I entered that room I felt jubilation. Utter ecstasy. Nothing else. I had no premonition I would find them on that bed together, she and that hulk. I had no idea until that incredible moment that this room was their refuge, not hers alone. Or, worst of all, that when caught shamelessly sprawled beside him in their lovemaking, she would only smile pityingly at me.

"How could I be prepared for any of that? After all, those dreams were mine. How could I ever imagine they would be invaded by any gross stranger? And now—"

"Yes?"

"Now that I know the truth I can't turn my mind away from it. Awake or asleep, all I can think of is that she was taken from me. Violated. And with her eager consent. God almighty, since I found my way into that room I've lived only with the picture of them in my mind. I can't live with it any longer."

"So. Then it must be exorcised, Albert, must it not?"

"Yes."

"At last we come to the decision-making. And is it to be my decision to make, Albert? Mine alone?"

"Yes."

"You will accept it without question?"

"Completely."

"Good. Then I will state the case directly. It is obvious that someone must pay the penalty for your betrayal, Albert. As a sane and intelligent man you must know that a blood sacrifice offers the only possible solution in a case like this. The only one. Under any conditions it would be impossible for you to be released from your agony while your betrayers maintain their obscene relationship. Yes. One or the other must be eliminated. But which? The intruder?"

"And then what, Doctor? Another such intruder to take his place in that room? Another crisis? Now that I know what the girl really is— what she's capable of—can I expect more than that?"

"True. Then you plainly see she herself must be sacrificed."

"Yes."

"So. And you also understand how it must be done?"

"Yes. With a blade, naturally."

"Naturally. A blade of the finest steel. That is traditional, and there are times when one sees the wisdom behind these timeworn traditions." The doctor picked up the letter opener from his desk and regarded it with admiration. He turned it slowly back and forth so that sunlight from the window flowed up and down the blade. "The finest steel, a tradition in itself. More than eight inches of it, Albert. More than enough for its purpose.

"And you realize, of course, that the first killing blow deep between the lower ribs does not mean the completion of the ritual. There must be total release of the emotions immediately afterward. A frenzied hacking until the lovely image is made a horror. A full measure of blood must flow to wash away betrayal. Remember, Albert, the therapeutic value of the act lies in that."

"Yes. Of course."

"Then," said the doctor, "all that is left is action."

He unlocked the door and opened it slightly on the drafty ground-floor corridor of the old brownstone. And, when in answer to his call, Miss Sophia Kaloosdian, doe-eyed, raven-haired, swan-necked, a large wad of chewing gum working rhythmically in her jaws, left her desk in the outer office and came to see what he wanted, he was waiting for her with smiling confidence, the hilt of the letter opener gripped tight in his fist and hidden behind his back.

The confidence was not misplaced. Dr. Albert Schwimmer may have been short, fat, nearsighted, and with a perpetual sniffle, but he was very strong.

A Place of her Own

JOYCE HARRINGTON

*J*f you asked me when she first showed up on the corner, I couldn't tell you. One day she just started being a regular part of the scenery, like Carvel's and Waldbaum's, and then she was always there. Summer and winter, rain or shine, she was there sitting on the sidewalk, like patience on a monument. In the good weather she'd sometimes go across the street to the opposite corner where there was a tree and a mailbox and sit between them. But most of the time she would be scrunched down in a little covered-over space, like a shallow cave, right between Carvel's and the bank. That was her place.

I was surprised that the bank let her stay there where everybody going in or coming out could see her. Not good for business, if you know what I mean. I thought about saying something to the manager, but it wasn't my bank.

Once in a while she'd be gone. The first time I went by and she wasn't there I said to myself, "Oh, boy! A good thing. Somebody picked her up. The police or the loony squad. Either way, a good thing. She's not making a disgrace of the neighborhood."

But the next day she was back, crouching in her cave, drinking coffee from a paper container and staring around with her crazy eyes. I can tell you, it gave me a shock to have those eyes staring at me when I wasn't expecting it, but I just walked on as if nothing had happened. I never missed a day of work in my life, and the only times I was ever late was when the subway got itself messed up. By the time I got to the station my heart had stopped pounding and all I could think about was squeezing onto the train.

After that I was always ready for her. I could see from a block away if she was there, and I could walk fast and keep my eyes looking the other way. Or I could walk on the other side of the street. But ready or not, something always made me look at her. Not right in the face, but at some part of her clothes or her feet or the top of her head. I couldn't go by without one quick look.

She always wore a coat, summer and winter. Sometimes she had it all buttoned up, other times slung over her shoulders like a model in a magazine. Underneath the coat she wore sweaters. Even on summer days when the temperature got in the nineties and everybody else was dying from the heat, sweaters. And baggy dirty slacks. I got the impression she wore a couple pairs of slacks at once. She looked like a great big bundle of old clothes. If you didn't look at her face, you could just walk by like she was some pile of garbage waiting to be picked up.

I took my vacation in August and went to Ohio to visit my married daughter, Ellen. I have to go to her. She won't come to visit me. When she got married, she said to me, "Momma, I hope you won't be hurt, but I'm getting out of this crummy town and I'm never coming back."

Well, I'm not hurt. Why should I be? It's pretty where she lives. Grass and trees around the house. Everything clean. She has a nice new car to drive around in. The kids, God bless them, almost grown up and never sick a day in their lives. Only they hardly remember me from one visit to the next. Their other grandmother lives nearby. She's a nice lady, I guess. The kids show me all the presents she gives them— ten-speed bicycles, a record player for Kathy, Timmy's racing-car setup in the basement. Those are nice things to give your grandchildren. I brought them presents, too—small things I could carry on the plane. Nothing special.

This time Ellen said to me, "Momma, you've been working over thirty years in that store. You could retire anytime you want. Wouldn't you like to stop working and come and live with us?"

She doesn't understand. It's not just a store. After her father died, rest his soul, I was lucky to get a job there. Ellen was only five years old. What does she remember about that time? But I remember how frightened I was the day I walked into the Personnel Office. Artie was a good man, but he didn't leave any insurance or anything else. He never expected to be taken off so young. So I had to get a job, quick, and I'd never worked a day in my life.

I was so nervous that day when they showed me how to work the cash register. Artie used to give me just enough money to buy food with and everything else he took care of himself. So it scared me to have all that money that wasn't mine passing through my hands every day. But I got used to it after a while, and I got used to having money of my own, too. So much for the rent, so much to live on, so much to save. And it's a good thing I saved because when Ellen got grown up, she wanted to go to college and that's where she met her husband. So it all worked out. If it wasn't for the store, Ellen wouldn't be living in her pretty house, with a dentist for a husband and two fine kids, and she ought to understand that.

Sometimes I think she's a little ashamed of me. Once, when I was there visiting, she had some of her neighbors over for coffee in the afternoon, and when she introduced me, she said, "This is my mother. She's a buyer for a big New York department store." Well, it was only a little lie, but I felt my face getting red. I couldn't correct her. That would only have made things worse. So I just smiled and hoped nobody would be interested enough to ask me any questions about my job. They weren't. Fact of the matter is, I am a saleswoman in the Ladies Foundations Department and that's where I've been for over 30 years. I'm not ashamed of it even if Ellen is.

When my vacation was over and she was driving me to the airport, she brought it up again. "You're too old to keep on working, Momma," she said. "Peter and I talked it over and we'd be happy to give you a home with us. I worry about you all alone in that awful little apartment. There's so much violence these days. You'd be safe out here with us."

Well, I had to bite my tongue to keep from saying what I wanted to say. The "awful little apartment" had been my home for more years than I had worked in Ladies Foundations. It was the home that Artie and I made together when we were young and I wasn't about to leave it now that I'm old. It had been Ellen's home, too, although she didn't seem to want to remember that she'd had some happy times there and there was always good nourishing food on the table.

What I said was, "I still have your bedroom suite. Good as new. Maybe Kathy would like to have it for her room. I could ship it out."

She laughed. "My God, Momma! Get rid of it. Give it to the Salvation Army. All pink ruffles and flounces, wasn't it? I can't believe I used to pretend I was some kind of movie star in that room. No, thanks. But whenever you're ready, you just get rid of all that junky old furniture and we'll set you up with a room of your own, a television, everything you need. Peter says we might be able to put in a swimming pool next year."

I thought about those things on the plane, and I thought about what I would really want to do with myself when the time came that I wouldn't be getting on the subway every morning and going to the store. It wasn't yet, but it would be soon. Three more years? It would be nice being right there to watch Kathy and Timmy grow up and get married. But the fact of the matter is that outside of Ellen herself, I've never been around teen-aged kids very much. They seem kind of large and noisy. And I have a television. Small, but perfectly good. I got it on sale at the store, which, with my discount, made it a very good buy. And what would an old lady like me want with a swimming pool? I haven't been in swimming since Ellen was 15 and we went for a week to the Jersey shore, and even then I only got my feet wet up to my knees.

I took a cab from the airport. Expensive, but I was tired, and the next day was already Monday and the end of my vacation. I'd have to go back to work. It was a heavy evening, humid and overcast, and the whole world was a dirty gray color. By the time we got off the expressway, it had begun to rain and the cab driver, like everyone else trying to squeeze through the weekend traffic, was scowling and muttering curses. For a moment I thought maybe Ellen was right and I ought to pack up and leave all this behind.

But then we swung onto a familiar street and home was only a few blocks away. I leaned forward to give the driver directions and through the rain-streaked windshield I saw her. She was crouched down in that little sheltered corner by the bank, a sheet of plastic tucked in around her knees. All around her she had boxes and shopping bags tied with string, and parked at one side she had a Waldbaum's shopping cart piled high with God knows what kind of rubbish. And right in the middle of all this she squatted, staring out into the rain. She stared right into the cab as we drove by and I felt sure she recognized me. It seemed as if she shouted something, but I couldn't hear her.

The driver said, "Which way, lady?"

So I told him where to turn, and in less than a minute I was paying him off with a good tip because he helped me carry my luggage up to the door. Before he left, he said, "How do I get out of this crummy neighborhood?" So I told him that and then I dragged my luggage indoors.

Home. I looked around the lobby and it was just the same as it always was. But for some reason I began to remember that years ago there used to be a red-leather settee and a couple of armchairs over against the wall. There was nothing there now. I couldn't remember when they'd been taken away. Then I remembered that on the wall, over the settee, there used to be a picture. Horses, I think. Or sailboats. Something outdoorsy. Now, if you looked very closely you could just about make out where it had hung, but the wall was so dirty everything had blended into the same shade of grimy green. The floor was dirty, too, and not just because it was raining and people had been tracking it up with wet feet. Whatever happened to the rubber mat the super used to put down when it rained? I guess a lot of things had changed over the years, and I'd just never noticed.

I pushed the button for the elevator, and while I was waiting I glanced over at the mailboxes. My neighbor across the hall, Mrs. Finney, had been picking up my mail while I was away, so there was no reason for me to check my mailbox. Still, I noticed that some of the little metal doors were bent and hanging loose. Not mine, but some of the others. How long had they been like that? And why didn't the super get them fixed?

Next to the mailboxes a sign had been taped to the wall. From where I stood I could read the big print at the top. It said: ATTENTION ALL TENANTS, and there was a lot of small print underneath. I was about to go and look at it, but the elevator door opened, so I dragged my luggage on and pushed the button for the sixth floor.

I don't know if it was because I was so tired, or because of the change coming from Ellen's pretty house with the trees and grass around it, or because I was finally seeing things the way they really were, but when I got inside my apartment and turned on the lights I could have cried. Nothing had changed in my apartment. Everything was just as I had left it. It wasn't even dusty or bad-smelling because Mrs. Finney, when she brought in the mail, would always open the windows and give the place a quick once-over, which I would do the same for her when she was away. No, it was something else, something inside me that turned on like a searchlight and made everything look shabby and old. Worn out. Like Ellen said, junk.

The living-room suite, that Artie and I bought with the money his folks gave us for a wedding present, was covered with summer slipcovers just like every summer. The slipcovers weren't as old as the furniture. I got new ones every few years or so from the store. How long ago did I get these? Whatever, there were holes in them and the brown plush underneath was showing through. That made me think of the places on the couch cushions and the arms where the brown plush was worn down to the shiny material. Old, right? Junk.

Same thing with the rug, the coffee table, the bookcase with Ellen's old books in it, even the draperies at the windows. Everything was old, shabby, faded, chipped, ready for the junk collector. Even the television was an old black-and-white set that I'd bought back in the days of Uncle Miltie and Howdy Doody. For Ellen.

I went into Ellen's room. I don't know what made me keep her room just the way she'd left it. Maybe I always thought she'd come back for a visit, in spite of what she said. The bedroom suite was a present I got for her when she started high school, so she'd feel like a young lady, no longer a baby, and have girl friends over to visit. I remember how proud she had been of her room.

This time I didn't turn on the overhead light. Maybe that's what made the living room look so awful. I walked into the room to where there were two little pink-shaded lamps sitting on the vanity table. I turned on one of those instead. The room was small, I have to admit that—smaller than the room I'd stayed in at Ellen's house. And most of it was taken up with the bed. I'll never forget the look on her face the day the delivery truck from the store came and the men carried that furniture upstairs and even helped put the bed together. When she saw them put the canopy on top, I thought she would never stop smiling and dancing around and squealing. "Oh, Momma! It's beautiful! I love it!" Those were her exact words. I guess people change.

Now, in the rosy glow from the vanity lamp, I could see that the canopy was sagging and the pink quilted bedspread and dust ruffle had turned the color of old underwear. The pink net skirt on the vanity table, which I'd made myself, was droopy and frayed at the bottom, and the white paint on the bedposts and on the chifforobe was dingy and gray. Maybe if I scrubbed it down . . .

The door buzzer sounded. I got my face ready with a smile because right now it would be very good to have some company and forget all this gloom that was making me feel like a worn-out piece of junk myself. But before I got to the door I took the smile away just in case it was some creep going through the building looking for old ladies to molest. Don't laugh. It happened in the next block. Thank God the

landlord put peepholes in all our doors. I looked through and it was
Mrs. Finney from across the hall.

Right away when she came in she said, "Did you eat yet, Lillian? I
brought some Danish."

That's Grace Finney. Always worrying about whether people got
enough to eat. A good person.

"I ate on the plane, but I could have some Danish. Why don't I make
some coffee?"

She followed me into the kitchen, and again I noticed things, like
the worn spot on the linoleum in front of the sink and the scars on
the table that made it look like it had been through the wars. But I put
it all out of my mind so I could tell Grace about Ellen and her family
and how well they were doing. She put the Danish down on the table
while I filled the kettle and got out the instant coffee.

"Did you read your mail yet?" she asked. "No. I can see you didn't.
Wait a minute."

And she raced out to the living room where the mail was stacked on
the coffee table and came back waving an envelope.

"Wait'll you see this," she said. "And there's nothing we can do about
it. Not a damn thing."

It was unusual for Grace Finney to swear. She prided herself on being
a lady and got her hair done every Saturday morning at Gwen's around
the corner. So it must be something really bad.

I looked at the envelope.

"Open it. Open it," she said.

It hadn't come through the mail. There was no stamp on it and no
address. Only my name, Mrs. Lillian Curry, written out in big black
letters.

"We all got one," she said. "It came right after you left. It's a shame.
A crying shame. Read it."

I opened the envelope. Inside was a single sheet of paper. I pulled it
out and right away across the top I saw: ATTENTION ALL TENANTS.

"What is this?" I said. "I saw it downstairs but I didn't stop to
read it."

"Read," she commanded. "You'll cry. If I tell you, I'll get so mad I
don't know what I'll do. Old Mr. Zukowski in 2D, when he read it, he
had a heart attack and he's still in the hospital. Nobody knows if he'll
ever get out alive."

So I read. And then I turned the kettle off. And then I sat down on a kitchen chair, the one that wobbled a little. Coming on top of the way I was feeling, I didn't know whether to laugh or cry over what the piece of paper said. I guess it's safe to say I was stunned, because I just sat there with my head going around and the words on the paper getting all blurry when I tried to read it again to make sure it was really true.

What it boiled down to was this. The building had been sold and the new owner was going to tear it down. All the other apartment buildings on the block, too. In place of a lot of rundown little buildings he was going to put up a brand-new giant building with lots more apartments. We all had to get out within two months, because after that all the services would be shut off. We could all come back if we wanted to and get apartments in the new building. At the end they tried to take the curse off it by saying what a great thing it was for the neighborhood and how projects like this would help put an end to urban decay.

Urban decay. Junk. Everything was turning into junk. They wanted to turn us all over to the junk collectors. Buildings, bedroom suites, people, even an old dog wouldn't be safe. Could they give me a new body, a new life to live in the new building? I could feel words choking in my throat, and I must have made some kind of noise, because Grace was shaking me and bending over to stare in my face.

"Are you all right?" she demanded. "Don't you go having a heart attack on me. Here, I'll make the coffee."

She rattled around and pretty soon a cup of black coffee was on the table beside the Danish.

"Eat," she said. "It's from Dubin's."

So I ate a bite of Danish and I sipped some coffee. And I have to admit I felt better, but still not clear in my head.

"I'm leaving," said Grace. "I'm not waiting around while this place turns into a ghost building and the scavengers start breaking the windows and stealing the pipes off the walls. The moving truck is coming in the morning. I found a place out in Queens. The rent is more, but at least it's clean and they won't be tearing it down around my ears. You ought to leave, too."

"But I just got back."

"Yeah, I know. It's a shock. You need a little time to get used to the idea. But don't wait too long. You know what happens to empty buildings. It's not safe."

"Where is safe? Ellen wants me to go out and live with them. She says it's safe."

"She's a good daughter, Ellen. You ought to go. I wish I had a daughter like that. All I have is that bum, my son, who can't even hold a job. Forty years old and still trying to figure out what to do with his life. Well, I have to go. I still have a lot of packing to do. I just didn't want you to be alone when you got the news. You'll be all right now? Have the rest of the Danish for breakfast."

I sat there at the table for a while. The coffee got cold and a roach got brave and ran across the drainboard. I didn't even get up to chase him. I always keep my kitchen spotless, no food lying around, so the roaches won't come. But they come anyway. You can't get away from them in these old buildings. Maybe the new building wouldn't have any roaches. Maybe I could find a place to stay in the neighborhood, a room somewhere nearby, and move into the new building when it gets finished.

That's what the piece of paper said, that we could all move back in and have nice new apartments. But what about the rent? New apartments don't come cheap. And what would I do with my furniture in the meantime? How long does it take to build a giant apartment house? A year, two years? Come to think of it, how would my junky old furniture look in a brand-new apartment? Come to think of it, would I live that long?

I shivered. It wasn't cold, only like the old saying goes, somebody was walking on my grave. Wherever that would be. I'd never thought about that before, but now it came through like a *Daily News* headline. A place to die. I wouldn't be looking for a place to live. I'd be looking for a place to die.

It was crazy, but the thought made me feel better. I wrapped the Danish up in plastic and put it in the breadbox. And then I went to polish my shoes. Tomorrow was Monday, and I never went to work on Monday without polishing my shoes.

In the morning I put on a black dress. I know things are different now, but back when I started working in the store we all had to wear black dresses and I never got out of the habit. Sometimes I'll wear brown or navy blue, but that's as far as I'll go. Not like some of the other girls who wear pantsuits in turquoise or lavender. It wouldn't be right.

I ate the rest of the Danish I had started and had a cup of coffee.

There wasn't much else to eat, and I would have to stop at Waldbaum's on my way home. There was one Danish left over, so I put it in a bag to take with me for my coffee break. When I left the building, the moving truck was already in front and Grace Finney's upright piano was standing on the sidewalk. She could only play *Chopsticks*, but she'd bought it years ago when her boy said he wanted to study music. He'd never even learned *Chopsticks*, but Grace hung on to the piano and used to let Ellen play whenever she wanted to. I walked away fast. I didn't want to be late for work on my first morning back from vacation.

The subway station was three blocks away, and as soon as I turned the corner I saw her. I didn't see her exactly, but I saw her shopping cart parked in its usual place outside the bank, so I knew she was there. I kept on walking fast, and I kept watching the toes of my shiny black shoes going one, two, one, two in front of me. I didn't look up when I passed her, and I don't know what made me do it, but I put the bag with the Danish in it on top of the mound of old junk in her shopping cart. I was trembling so bad when I got to the change booth, I could hardly pick up my tokens.

The only thing different about the store when I got there was that they had the new fall merchandise on display. When I had left, they were getting rid of the last of the summer stuff. But Ladies Foundations .doesn't change much from season to season. A girdle is a girdle, even though they keep coming out with new kinds of fabrics and new styles. It felt good to be back, and right away before the opening bell rang I started checking over the shelves and drawers so I'd know if we were running low on any sizes.

Miss Kramer, the floor manager, came by before I'd gotten very far, and she said, "Good morning, Lillian. Welcome back. Did you have a good vacation? I'd like to see you in my office if you have a few minutes."

So I said, "Good morning. Thanks. Yes. I'll come right now."

I followed her across the floor and into the corridor behind the fitting rooms where her office was, all the way wondering what she wanted to talk to me about. It had been over a year since my last raise, so maybe that was it. I could sure use a raise if I was going to have to find a new apartment. I had a little money saved up, but the way prices were going higher all the time, it was getting harder and harder to save anything.

"Sit down, Lillian," she said.

So I sat down in the little straight chair in front of her desk and she sat down in the swivel chair behind her desk. She looked at me for a second and then she started flipping through some cards in a metal box. She pulled one out.

"Lillian," she said, "you've been with us for over thirty years."

"Yes," I said, feeling proud and smiling a little. It was sure to be a raise. It always started like that; how long you've been there and what a good employee you were and how you've earned a little extra in your paycheck.

"And you've been in Ladies Foundations all that time," she went on. "You've received five letters of commendation from the President, your attendance record is perfect, and your sales record is steady."

I just nodded and held my breath. I couldn't say a word. It was coming now. I just wondered how much it would be. My hands were getting clammy and I wished I had brought a handkerchief.

Miss Kramer took a deep breath, bulging out her chest, and looked at the wall behind my head. "Lillian," she said, "you're sixty-two years old. Have you thought about how you will spend your retirement years?"

"What!" I said. "No! There's plenty of time for that."

"Well, that's just the point," she said. "There isn't plenty of time. We're cutting back on staff, and we'd like you to take early retirement."

It was like a knife cutting into my heart, cutting off the blood, cutting off the air to my lungs. I couldn't breathe. I got cold all over. There was a pain somewhere inside that wouldn't stay still and wouldn't let go.

I must have scared Miss Kramer. She must have thought I was going to faint or have a stroke or something. She got up out of her chair and ran around her desk and held me by the shoulders.

"Lillian," she whispered, "are you all right? Do you want to lie down?"

"No," I said. And I shook myself a little, so she would let go. I couldn't let her see that I was weak enough to fall off the chair, so I held on to the seat with both hands.

She backed off a little but kept her eyes glued to my face. "Do you understand, Lillian?" she said. "You've worked a long time and you've been a good employee, but now it's time for you to take it easy. You'll get your pension and you'll always have your discount. And we'll keep up your medical insurance. We're not going to throw you out and forget about you. You'll always be a member of the family."

"No," I said. "I won't go. You can't make me. What about my regulars? They always ask for me."

"Lillian, nothing lasts forever. If I were you, I'd be glad to have a chance to rest and do what I want to do. Don't you have a daughter and grandchildren somewhere out west? Think how glad they would be if you could spend more time with them."

"No. I don't want to go out there and be an old lady stuck in a room with nothing to do. I've always worked. I'm a good worker. You said so yourself. These young kids, what do they know? Here one day and gone the next. Not me. I'm not going. You can't make me go. I'll talk to the President. He knows you can't run that department without me."

She sighed and sat back down in her chair. "Lillian," she said, "don't make it hard for yourself." She picked up a sheaf of papers and handed it to me. "Here's your retirement computation all made out and signed by the President. He'd like to wish you well himself, but he's out of town this week. Now if you'll just hand in your identification card, I'll give you your final paycheck and you'll be free to pursue a life of leisure."

"Just like that? Out?" I couldn't believe it. "You don't even want me to work today? Out on the street? No place to go? Nothing to do? After I polished my shoes?"

"There'll be a Christmas party for retirees. You'll get an invitation. Now if you'll excuse me, we're getting ready for Labor Day and you know what that means."

"You couldn't let me stay and help out?"

She didn't answer. Now I really wished I had brought a handkerchief. But I held back the tears and we walked back to my counter. I got out my pocketbook, handed her my I.D. card, and she gave me the check and that was that.

I stood there behind the counter for a minute, but then I started feeling funny, like I didn't belong which, of course, I didn't any more. I walked around to the other side of the counter, trying to feel like a customer, but that didn't feel right either. I wanted to say goodbye to the other girls in the department, but I was afraid that if I did I'd really start crying and that wouldn't do any good. So I just drifted away across the floor as if I was only going to the ladies room or the cafeteria for a cup of coffee.

That was the way to do it—a little bit at a time. I walked around the floor, through Sleepwear and Daywear and Robes, and I saw a lot of familiar faces behind the counters getting ready for business. But I might have been invisible for all the notice they took of me. I guess the word had got around.

By the time I got to the escalators, customers were beginning to spread through the store, so I just went along following this group or that group. All morning I wandered through the store, up and down the escalators, visiting all my favorite departments. But I didn't buy anything and I didn't speak to a soul. At lunchtime I ran out to the bank and cashed my check. I couldn't eat in the employees' cafeteria any more, but I did the next best thing. I ate in the restaurant on the fifth floor.

In the afternoon I spent a lot of time looking at things that Kathy and Timmy would like. And then I went to Home Furnishings and thought about how I would like my new apartment to look. I stayed there until quitting time.

After I got off the subway, I stopped at Waldbaum's. I bought a barbecued chicken, some cottage cheese, a head of lettuce, and two tomatoes. The street was full of people going in and out of shops and hurrying home from work. I was hurrying home from work, too, but not so fast that I didn't notice her. She was in her usual corner by the bank, staring and smirking at the people going by. I stopped, and for the first time I looked right at her. She didn't like that. She shook her fist at me and growled some words I couldn't understand.

I said, "Do you want something to eat?"

I didn't wait for her to answer. I think she was as surprised as I was that I had spoken to her. I pulled the barbecued chicken out of the bag and stooped to lay it in her lap. Getting that close to her was a revelation. She smelled. Well, of course, she did, poor thing. There aren't any bathtubs on street corners. Then I went home.

The moving truck was gone, and that meant Grace was gone. There really wasn't anyone else in the building I was on friendly terms with. No mail in the mailbox. Who was there to write to me except once in a while Ellen and once a month Con Edison? The building already seemed deserted. My footsteps made a hollow sound in the lobby and the elevator groaned like it had rheumatism. I wondered how many besides Grace had already moved out. Maybe I was the only one left.

I made a little cottage-cheese salad for my supper and went to bed as soon as I had washed my plate and one fork. Ellen was right about one thing, I wasn't getting any younger. My black shoes were good and strong and had low heels, but even so, my feet hurt and my legs ached clear up to my knees from standing up and walking around all day. I fell asleep thinking about the Labor Day sales and how busy we would be at the store.

In the morning I got up and took a shower just like always, put on my black dress and my black shoes that still had a good shine to them, and got ready to go to the store. I always put on a little makeup, not a lot because an old lady with a face full of makeup looks like death warmed over, but just enough to show I cared about my appearance. This morning I took a good hard look at myself. I had gray hair, and so did she. Blue eyes, both of us. My skin, wrinkles and all, was pale and soft with only a few age spots, while hers was coarse and red. Otherwise, we might have been sisters. I wondered if she'd eaten the chicken.

When I left the building, a man was hauling in the garbage cans. He wasn't the regular super, but I stopped to talk to him anyway.

"Where's Victor? Is he sick?"

"Who?"

"Victor. The super."

"Gone. All the supers gone. The whole block. They fired all the supers. Me, I just come around and do the garbage cans. But not for long. Another week or two, then no more. You got garbage, you gotta get rid of it yourself. Better you should get out, lady. You got a place to go, go. It ain't safe around here no more. Last night they broke in next door and cleaned out the empty apartments. Light fixtures, toilets, it's a wonder they don't take the wallpaper off the walls. Damn ripoff artists!"

He sent the garbage cans crashing down into the areaway as if they were the thieves in question. I walked away toward the subway. I certainly didn't want to be late today, not with Labor Day coming up next weekend. A place to go. I always had a place to go. The store was my place. I would always be safe there.

When I got to the corner by the bank, she was standing up. I think she was waiting for me. I had never seen her on her feet before, and I was surprised to see how tall she was. Somehow I'd always thought of her as bent and stunted, a dwarf, but she was at least as tall as I am, maybe an inch or two taller.

"Wait," she croaked. She rummaged in her shopping cart and came up with a bright yellow bundle. "Take it."

"No," I said. Even though it was a summer morning and already hot and sticky, I felt a chill.

"Take it," she growled, and shoved it into my hands.

I shook it out. It was one of her sweaters, a yellow orlon cardigan, wrinkled and raveling, with buttons missing.

"Put it on."

She looked so fierce that I didn't want to risk making her angry with me. I put it on. The surprising thing was that my flesh didn't crawl from contact with the filthy thing. Instead, I felt a kind of warmth spreading all through my shaking body.

"Nice," she said. "You keep it."

I said, "Thank you. I have to go now." And I went on to the subway.

The guard wouldn't let me go in the employees' entrance. I had to go around to the front and wait for the store to open. That was the first thing. The second thing was that after I'd been in the store for about an hour I noticed one of the store detectives following me. I knew her, a nice girl who'd helped me out several times when ladies would try to put on two or three girdles and walk out.

I stopped and said, "Why are you following me?"

"I'm not following you," she said.

"Yes, you are. Do you think I'm going to steal something?"

"No," she said. "Look, Mrs. Curry, why don't you go home. They're afraid you might do something crazy. They saw you walking around yesterday and we all have orders to watch out for you."

"Do I look crazy?" I asked her.

"No," she said, but her voice wavered and I could see her taking in the yellow sweater. Then I realized that I'd forgotten to put on any makeup that morning and maybe I hadn't even combed my hair.

"Okay," I said. I wasn't going to wait around for a third thing to happen, and I could see Miss Kramer sailing across the floor with a hard look on her face. I got on the down escalator.

It was strange getting on the subway in the middle of the day. No crowds, I even got a seat. I noticed that people avoided sitting next to me. The yellow sweater was like some kind of magical cloak that made a little wall of privacy between me and everyone else. I thought that over all the way home, that and the fact that the store really wasn't my place any more and I would have to find some place that was mine.

When I got to the corner near the bank there she was. Some kids

were teasing her, bouncing a ball off the wall and making it go as close
to her as they could without actually hitting her. She crouched in her
corner with her eyes closed, trying to ignore them, but her lips were
moving a mile a minute and she sure wasn't saying her prayers. I felt
sorry for her and at the same time glad, because for some reason when
I stopped at Waldbaum's I had picked up double what I needed for my
dinner. Two little steaks instead of one, not sirloin or anything like
that. Just minute steaks, but they taste okay if you put some steak sauce
on them. Two nice potatoes to bake in the oven and some frozen peas.
I guess I was thinking that I could eat one steak today and one tomorrow, but now I thought, "Why not have some company? Mrs. Finney
is gone and there's nobody to talk to, and maybe this one could do
with a decent meal. It would be my good deed for the day."

I shooed the kids away. They went, but not before they called me
some names I'd never heard before and I thought I had heard everything. When I turned back to look at her, she was looking at me. And
smiling. At least, I think it was a smile, but it was hard to tell because
one side of her mouth went up and the other side went down and there
were a couple of teeth missing in the middle. But she seemed friendly
enough.

I said, "Hi. Was the chicken okay?"

She growled something and started rummaging in one of her boxes.
What she pulled out was a plastic bag, the kind that hot-dog buns
come in, and she handed it to me still growling and smiling and getting
very excited. I looked in the plastic bag. It was full of chicken bones,
big ones and little ones, all the meat chewed off clean as a whistle. I
guess she was saying thank you and wanted me to know that she had
really polished off that chicken.

"Well," I said, "that's nice."

I didn't know what to do with the chicken bones. I didn't want to
put them in the trash barrel on the corner right in front of her eyes,
just in case she meant them as a present for me and I would hurt her
feelings. So I put them in my Waldbaum's shopping bag. Her smile got
even bigger, and she started nodding and making gobbling noises and
pointing at my shopping bag. I got the idea.

"You want something else to eat?"

Oh, boy! Talk about hitting the jackpot! Her eyes got bright and
nearly bugged out of her head, and spit started drooling down the
corners of her mouth.

"Well, okay," I said, "but you'll have to come home with me so I can cook it."

That stopped her. She closed her eyes, sank back into her corner, and pulled her coat collar up around her ears.

"Suit yourself," I said. She was acting like a little kid, so I'd just have to treat her like one. "Come or don't come. It's up to you. I'm going now."

I crossed the street, but I hadn't got more than half a block away before I heard the shopping cart rattling and bumping along behind me. And that's the way we went home, me walking along in front pretending I didn't know she was following, and her pushing her shopping cart loaded up with everything she owned, which was junk.

When we got inside the lobby of my building, I kept on pretending she wasn't there, and when the elevator came I got on it and so did she without saying a word. But when we finally got inside my apartment I couldn't keep it up any more.

"Well, here we are," I said.

She didn't say anything, but she started looking around and picking things up and putting them down. I didn't mind because it was all going to have to go anyway, and if she broke something what did it matter because it was all just as much junk as what she had in her shopping cart. Which was parked just inside the door.

"I'm going to cook now," I said. "The bathroom's over there if you want to wash up."

So I went in the kitchen and did what I had to do. Potatoes in the oven, set the table, get out the frying pan. I had some sherry left over from Christmas. I'm not much of a drinking person, but every once in a while I liked to have a glass or two with Mrs. Finney. Might as well get rid of it, I thought. So I went into the living room to ask if she'd like some. She wasn't there. I thought maybe she got nervous and left. Nothing to be nervous about. But then I saw the shopping cart still there, and not only that, but she had put my pair of china robins that I'd won at the bingo at church years ago right on top of the heap of stuff in the cart.

"Well, that's okay," I said to myself, "if it makes her happy. It all has to go and it might as well go that way."

She came out of the bathroom and her face was about ten degrees cleaner, although the rest of her still didn't smell too good.

"Want some sherry?" I asked her.

She smiled that crazy crooked smile and croaked out a word that sounded like "Yes."

So back in the kitchen I went and got out some glasses and the bottle, and while I was doing that I got so angry because a couple of roaches crawled out of the breadbox.

"Dammit!" I said, although I hardly ever swear, and I quick got the roach powder out from under the sink. Boy, did I let them have it! I buried them in it. And I watched them curl up and tip over on their backs with their legs waving in the air. And then I poured the sherry. I had to stir hers around a lot because the way it is with oil and vinegar, it's the same with sherry and roach powder.

It wasn't that I thought she was a roach or something horrible. She was really kind of nice to have around. She didn't talk too much, and she had a sense of obligation which she showed by giving me her yellow sweater. The only thing was, there wouldn't be room for the two of us in the corner by the bank, and I didn't want to leave the old neighborhood, not even to go to Queens where Grace Finney was.

Well, she drank her sherry up right away, in one gulp, and held out her glass for more. So I went back in the kitchen to get her some more. And then some more. Pretty soon the bottle was empty. So was the roach-powder box.

I threw them both in the garbage and checked on the potatoes baking in the oven. They weren't done yet. I went back in the living room and she was sort of toppled over on the couch kind of snoring and blowing bubbles out of the side of her mouth.

I said, "If you're tired, why don't you come and lie down?"

I pulled her up and made her get off the couch. It wasn't easy, what with her being almost a dead weight and the smell and all. But I took her in my bedroom and let her flop down on my bed. She looked at me once, and I think she looked kind of happy. She gave a little growl and closed her eyes and that was that.

The potatoes still weren't done, so I decided the least I could do was make her look halfway decent. I took her shoes off. She was wearing an old pair of sneakers with holes at the toes, tied with string. No socks. Her ankles were crusty with dirt. I got a basin of hot water and soap and towels and a scrub brush. It was hard work, getting all those clothes off her and cleaning her up. And it was sad how thin she was underneath everything. I washed her like a baby and when I got finished she was as clean and fresh as a baby. I even washed her hair. And then

I dressed her in one of my own flannel nightgowns and straightened her out on the bed and covered her up. She looked like she was sleeping, so I tiptoed out of the room.

Boy, was I hungry! By then the potatoes were done, so I put both steaks in the frying pan and boiled up the water for the peas. And believe it or not I ate everything. Every bite. Then I cleaned up the kitchen, because you never can tell. I wouldn't want to go off and leave a mess behind for someone else to see. I'd been thinking about it all, you see, and what I thought was this. She had a place in the world and now she didn't need it any more. I had no place in the world and I needed one. Now I would take her place, and she could have my old place, which was no place.

And what would happen when they find her? Who can tell the difference between one old lady and another? Who cares? They'll write to Ellen and tell her, "We found your mother." Maybe she'd come, maybe she wouldn't. Maybe she'd cry a little, and have the body shipped out there to be buried. I don't want to be buried out there, dead or alive. If she comes here and says, "That's not my mother," they'll say, "Then who is she? We found her in your mother's apartment." But she won't come. Anyway, maybe they'll never find her. If I know them, they'll just tear the building down and cart the rubble off to New Jersey, her included.

And all the time I'll be laughing. I'll be there in my corner. She'll be there. We'll be there. I never knew her name. That's all right, though. We'll have a new name. Or no name. Who needs a name? I have this nice shopping cart and a place to go to.

She's always there, crouching down in the little covered-over space next to the bank on the corner. Rain or shine, winter or summer, she's there watching the people go by. It's not a bad life, and you learn a lot about human nature. It's amazing, the good stuff that people throw away. If it gets cold, there are places to go to keep warm, but after a while you get so you don't feel the cold. One thing, though. I always keep my shoes polished.

Dead Man's Switch

BILL CRENSHAW

Security in the building was good, better than Aikens had expected, and he took some pleasure in that, not only because he
was good too and prided himself on rising to challenges and winning,
but also because the harder the problem, the more he had to concentrate, and the more he had to concentrate, the less chance he had of
going crazy, which is where he thought he was going to go if he
couldn't get to the upper offices and make Wilbur back off.

He could get in and out of buildings easy and without leaving any
two witnesses who could agree even on height, and he had double-
suited before, that was no problem, but it wasn't enough this time. This
time he wanted to show off to himself, needed to prove his control, so
this time he triple-suited, getting inside the building in Mike's Meats
coveralls, authentic down to the frayed cuffs, carrying a clipboard as
he followed some seconds behind the real delivery man, asking breathlessly which way they had gone.

Under the coveralls he wore a Southern Security uniform, complete
with an empty .38 high on the waistline.

He left the staff restroom of the fifth floor four-star restaurant as a
security guard and worked his way up at a leisurely pace.

Under the uniform he wore a seven hundred dollar pinstriped three-
piece suit. He'd be wearing that when he saw Wilbur, and in the suit
he also wore a small tape recorder and a tie-tac mike and a surprise.
He looked fifty pounds heavier than he was, but his movements were
natural and sure with no hint of stiffness. He had practiced. He could
triple-suit in Atlanta in August without sweating.

He could have gotten into the Omega Building simply by registering as a guest in the hotel wing or wearing his three-piece up the glass elevator to the executive offices, but neither route would have led very far and he needed access to the service elevators and back hallways he had studied so carefully in the assessor's office, and he needed the challenge, the fear, the possibility of getting caught, the possibility that kept him sharp. Because it was possible to get caught, he wouldn't.

And he knew, of course, that he was walking into a trap. The newspaper story was too obvious, had to be a plant, bait to lure him to Atlanta, to this building, to the thirty-eighth floor, to Wilbur. Aikens was counting on the trap. He'd use Wilbur's trap to trap Wilbur.

Darlene didn't understand, was afraid, had tried to talk him out of it. She'd jumped cities five times with him and would again, she said, would do anything, go anywhere to be with him, touch him, love him. Darlene didn't understand that he had been running for her and that in a way he was going for her so that they could stop running, could stop sleeping with a hand under the pillow on his squatty .32 automatic. They'd done that for five and a half months now, five and a half months of hell, and Wilbur was the devil. Had to be Wilbur, no question. Who would have thought that he would keep looking during all these years, but who else could it be? Hadn't Wilbur already tried to kill him, grabbing a cop's pistol on the courthouse steps after the verdict? Hadn't he seen the look on Wilbur's face as the cops wrestled him down? Had to be Wilbur, and after six years Wilbur still meant business, and for a businessman, business was business.

So Darlene should understand that he was doing it for her, too, but she didn't, or if she did she didn't care. She was afraid to let him out of her sight, like he would disappear or something.

"We can leave the country," she'd said last night, her tears hot on his chest.

"He found us in Tijuana. He'd find us again."

"Oh, Avery," she'd whispered in that throaty husk he loved, "I wish you hadn't croaked his kid."

And Aikens had gotten mad at that. He hadn't croaked the kid. The kid had died. It wasn't the same thing.

He was sorry about the kid—that hadn't been part of it, and it wasn't his fault, as far as he could see. When an eight-year-old starts talking about being sick and having diabetes and giving himself shots or he'll die, you got to figure that it's one of those stories that talk shows are always telling you to make up in case you get kidnapped or something, like telling women to ram their fingers down their throats and vomit on the alleged rapist or say you've got AIDS or something. It was all part of the same scam, Aikens thought, that kept guys like him down and out and guys like Wilbur up and in. He felt in his own way that the kid had died on purpose just to get even with him, just to spoil all that money.

Something was always spoiling things for him, Aikens thought. Every time he hit the number, somebody sucker-punched him. He'd been so careful with the kid, taken time for details, never showed the kid his face, hadn't left a trace of hard evidence that could link him to the snatch. He'd even used the kid himself to give instructions on the phone so they couldn't record him or voiceprint him or anything. And then, as soon as he gets the money almost, he sees that the kid is out cold and he reads in the paper that the kid never woke up, just kind of drifted on off wherever you go. After all that planning, he dies and spoils it, just like something always did.

Even Darlene. He'd hardly found her when something tried to ruin it. Darlene, good God almighty, Darlene, what could explain that? Here he was finally, with a woman who loved him, really loved him, not just any woman, but a real woman, beautiful, and she didn't love him because of his money, which he'd been careful not to tell her about too soon, or because of his connections, which she didn't know about, but because of him by himself, who he was. She'd do anything for him, in bed or out. She needed him, clung to him like her life depended on it, like a drowning woman, but she was strong, too, he could tell that, feel it under that soft skin, strong like steel, or he wouldn't bother with her.

And just when she had changed his life, the Wilbur thing began. A couple of phone calls that were dial tones, a sympathy card in the mail, then a whistle-smoke bomb under the car, keyed to his ignition. Kid's trick. Any little twerp in the neighborhood could have done it. But the message was clear—this could have been a bomb, Aikens. He didn't need a picture drawn, he could see the writing on the wall. Somebody was playing cat and he was the mouse and he knew that sooner or later the cat gets tired of playing and bites down hard. What the hard part was was waiting for the bite.

But he could wait. He could play the game with the best. Except for Darlene, she couldn't, she was his weakness now, which was maybe a coincidence. "Or maybe," he told Darlene as they stared from their bed to the car lights swinging across the brick wall of the building across the alley, "maybe it's a sign of Wilbur's hate that he watched and watched until I had more to lose than money or living, until I could lose somebody else, and then he knew it was time to take what he thought he was owed for his boy." Darlene had kissed his cheek gently, and they made love, and that had made it worse somehow because then he worried what if they shoot me now.

Aikens resented her at times for making him weak, vulnerable in ways he had not imagined he could be. He found that the razor's edge was more frightening than exhilarating; he lost sleep, lost weight, lost, he thought, hair. His hand trembled; it never had before.

He whimpered in his sleep, good God almighty, whimpered, she said, what kind of man does that? But he could still take it, he told himself, didn't like running but could run forever if he had to, or as long as the money lasted. But then they'd tried to snatch Darlene.

He had been sleeping fitfully, wrestling with formless nightmares, waking suddenly as he realized that the scream was not in his dream. He had slammed into the hallway yelling and firing his pistol at the ceiling, heard a sudden sob from the stairwell and heavy footsteps running down, leaned over the rail to see Darlene hunched below him, clinging to the banister, a thread of blood at the corner of her mouth. It was the blood that got to him, made it real. He helped her back up the stairs, snarling at the half-faces at the half-opened, still-chained doors. He had washed her mouth as if she had been a child. They had skipped town that night, and on the road at four in the morning, Aikens realized that he had decided to turn his back to the wall and fight.

Then there was the picture in the paper and Wilbur in Atlanta, just two and a half hours away from where they were in Greenville, South Carolina, Wilbur moving his home and offices into the newest Atlanta multi-tower, moving jobs and money to Georgia. It was an invitation, regrets only. Aikens thought, *No regrets*, and found as he planned that his hand stopped trembling, and only then did he realize how much all of it had gotten to him, and when he realized that, he smiled.

There was always a chance that the newspaper story was not an invitation, was just a coincidence, and that Wilbur would be in a building with serious security, so he had triple-suited just in case. And if it was an invitation, if Wilbur did want to see him, then he could get in easy, but then a trap would be waiting for him, so he had triple-suited for that, too, playing it straight because you're never wrong playing it straight, being careful, watching your back. Check all the angles, never be surprised. That's where the dead man's switch came in.

He stood in front of the service elevator on the twelfth floor, hitching his thumbs in his belt as he'd seen security guards do, rocking back and forth on his heels, lips pursed as if whistling a tune to himself. A secretary clicked down the hall, brisk and efficient even as she left for the day. He touched his glossy visor with two fingers as she passed. "Have a good weekend," he said. She ignored him. He pursed his lips and pushed the up button again.

He got off the elevator on the twenty-seventh floor and turned left to the restroom where he had hidden a briefcase in the suspended ceiling the day before. He checked the stalls. Empty. He locked himself into the last stall, stood on the toilet, and pushed the panel aside, waving away the tiny brown fibers that floated suddenly around his face like gnats. He retrieved the briefcase, then took off the security guard uniform and stuffed it in the ceiling. The briefcase was empty, a prop needed only because it would be conspicuous in its absence. He put a couple of rolls of toilet paper inside to give it some weight so that it would move right. Attention to detail, mind the little things because the little things will trip you up. He hefted the briefcase. It felt right. Then he checked the bomb.

He wore two small but sufficient charges, one in each inside breast pocket of his suit jacket. They were wired through the lining to a battery pack in his left lower pocket and wired from there through the lining down his left sleeve to the dead man's switch made from a home video game joystick. The joystick tube would fit concealed in his hand, his thumb constantly depressing the rewired firing button. After the bomb was armed, it would explode if he released that button, like if he died suddenly. Dead men tell no tales, but he'd take Wilbur out with him if Wilbur tried anything.

And Wilbur would know that, of course, at the right time.

Aikens had no intention of blowing himself up. He had too much to lose. But he knew he couldn't fake a bomb, danger gave the edge, he had to know he could blow up for real. Acting isn't the same as real. And anyway, this was insurance, a deterrent, a policy of mutually assured destruction that guaranteed the safety of all involved. Nobody was supposed to die. That was the point.

He grimaced in the mirror at the ceiling fibers on the shoulders of his suit and used the hot blast of air from the upturned nozzle of the hand dryer to help brush them off. Someone came in, grunted a greeting. He grunted back, combing his hair, then left.

He knew he looked the executive type because anybody looked the executive type in pinstripes and razor cut hair, like in that magazine that took bums out of flophouses and gutters and dressed them up like company biggies and if they kept their mouths shut who could tell? He walked with leisurely purpose, deliberate but relaxed, confident, preoccupied with important matters. Wilbur's office was glass fronted and dead ahead at the hall junction, and the secretary was taking her own sweet time about leaving, he'd be there before she was gone.

"Goodnight, Mr. Wilbur," he heard her call as she turned back toward an inner door. "Have a good weekend." She dawdled and he got to the junction before she left and he turned right at the junction and hoped that she would turn left, toward the nearest elevators. She did. When he heard the elevator's *ding*, he turned back, started the tape recorder, and walked straight into the offices of M. J. Wilbur and Associates as if he had an appointment, which he thought he did.

There he was, sitting under a hot white cone of light from his desk lamp, hunched over some folders. He was careless, or pretending to be, not looking up, just keeping on keeping on. Aikens didn't shut the door.

"Something else, Vicki?" said Wilbur.

Aikens said nothing, waited, concentrated on breathing slowly and looking cool, all business. Wilbur finally raised his head, looked over the top of round half glasses. Aikens hated glasses like that, weak glasses, booky glasses. Glasses like that invited trouble.

"Did Mrs. MacDonald let you in? Do you have an appointment?"

Aikens tensed as Wilbur turned to his left, reached for a fat black pen with his left hand, ran it down his appointment calendar. Aikens watched every move, every hint of motion, might be a gun in the drawer or a call button under the edge of the desktop, or it could be just what it looked to be. Aikens was ready to move fast, but he wanted a clear read on Wilbur before he said anything.

Wilbur turned from his calendar and looked back over the top of his glasses. "You'll need to call Mrs. MacDonald on Monday for an appointment. Please shut the door as you leave." He bent back over his folders.

Aikens wasn't buying it. He could see that Wilbur wasn't reading, really, could see his fist wrapped around that fat pen, could see sweat bead in the glare of the desk lamp. Wilbur was nervous, too fidgety, dangerous. Aikens knew it was his turn to move. He decided to go direct.

"Cut the crap, Wilbur," he said. "You know who I am." And he stayed frozen, this was a flashpoint, he'd called a bluff and anything could go down, he was ready. If Wilbur moved for a gun, he'd be out the door before Wilbur popped off a round and he'd go straight to the cops with the tape, what an irony. But if Wilbur had just wanted him dead, he could have had that wish long ago, so Aikens was betting no gun, not yet, still cat and mouse. Both men were stone, eyes locked, Wilbur squinting against the glare.

"I know who you are," Wilbur said. There was Muzak from somewhere. Wilbur didn't move.

"I'm going to sit down now," said Aikens, nodding toward the leather chair in front of Wilbur's desk. "You just sit still." He shut the door and crossed to the chair, eased into it, and set the briefcase down on the floor to his right, watching Wilbur all the while. The silence continued. Aikens felt good, felt that adrenaline rush, that edge. Everything was sharp. He smiled.

"What do you want?" asked Wilbur.

Aikens could almost see the venom in his voice, and he let his smile widen. "That's my line," he said. "What do *you* want? Why are you hounding me?"

"Why shouldn't I just call security and have you thrown out?"

"Because you went to so much trouble to get me here."

"You're crazy."

"Do it, then," said Aikens, waving the back of his hand toward the phone as if dismissing it. "Call."

Aikens didn't like hitting another flashpoint so soon, liked them spaced regular and three or four minutes apart at least so you could gauge the stakes better, see what the other guy was hoping to win and was afraid to lose. Then you knew what to do. But this was coming too quick, before he got a handle on Wilbur, and the whole idea was to get something on tape that he could use as blackmail, use to force Wilbur back into his high rise and off the streets, back where he belonged.

And he could tell that whatever Wilbur had expected from this meeting, if Wilbur had in fact set up this meeting, whatever he'd expected, this wasn't it, because he was fighting for control, working his jaw muscles, white-knuckling that pen, tensing his arm muscles. Wilbur wasn't dealing with this well at all.

Who am I kidding? thought Aikens, because he could tell that he wasn't dealing with it well either, that the euphoria that had been building ever since he had decided to confront Wilbur was draining fast, leaving him empty, like a sucked orange. Only the dead man's switch left him in control of anything and that was because the dead man's switch controlled ultimately, like doctors and lawyers and judges and such controlled ultimately, because they could control somebody's life. It was bottom line control, the kind that Wilbur would understand, and it was all Aikens had, and as long as he had the dead man's switch, he could hold on, but he had to leave the office sometime and when he did he had to know that the nightmare with Wilbur was over, because that's what it was, a nightmare, he could admit that now as he sat on what seemed to him the peak of an ice mountain, tilting down toward the beginning of a long slide, because it *was* a nightmare and he couldn't live it any more, so one way or the other Wilbur would quit or he would go crazy.

He felt light-headed. He had to regain control.

"You should know," he said, halting involuntarily when Wilbur's eyes snapped into focus on him, "you should know that I'm wired with a dead man's switch and that if anything happens to me I'm wearing enough black powder to put this office out into the street." He held up his left hand to show Wilbur the joystick and the mashing thumb.

And Wilbur just sat there a minute or two it seemed like and looked from Aikens' eyes to his thumb and back again, which was not at all the reaction Aikens wanted. Then Wilbur started smiling like the smile was coming on his face whether he wanted it to or not and he picked up a paper clip in his right hand and kind of flipped it backhanded with his index and middle fingers at Aikens' head, and he said, "So let it go."

"Hey!" said Aikens.

Wilbur flicked another paper clip at him. "Come on, let it go." He flicked another; Aikens flinched aside; Wilbur picked up a pencil. "Let it go, Aikens."

"Don't push me," said Aikens, reaching for his briefcase, "or I will."

Wilbur laughed aloud at that and threw the pencil spinning like a knife. It bounced off the briefcase that Aikens raised suddenly between them. Wilbur reached for a stapler.

"Hey!" Aikens shouted and twisted out of the chair. The stapler scarred the leather cushion.

"Let it go, Aikens. You can do it. C'mon." He threw a coffee mug.

It caught Aikens in the left shoulder. Aikens ducked and a second mug crashed into the wall beyond. He crouched behind the chair, shaking with anger and confusion. Wilbur was crazy, would get them both killed. A fat book arced high over the chair like a mortar shell and smacked down beside him. Did Wilbur think this was some kind of game?

"Let it go," Wilbur squealed through his laughter.

Aikens sprang to his feet, enraged, afraid. "It's a dead man's switch, you idiot," he shouted. "If you want me to let go, you'll have to kill me."

Wilbur's laughter roared back. "Oh, macho," he hooted. "I love it when you're macho." And he threw a glass paperweight with a piece of pink coral embedded inside and it hit Aiken on the left wrist and it was all Aikens could do to keep his thumb down. With his right hand he reached into his coat and ripped at the wires until he pulled one free of the battery.

"You're crazy," he said and turned and started for the door, heard the drawer slide open, knew that Wilbur had pulled a gun even before the porcelain lamp by the door broke and sagged and shattered as the bullet passed through.

"Sit down," said Wilbur. He was holding a pistol, a .32 it looked like. Aikens sat, wondering if the shot had been loud enough to attract security, hoping that it had been. This wasn't right, none of it was right, he had only come to get the man to leave him and Darlene alone and now he might be killed. He'd been counting on not being killed, on confronting the little man with the big bucks one-on-one without the goons he hired to do his hassling, but this wasn't part of it. He hadn't even brought a gun himself, Darlene had said no guns, that was just asking for trouble, and he had agreed, but he hadn't told Darlene about the dead man's switch or she wouldn't have let him come at all. And now he didn't have the dead man's switch and he didn't have a gun, and there was nothing that even resembled euphoria left.

Wilbur leaned forward across his desk, deep into the white cone of light, and laid the gun down just in front of his right hand. "Now," he said, "what do you want?"

Aikens knew that this was a different kind of flashpoint, that it was his turn now, that he had to seem in control even if he were not. He had a goal; he had to concentrate on that, on not only getting out alive, but on getting Wilbur to quit, and he had to concentrate on

Darlene or he might be stupid and he couldn't afford to be stupid now. Still, the gun was there, three, maybe four feet, a good lunge and grab and he'd be back in control, but it was only six inches from Wilbur, nothing doing yet.

"Well?" said Wilbur. The tone lacked patience.

"I came to get you to back off," said Aikens. "Leave me alone. I didn't have nothing to do with your kid. I can understand how you feel about him, but I didn't do nothing, you know? I mean, I know my life hasn't been what you'd call straight, but it's been business, like yours, business, and in business you protect. I'm big on protection, and even if I had snatched your kid, which I didn't, you understand, though I'll admit I've considered that kind of job, even if I had snatched him I'd protect myself and the way to do that is to protect the kid, right? I mean stands to reason, 'cause you get busted for snatching that's one thing, but if somebody dies, that's something else, isn't it?"

"Murder."

"Yeah, right, who needs that? I'm in it for the money, you know, and I'm not greedy, so I don't do jobs that might have murder connected. I understand your grief, Wilbur, I do, and I know that you need some-body to blame, and that's me, because I work the other side of the street and things looked suspicious about me for a while there, but like the judge said, there was no connection between me and the kidnap-ping, which was why he threw it out. And I know it's the other side of the street, but it's the same street, if you know what I mean, only maybe on my side we call spades spades."

It was the silence that Aikens feared most now, so he filled the air with his voice, trying to sound calm, but pleading a bit, just enough, he hoped, to let Wilbur get the idea that Wilbur was in control now, that Aikens was at his mercy, and yet showing too a bit of independent spirit because if Wilbur was like him at all, he didn't respect things soft, like slugs, and would just as soon squash them as not. Things had to have a hardness somewhere or they didn't deserve to live, so maybe the kid should have died. Wilbur should see that, but people like Wilbur and Aikens and Darlene should live because they had that hardness somewhere at their core. Wilbur had to respect that.

But he also knew that Wilbur might be crazy, probably was, so maybe he couldn't count on him to respect a hardness at the core; maybe he wanted Aikens to crawl like a slug, and Aikens didn't think he could do that, even if it meant not ever seeing Darlene again, good God almighty, Darlene, if only he'd listened to her, if only he could see her again. What was this macho crap anyway? He could have popped Wilbur himself, except that he might take a fall for it and he'd lose Darlene anyway, so he didn't. Everything he had done for six months had been for Darlene. He needed her. If only he knew what Wilbur wanted to hear, he could tell him.

"So," he continued, "I don't think you ought to bother me any more or kill me."

Wilbur just sat there in that cold white cone of light, the shadows in his eyes deep in the sockets. "I wish I could kill you," he said, "but I can't. I tried to once more after the courthouse steps. I guess you should know that. I was going to get you during a transfer like Ruby got Oswald, but they kept putting the transfer off and I thought about it more and more and realized . . . a lot of different things. That I might hit someone else, for one thing, some poor cop who hated you as much as I did, or who didn't hate you at all, perhaps, but who was just doing his job. What if I hit him? And I also realized those clichés. By realized I mean I fully understood them intellectually and emotionally, here and here." He touched his head and his stomach with a forefinger. "You have to experience these things, perhaps, to understand these clichés fully. Isn't that ironic? The clichés are supposed to substitute for that experience, but without the experience, they're relatively meaningless."

He broke off, staring blankly before him. Aikens wanted him to keep talking, this was exactly the kind of stuff he could take to the cops, a threat on his life, and he could ditch the blasting caps and black powder and batteries before he went to the cops and claim that he'd only taken the joystick as a bluff because he feared for his life. He needed more, but this was a good start.

"What clichés?" Aikens asked.

Wilbur answered without changing his position. "Killing you wouldn't bring my boy back. Two wrongs don't make a right. Revenge is not justice. That sort of thing. They're true. So finally I realized that I couldn't kill you."

For the tape, Aikens had to ask it. "Then why'd you just take a shot at me with that .32 automatic?"

Wilbur's eyes snapped up again and into focus and he smiled slightly. "I didn't want you to leave," he said. He smiled more broadly, inviting.

Aikens smiled back. "You know," he said, "phone calls and nasty letters and smoke bombs in my car and trashing my room and rocks through windows is one thing. But when you get rough with Darlene, that's something else. You of all people I know should know how it is when an innocent person gets hurt, even if If had been the one who kidnapped your son, I mean, which I wasn't."

"My wife died, did you know that?" said Wilbur. "About six months after the trial. Just died, got sick and died. Now why do you think she did that?"

There was no answer to that, Aikens knew. That was an accusation, dangerous.

"I'm sorry about your wife, truly. If you knew me, you would know that I wouldn't wish bad on anybody."

"Oh, but I *do* know you, Aikens." said Wilbur, rocking back a little in his chair, a little out of the cone of light, a little away from the gun, teasing. "I know everything about you. I know what you eat for breakfast and how often you brush your teeth. I know what beer you like and how you like your sex and how you make little noises in your sex and in your sleep. I've even got some of those little noises on tape. Would you like to hear them?" He rocked forward and punched a button on a cassette recorder. "You know, most people are surprised when they hear themselves on tape. They don't sound like themselves, often don't even recognize themselves. See what you think."

Aikens recognized himself, himself and Darlene, and that meant that this son of a bitch had invaded every aspect of their lives, every little corner of their privacy, of their brains. Whatever he felt inside him he couldn't name, but it was white hot and moving fast. And Wilbur was tormenting him again, laughing at his helplessness, his impotence, he was right in front of the guy and there was nothing he could do because Wilbur was leaning across the desk and the gun was closer to him and Aikens would just have to take it if he ever wanted to see Darlene again.

"Who'd you get to climb out of the toilet to record that?" he snarled, his voice quaking. "You can always find somebody who'll do anything for money, no matter what kind of scuz job it is, can't you?"

"I think we understand each other at last, Aikens, I really do." And he rocked back again in the chair, and Aikens had the gun in his hand before the springs even squeaked good.

"That's it, you bastard," said Aikens, grinning, with the gun pointed at Wilbur's guts. "I can tape, too, and I've got all of this on tape myself, and I'm going to the cops. Won't that be a fine how-do-you-do when this scandal breaks, wiretapping, spying, threatening, pulling a gun, assault and battery with intent. This is going to look real fine. And me and Darlene will be laughing all the time."

"I hardly think so," said Wilbur from the shadow beyond the cone. "I know more about you than you do me. I know you killed my only child. I know you got away with it because you're so very good with details, because there's no evidence to link you to your jobs. I want you punished, and I know what will punish you, besides the jail term you'll be serving soon, I mean. What will punish you is this. I hardly think you and Darlene will be laughing together any more. No, I haven't killed her. I've merely paid her. She works for me. A thousand dollars a day for the last half a year plus a fifty thousand dollar bonus if only one of us leaves this room alive. You're quite right. There is always someone who will do anything for money."

"You're lying," said Aikens, but there was a cold growing outward from his center.

"No, I'm not, as you'll realize when you think about it. Nothing else makes sense. These are her reports." He swept his right hand over the folders on his desk. "She made those tapes. Take it all with you. She finds you quite disgusting, by the way."

Aikens leaned way across the desk and fired once. Wilbur flinched in the shadow, then he smiled and rocked forward into the light, onto his desk, dead.

Aikens fought for control, fought not to run. Wilbur was right. He was careful. He had just screwed up, but he was careful, could make up for it now. Good thick walls and closed solid doors, Wilbur's shot at the lamp wasn't heard, hadn't brought help; neither would this. He had time to wipe fingerprints, to take the tapes and reports, which couldn't be from Darlene, the bastard was lying and deserved what he got. Time to clean up all the evidence, to walk away clean. Make it look like a suicide. He'd fired close enough to leave powder burns on the shirt, he could wipe his prints and wrap Wilbur's fingers around the gun. The cups and paper clips and paperweight would look like they'd been thrown around by a man depressed enough to kill himself maybe. It would work.

Aikens opened his briefcase on the desk and stuffed in the tapes and folders with the toilet paper, moving quickly but carefully, a good rhythm, not stopping to see if they could be from Darlene because they couldn't be, it was just Wilbur baiting him, tormenting him, pushing, almost as if he had wanted to be shot.

He moved around the desk to the body, wiped the gun clean with a Kleenex, held it by the barrel with the Kleenex and reached for Wilbur's hand. Which hand? Details, pay attention to details. Was Wilbur right- or left-handed? He'd thrown things with his right but he'd held that fat pen in his left. Left hand, then.

Aikens reached across for the left hand and noticed several things at once, noticed that the fat black pen now lying on the blotter before Wilbur's cupped left hand wasn't a pen at all, looked more like his joystick than a pen, right down to the button on top of the barrel, and he realized that the gun he was holding was in fact his own gun, the one he'd left with Darlene, and just as he realized that the fat pen was a dead man's switch wired to an alarm, three Southern Security guards burst in wearing their .38's high in their hands.

He wondered for an instant if Darlene would be waiting when he got out, but then the completeness of Wilbur's revenge crushed down upon him.

The Girl of my Dreams

DONALD E. WESTLAKE

Yesterday I bought a gun.

I'm very confused; I don't know what to do.

I have always been a mild and shy young man, quiet and conservative and polite. I have been employed the last five years—since at 19 I left college because of lack of funds—at the shirt counter of Willis & De-Kalb, Men's Clothiers, Stores in Principal Cities, and I would say that I have been generally content with my lot. Although recently I have been finding the new manager, Mr. Miller, somewhat abrasive—not to overstate the matter—the work itself has always been agreeable, and I have continued to look forward to a quiet lifetime in the same employment.

I have never been much of a dreamer, neither by day nor by night. Reveries, daydreams, these are the products of vaulting ambition or vaulting desire, of both of which I have remained for the most part gratefully free. And though science assures us that some part of every night's sleep is spent in the manufacture of dreams, mine must normally be gentle and innocuous, even dull, as I rarely remember them in the morning.

I would date the beginning of the change in my life from the moment of the retirement of old Mr. Randmunson from his post as manager of our local Willis & DeKalb store, and his prompt replacement by Mr. Miller, a stranger from the Akron branch.

Mr. Miller is a hearty man, cheeks and nose all red with ruddy health, handshake painfully firm, voice roaring, laugh aggressive. Not yet 35, he moves and speaks with the authority and self-confidence of a man much older, and he makes it no secret that some day he intends to be president of the entire chain. Our little store is merely a stopover for him, another rung upward on the ladder of his success.

His first day in the store, he came to me, ebullient and overpowering and supremely positive. He asked my opinion, he discussed business and geography and entertainment, he offered me a cigarette, he thumped my shoulder. "We'll get along, Ronald!" he told me. "Just keep moving those shirts!"

"Yes, Mr. Miller."

"And let me have an inventory list, by style and size, tomorrow morning."

"Sir?"

"Any time before noon," he said carelessly, and laughed, and thumped my shoulder. "We'll have a great team here, Ronald, a first-rate team!"

Two nights later I dreamed for the first time of Delia.

I went to bed as usual at 11:40, after the news on channel six. I switched out the light, went to sleep, and in utter simplicity and clarity the dream began. In it I was driving my automobile on Western Avenue, out from the center of town. It was all thoroughly realistic—the day, the traffic, the used-car lots along Western Avenue all gleaming in the spring sun. My six-year-old Plymouth was pulling just a little to the right, exactly as it does in real life. I knew I was dreaming, but at the same time it was very pleasant to be in my car on Western Avenue on such a lovely spring day.

A scream startled me, and my foot trod reflexively on the brake pedal. Nearby, on the sidewalk, a man and girl were struggling together. He was trying to wrest a package from her but she was resisting, clutching the package tight with both arms around it, and again screaming. The package was wrapped in brown paper and was about the size and shape of a suit carton from Willis & DeKalb.

I want to emphasize that everything was very realistic, down to the smallest detail. There were none of the abrupt shifts in time or space or viewpoint normally associated with dreams, no impossibilities or absurdities.

There was no one else on the sidewalk nearby, and I acted almost without thinking. Braking my Plymouth at the curb, I leaped out, ran around the car, and began to grapple with the girl's attacker. He was wearing brown corduroy trousers and a black leather jacket and he needed a shave. His breath was bad.

"Leave her alone!" I shouted, while the girl continued to scream.

The mugger had to give up his grip on the package in order to deal with me. He pushed me away and I staggered ineffectively backward just as I would do in real life, while the girl kicked him repeatedly in the shins. As soon as I regained my balance I rushed forward again, and now he decided he'd had enough. He turned tail and ran, down Western Avenue and through a used-car lot and so out of sight.

The girl, breathing hard, still clutching the package to her breast, turned to smile gratefully on me and say, "How can I ever thank you?"

What a beautiful girl! The most beautiful girl I have ever seen, before or since. Auburn hair and lovely features, deep clear hazel eyes, slender wrists with every delicate birdlike bone outlined beneath the tender skin. She wore a blue and white spring dress and casual white shoes. Silver teardrops graced her graceful ears.

She gazed at me with her melting, warm, companionable eyes, and she smiled at me with lips that murmured to be kissed, and she said to me, "How can I ever thank you?" in a voice as dulcet as honey.

And there the dream ended, in extreme closeup on my Delia's face.

I awoke the next morning in a state of euphoria. The dream was still vivid in my mind in every detail, and most particularly I remembered the look of her sweet face at the end. That face stayed with me throughout the day, a day which otherwise might have been only bitter, as it was on that day Mr. Miller gave the two-week notice to my friend and co-worker Gregory Shostrill of the stockroom. I shared, of course, the employees' general indignation that such an old and loyal worker had been so summarily dismissed, but for me the outrage was tempered by the continuing memory of last night's wonderful dream.

I never anticipated for a second that I would ever see my dream girl again, but that night she returned to me, and my astonishment was only matched by my delight. I went to bed at my usual hour, fell asleep, and the dream began. It started precisely where, the night before, it had ended, with the beautiful girl saying to me, "How can I ever thank you?"

I now functioned at two levels of awareness. The first, in which I knew myself to be dreaming, was flabbergasted to find the dream picking up as though no day had elapsed, no break at all had taken place in the unfolding of this story. The second level, in which I was an active participant in the dream rather than its observer, treated this resumption of events as natural and inevitable and obvious, and reacted without delay.

It was this second level which replied, "Anyone would have done what I did," and then added, "May I drive you wherever you're going?"

Now here, I grant, the dream had begun to be somewhat less than realistic. That I should talk with this lovely creature so effortlessly, without stammering, without blushing, with no worms of terror crawling within my skull, was not entirely as the same scene would have been played in real life. In this situation, in reality, I might have attacked the mugger as I'd done in the dream, but on being left alone with the girl afterward I would surely have been reduced to a strained smile and a strangled silence.

But not in the dream. In the dream I was gallant and effortless, as I offered to drive her wherever she was going.

"If it wouldn't be putting you out of your way—"

"Not in the least," I assured her. "Where are you going?"

"Home," she said. "Summit Street. Do you know it?"

"Of course. It's right on my way."

Which wasn't at all true. Summit Street, tucked away in the Oak Hills section, a rather well-to-do residential neighborhood, was a side street off a side street. There's never any reason to drive on Summit Street unless Summit Street is your destination.

Nevertheless I said it was on my way—and she accepted pleasantly. Holding the car door for her, I noticed my Plymouth was unusually clean and I was glad I'd finally got around to having it washed. New seat covers, too, very nice-looking; I couldn't remember having bought them but I was pleased I had.

Once we were driving together along Western Avenue I introduced myself. "My name's Ronald. Ronald Grady."

"Delia," she told me, smiling again. "Delia Wright."

"Hello, Delia Wright."

Her smile broadened. "Hello, Ronald Grady." She reached out and, for just a second, touched her fingers to my right wrist.

After that the dream continued in the most naturalistic manner, the two of us chatting about one thing and another—the high schools we'd attended and how odd it was we'd never met before. When we reached Summit Street, she pointed out her house and I stopped at the curb. She said, "Won't you come in for a cup of coffee? I'd like you to meet my mother."

"I really can't now," I told her, smiling regretfully. "But if you're doing nothing tonight, could I take you to dinner and a movie?"

"I'd like that," she said.

"So would I."

Our eyes met, and the moment seemed to deepen—and there the dream stopped.

I awoke next morning with a pleasant warm sensation on my right wrist, and I knew it was because Delia had touched me there. I ate a heartier breakfast than usual, startled my mother—I have continued to live at home with my mother and an older sister, seeing no point in the additional expense of a place of my own—startled my mother, I say, by singing rather loudly as I dressed, and went off to work in as sunny a mood as could be imagined.

Which Mr. Miller, a few hours later, succeeded in shattering.

I admit I returned late from lunch. The people at the auto store had assured me they could install the new seat covers in 15 minutes, but it actually took them over half an hour. Still, it was the first time in five years I had ever been late, and Mr. Miller's sarcasm and abuse seemed to me under the circumstances excessive. He carried on for nearly half an hour, and in fact continued to make reference to the incident for the next two weeks.

Still, my hurt and outrage at Mr. Miller's attitude were not so great as they might have been, had I not had that spot of warmth on my wrist to remind me of Delia. I thought of Delia, of her beauty and grace, of my own ease and confidence with her, and I weathered the Miller storm much better than might have been expected.

That night I hardly watched the eleven o'clock news at all. I stayed till it ended only because any change in my habits would have produced a string of irrelevant questions from my mother; but as soon as the newscaster had bid me good night I headed directly for my own bed and sleep.

And Delia. I had been afraid to hope the dream would continue into a third night, but it did, it did, and most delightfully so.

This time the dream skipped. It jumped over those dull meaningless hours when I was not with Delia, those hours as stale and empty as the real world, and it began tonight with me back at Summit Street promptly at seven, and Delia opening her front door to greet me.

Again the dream was utterly realistic. The white dinner jacket I wore was unlike anything in my waking wardrobe, but otherwise all was lifelike.

In tonight's dream we went to dinner together at Astoldi's, an expensive Italian restaurant which I had attended—in daylife—only once, at the testimonial dinner for Mr. Randmunson when he retired from Willis & DeKalb. But tonight I behaved—and felt, which is equally important—as though I dined at Astoldi's twice a week.

The dream ended as we were leaving the restaurant after dinner, on our way to the theater.

The next day, and the days that followed, passed in a slow and velvet haze. I no longer cared about Mr. Miller's endless abrasiveness. I bought a white dinner jacket, though in daylife I had no use for it. Later on, after a dream segment in which I wore a dark blue ascot, I bought three such ascots and hung them in my closet.

The dream, meanwhile, went on and on without a break, never skipping a night. It omitted all periods of time when I was not with my Delia, but those times spent with her were presented entirely, and chronologically, and with great realism.

There were, of course, small exceptions to the realism. My ease with Delia, for instance. And the fact that my Plymouth grew steadily younger night by night, and soon stopped pulling to the right.

That first date with Delia was followed by a second and a third. We went dancing together, we went swimming together, we went for rides on a lake in her cousin's cabin cruiser and for drives in the mountains in her own Porsche convertible. I kissed her, and her lips were indescribably sweet.

I saw her in all lights and under all conditions. Diving from a tacketa-tacketa long board into a jade-green swimming pool, and framed for one heartbeat in silhouette against the pale blue sky. Dancing in a white ball gown, low across her tanned breasts and trailing the floor behind her. Kneeling in the garden behind her house, dressed in shorts and a sleeveless pale green blouse, wearing gardening gloves and holding a trowel, laughing, with dirt smudged on her nose and cheek. Driving her white Porsche, her auburn hair blowing in the wind, her eyes bright with joy and laughter.

The dream, the Dream, became to me much finer than reality, oh, much much finer. And in the Dream there was no haste, no hurry, no fear. Delia and I were in love, we were lovers, though we had not yet actually lived together. I was calm and confident, slow and sure, feeling no frantic need to possess my Delia now, *now*. I knew the time would come, and in our tender moments I could see in her eyes that she also knew, and that she was not afraid.

Slowly we learned one another. We kissed, I held her tight, my arm encircled her slender waist. I touched her breasts and, one moonlit night on a deserted beach, I stroked her lovely legs.

How I loved my Delia! And how I needed her, how necessary an antidote she was to the increasing bitterness of my days.

It was Mr. Miller, of course, who disrupted my days as thoroughly as Delia soothed and sweetened my nights. Our store was soon unrecognizable, most of the older employees gone, new people and new methods everywhere. I believe I was kept on only because I was such a silent enduring victim for Mr. Miller's sarcasm, his nasal voice and his twisted smile and his bitter eyes. He was in such a starved hurry for the presidency of the firm, he was so frantic to capture Willis & DeKalb, that it forced him to excesses beyond belief.

But I was, if not totally immune, at least relatively safe from the psychological blows of Mr. Miller's manner. The joyful calm of the Dream carried me through all but the very worst of the days in the store.

Another development was that I found myself more self-assured with other people in daylife. Woman customers, and even the fashionably attractive and newly hired woman employees, were beginning to make it clear that they found me not entirely without interest. It goes without saying that I remained faithful to my Delia, but it was nevertheless pleasurable to realize that a real-world social life was available to me, should I ever want it.

Not that I could visualize myself ever being less than fully satisfied with Delia.

But then it all began to change. Slowly, very very slowly, so that I don't know for how long the tide had already ebbed before I first became aware. In my Delia's eyes—I first saw it in her eyes. Where before they had been warm bottomless pools, now they seemed flat and cold and opaque; I no longer saw in them the candor and beauty of before. Also, from time to time I would catch a pensive frown on her face, a solemn thoughtfulness.

"What is it?" I would ask her. "Tell me. Whatever I can do—"

"It's nothing," she would insist. "Really, darling, it's nothing at all." And kiss me on the cheek.

In this same period, while matters were unexpectedly worsening in the dream, a slow improvement had begun in the store. All the employees to be fired were now gone, all the new employees in and used to their jobs, all the new routines worked with and grown accustomed to. Mr. Miller seemed also to be growing accustomed to his new job and the new store. Less and less was he taking out his viciousness and insecurity on me. He had, in fact, taken to avoiding me for days at a time, as though beginning to feel ashamed of his earlier harshness.

Which was fine but irrelevant. What was my waking time after all but the necessary adjunct to my dream? It was the dream that mattered, and the dream was not going well, not going well at all.

It was, in fact, getting worse. Delia began to break dates with me, and to make excuses when I asked her for dates. The pensive looks, the distracted looks, the buried sense of impatience, all were more frequent now. Entire portions of the dream were spent with me alone—I was *never* alone in the early nights!—pacing the floor of my room, waiting for a promised call that never came.

What could it be? I asked her and asked, but always she evaded my questions, my eyes, my arms. If I pressed, she would insist it was nothing, nothing, and then for a little while she would be her old self again, gay and beautiful, and I could believe it had only been my imagination after all. But only for a little while, and then the distraction, the evasiveness, the impatience, the excuses, all would return once more.

Until two nights ago. We sat in her convertible beneath a full moon, high on a dark cliff overlooking the sea, and I forced the issue at last. "Delia," I said. "Tell me the truth, I have to know. Is there another man?"

She looked at me, and I saw she was about to deny everything yet again, but this time she couldn't do it. She bowed her head. "I'm sorry, Ronald," she said, her voice so low I could barely hear the words. "There is."

"Who?"

She raised her head, gazing at me with eyes in which guilt and pity and love and shame were all commingled, and she said, "It's Mr. Miller."

I recoiled. "*What?*"

"I met him at the country club," she said. "I can't help it, Ronald. I wish to God I'd never met the man. He has some sort of hold over me, some hypnotic power. That first night he took me to a motel and—"

Then she told me, told me everything, every action and every demand, in the most revolting detail. And though I squirmed and struggled, though I strained and yearned, I could not wake up, I could not end the dream. Delia told me everything she had done with Mr. Miller, her helplessness to deny him even though it was *me* she loved and he for whom she felt only detestation, her constant trysts with him night after night, direct from my arms to his. She told me of their planned meeting later that very night in the motel where it had all begun, and she told me of her bitter self-knowledge that even now, after I knew everything, *she would still meet him.*

Then at last her toneless voice was finished and we were in silence once again, beneath the moon, high on the cliff. *Then* I awoke.

That was two nights ago. Yesterday I arose the same as ever—what else could I do?—and I went to the store as usual and I behaved normally in every way. What else could I do? But I noticed again Mr. Miller's muted attitude toward me, and now I understood it was the result of his guilty knowledge. Of course Delia had told him about me—she'd described all that to me during the confession, relating how Mr. Miller had laughed and been scornful to hear that "Ronald the sap" had never been to bed with her. "Doesn't know what he's missing, does he?" she quoted him as saying, with a laugh.

At lunchtime I drove past the motel she'd named, and a squalid place it was, peeling stucco painted a garish blue. Not far beyond it was a gunsmith's; on the spur of the moment I stopped, talked to the salesman about "plinking" and "varmints," and bought a snub-nosed Iver Johnson Trailsman revolver. The salesman inserted the .32 bullets into the chambers, and I put the box containing the gun into the glove compartment of my car. Last evening I carried the gun unobserved into the house and hid it in my room, in a dresser drawer, beneath my sweaters.

And last night, as usual, I dreamed. But in the dream I was not with Delia. In the dream I was alone, in my bedroom, sitting on the edge of the bed with the gun in my hand, listening to the small noises of my mother and sister as they prepared for sleep, waiting for the house to be quiet.

In last night's dream I had the gun and I planned to use it. In last night's dream I had not left my Plymouth in the driveway as usual but half a block away, parked at the curb. In last night's dream I was waiting only for my mother and sister to be safely asleep, when I intended to creep silently from the house, hurry down the sidewalk to my Plymouth, drive to that motel, and enter Room 7—it's always Room 7, Delia told me, always the same room—where it was my intention to shoot Mr. Miller dead.

In last night's dream I heard my mother and sister moving about, at first in the kitchen and then in the bathroom and then in their bedrooms. In last night's dream the house slowly, gradually, finally became quiet, and I got to my feet, putting the gun in my pocket, preparing to leave the room. And at that point the dream stopped.

I have been very confused today. I have wanted to talk to Mr. Miller, but I've been afraid to. I have been unsure what to do next, or in which life to do it. If I kill Mr. Miller in the dream tonight, will he still be in the store tomorrow, with his guilt and his scorn? If I kill Mr. Miller in the dream tonight, and if he is still in the store tomorrow, will I go mad? If I fail to kill Mr. Miller, somewhere, somehow, how can I go on living with myself?

When I came home from work this evening, I didn't park the Plymouth in the driveway as usual, but left it at the curb, half a block from here. My mind was in turmoil all evening, but I behaved normally, and after the eleven o'clock news I came up here to my bedroom.

But I was afraid to sleep, afraid to dream. I took the gun from the drawer, and I have been sitting here, listening to the small sounds of my mother and my sister as they prepare for bed.

Can things ever again be as they were between Delia and me. Can the memory of what has happened ever be erased? I turn the gun and look into its black barrel and I ask myself all these questions. "Perchance to dream." If I arranged it that I would never awake again, would I go on dreaming? But would the dream become worse instead of better?

Is it possible—as some faint doubting corner of my mind suggests—even remotely possible, that Delia is not what she seems, that she was never true, that she is a succubus who has come to destroy me through my dream?

The house is silent. The hour is late. If I stay awake, if I creep from the house and drive to the motel, what will I find in Room 7?

And whom shall I kill?

East Wind

DAPHNE DU MAURIER

*N*early a hundred miles west of the Scillies, far from the main track of ships, lies the small, rocky island of St. Hilda's. Only a few miles square, it is a barren, rugged place, with great jagged cliffs that run steep into deep water. The harbor is hardly more than a creek, and the entrance like a black hole cut out of the rock. The island rises out of the sea a queer, misshapen crag, splendid in its desolation, with a gray face lifted to the four winds. It might have been thrown up from the depths of the Atlantic in a moment of great unrest, and set there, a small defiant piece of land, to withstand forever the anger of the sea. Over a century ago few knew of its existence, and the many sailors who saw its black outline on the horizon imagined it to be little more than a solitary rock, standing like a sentinel in mid-ocean.

The population of St. Hilda's has never exceeded seventy, and the people are descendants of the original settlers from the Scillies and Western Ireland. Their only means of livelihood used to be the catching of fish and the cultivation of the soil. Today things are greatly changed, owing to the monthly call of a coastal steamer and the installation of wireless. But in the middle half of the last century, years would sometimes pass without communication with the mainland, and the people had degenerated into quiet, listless folk, the inevitable result of intermarriage.

There were no books then, no papers, and even the small chapel that had been built by the original settlers had fallen into disuse. Year in, year out, the life remained unchanged, with never a new face or a fresh thought to break the monotony of the days. Sometimes, on the horizon, the faint glimmer of a sail would be seen, and the people would gaze with wonder in their eyes, but slowly the sail would become a far-off speck, and the unknown ship pass into oblivion.

They were peaceable folk, these natives of St. Hilda's, born to a quiet, untroubled existence as monotonous as the waves that broke against their shores. They knew nothing of the world beyond the island, they saw no more momentous happenings than birth and death and the changes of the seasons. Their lives were untouched by great emotions, by great sorrows. Their desires had never been lit, but lay imprisoned within their souls. They lived blindly, happily, like children, content to grope in the dark and never to search for the something that lay beyond their darkness. Some inner sense warned them that in their ignorance dwelt security, a happiness that was never wild, never triumphant, but peaceful and silent. They walked with their eyes to the ground; they had become weary of looking upon a sea where no ship came, of lifting their faces to a sky that seldom changed.

Summer and winter passed, children grew into men and women—there was no more in life than these things. Far away lay the other lands dwelt in by strange people, where the life was said to be hard and men had to fight for their existence. Sometimes an islander would sail away, shaping his course for the mainland and promising to return with news of the rest of the world. Perhaps he was drowned, or picked up by some passing ship; no one could say, for he never came back. No one who left the island returned. The few ships that so rarely visited St. Hilda's came once only and passed not again.

It was almost as if there were no such place, as if the island were a dream, a phantom creation of a sailor's brain, something rising out of the sea at midnight as a challenge to reality, then vanishing in surf and mist to be forgotten, to be half consciously remembered years later, flickering for a bewildered second in a dusty brain as a dead thought. Yet to the people of St. Hilda's the island was reality, the ships that came and went were their phantoms.

There was only the island. Beyond it lay the ghostly, the intangible. The truth was in the seared rock, in the touch of the soil, in the sound of the waves breaking against the cliffs. This was the belief of the humble fisherfolk, and they cast their nets during the day, and gossiped over the harbor wall at evening with never a thought of the lands across the sea. At dawn the men set off to fish, and when their nets were filled they would return to the island and climb the steep path that led to the fields, to work with stolid patience at the soil.

The group of cottages was clustered together at the water's edge, with seldom more than two rooms to contain an entire family. Here the women bent over their fires, cooked, and darned their men's clothes, talking peacefully from dawn till dusk.

One cottage stood apart from the others, built high on the cliff and looking down upon the creek. Today only the site remains, and instead of a cottage stands the ugly wireless station; but sixty years ago this was the home of the chief fisherman of St. Hilda's. Here Guthrie dwelt with his wife Jane, living as children, content in each other, unmindful of desire, ignorant of distress.

Guthrie stood on the cliffs at twilight, watching the sea. Below him in the harbor the fishing boats rocked, moored for the night. The men gossiped over the harbor wall and the sound of their voices rose to him, mingled with the thin cries of children. The little quay was slippery with spray and blood and the scales of dead fish. The smoke curled from the chimneys, a thin blue column, twisting and turning in the air. From the door of his cottage came Jane, her hands to her eyes, searching for him. "Come away down!" she called. "The supper's been ready an hour since. Ye'll find un spoilt, as likely as not."

He waved his arm and turned, pausing to glance at the horizon for the last time. The sky was speckled with white loose-flocked clouds, and the sea, changing from the oily smoothness of the day, was running past the harbor in a low swell. Already there was a wash upon the rocks, at the eastward entrance. A soft humming sound came to his ears, as the sea gathered force, and a cool breeze played with his hair. He ran down the hill to the village, and cried to the fishermen who were standing by the wall.

" 'Tis the East Wind startin'," he told them. "Can't ye see the sky like a fish's tail, and the big lumpin' sea awash on the rocks? Before midnight there'll be a gale to blow your heads off, and the sea angrier than the devil himself. Look to the boats."

The harbor was sheltered from the wind, yet the vessels were moored securely fore and aft to prevent the possibility of their breaking adrift.

After he had seen that everything was safe for the night, Guthrie climbed the path to his cottage on the cliff. He ate his supper in silence.

He felt restless and excited; the quiet atmosphere of the cottage seemed to oppress him. He tried to occupy himself in mending a hole in one of his nets, but he could not give his mind to the task. The net slipped from his hands; he turned his head and listened. It seemed as if a cry had risen out of the night. Yet there was nothing, only the low hum of the wind, and the sound of surf breaking upon the rocks. He sighed and gazed into the fire, oddly disturbed, his soul heavy within him.

In the bedroom, with her head by the window, Jane knelt, listening to the sea. Her heart beat strangely, her hands trembled, she wanted to creep from the cottage and run onto the cliffs where she would feel the true force of the wind. It would strike upon her breast and sweep the hair from her face, she would hear the singing of it in her ears, she would smell the salt tang of the spray as it stung her lips and her eyes. The longing came upon her to laugh with the wind, to cry with the sea, to open wide her arms and be possessed by something which would envelop her like a dark cloak and prevent her from straying far away on the lonely cliffs amongst the tall grass. She prayed for the day to dawn, not gently as was its custom, but fiercely, with the sun burning the fields and the wind sweeping the white-edged seas, bringing destruction. She would stand and wait upon the shore, feeling the wet sand beneath her naked feet.

A footstep sounded outside the room and she turned with a little shiver from the window. It was Guthrie. He gazed at her solemnly and bade her shut out the sound of the wind. They undressed quietly and lay beside each other in the narrow bed without a word. He could feel the warmth of her body, but his heart was not with her. His thoughts left his form, imprisoned there at her side, and fled into the night. She felt him go, yet minded not. She put away his cold hands from her, and gave herself to her own dreams, where he could have no entrance.

Thus they slept together in each other's arms, yet separately, like dead things in a grave, their souls long vanished and forgotten.

When they awoke, the dawn had broken in the sky. The sun shone blindly from a blue heaven, scorching the earth. Great seas, tipped with foam, crashed against the cliff and swept the rocks outside the harbor, and all the while the East Wind blew, tossing the grass, scattering the hot white sand, forcing its triumphant path through the white mist and the green waves like a demon let loose upon the island.

Guthrie went to the window and looked out upon the day. A cry came from his lips and he ran from the cottage, unable to believe his eyes. Jane followed him. The folk in the other cottages had risen, too, and stood staring at the harbor, their hands lifted in amazement, their excited voices filling the air with sound yet fading away, indistinguishable from the wind. For there in the harbor, dwarfing the little fishing boats with her great spars, the sails stretched upon her yards to dry in the morning sun, lay a brig at anchor, rocking against wind and tide.

Guthrie stood on the quay amongst the crowd of fishermen. The whole of St. Hilda's was gathered there to welcome the strangers from the brig. Tall, dark men they were, these sailors from beyond the sea, with narrow almond eyes and white teeth that gleamed as they laughed. They spoke in a different tongue. Guthrie and his fellows questioned them, while the women and children surrounded them with gaping mouths, gazing into their faces, feeling their clothes with timid, wondering hands.

"How did ye find the entrance to the harbor," cried Guthrie, "with the wind an' the eye in league together against ye? 'Tis the devil himself that hath sent ye here maybe."

The sailors laughed and shook their heads. They could not understand what he said. Their eyes wandered beyond him and the fishermen to the women. They smiled and spoke amongst themselves, happy at their discovery.

All the while the sun beat down upon their heads and the East Wind blew, scorching the air like a breath from hell. No man went forth to fish that day. Great mountainous seas thundered past the harbor mouth and the fishing boats remained at anchor, small and insignificant beside the strange brig.

Something of madness seemed to fall upon the people of St. Hilda's. Their nets lay neglected and unmended beside their cottage doors, the fields and flowers remained untended on the hills above the village. There was no interest in their lives but the sailors from the ship. They clambered upon the brig, leaving no part of her unvisited, they touched the strangers' clothes with excited, inquisitive fingers. The sailors laughed at them, they hunted in the sea chests and gave the men cigarettes, they found bright scarves and colored kerchiefs for the women. Guthrie led them out upon the cliffs, swaggering a little like a young boy, a cigarette between his lips.

The fishermen threw wide their cottage doors, jealous of one another's hospitality, each one desirous of extending the greatest welcome.

The sailors soon explored the island; they thought it a poor, barren place, without interest. They descended to the shore and formed themselves into groups on the quayside, yawning, idle, hoping for a change of weather. The time hung heavily upon their hands.

Still the East Wind blew, scattering the sand, turning the earth to dust. The sun blazed from a cloudless sky, the big seas swept round the shores, green, foam-flecked, twisting and turning like a live thing. The sun set streaky and windswept, pointing orange fingers to the sky. The night came, warm and alive. The very air was restless. The sailors found the disused chapel at the end of the village and encamped there, fetching tobacco and brandy from the brig.

There seemed to be no order amongst them. They had no discipline, they obeyed no rules. Two men only remained on the brig to watch. The fisherfolk wondered not at their conduct; their presence on the island was so wonderful and rare a thing, nothing counted but this. They joined the sailors in the chapel, they tasted brandy for the first time. The night rang with cries and song. The island was a new place now, broken of peace, swayed by suggestion, and filled with strange desires.

Guthrie stood amongst his companions, his cheeks flushed, his cold eyes bright and foolish. He held a glass in his hand, he swallowed the brandy with deep, contented draughts. He laughed with the sailors, wildly, without reason; what did it matter if he could not understand their words? The lights swayed before his eyes, the ground sloped beneath his feet, it seemed as if he had never lived before. The wind could shout and the sea thunder and roar, the world called to him now. Beyond the island lay the other lands, the homes of these sailors. Here he would find life, and beauty, and strange, incredible adventures. No more would he bend his back, toiling at the useless soil. The songs of the sailors rang in his ears, the tobacco smoke blinded his eyes, the brandy seemed to mix with the blood in his veins.

The women danced with the sailors. Someone had found a concertina, and a fiddle with three strings. Crazy tunes broke into the air. The women had never danced before. They were whirled from their feet, their petticoats flying out behind them. The sailors laughed and sang, beating the measure with their feet upon the floor. The fishermen lolled stupidly against the walls, drunken, happy, careless of time. A sailor came across to Jane and smiled, holding out his arms. She danced with him, flushed, excited, eager to please.

Faster, faster went the music, and faster flew their feet around the room. She felt his arm tighten round her waist, and was aware of the warmth of his body against hers. She could feel his breath upon her cheek. She raised her head and met his eyes. They looked into hers, seeing her naked, and he moistened his lips with his tongue. They smiled, reading each other's thoughts. An exquisite shudder, like the touch of a cool hand, ran through her. Her legs felt weak beneath her. She lowered her eyes, conscious of desire, and turned to see if Guthrie had noticed, guilty for the first time.

And the East Wind blew against the church, shaking the roof, and the surf broke and thundered on the shore.

The next day dawned the same, hot and relentless.

The wind did not weaken in its power, nor the sea lessen in its fury. The brig still rolled at her moorings amongst the fishing boats. The fishermen leant with the sailors against the harbor wall, drinking and smoking, without thought, without energy, cursing the wind. The women idled at their cooking, neglected their mending. They stood at the doors of the cottages, new scarves round their shoulders, scarlet handkerchieves upon their heads, impatient with the children, restless, waiting for a smile.

The day passed thus, and another night, and yet another day. The sun shone, the sea shuddered and crashed, the wind blew. No one left the harbor to fish, no one worked on the land. There seemed no shade on the island, the grass lay brown and withered, the leaves hung parched and despondent from the few trees. Night fell once more and the wind had not ceased. Guthrie sat in the cottage, his head between his hands, his brain empty.

He felt ill and tired, like a very old man. Only one thing could prevent the sound of the wind from screaming in his ears and the heat of the sun from scorching his eyes. His lungs were dry, his throat ached. He staggered from the cottage and went down the hill to the church, where the sailors and the fishermen lay in heaps upon the floor, the brandy running from their mouths. He flung himself amongst them and drank greedily, senselessly, giving himself to it, forgetting the wind and the sea.

Jane closed the cottage door behind her and ran out onto the cliffs. The tall grass bathed her ankles and the wind leapt through her hair. It sang in her ears, a triumphant call. The sea flung itself upon the rocks below and loose flecks of foam scattered up toward her. She knew that if she waited he would come to her from the chapel. All day his eyes had followed her as she walked amongst the sailors by the harbor wall. Nothing mattered but this. Guthrie was drunk, asleep, forgotten, but here on the cliffs the stars shone upon her, and the East Wind blew. A dark shadow appeared from behind a clump of trees. For one moment she was afraid. One moment only.

"Who are you?" she called, but her voice fled to the wind.

The sailor came toward her. He flung off her clothes with deft, accustomed fingers; she put her hands before her eyes to hide her face. He laughed, and buried his lips in her hair. She stood then with arms outstretched, waiting, naked and unashamed, like a white phantom, broken and swept by the wind. Down in the chapel the men shouted and sang. They fought amongst themselves, mad with drink. One fisherman threw a knife and pinned his brother against the wall. He writhed like a serpent, screaming with pain.

Guthrie rose to his feet. "Quiet, you dogs!" he shouted. "Can you not drink in peace, and leave men to their dreams? Is it like this you wait for the wind to change?"

Jeers and laughter drowned his voice. A man pointed a trembling finger at him. "Aye, talk of peace, Guthrie, you weak-limbed fool. With your wife even now shaming your bed with a stranger. We'll have new blood in the island, I reckon." A chorus of voices joined in, laughing, and they pointed at him. "Aye, Guthrie, look to your wife!"

He leapt at them with a cry of rage, smashing their faces. But they were too many for him, they threw him from the chapel, flinging him onto the rough quayside. He lay stunned for a moment, then shook himself like a dog and rose to his feet. So Jane was a wanton. Jane had deceived him. He remembered his wife's body, white and slim. A haze of madness came over him, mingled with hatred and desire. He stumbled through the darkness, up the hill to the cottage. There was no light in any of the windows; the rooms were empty.

"Jane," he called, "Jane, where be ye hidin' with your damned cur lover?" No one answered. Sobbing with rage, he tore an axe from the wall—a great clumsy tool, used for chopping firewood. "Jane," he called once more, "come out, will ye?"

His voice was powerless against the wind that shook the walls of the cottage. He crouched by the door and waited, the axe in his hands. Hours passed and he sat in a stupor, awaiting her return.

Before dawn she came, pale and trembling, like a lost thing. He heard her footfall on the path. A twig snapped under her feet. The axe uplifted.

"Guthrie," she screamed, "Guthrie, let me alone, let me alone." She spread her hands in supplication, but he pushed them aside and brought the axe down upon her head, crumpling her, smashing her skull. She fell to the ground, twisted, unrecognizable, ghastly. He leant over her, peering at her body, breathing heavily. The blood ran before his eyes. He sat down by her side, his senses swimming, his mind vacant. He fell into a drunken sleep, his head pillowed on her breast.

When he awoke, sober, himself again, he found her dead body at his feet. He gazed at it in horror, not understanding. The axe was still upon the floor. He lay stunned, sick and frightened, unable to move. Then he listened, as if for an accustomed sound. All was silent. Something had changed. The wind. He could no longer hear the wind.

He staggered to his feet and looked out upon the island. The air was cool. Rain had fallen while he slept. From the southwest blew a cool, steady breeze. The sea was gray and calm. Far on the horizon lay a black dot, her white sails outlined against the sky.

The brig had gone with the morning tide.

Dr. Temple is Dead

WILLIAM BANKIER

loria Temple poured some whiskey into her glass without spilling a drop. This was progress; twenty minutes ago she had
knocked over the glass with the neck of the bottle and had spent the
time since cleaning up her father's desk. It was the fine walnut desk
with inlaid green leather and gold embossed top, the one he sat behind
when he saw his patients. Once she was started with the sponge and
cloth, she went ahead and polished the front and side panels, even the
round feet half buried in the pile of the bottle-green broadloom.

Gloria knew she was compulsive when it came to cleaning up a mess.
Her session in the bathroom earlier was another example; starting with
her father's straight razor, she had gone on to wash and polish the
comb, brush, and shaving mug, even though he would never use them
again. Still, there were worse habits and it made her feel better to get
things organized.

Now Gloria drew the telephone toward her and dialed, checking
after each digit to make sure she was getting the number exactly as it
was written on the patient's card in her father's neat hand. The patient
was Mr. Kamen, S. J., and his appointment was for nine o'clock in the
morning—the first on tomorrow's schedule.

As the telephone rang, Gloria sipped whiskey. It was essential that
she get through to these people. It would be chaos if they began showing up and found no Dr. Temple.

"Hello?"—a sluggish, middle-aged voice.

"Mr. Kamen?"

"Speaking."

"This is Gloria Temple, Dr. Temple's daughter."

"Yes?" A defensive note crept in.

"I'm sorry but I have bad news. My father is dead. I thought I should tell you right away because I know you were expecting to see him tomorrow."

"Dead? What happened?"

"He took a nap late this afternoon. I went in to call him and found him lying there. He was—he was all right. I mean there was no suffering. He died very suddenly and very peacefully in his sleep."

There was silence on the line. Then: "But what am I going to do? Who will I see? Dr. Temple is the only one who understands my—"

"I know. This is going to be difficult for you and all the other patients until you can get re-established with another analyst. But I'm sure my father's colleagues will help and you'll be hearing from one of them soon. If you need help in the next few days, I suggest you call Mt. Hope Hospital. They can advise you."

Gloria put down the phone on a stunned Mr. Kamen. Her glass was almost empty—she was sure she had poured more than that. As she refilled it, she realized that her father was not going to come into the room and take away the bottle. She was free to drink herself to death, the end he had so often predicted for her. There must be worse ways to go.

Gloria remembered the body on the bed and realized she ought to telephone somebody about it. Police probably; they had ambulances. But the patients came first—how often had she heard her father say that? Five years ago, when her mother was still alive, Mrs. Temple used to complain: "You paid taxes on more than a hundred thousand dollars last year, Raphael. We don't need all that money. We need a husband and father."

As always, Dr. Raphael Temple produced his mild smile and let the argument blow away. "I'm not selling shoes," he would say. "These people are sick, they need me. The patients come first."

Gloria loved her father. He was the handsomest, kindest man she had ever known. She could recall the early years when she was in primary school and he was still getting started. He was at home more in those days, and they went for walks after supper and on weekends. He held her on one arm outside the apartment building as the sun went down and she could smell his cologne and feel the heat from his face. It was like being held by a big warm tree.

Then he became busy so she got busy too and they saw less of each other. For a few months after her mother's funeral she thought they were drawing together again. He rang her at the agency where she worked and they met for lunch. They went to a couple of plays and attended an important indoor tennis match. She was 24 years old now and he was still so youthful-looking that they made an attractive couple.

Until Abigail Peterson came along. Gloria never learned where he found Abigail, nor did she care. The hell of it was that the buxom architect began to dominate Raphael Temple's life. He found time for *her* all right. His first vacation in six years was spent in Bermuda with that Peterson person—he brought back snapshots to show the fun they had. Blonde indecent cow!

Gloria dialed the next number. This was Mrs. Easterby whose appointment was for eleven the next morning. "Mrs. Easterby? It's Gloria Temple, Dr. Temple's daughter."

"What's wrong?"

"I have bad news. My father died suddenly this evening. Since your appointment is for tomorrow morning—"

"Is this some sort of joke?" Mrs. Easterby could not believe the message because the voice on the telephone sounded drunk and belligerent.

"It's no joke." Gloria reined back her feelings. She was still able to do this when necessary; her sessions with Dr. Sills had helped in that direction. "Dr. Temple died in his sleep a short while ago. All appointments have had to be canceled." She went on to explain the emergency arrangements and finally hung up on Mrs. Easterby who sounded on the verge of tears.

What would Dr. Sills say about Gloria's falling off the wagon this way? Her feelings for Morton Sills were almost as strong as those for her father—in fact, they were all mixed up together, and she recognized this for the truth. It was the subject of many of their early sessions when she had submitted at last to her father's persistent suggestions that she see someone.

"This jealousy of yours towards Abigail is not healthy, dear," her father told her. "A certain amount of resentment is normal. But you are far beyond that level. It's no good my talking to you—a third party is needed. Let me give you Mort Sills's number. Call him, you'll like him."

She did like Dr. Sills from the very beginning. He was quite similar to her father physically—a man in his late forties with salt-and-pepper hair and a heavy face with pleasant wrinkles beside the eyes. After an initial period of deep reserve she broke the ice and found she was able to talk easily. But still she talked only about comparatively trivial things; her essential hostility remained buried so deeply that she herself only suspected its existence.

In time the usual transference took place and Dr. Sills became the most important man in her life. She called him Mort, he called her Gloria. She maneuvered him into meeting her for coffee and vowed that she intended to go on seeing him after her therapy was finished. As always, he listened quietly, not saying much, as if the very fact of the words flowing out of her was enough.

It was not enough. It would never be enough.

Phone call by phone call, Gloria made her way through the appointments calendar. It began to look as if the bottle was not going to see her to the end of the list. Fair enough; she had advised the patients for the next four days. The rest could be telephoned tomorrow.

She got up from the desk and walked to the couch. She sat down. Then she lay back and closed her eyes. There was a couch in Mort's office but she always spent the fifty minutes sitting in a chair. They never used the couch—except for that one time. Had it really happened? The whiskey and her own confusion were loosening Gloria Temple's hold on reality. The things she wanted from Mort and the things that had actually taken place between them were beginning to blur together.

No sense falling asleep in her father's office. Gloria got up and staggered as she moved back to the desk. There was something else she had to do—what was it? Yes, call the police and have them come and take away the body.

The police would be unhappy, she realized, at being brought in so late. There had been light in the apartment when she made the discovery but now the windows were dark. A thought struck her. What if he was not dead after all? What if they came in response to her call and found him sleeping? That would be an embarrassing situation. And all those patients to be rung back, all of them thinking the doctor's daughter must be crazy.

The idea of her father waking from a much-needed nap took over in Gloria's mind. She saw him sitting up on the bed, his hair tousled on the sides, his voice confused. She started to cry, heavy tears streaming down her cheeks, the first release since it happened.

She took the empty bottle to the kitchen and set it out on the back landing beside the bin. She dried her face with a dish towel. Then she walked down the corridor to the bedroom door, opened it, and went into the darkened room.

She knew from the silence that he was really dead. She was alone in the world. No more father, the best there was even though he had switched his affections to Abigail Peterson. And now no more Morton since his insistence that their relationship had grown too close for comfort.

"I'm more to blame than you are, Gloria," she remembered him saying. "I should have seen it coming and should have avoided it. I guess I'm only human. I'm sorry. Here's the name of a colleague who has time for another patient. Call him, he's a good man." That was what she was being given in place of his love—a scrap of paper with a name on it.

She went to the bed and looked down at the body, the salt-and-pepper hair against the shadowy pillow, the blanket drawn up to the chin. She lay down on top of the blanket and closed her eyes. In a minute, when she felt better, she would call the police.

The sound of the door opening did not disturb her but when the overhead light snapped on, she sat up. She was confused, dragged out of deep sleep. Her father crossed the room, setting down his suitcase.

"Gloria? What the hell—"

"Daddy?"

"You're drunk, aren't you? I go away for one night and you—" He glanced at a crumpled slip of paper on the bureau, smoothed it out, and read the scribbled name of a psychiatrist he knew vaguely. His daughter's companion had not moved. Dr. Temple approached with an expression of curiosity on his face. "I don't much appreciate your using my bed—"

He stood still for a moment, then reached down and drew back the blanket. She watched his reaction as he stared at the slashed throat and the bloodstained sheets. "Good God, no," Dr. Temple said. "Mort."

Gloria felt like laughing, so she did. "Oui," she said in high-school French. "Il est mort."

From the Balcony

CHRISTIANNA BRAND

From the balcony up there they could see right down into her house. And she knew that they talked about her. The old woman sat out on every fine day in her wheelchair, peering down through the railings with nothing else to do but watch.

"I knew it," said the old woman. "There she goes again! Dipping a great hunk of bread into the curry sauce."

"Tasting it," said her daughter with a sneer.

"Gobbling it," said the old woman. "Then she'll sit down to her supper and eat a great dob of it on a mound of rice. No wonder she's fat." She herself, long ailing, was very thin.

"Fat?" said the daughter. "She's disgusting." *She* was not thin but slim. She ate sensibly, carefully keeping herself slim. Her husband loved and admired her for her beautiful figure.

"What can the husband think, married to such a mountain of flesh?" Mrs. Jennings was not a mountain of flesh but she was overweight and it was true that her husband found her unlovely in consequence.

"Aren't you having any curry?"

"No, I picked when I was cooking. I must pay for it."

"Well, that makes a change," he said, finishing up her share.

"I thought you'd rather admire me," she said, trying a little joke.

"It's a long time since I did that," he said.

They were out there again next day, the old woman in her chair, the rest popping in and out, waiting on her—the old grandfather, the daughter and her husband, a couple of teenage kids. The Family, Mrs. Jennings called them to herself, with a capital F. They could see everything. They could see into the kitchen, all the front rooms, upstairs and down, even part of the garden at the back of the house. Mrs. Jennings' garden had a tiny swimming pool. "Don't tell me she's going in!" said the boy, coming out with a glass of nice cold milk for Gran'ma. "What'll the displacement be?"

"Flood the garden," said his sister, sniggering.

"That I *would* like to see," said the old woman. "Her in one of them bikinis."

Mrs. Jennings in fact did not venture into the pool. "Those people would have been watching me," she said, excusing herself to her husband when he came home. "Saying things about me."

"Some old trout in a wheel-chair?" he said. "What the hell does she matter?" The Family were a frequent source of disagreement, sometimes she thought the original cause of it all. Was it not her complaints about them that had first drawn his attention to her increase in weight, so gradual a process that he had hitherto been blind to it?

"So you didn't go for a wallow?" he said. "Pity. It might tone up that flab of yours."

"Yes, I know. So I came in and did some hard housework instead."

"Well, she's given that up. Now we'll begin on some housework," said the old woman to her granddaughter, looking down into the drawing room. "You wait—twenty minutes and she'll be on the sofa, gorging biscuits."

It was true that, carrying so much overweight, Mrs. Jennings got easily tired doing housework. But I'm not going to eat anything, she said to herself. I know that old hag up there watches everything I touch. She couldn't resist a cup of coffee, however, and an hour later she was still stretched out on the sofa, doing the crossword. "A bit more exercise would do her good," said the old grandfather. "All that money—better for her to be a bit hard up, have to go out to work. *And* on foot," he added, almost savagely.

"And how did you bestir yourself today?" asked Mr. Jennings, sitting down to a well filled dinner plate. He was not such a beauty himself, reflected Mrs. Jennings—not as svelte as all that. "I did a big household shop," she said. Only at the last minute had she succumbed and taken a taxi home. "All by bus," she said, fibbing. "Parcels and the lot."

"I bet," said Mr. Jennings on an unlovely, jeering note.

"Well, nearly all. Oh, and I took your suit to the cleaners. There was a letter in the pocket. I put it on your desk."

He went a shade pale. "Having had a good look at it first?"

"No, I didn't," she said. "I don't read other people's letters."

"All women read other people's letters," he said. "Especially their husbands'."

"Well, I don't and I didn't. Why should I?"

"I simply took the girl out to lunch," he said, defensive.

"The girl? What girl?"

"The girl in the letter. A thin girl," he said.

"Got a girl friend now," the old woman was saying, cozy now indoors in the sitting room. Friends had come in for coffee and the Family were regaling them with the continuing story of That Woman Opposite. "Brought her home the night old Fatso was away—whatever took her away, but she was gone for the night. And in they come, like a couple of rabbits to the burrow, him and this floozie with him. You could follow the lights—lights on in the hall, lights on in the sitting room, lights out in the sitting room, lights on up the stairs, lights on in the bedroom, lights off in the bedroom—"

"What's she like?" asked the grandchildren.

"Thin," said the old woman.

So now she really went to work, dieting hard. It was a weary business all the same, depriving yourself, starving yourself, losing weight, yes, but so gradually that nobody noticed it—never really anything to show. "Well, you're not all that fat," said her doctor. "Lose a couple more and you'll be a sylph." A couple more stone he meant.

"I'm eating literally nothing."

"What's nothing?" he said.

"No meals," she said. "But I pick when I'm cooking. I lick the spoon. Well, I can't help it. I've got to cook rich things for my husband and I have to taste while I'm going along, haven't I?"

"Why must you cook rich things for him? Couldn't he manage on something less destructive to *you*?"

"Oh, no—he loves those things. He wants everything cooked in cream. And I've got to give him what he wants."

"I expect it's really because you like licking the spoons," he said, laughing.

"Licking the spoons," said the old woman's daughter, leaning over the balcony rail to look down into the lighted kitchen. "See her? Half a pint of double cream that looks like to me—and there she is, dipping the spoon in every other minute, licking away. And chocolate sauce, that'll be for the ice cream; hot chocolate sauce, that's her favourite. Some stuff she puts into it, fetches the bottle from the dining room, and then licks great spoonfuls to see she's got it just right . . ."

"What's this muck?" said Mr. Jennings that night. "It's got far too much kirsch in it. You haven't got it right."

"I'm trying to keep off tasting all the time."

"Yes, well while you're on that lark I'll have my dinners elsewhere," he said.

So there was no more tasting. Sick with knowledge of her own lack of appeal, Mrs. Jennings accepted his absences, increasingly frequent and prolonged. And since she made no objection, he shrugged and went his way. "He's left her," said the Family, adding pity to contempt. "Well, almost. He keeps up the outward pretense. But it won't be long now."

Mr. Jennings kept up the pretense because it suited him to do so. The thin lady was keeping up pretenses of her own. But at home he troubled not at all. "If you don't like it," he said, "look in the mirror. Just ask yourself, whose fault is it? You're disgusting."

"It's her own fault," said the people opposite . . .

She began to diet in real earnest. Now that the tasting was over, it wasn't any great hardship. She had spoken the truth when she said that she by no means grossly overate or indeed overate at all—not by standards other than her own. It was simply that with her particular metabolism she more easily put on fat. And with so little cooking to be done for her husband, the weight loss became, if gradual, at least very steady. "I live almost entirely on salads now," she told her doctor.

*   *   *

"If she eats any more of them greens," said the old woman on the balcony, watching her stagger home laden with lettuces, "she'll turn into a rabbit."

"Lashings of salad cream," said the daughter, who never touched anything herself but a dab of malt vinegar. "What'll you bet?"

"But she's losing!"

"Skinny," said the old woman. "Much more of it and she'll be *skinny*."

"Doesn't suit her," said the husband. "She was better fat."

"She was never all that fat. What's she messing herself about for?"

"Never get him back that way," said the Family, comfortably.

"You were a lot too fat," said Mrs. Jennings' husband on one of his now rare visits home, "and now you're a lot too thin."

"Don't you like me thin?"

"I don't like you at all," he said.

"Oh," she said, shocked. She ventured: "You used to like me once. When I was slim."

"You're not slim now," he said. "You're gaunt."

"She'll take to the drink," said the old grandmother. "You watch!"

She had given up even the six o'clock half glass of sherry. Now, sad and lonely, faced with an evening meal of yet more lettuce, she took to the habit again. A half glass—a whole glass—a couple of glasses: before the evening salad, before the lunchtime salad, at eleven o'clock. "I see they're delivering from the wine shop regular," said the grandfather. "And the hard stuff. Not sherry any more and that derbonny."

"You're not drinking too much?" said her doctor.

"Only what they call 'socially'."

"I'm not too sure it isn't a drop more than that."

"You've been talking to the people opposite," she said.

"The people opposite?"

"In the flats. They watch me from the balcony there."

"Well, *I* don't know them, do I?" said the doctor. "How could I talk to them?"

"They watch me all the time. Criticize me among themselves."

"How do you know?" he said.

"Well, I'm sure. What else would they watch me for? There's an old lady, an invalid—she sits in her chair and watches me through the railings of the balcony. She's got nothing else to do. And the Family come in and out and they talk about me."

"How do you know they talk about you? You can't hear them."

"What else would they talk about? Hanging over the balcony up there, looking down, watching me. What else has the old woman got to interest her? She talks about me to them and then they all talk about me together. There's nothing I do they don't know about. They've watched me get fat and stay fat. And get thinner and get fat again and now get too thin and stay too thin. I'm so fixated on salad stuffs now, I seem never to eat anything else. I expect they know that too. Everything I do, they see and comment on."

"Maybe they talk kindly?"

"No, they don't. Why should they? They've seen me drive my husband away, making myself so unattractive. They've seen him with his mistress. He brought her to the house once—I smelt her scent on my pillow—"

"Perhaps they criticize *him?*"

"No, they don't," she said. "Why should they?" she said again. "You can't blame him."

But in her heart, she blamed him. She had tried very hard and he had been cruel. She thought to herself with fear that by now she was beginning to hate him.

"Well, well," said the doctor. There seemed nothing else to say. But he did advise: "Go easy on the booze, my dear."

"Alcoholics Anonymous any day now," said the old woman from her wheelchair.

In the doctor's waiting room Mrs. Jennings had leafed through the magazines. "Go out and get a new hairdo," they all advised, as a way to reclaim lost love. "Have a facial, dress yourself up a bit glam." She went out and got a new hairdo, had a facial, bought some brightish new clothes.

"What in God's name are you doing to yourself now?" said Mr. Jennings on the next of the rare visits.

She had had a little drinkie and now she embarked upon another of her humble jokes. "I read in a magazine that the way to get back my husband's love was to make myself look glamorous."

"Well, you've made yourself look a freak," he said.

More than one little drinkie, actually—several little drinkies. She tottered up to her feet, took the decanter by its stout glass neck, and lifted
it above her head. He gave her one look of stunned amazement and,
as the bottle hit him, stepped back and fell, grazing his temple on the
hard edge of the marble mantelpiece.

She put back the decanter slowly on its tray and knelt down beside
him. After a little while she realized that he was dead.

Wonderful how it sobered you up. One minute you were halftight,
reeling, stupefied, boiling with the pain and indignation of the ultimate
insult, and all of a sudden you were cool again, cold again, aware and
very much afraid. But thinking, quickly. I hardly touched him. Well,
yes, I hit him—but he scraped his head on the mantelpiece as he fell.
He'd had a few drinks before he came home, we were just talking, he
slipped and fell backwards, he banged his poor head. I didn't hit him,
I didn't touch him, it's nothing to do with *me*.

And she picked up the decanter and wiped from its neck any grip
marks that might be there, handling it as though it had been used
merely for pouring out whiskies, and put it back on its tray. And knelt
down again—and touched with her finger the blood oozing from his
head wound, and tweaked out a gray hair. And stood up and smeared
her finger against the edge of the mantelpiece, holding the hair against
it so that it stuck there. It was horrid, doing it, but she knew, as she
had known at the doctor's with a flash of insight, that in fact she no
longer loved him, wouldn't really have wanted him back. To touch him
did not terribly upset her.

It will be nicer without him, she thought. I can move away where I
won't be looked down on or be talked about by those horrible people
out on the balcony.

Out on the balcony! On this sunshiny evening they would be out
on the balcony, leaning over, peering into her window: seeing it all!

"He's fell over," said the old woman. "He's lying there. She's—what's
she doing now?"

"Leaning over him," said the daughter. "He's dead, she can see he's
dead. She's killed him."

"Hit him with that there glass bottle," said the daughter's husband.
"What's she up to now?"

"Wiping the neck of it," said the granddaughter.

"Covering up her traces," said the grandson eagerly.

"Kneeling down again. She's— Well, I never!" said the daughter. "What's all this for?"

"Blood on the mantelpiece. She's going to pretend he hit his head there. Going to pretend he was drinking and fell over. Just slipped and fell, she never hit him, it's nothing to do with *her*. I'll tell you what," said the old grandfather slowly, "I think we should inform the police—"

Mrs. Jennings stood listening. She could almost hear them now, she knew so well what they would be saying. After a little while, she went to the telephone. "Police? Would you come round?" She gave her address. "I think I've just killed my husband. He's lying here dead." She replaced the receiver and went and stood at the window, looking up at them. "I don't know why I said 'I think'," she said, "you'll tell them anyway."

"Police?" the daughter's husband was saying. "You'd better come round. We've just seen a murder committed."

"Yes, it was I who phoned you," said Mrs. Jennings when the police arrived. "But you've had another call, from the people opposite. Up there, in the balcony flat. They watch me," she said. "Everything I do, they know all about me!" She glanced down her fleshless frame in the too-smart new clothes at the dead body on the floor. "Everything," she said. "They spy on me, they criticize. I never get away from them. They've ruined my life. If it hadn't been for them I don't think this would have happened."

The officer made a sign to his sergeant and knelt down beside the body, glanced up at the mantelpiece, at a grey hair on the edge of it and a smear of blood. "Did he fall against this?" he suggested, standing up, easing his cramped back. "Step back, trip over the mat, something like that? Hit his head as he went down?"

"Do you mean—an accident?" she said.

"Well, that's the way it looks. Is there something," he asked, made very curious by the tone of her voice, "that you'd like to tell me?"

"They'll tell you anyway. The people opposite. It wasn't an accident. I picked up the decanter and hit him with it. He insulted me. Just once too often. He insulted me."

"You hit him?"

"With the decanter. He dodged back, trying to avoid it, and then he

fell and hit his head, but only a little bit, against the mantelpiece. But
I hit him first."

"You mean, to—"

"Oh, yes, to kill him. I might as well admit it," she repeated, "they'll
tell you anyway."

"The people opposite?"

"They'll have been watching. They're always watching. The old
woman in her wheelchair—what else has she got to do? And the Family.
Always talking about me. Can't you hear them," said Mrs. Jennings,
"talking about me?"

"Who was she telephoning?" said the old woman.

"Police most likely. She knew we'd tell anyway."

"It began with her putting on all that weight," said the daughter.

"It began with me putting on weight," said Mrs. Jennings. "That's
what they're saying. Can't you hear them? 'She knew we'd tell anyway,'
they're saying. Always watching me, always talking about me. But for
them, I could have pretended this was an accident, I might have gotten
away with it. But they wouldn't have that. Better ring the police, they
said. It was the daughter's husband rang you, I heard him. We've just
seen a murder committed, he said—I heard him. I hear them all the
time. They watch me and talk about me. Can't *you* hear them? Listen!"

"They've stopped now," said the policeman.

"No, they haven't—they're chattering on, chattering on—"

A policewoman had arrived and now put an arm lightly about her
shoulders.

"Where is she taking me?"

"Where you won't hear them talking. You don't have to worry, love—
you won't have them watching any more."

"They'll watch you taking me."

"No, no—they've all gone inside. There's no one on the balcony
now."

"You can't hear them talking? They'll still be talking."

"Well, now you mention it, I think I can," he said. "But nicely. Sorry
to see you go, they're saying. Such a nice lady, really, they never meant
anything against you; be sorry to see you go—" Tenderly clucking, he
urged her gently towards the door, the woman's arm still about her
shoulders. But when she was gone, he said to his sergeant, "No family?"

The sergeant shook his head. "Single-room bed-sits, sir. One elderly lady on that floor, lives alone. Neighbor calls in, wheels her out onto the balcony with a thermos flask and some sandwiches for the day."

"No one else calls?"

"No one, sir. No friends, nobody. Sad for her, poor old girl," said the sergeant. "She's blind."

Ted Bundy's Father

RUTH GRAVIROS

With his tendency to tune out the distasteful, Warner Chadason couldn't remember when he'd first heard or read about Ted Bundy. He'd had little personal experience with crime in his sixty-four years—the hit-and-run death of a classmate when he was in grammar school, a series of petty thefts on board ship when he was in the Navy, the burglary of the first house he and Jane had rented when they were married, the non-fatal shooting last summer of the manager of the store where they bought their liquor out on Route 138.

Except for several brief skirmishes in the North Atlantic in 1944, he had enjoyed an unthreatened life, growing up in an affectionate, comfortable home in the same serene town on the Rhode Island coast where he again now lived. His parents and his middle brother were gone, marriage had taken both sisters to distant parts of the country, and his oldest brother, a retired violinist with the Rhode Island Philharmonic, lived in Providence.

Warner's enthusiasms had always been simple. Beyond bringing up a family and his work as a marine biologist, he enjoyed reading, music, and fixing things. Wherever he'd lived since he was a teenager, neighbors had called on him for help with mechanical problems. Far from resenting it, he was sorry when lack of time sometimes made it impossible to see a repair through himself. He savored the hour or so with Jane over drinks before dinner every evening, neglected his health a little, and avoided television, aware that with his passive nature he could easily watch to excess. One evening when he'd discovered himself idly watching *Wheel of Fortune* with Jane and their visiting daughter Pat, whose husband was teaching an evening class, he jumped to his feet, said, "Let me out of here," and headed for his study. "Too much for you, Daddy?" Pat said. Jane laughed. "Can't take it, eh?"

So when *had* his awareness of Bundy begun? The question of capital punishment had always been a bone of contention between Jane and himself. Maybe it was during one of their disputes about it. He was against the death penalty, no matter how horrible the crime or the criminal. "It's not a civilized solution, it doesn't address the problems these people are acting out," was his unequivocal stand. He did recall one evening early in the fall, the appetizing aroma of the lamb roast in the oven urging them toward one last drink before moving to the table, Jane spoke of Ted Bundy as if Warner naturally knew who he was. "If we lived in another part of the country," she said, "one of the girls, or all three of them, could have been his victim. I think you'd feel differently about it then."

Pat was thirty-five, Susan was thirty-three, and Elaine was twenty-eight. "They would have been exactly the right age and type of most of Bundy's victims when he was on his rampage in the Seventies," Jane said.

"The right type?"

"Intelligent, attractive, kind."

Warner frowned. "If I did go for the death penalty because any of the girls were his victim, it would be because I couldn't be impartial."

"You can't keep your distance from such an important issue because it hasn't happened to you!"

"I'm not saying the man shouldn't be locked away for the rest of his life. I'm not even concerned about whether he lives or dies. But taking his life makes monsters of *us*. And it won't bring back his victims."

"He *has* been locked away, Warner, and he's escaped twice. In Colorado he jumped out of a second-floor window in the courthouse where he was about to go on trial, and later, when he was recaptured, through the ceiling in his jail cell. And he went on to Florida and killed and hurt some more young women. The ones who lived will never be the same. And even now on Death Row, they have to keep changing his cell because of his attempts to escape. It's all a game to him. Killing the girls was just the beginning. He's playing games with everyone: the police, the press, the psychiatrists, the courts, the taxpayers—"

Jane was the most persuasive woman Warner had ever known. When she walked into the lab at Woods Hole back in 1949 as a summer intern from Vassar, he'd known she'd be capable of dissuading him from some long-held convictions—which she had, for the most part painlessly. It was possible, he sometimes thought, that he'd married her as much for that quality in her as for the powerful physical attraction between them.

Her insistence on planned parenthood as a requisite to their marriage was a case in point. She wouldn't consider starting a family until they had sufficient means to give a child a healthy start in life. It was essential not only to their peace and happiness, she said, but to the peace and happiness of any children they would have—even to the peace and happiness of the community. "The unwanted child is the unwanted citizen," she'd concluded, never afraid of sounding the zealot. It was part of her passion. For all their reserved behavior in public and with the children, they were deeply passionate in private. He was, in his marriage, a very fortunate man, he knew, and Jane had made it clear every day of their years together that she considered herself as lucky as he did.

The children's slowness to marriage Jane attributed to the times— another judgment Warner could see to be true. His graduate students and the children of his friends and colleagues were definitely different in that respect from his generation. They seemed to fall in love just as haphazardly, but they were far more adept at protecting themselves from a chancy future. The case of buck fever he'd witnessed back in the Forties had no counterpart in the Eighties.

Susan, their only child to marry young, was divorced and living in New Hampshire with her nine-year-old daughter Jess, not far from her former husband, whose lifestyle seemed able to accommodate little more than his carpentry jobs, skiing, drinking with his friends, and occasional "quality time" with his daughter. Pat had married at thirty-two. She and Bill, who taught drama at the university, were expecting their first child in March. Elaine, heedless of herself as the family beauty, so far seemed to thrive on her life as a journalist living alone in New York City. Over Thanksgiving weekend—which also happened to be the weekend of Warner's birthday this year—Tom, their fourth child, an associate professor in the humanities at the University of Chicago, had brought home a spirited young Dutch woman and announced their engagement at the holiday dinner. Meta was a psychologist with three years' more seniority on the faculty. Elaine declared herself to be delighted with

Tom's catch but concerned that the weight of the family was falling so heavily toward the academic. "What's going on here?" she demanded.

"What can I tell ya?" Tom assumed *Saturday Night Live's* Dennis Miller's sweet smirk. "Knowledge is power."

"So think gossips and blackmailers, too." She shook her face close at him. "And spooks."

"And journalists," her brother said, sealing it with a kiss to her resolute jaw.

Warner spent a good part of the day after Thanksgiving helping Mark Roper, who had a glamorous house out near the beach, repair the damage after a plumbing leak that had all but ruined the Ropers' holiday. There was a half hour of daylight left when he drove in and saw Jane and most of the others settled in the old Adirondack chairs in the spacious fir-sheltered yard, bundled up in heavy jackets, drinking hot toddies. As he turned off the ignition and climbed out of the car, Jane poured from the thermos at her feet. "Welcome, pilgrim," she said, winding a cloth napkin around the glass and handing it to him.

"Hello, everybody." He took it from her to one of the empty chairs in the circle of conversation. Elaine was saying. "He murdered more women than we'll probably ever know. *He's* probably lost count."

"Don't you believe it," said Meta.

"When he was captured after killing that young girl in Florida, he told detectives he'd killed in six states, not four, and that they should add a digit to the FBI estimate that he was responsible for thirty-six murders."

"I wouldn't object to a change of subject," Jane said, taking the rubber ball Luther, the labrador, had been holding in his mouth for her attention and tossing it toward the woods with a skilled arm.

"His is an amazing case of malignant narcissism." Meta's eyes behind her eyeglasses were bright. Did she know how pretty she was, Warner wondered, the blonde braid below her handknit cap, so careless and healthy and young?

"Have they any idea even now what's genetic and what's not?" Jane asked her.

"Ha. We like to think we know. In Mr. Bundy's case, perhaps being born a white illegitimate child in the U.S. in nineteen forty-six when extramarital sex was still taboo, and being raised first in a household where he was led to believe his grandparents were his parents and his mother was his sister, then at the age of three being taken from the couple he thought were his parents by the sister a long distance away, where she soon presented him with a new 'father,' would prompt more than enough trauma to make any genetic factors irrelevant."

"Jack Nicholson grew up with that same mother-sister fiction," Elaine pointed out, "and he seems to have turned it into marvelous creativity."

Tom laughed. "He knows how to *play* malignant narcissism, for sure."

Elaine and Susan were pensive. "I wonder what makes the difference in how people react to desperate beginnings," Elaine said.

"The adults involved, I would think." A breeze blew up and Meta looked reflectively at the swaying trees. "Even if they can't be honest with a child regarding the facts, if they really love the child and show it in appropriate ways it should make a difference."

They celebrated Warner's birthday with dinner at their favorite restaurant in Newport on Saturday night. Through Sunday, the days and nights remained crisp and dry, with an ongoing fire in the living-room fireplace, impromptu conversations everywhere to be found in the house. Only one of these, to Warner's knowledge, disturbed the tranquility of the weekend.

Sunday morning, while the others slept late, only Susan, who was an insomniac, was awake to share breakfast in the sunroom with Warner and Jane. Susan, cursed with depression most of her life, had grown increasingly moody and fractious since her exuberant arrival in her battered Volvo on Wednesday night.

"I can't wait to get back and see Jess," she said gloomily.

"We can't wait to see her at Christmas," Jane assured her. "Have another popover."

" 'Have another popover.' My daughter finally comes up in the conversation and you say 'have another popover.' "

"I'm sorry, dear. I can't say we've missed her this weekend as much as you must have, but believe me we'd have loved for her to be here. You know we wish you'd move back to Rhode Island."

"She needs her father, too."

"Yes, of course she does. Susan, if we haven't spoken of her as often as we might it's not a case of out of sight out of mind, it—"

"I feel so out of it with all of you, you know?" Susan glared at each of her parents in turn and then focused her misty-eyed anger at the stack of firewood on the drive outside the window. "Last night at dinner

I could have barfed at the new bonding going on across the table between Tom and his girl friend and the old bonding going on between Pat and Bill—like they couldn't wait to get back to their respective beds to hash about the rest of us."

"You'll marry again," Jane said—as Warner wished she hadn't even before Susan turned on her, furious.

"That's so typical, Mother! I'm not talking about me, I'm talking about them! You think you understand more than you understand—like Tom's smug little *clairvoyant* from the Netherlands. She has all the answers!" She returned her gaze to the driveway. "My dear brother's going to marry a girl just like the girl that married dear old Dad." Then, with the eye contact of a great actress, she told them both, "I'll leave you to *your* bonding, I've got to pack." She started out of her chair.

"Oh, shut up." Jane reached for her wrist and brought her back down. "Susan, I know that when you hurt, you want to hurt. And I know your father and I have made mistakes as parents and we're still making them—"

"What? Just by being models of contentment?" Susan said sarcastically. "Don't be silly. How could I object to that?"

"You could object to it, dear, if your courageous choice of a husband didn't live up to your expectations. Sam was a decent choice. He's a good man. But he's apparently not ready to be a husband and a father, and he may never be ready. You've dealt with that beautifully—"

"Spare me."

"I'm not being condescending."

"Oh, no? Spare me that, too."

Warner pushed back his chair, brought his half empty plate and coffee cup to the kitchen, and leashed Luther for their morning walk.

When they returned a half hour later, Susan and Jane were still talking intensely but more quietly at the table. As Warner hung up his jacket in the mud room, thinking of how and where and whether to escape, he heard Susan complain that she bore the brunt of Sam's desertion in Jess's eyes, that all mothers bear the burden of a child's blame when a father is abusive or indifferent or absent and there wasn't a *word* for the unfairness of it.

Jane worked as a volunteer two days a week at a local thrift shop, the proceeds of which fed half a dozen charities. She was an insatiable reader and donated, borrowed, and returned books every day she went in. Several weeks before Christmas, she looked up after dinner from a copy of a dogeared paperback she was reading, thought a while, and said, "Bundy's game was easy for him to win because he didn't play fair. His victims weren't aware of the game—they hadn't been brought up to even dream they were being hunted when he came along in his well mannered way with his casts and his crutches and asked for their help."

"What's this obsession everyone has with this guy?" Warner objected. "Mass murder's a pretty morbid subject to begin with, and he's not the only one around."

"Well, for one thing he's due for execution soon. I should think that would be of interest to you, morbid as it is, you're so dead set against capital punishment."

Warner folded his newspaper closed. "What's the book?" He could see the author's name, Ann Rule, on the well cracked binding from this distance, but not the title.

"It's called *The Stranger Beside Me.* The author's written other true-crime books and just happens to have known Ted Bundy since nineteen seventy-one when they were both night volunteers at a suicide-prevention clinic in Seattle. She was an unpaid volunteer, he was a paid work-study student."

"He was born in Seattle?"

"No, he was born in a home for unwed mothers in Burlington, Vermont, in late nineteen forty-six. His mother left him there alone for a few months, then returned to get him and bring him home to live with her parents in Philadelphia."

"And she pretended to be his sister," Warner remembered. "What about his real father?"

"His mother won't say, except that he was a sailor."

"There were a lot of us around then," Warner smiled.

"Abortion was illegal, of course, and anyway her family's religion forbade it. When she took him to Washington state, she started to use her middle name, Louise, instead of her first name, Eleanor."

"When did she tell him the truth about it?"

"She didn't. He knew something wasn't right—of course he would, a *sister* taking him away from his *parents*? When he was twenty-two he came back East and traced his birth to Vermont. He went to Burlington, asked for his birth certificate under her name before she married John Bundy out in Washington, and there it was. It had to be some kind of shock."

"I can imagine," Warner said—then, as Jane returned to the book, he thought, No. No, I can't.

As Christmas drew closer and the university suspended classes, Warner helped Jane with the usual errands. Tom was flying to Apeldoorn with Meta to spend the holidays with her family, but Elaine was coming up by train from New York, possibly with a new suitor (but probably not, she said), and Susan was driving down from North Conway with Jess.

One rainy morning, Jane's Olds wouldn't start and Warner drove her to the thrift shop on the Post Road. As she climbed out and reached back for the shopping bag of books she was donating and returning, he spotted the Ted Bundy book at the top. "Let me have a look at that before you return it," he said. That something inside him leapt at the prospect startled him.

That he was interested in reading it at all surprised Jane. "Do you want to pick me up at four-thirty?" she said, transferring the book from the bag to the passenger seat. "We have that heavy food-shopping to do."

He stopped at the lab for some papers and any mail, then drove home, made a cheese sandwich, poured a beer, and went to his study with the book.

Even reading comprehensively, Warner was a fast reader, and reading the book without skipping a detail he was halfway through it by midafternoon. He had stopped more than once to study the eight pages of photographs of Bundy, several of his victims, the scene of one of the crimes, a police sketch made of him in 1974, mug shots of him in 1975. At his most bedraggled, his hair curly and brown, his smile open, he was more attractive than average, even appealing. Warner could see he'd be very easy to relate to and trust on first meeting.

He was 5'10", which was surprising since his mother—of whom there was no photograph—was only a few inches over five feet. The more Warner read about his pretensions, his loving Mozart and good wines and gourmet food, the more impatient he became with the superficiality of the man. And as he read about the murders he had been convicted of and confessed to, the sicker he felt about Bundy. When the clock told him it was time to pick up Jane, he was relieved to take off his reading glasses and put the book aside.

As he went to the door, he stopped to take a brief, uncharacteristic glimpse of himself in the hall mirror—tall, his crisp salt-and-pepper hair still abundant.

If Bundy's mother was so short, he reflected as he unlocked the car a few minutes later, his height must have come from his father.

When they returned from shopping, Jane heated the pizza they'd picked up for dinner and served it with a green salad and wine. Warner didn't mention the cheese sandwich he'd had for lunch. He'd never had a cholesterol problem, but he was aware he was pushing it.

After coffee, Jane began her serious holiday cooking. She would start with the desserts tonight and tomorrow, and when the holidays rolled around a week from now she would have frozen or wrapped enough hors d'oeuvres, casseroles, bread, cookies, and desserts to see friends and themselves into the new year.

By the time the ingredients were organized and the oven was on temperature, Warner, in his study, was on page 397 of *The Stranger Beside Me*:

"Ted loved *things* more than he loved people. He could find life in an abandoned bicycle or an old car and feel a kind of compassion for these inanimate objects—more compassion than he could ever feel for another human being." For the first time, Warner perceived Bundy involving himself in a genuine interest, not one he manufactured to impress. The skills must have served him well in his escape attempts.

Forty-five more pages and he'd finished. From the kitchen came the sound of foil tearing, of the oven, cabinet, and refrigerator doors opening and closing. Luther was in a deep sleep across the threshold, where he perversely liked to lie. Warner thought a while, then opened the book to study the photographs once again and to reread parts of the second chapter about Ted Bundy's start in life.

Eleanor Louise Cowell. The surname seemed familiar but far from certain. Her illegitimate boy was born on November 24, 1946. Even allowing for the widest obstetrical vagaries in a full-term birth, he was most likely conceived in February of that year.

In February 1946, Warner had spent his last weekend furlough prior to his discharge from the Navy in Philadelphia, off the tanker on which he'd spent most of his almost two years of college-interrupted service. Within the month, he was headed home to Rhode Island, a degree, and, five years later, marriage.

*   *   *

His left hand and forearm were heavily bandaged because of second-
and third-degree burns he'd suffered in a fall against a boiler during a
heavy storm off Nova Scotia. But his sense of freedom at his imminent
release had more than compensated for the pain. He and his best buddy,
Alex Kessel, had signed off and begun the weekend together, but Alex,
who was engaged to be married in May, went wild on the Friday night
and spent most of Saturday sleeping off a whopping hangover in their
hotel room.

After seeing to Alex's needs, Warner set out alone to see the city of
brotherly love. In the hotel coffee shop, he ordered orange juice, scrap-
ple (which he'd never had before), and eggs. He went on to the zoo,
then to the Museum of Art. It was there that he'd noticed this tiny,
dark-haired girl, first studying a painting and then studying him. She
spoke to him first, asking him about his bandages. She told him how
to care for burns and the importance of keeping them clean and the
bandages dry. He thought she was a nurse at first, but she said no, she
wasn't.

She hadn't, he recalled, answered any of his friendly personal questions in detail. She told him her name was Ellie—if she gave a last
name it was lost to him. Remembering her and his feelings now,
Warner was newly impressed by her strange secrecy and by the
sadness of their predicament. She didn't know what to do with her
day and neither did he.

He suggested a movie and then, if she had no other plans, dinner.
She had no plans, she said—a movie and dinner would suit her fine.
They walked to where she knew the nearest theater to be. *To Each His
Own*, which neither of them had seen, was playing, and though it held
no attraction for him he could see she was drawn to it, so he reached
for his wallet and paid for the best seats.

Afterward, he asked if she would be interested in a shore dinner and
she said yes, she loved cole slaw, didn't he love cole slaw? Did he know
it was sugar of all things that gave it that special taste?

The seafood restaurant they found was spacious and popular, with
roomy booths and sawdust on the floor. They each had a cuba libre
while they waited for their fried clams and although Warner couldn't
actually remember what they'd talked about, he expected he'd done
most of the talking and that it had been about his experiences on board

ship, *his* interests, *his* aspirations. She wasn't shy so much as quiet and had given him the impression she preferred to listen and make the occasional—sometimes stupefying—comment.

She lingered so long over her ice cream and coffee, he guessed correctly that she was disinclined to go home and so he suggested that since the weather was on the mild side she, as a native Philadelphian, give him a walking tour.

First they observed the action on Market Street. Many servicemen during the war, Warner thought, had gone berserk on weekend leave because of the danger or boredom they were going back to—now they were going crazy for different reasons. The prospect of the real freedom soon to come, maybe, or the loss of their innocence or of their buddies—or, as in Alex's case, fear of a new commitment. He couldn't begin to say from his own experience what really drove the others.

From the busier streets, Ellie led him out past the length of Franklin Field to a college campus—which of Philadelphia's colleges another detail Warner couldn't recollect. It was while they were wandering there that she took him by complete surprise. They were alone on a path close to a dark two-story red-brick building when she faced him under a low-wattage streetlight, slid a hand under his pea jacket, under his winter middy, under his white T-shirt, and gave him an extended look that told him this was what the day had been leading to and that this was the place.

He followed her back around the side of the building and two steps up behind a row of white pillars to the deserted concrete terrace. Nothing about her previous, almost puritanical presentation of herself—her careful manners, the gray cloth coat over the black jumper and long-sleeved, high-necked white blouse—had prepared him for the ardor with which she met him, or the lust she evoked in him—a lust he'd never remotely, even in his loneliest fantasies, experienced until then.

The blank he draws now of almost everything that night after her climactic "*Oh!*" is terrifying. He does remember not seeing her home—at her insistence—and wondering if she could after all be married, or if it was his uniform she was ashamed of. He vaguely recalls wanting to phone her the next day before he and Alex returned to the ship, but she had left him with no information about herself and asked for none from him. Just as she had asked for no protection.

*   *   *

In 1969, while Ted Bundy was attending classes briefly at Temple University, a young woman was stabbed to death in the stacks of the library. Her murderer was never found.

In July 1971, in Burlington, Vermont, a young woman of twenty-four was beaten, raped, and strangled in her apartment. She had been working that summer at a motor inn directly next door to the home for unwed mothers where Ted Bundy was born twenty-five years earlier. The only indication that Bundy might have been in Burlington at the time, aside from his unaccountability elsewhere, was a notation in the dog catcher's records that someone named Bundy had been bitten by a dog that week.

Were Pennsylvania and Vermont the additional states Bundy meant when he laid claim to two in addition to Washington, Utah, Colorado, and Florida?

"You can't pronounce it centri*fugal* just because you want to," Elaine told Jess from her armchair. "It's cen*tri*fugal. You have to pronounce words properly or you don't get no respect." Jess, tall for nine, sat posture-perfect on the floor by the still aromatic Christmas tree, considering her aunt doubtfully. "Besides, cen*tri*fugal is more fun to say."

"I don't think so."

Elaine bounced her head against the back of the chair. "What can I tell ya, Tom?" she addressed her absent brother. "Knowledge is painful."

"Why *I* don't teach," Susan said from where she lay on the sofa, a chic-funky felt hat crunched low on her head.

"Why I don't teach, too," agreed Elaine. She smiled at Jess. "I just preach, right?" It was Monday afternoon, the day after Christmas. She would be getting an early train back to New York in the morning. Susan and Jess were staying until Friday. She pulled herself out of the chair. "Well, it's my last chance to see the Canadian geese down by the salt marsh. Does anyone want to come with me?"

"*I* do." Jess was on her feet.

"I'm too comfortable," Susan told them, gazing into the fire and then at Elaine. "I'm sorry." Jess was already in the kitchen, asking if she could borrow her grandfather's binoculars.

"Listen, an outing for me is an everyday for you."

"And vice versa."

"So when are you coming to New York again? I've got two bedrooms now. Come and go as you please."

"With Jess?" Susan meant that was unlikely.

"With or without Jess. Either would be wonderful."

She meant it, Susan thought as Jess and Elaine slammed out the back doors. She didn't like remembering how relieved she'd been to find that Elaine was alone when she and Jess arrived on Friday, but she was in a self-forgiving mood and conceded that she had barely recovered from the Thanksgiving-weekend realization that the family was partnering out and she was being left behind. The first shall be last, etc.

Her father had been gone for hours, rescuing some students who had elected to stay over for the holidays and were having a problem at the lab. Her mother was concocting a fish chowder for dinner. The living room was a tangle from the day before. Maybe she could make herself useful and restore some order.

She rolled off the sofa onto her feet, taking off the hat, her gift from Elaine—from Putumayo, whose clothes Susan insisted were made with her specifically in mind. She looked around for a big box for the debris. The largest contained the portable fireplace her father had given her mother to make more comfortable the late-day and -night outdoor sits she liked so much. They might want to keep it in the carton.

Searching further, she found the box with her father's gifts to her—a covered trashcan for the kitchen, because of a problem she was having with mice, inside it an ultrasonic-sound device that was supposed to drive pests away. It would do. She began gathering the discarded wrappings into it, setting aside any genuine ribbon of usable length in case her mother wanted it. If she didn't, Jess would.

"Here, let me help," Jane said, coming from the kitchen and kneeling beside Susan, who was reaching under the tree to realign a tumble of gifts.

"I see Father did his Christmas shopping at Payson's Hardware as usual," Susan observed.

"Jess told us on the phone you have 'horrible mice.'"

Susan shuddered. "They're making me paranoid. I'm all the time looking for sign of them. They're like tiny Houdinis." She stopped and looked at her mother. There had been an abstracted quality about her all weekend that Susan found disturbing. "Is there something wrong between you and Father?"

"Wrong!" Jane looked at her, alarmed. She slid some boxes around on the rug and stood up. "I've got to take out the bread," she said with a toss of the head that said "Come with me."

Lifting two hot loaves from the oven, a pair of quilted mitts on her hands, she said, "Something's bothering him. I don't know what it is."

"For how long?"

"A week." She started to glaze the bread with butter and gave Susan a wan smile. "Only a week."

"I hate to admit this," Susan said, inclining her head to her mother's flushed cheek, "but I like it better when you're both happy." She moved across the kitchen to the table and sat. "What did these students call him away for, anyway?"

"Oh, just the autoclave again. They're not used to it. They were sterilizing the equipment for their tests and it malfunctioned. They were in a panic it was going to explode."

"Sounds familiar." How many times over the years Susan had heard her father on the phone saying, "Ground yourself well, unplug it, and I'll come by in an hour or so when it's cooled down."

"They keep building better mousetraps. When are they going to build a better autoclave?" Susan said. Then: "Don't they ever call on someone else to go fix it?"

"Why should they? He always says yes."

"Never be an expert." Susan took a pine branch from the arrangement in an old jar on the table and pinched the berries. "I have a streak of laziness two miles wide. Look at this family. I don't know where you got me."

"You don't?"

"I married Sam because I thought he was as lazy as me. In some ways he is, but he's up for every odd job anybody hands him. Wouldn't it be funny if I really married him because he's like Father?"

When Jess and Susan left at the end of the week, the house seemed not only emptier than usual, it seemed emptier longer. Warner's dark mood failed to lift and it seemed to Jane that the light had gone out of his eyes, that his skin was unhealthily darker. She wanted to suggest he see a doctor. It would have been ideal to be able to say it was time they both had a checkup, but she had had a thorough checkup as recently as September.

Late one evening toward the end of January, she came downstairs from an evening of estimating the taxes for the thrift shop and found him daydreaming in front of a dreary TV sitcom.

"What's on television?" she asked.

"Nothing too exciting," he said.

Ordinarily she would have clutched her heart and said. "Thank God," but he wasn't up for it and neither was she. Instead she went to the kitchen and brewed some tea for the *Eleven O'Clock News*.

In the middle of which Warner jumped from his chair with a stricken look, told her he thought he'd left an important matter unattended at the lab, he might be late getting back, put on his windbreaker, and was gone.

Dear God, she thought as the beams from the headlights flashed past the window, what now? What devil was driving him so far away from her?

With all the overhead fluorescents on and the night pitch-black beyond the windows, the laboratory was deathlike. Warner had shot the inside lock and gone directly to the autoclave—the highly pressured, overworked soul of the place. The heat it generated was tremendous and most of the faculty and students were afraid of the damage it was capable of. He had seen some very mean burns from it and was himself wary of such accidents after his at sea all those years ago.

Forty-two years ago.

Ted Bundy was to die in the morning at the age of forty-two. It had been announced on the news, as he had expected it would be. What he had not expected was a videotaped interview with him made earlier tonight at the maximum-security prison in Florida. Wearing what looked to be a shrimp-colored T-shirt over a white long-sleeved jersey, his handcuffed hands clasped together in front of his mouth as he listened to the interviewer's questions, he didn't look that age. Nor did he appear arrogant. When the man interviewing him—a minister, did they say?— asked what he thought should be done about mass-murderers like himself, he'd said, "Don't get me wrong, I don't want to die—but I think society should do whatever it has to do to protect itself." Was this a last-minute bid for mercy, Warner wondered, and was the claim he made about his obsession with hard-core pornography being the trigger for the killings as true as only he could know it to be, or was he playing yet another game with a world he did not love? Warner thought it was too simplistic an explanation for him killing as he did. He had to feel such an injustice had been done to him sometime in his life that he couldn't hurt enough to satisfy his rage.

People who favored the death penalty, it occurred to Warner, and those who put themselves on line for it seemed to share an inability to see beyond their terrible grievances. He was certainly no more merciful than Jane. Luckier, perhaps, in a kind of sightedness that either could see beyond what she saw or not as far. Watching the interview with her, he had known they would have to discuss it when the news was over and he couldn't bear the thought of it. Nor could he bear to watch the rest of the interview itself, reading the terror in Ted's face in spite of the medication he must have been given—his mouth had been dry as he gave his carefully deliberated answers. How did a condemned prisoner live through his or her last hours? How did those who loved them? Why were they put through the long night?

The books and articles he had read about Bundy and other mass-murderers since he'd finished *The Stranger Beside Me*, in their attempts to shape some sense from their behavior, had only added to Warner's confusion. He was impatient when they focused on Louise Bundy as at the root of her son's pathology. Even though she had behaved peculiarly with Warner, even though she hadn't wanted any kind of protection, he couldn't excuse himself. True, she'd said no, but he could have insisted. That might have frightened her, but on the other hand she may have needed that kind of reassurance. He'd had an obligation to anticipate the possibility of a child and to protect against it. These past weeks he had looked up James Agee's comment in one of his letters to Father Flye, the Episcopal priest whose long friendship with the author dated back to when Agee was his student at St. Andrew's School in Tennessee. Jane had quoted it to him back when the *Letters* were first published in the Sixties.

"I very much trust in the blindness of nature," he'd written, "but there is a great deal in that blindness which is repellent, too. Begetting a child is at least as serious an act as murder."

They had seen *To Each His Own* that same evening! Olivia de Havilland had won the Oscar for playing the mother of an illegitimate baby in the movie. He had thought it pure soap opera and had in fact fallen asleep through part of it. Ellie, this strange creature from some nether world like the Marianas trench, as he had since come to think of her, had had tears in her eyes when the lights came back up in the theater. But in the movie Olivia de Havilland had put the baby out for adoption—why hadn't Ellie? And why had she left Ted alone for two months at the Vermont home before returning to claim him and bring him to her parents' home in Philadelphia? In one of the books Warner had read, it was estimated that half of all our knowledge is locked in our first year of life. With his fate uncertain those first three months, no one to bond to, and God only knew what happening the remaining nine months, Ted's destiny and that of his victims could well have been decided by his first birthday.

"It's a tragedy for this court to see such a total waste of humanity that I've experienced in this courtroom," the avuncular judge who was the first to sentence Ted to death in Florida had said. "You're a bright young man. You'd have made a good lawyer, and I'd have loved to have you practice in front of me. But you went another way, partner. Take care of yourself. I don't have any animosity toward you—I want you to know that."

That his hours with Ellie had been born of a kind of mild desperation, Warner had only recently acknowledged, and that everything he remembered and read about Louise Bundy told him that marriage with her would have been disastrous, couldn't absolve him of his absence in the boy's formative years. If he had given him a grounding and Ted had become a monster nevertheless, Warner could consider laying more of the blame elsewhere, or on the system. As it was, he recognized now, he was part of the system. The man he had thought he was—considerate, rational husband, father, mentor, neighbor—did not really exist.

Had anyone been observing Warner from outside since his arrival, they would have wondered at his almost catatonic stance before the silent autoclave. But now they would see him straighten and seem to address the problem it presented.

When the unit had last malfunctioned in December, Warner, for reasons he hadn't fully admitted to himself until now, had repaired it only to meet its immediate functional and safety needs. Several pipes and the gauge needed replacement rather than first aid. He should have ordered the new parts and seen them installed by now, but he'd done neither. So that now all he had to do was remove the faulty parts, work at the already frayed cord so that it was dangerously exposed, pour water on the floor beneath the unit to simulate escaped steam, plug in the cord, grasp the exposed section, and precede his son to Hell.

* * *

The digital clock by the bed read 5:10. Jane had phoned the lab and Warner's office at the university with no luck. She knew he could have been at the lab and purposely not picked up. Instinct also told her not to go looking for him or to call the children.

Was it possible that Warner was lost to her forever? It could be happening, she knew that without having the slightest inkling why, and all she could do was wait for the news from some policeman or learn that this was simply another of the morbid apprehensions that had been hounding her since her sixtieth birthday. There was that, too, after all, to be considered in Warner's recent behavior.

She couldn't concentrate on anything but her thoughts. What Warner called "the great unread" in the bookcase by her side of the bed held no comfort for her tonight.

His ventures as a handyman, she thought. More often than not any more they were an effort at keeping the peace in the families of friends and neighbors who had foolhardily entrusted their cars, TV sets, lawn mowers, and sewing machines to each other. In trying to restore these things to the condition the lender perceived them to have been, he hoped to restore the amiability of the community.

Luther, who had kept a restless watch down by the back door most of the night, came upstairs and in from the hallway, leaning his face on the comforter—comforter himself, his dark gaze over his graying muzzle perplexed and concerned. "I've got two labs now," Warner had told him when he was a puppy, "but only one named Luther."

"I don't know, Luther," she said to him now. "I'd tell you if I knew, but I don't."

All she did know was that Warner had bounded from his chair in the middle of the interview with Ted Bundy. Pore over that as she had, she couldn't for the life of her see any significance in it at all.

She was down in the living room with a cup of coffee, Luther all but on her lap, when she heard a car turn into the driveway shortly after seven. As Luther ran barking to the door, Jane closed her eyes against the life that seemed to fall away from her in her fear of hearing the doorbell. Then there was the sound of the key in the lock and Warner let himself in. Bending wearily to hush Luther, he saw her. She ran to him from the chair and his arms closed around her. Hers encircled him in a grateful stranglehold.

In the pale cast of dawn, he had lost the name of action. But although he hadn't been able to end his life, he was left with serious doubt about the favor that would be to Jane. His recognition that all their life together had been a fool's paradise for him was not something he could shrug off. Had he had any conscience at all before he met her? Why had he aborted his plan for an accident? Did he not want to die? Had he not wanted to kill? Had he not wanted to be killed? There was that theory that those three elements are necessary for the commission of suicide, he remembered. Actually, he had no disposition for any of the three. More than that, though, the conscious thought that had stopped him was the certainty that Jane would know it had been no accident, however feasible it might seem to the police, the community, and perhaps the children.

He buried his face in her hair. They were both crying. And while she would probably never tell him why she was, he thought he knew. It would remain one of the few secrets they would ever have apart.

A few hours later on January 24, 1989, in a bar on the U.S. side of Niagara Falls, an observant stranger might have taken note of one of those ever-young, ever-attractive drifters, full head of curly hair, propped over a beer at the gummy counter, a loud, complacent woman at his side, both occupied with the news on the TV over the bar.

On the screen, crowds cheering a ghostlike white hearse moving through dawn light gave way to a replay of part of the Bundy interview of the night before.

"He sure was a good-looking guy," the woman said. "Just my type." She appraised her drinking partner. "He looks a lot like you, Gus. Look at him, Larry," she said to the bartender, "doesn't he look like Gus?" Larry checked the two faces out and agreed obligingly. "You could be father and son if you were older," she told Gus.

Gus smiled and stroked the stubble on his jaw, flattered at looking like the man on television and at being taken, as always, for younger than he was.

"Bastard never had a father," Larry commented, pouring himself the third cup of coffee that morning.

"My God, I can't get over it," the woman said, reaching for a cigarette. "You don't see a resemblance like this every day."

Just like her to go on and on about it, Gus thought, watching the dead man still talking on the television screen. And as he watched, the smile left his face and a penumbrous shadow fell across his calculating, worried eyes.

Meet Me by the Mannequin

CORNELL WOOLRICH

*A*ll the way up on the bus I kept wondering if she'd be glad to see me or not. I hadn't told her I was coming. For that matter, I hadn't told them at the other end I was leaving—not until after I'd gone. Just a note left behind in my room: *Dear Mom and Pop: I can't stand it here any more. I'm not going back to high school when it opens, I'm going to the city. I want to begin to really live. Please don't worry about me, I'll be all right. I'll look up Jean and stay with her. Love—Francine.* And that's what I was on my way to do right now.

My sister Jean hadn't been much older than I was when she left, just under eighteen. She hadn't told us much in her letters, but the little she'd said had made it sound wonderful to me. She told us she had a job, but she'd never said what it was. She must have been making a lot of money at it. I don't think there'd been a letter in the three years she was gone that hadn't had at least a twenty and sometimes as high as a fifty-dollar bill in it. But when I'd suggested running up to see her during my school vacation the summer before, she hadn't seemed to want me to come. It was so hot, she'd said, and I wouldn't like it. And when I insisted, she finally said she wasn't going to be there herself, she was going away. But then six months afterwards, in one of her later letters, she forgot she'd said that and mentioned something about being stuck in the city through the whole summer.

I wondered vaguely why she hadn't wanted her kid sister to visit her. I supposed she'd thought I wasn't old enough yet, or they needed me at home, or she felt I ought to finish high school first, and let it go at that. Older sisters aren't always so easy to figure out.

I had her address, the one we wrote her to, but it was just Greek to me. I wasn't worried about finding it though. I'd ask my way when I got there, and that'd be all there was to it.

The bus got in quite late and I was tired. I was hungry, too, and I only had twenty-two cents left, after paying my bus fare and buying a sandwich and coffee at noon. But of course I was going straight to Jean, so what difference did that make?

I climbed down and looked around the terminal. Wonderland was already beginning. I had a single bag with me, not much bigger than a telephone directory. I hadn't brought much, mostly because I didn't have much to bring. Who wanted country stuff when you were going to start life in the city, anyway?

I chose one of the many exits at random, and came out on an avenue that was sheer magic. It stretched as far as the eye could reach, and the buildings were tall along it, and neon signs all colors of the rainbow flashed against the night sky. I'd reached the Promised Land, all right.

I was so enthralled that I decided to put off asking my way to Jean's for a little while and do a little roaming around first. There was plenty of time, it was still early.

I'd walked along for about five or ten blocks, bag in hand, when I first saw the mannequin. It was in a lighted show window on the Avenue—Chalif-Bleekman's—where there were a row of them with sort of tea-colored faces and gold and silver wigs. It was the one on the end. The others all looked ritzy, but the one on the end had a sort of friendly smile on her face. Her expression seemed to say: "Hi, little girl. Welcome to the city. If you ever need a friend, or get in a jam, come around and tell me all about it."

I don't know how to explain what I mean. It sounds sort of crazy, I know. You have to be pretty young, and you have to be pretty imaginative—like everyone said I was back home—to get it. If you're hardboiled or cynical, you won't get it at all. It's like some people carry around a rabbit's foot, and others have a lucky coin with a hole in it. It's like some people believe in a lucky star, and others in a patron saint. This mannequin became my patron saint at sight. Oh, I knew it was just a wax figure that couldn't talk or hear or think. I wasn't that dumb. But that didn't alter the case any. Everyone has to have a little fantasy in their life. And I was lonely and didn't know anybody and it was my first night in the city. That was why, I guess.

Anyway, I stood there day-dreaming in front of it, and telling it all my hopes and fears and ambitions. Not out loud, of course. And it looked back with that understanding smile, as if it was trying to say: "Sure. I know. Don't worry, everything'll turn out all right. And if it doesn't, you know where to find me, I'll always be here, night and day." It was like a pact made between us, that first night, that was never to be broken afterwards.

Finally I had to move on. It was getting late, and I had to get up to Jean's. I put the pads of my fingers against the glass in a sort of parting gesture, and went on my way. The others all looked ritzy with their noses in the air, but *mine* had that same friendly, sympathetic smile to the end.

I saw a policeman rolling traffic stanchions out of the middle of the street, and I went over to him to ask my way. It's always safest to ask a policeman when you're in a strange city. I knew that much.

He scratched the back of his head when I handed him the scrap of paper that had Jean's address penciled on it. Then he looked me over, up and down, standing there in my country clothes with my little bag in my hand.

Instead of telling me where it was, he said: "Are you sure you want to go there?"

"Certainly," I said in surprise. "I'm—I'm supposed to."

He mumbled something under his breath that sounded like: "Ah, it's a shame—but what can a cop on traffic duty do about it?"

"Thank you," I said when he'd finished telling me which direction to take.

He shook his head as if he felt sorry for me. "Don't thank me," he sighed. "Sure and it's no favor I'm doing you."

I looked back and saw him still watching me and shaking his head. He seemed to have recognized the address, but I couldn't understand why he should feel so bad about my going there.

Even the twenties and fifties she'd sent home hadn't prepared me for the looks of it when I finally reached it. Why, she must be making money hand-over-fist to be able to afford living in such a place! I almost thought for a minute I'd made a mistake. I went over to the doorman to verify the number. Yes, it was the right one. I asked him which floor Jean Everton lived on.

He acted as though he'd never heard the name before. He went inside to consult a second uniformed man in the hall. Instead of waiting where I was, I went in after him. I was certain she lived here. She wouldn't have given this address in her letters if she hadn't. I was just in time to hear the second hallman saying under his breath: "Edwards, that's who it is. She sometimes gets mail here under the other name. I remember she left orders with me about that once." Then he looked at me and dropped his voice even lower, but I could still make out what he was saying. "Must be a new girl they're taking on. Better not let her go up the front way; they won't like it, they're open already."

The first one stepped back to me and whispered in a peculiar confidential undertone, as though it were a secret. "It's the penthouse you want. But you're not supposed to go in through the front like this; you'd get in Dutch if they ever caught you trying it, and so would we if we let you. You girls are supposed to use the back way. I'll show you where it is."

He took me outside and around to the side of the building, and through a delivery passage to a service elevator run by a grinning colored man. "Take her up to The Place," he said to him mysteriously.

"Up there?" the operator asked with a strange look.

"Up there." The doorman nodded secretively.

On the way up he turned to me and asked: "You ever been up there befo', miss?"

I said: "No, I never have."

He didn't answer, just said, "Um-um," and I caught him shaking his head a little, the same way the cop had.

He stopped the car finally and opened the door onto a little vestibule. There was only one other door, a strong-looking thing with a little peephole in the middle of it. I went unhesitatingly over to it and pushed a bell.

The kind-faced operator behind me seemed to close his car door almost reluctantly, as though he hated to leave me up there. The last I saw of him he was still shaking his head dolefully.

None of this really registered on me at the time. I was too excited at the prospect of seeing Jean. Besides, the city was such a whole new world to me that the way people acted was bound to seem strange at first, until I got used to it. That was all it was, I told myself.

The peephole opened and an eye peered out at me. A single eye, blue, and hard as agate. A little whiff of sachet seeped out through the hole.

A woman's voice said harshly: "Yes?"

I said: "Is Jean in there?"

The eye slid around in a half-turn, away from the opening. "Somebody to see Jean."

Chains clicked against steel and the door swung grudgingly open. I edged in timidly, bag in hand.

There were three women in there, but Jean wasn't one of them. It looked like some kind of a dressing-room. There was a mirror-strip along the wall, and a long table and chairs under it. They all looked at me. They were beautifully dressed, lovely to look at. But there was something hard and forbidding about them, I don't know quite what. There was a confused hum coming from somewhere nearby—like the drone of a lot of voices. Every once in a while it rose sharply to a crescendo, as though something exciting had just happened, then it would die down again to a breathless, waiting hush. Then start over.

"Where is she?" I asked uncertainly.

The answer was an ungracious snarl. "She's out in front, where d'ya suppose? You didn't expect to find her back here, did ya? We're open already." She snapped cigarette ashes at me with her thumbnail. "If you were sent here to work, you better get into your duds fast. You're an hour late."

I just stared stupidly.

She jackknifed her finger at my bag. "Brought your own clothes, didn't you? Well, whaddaya waiting for?" She gave me a shove that nearly overturned the nearest chair, and me with it.

"Gord!" she said to the others. "She's gonna be a credit to the place! Jean musta had a lapse of memory when she picked her out."

"Them dumb ones make the best come-ons," one of the others snapped back. "Didn't you ever know that? And since when does Jean do the picking anyway? She takes whoever Rosetti wishes on her, and likes it!"

There was a sudden peremptory slamming on the inside door, the one across the way from where I had come in, and they froze to silence. A man's voice called through: "Come on, you tramps in there, get going! Three of the tables need pepping up."

They jumped like trained seals through paper hoops, jostling each other in their eagerness to be the first out. The blur of noise rose sharply with the opening of the door. A phrase came through it.

"Twenny-one—red!" And then someone said, "Whee!" A minute later the door had closed again and I was alone.

A human being can be in a situation in which she never was before, and her instincts will tell her what her experience cannot. That happened to me now. They'd just called me dumb, and I was dumb. I didn't know the first thing about this place. I'd never been in one like it before. And yet I knew instinctively I didn't like it here. I wanted to get out without even waiting to see Jean. Something told me to. Something told me not to stay a minute longer.

It wasn't those three girls so much. Their bark was worse than their bite. It was something about the sound of that voice that had come through the door just now. There had been something evil in it. It was the sort of voice you hear in secret places, where secret things are done that never see the light of day. I remembered now the way the cop and the elevator operator had both shaken their heads. They'd known. They'd known something about this place.

There was no one in there with me at the moment, no one to stop me. All I had to do was take the chains off that door, slip out the way I'd come in, ring for the rear elevator. Then I remembered I only had twenty-two cents. But even that wasn't enough to keep me here. I could telephone Jean from outside and ask her to come out and meet me.

I had my hand out to the first chain, trying to get it out of its socket without making any noise, when I heard my name called in a frightened whisper behind me.

"Francie!"

Jean was standing in the opposite doorway. She came in quickly and locked the door behind her. There was something sick and choked in her voice. "They told me there was somebody back here asking for me—but you're the last person I expected to see!"

She had diamonds on her wrists and at her throat, and flowers in her hair, and champagne on her breath. She was old. Golden-haired and beautiful, and yet somehow old and tired-looking. Not like when she'd left home.

Her voice was a hiss of terror, like air whistling out of a punctured tire. "What got into you to do this? Why did you come here of all places? This is the last place on earth you should have come!"

"Why? I only wanted to see you."

She evidently didn't have time to explain. "Quick! Has anyone seen you?"

"Only those three girls—"

"I can shut them up. They work under me. Come on, get out of here fast!"

"But Jean. I came here to stay with you, to live with you."

"You don't know what you're saying! Stop arguing, someone may come in here any minute. I want you to take the next bus and go back home. I'd take you down and put you on it myself, only I can't leave here right now—"

"But Jean, I have only twenty-two cents."

She bent over, fumbled frantically with the side of her stocking, thrust a crumpled bill into my hand. It wasn't a twenty, it wasn't even a fifty this time. It was a hundred-dollar bill. I'd never seen one before. I didn't want the money, I wanted to stay. Not here in this place, but in the city. Now that she was with me, I wasn't frightened any more.

But she was pushing me toward the door through which I'd come in. She wouldn't listen to my protests. We never got to it. A muted buzzer sounded somewhere over our heads. It wasn't any louder than the sound a trapped fly makes in a bottle, but it made us both jump. And at the same instant the knob on the inner door that Jean had locked behind her began to rotate viciously. That same voice as before, the one that had sent cold chills through me, rasped angrily: "Jean, what're you doing in there? What's this door locked for? I need you out here—fast."

"Rosetti," she whispered sickly. "If he ever sees you—" Her grasp on my wrist was ice-cold.

She pulled me toward the side of the room so suddenly that I nearly went off-balance. There was a sort of built-in wardrobe occupying the entire side, with sliding doors that sheathed into one another. She clawed two of them apart, thrust me in against a welter of gold and tinsel dresses, then drew them together again. There was room enough to stand upright. Her panting, parting instructions came through the hair-breadth crack that remained.

"Stay in there until the coast is clear, then get out of here as fast as you can! If anyone should slide the doors open to take anything out, don't lose your head—shift with the doors and you'll be all right! Don't wait for me to come back, I mayn't be able to—"

I heard the sound she made unlocking the door, heard him bawling her out. "Take it easy, Rosetti. I had a run in my stocking," I heard her say placatingly.

I put my eye to the crack and got a look at him—or at least, a vertical strip of his face. He looked just like his voice had sounded.

"We're taking Masters into the argument room. Do a number and do it noisy, hear me? All *ta-ra*."

"Now?" she gasped, "with a place full of people?"

"That's what you're here for. Do your Western number." He gave one of the wardrobe doors I was behind a fling. I quailed, but managed to shift noiselessly behind it, out of the light that slipped in. I saw Jean's be-diamonded arm come plunging into the opening, take down a two-gallon cowboy hat from the shelf. Then she looped a lariat around her wrist, went over to a drawer, and took out a pistol.

Her face was very pale under the rouge. So was his, but for a different reason—not fear but malice.

She poised in the open doorway a minute. He signaled some musicians and they started an introduction. She gave her lariat a preliminary twirl, screeched "Yippee!" and shot the pistol into the air. Then she moved out of sight.

He closed the door after her, but stayed inside. He crossed swiftly to the outer door, the one that led to the service elevator, opened it, and let in a laundryman and his assistant, carrying an immense basket full of wash between them.

"Leave it here," he said. "Be ready for you in about ten minutes."

They went out again and he closed the door after them. Then he turned around and went out the other way. I saw his hand starting to grope into his coat as he pulled the door shut after him, as if he was taking out something. I heard somebody who must have been standing right outside waiting for him ask: "All set, boss?"

"All set," he answered, and then the door closed.

I waited a minute to make sure he wouldn't come back, and then edged out of the closet. Outside, in the distance, you could hear Jean's gun shots go off every once in a while. I opened the peephole on the outside door and looked through. The laundrymen were leaning back against the wall out there in the service passageway, waiting to take away the wash. I was wondering whether I should risk it and let myself out while they were there—whether they'd stop me—when without any warning the door behind me was flung open and a drunk came wavering in. He pulled the door shut behind him and leaned against it for a moment, as if trying to regain sufficient strength to go on.

He was a man in his early fifties, very handsome, with silvery hair. His collar and dress-tie were a little askew, the way a drunk's usually are. He'd had a flower in his buttonhole, but all the petals had fallen off, just the stem was left.

I was too frightened to move for a minute, just stood there staring stupidly at him. He didn't see me—he didn't seem to see anything. He forced himself away from the door that he had used to support him, came on toward where I was. I edged out of the way. Even then he didn't seem to be aware of me. His eyes had a fixed, glassy look and he walked in a funny trailing way, as though his feet were too heavy to lift.

He was holding a bunched handkerchief to his chest, over the seam of his shirt, and he kept giving a dry little cough. It seemed impossible that he hadn't seen me, but his eyes gave no sign, so I scuttled back behind the sliding wardrobe doors where I'd come from, and narrowed them once more to a crack, watching him fearfully through the slit.

His knees were starting to dip under him, but he kept on with painful stubborn slowness toward that outer door, moving like a deepsea diver under many fathoms of water. It didn't look as though he'd ever get there. He never did.

Suddenly Rosetti's voice sounded behind him. He had come in with two other men. One of them closed the door behind him, locked it this time, and sealed it with his shoulder-blades in an indolent lounge.

"Trying to find your way out?" Rosetti purred. "This is the way out."

Flame slashed from his hand, a thunderclap exploded in the room, and the drunk was suddenly flat and still.

The man holding up the door chuckled, "No wonder he couldn't make it, all the lead he was carrying with him. I bet he gained twenty pounds in the last five minutes."

Rosetti opened the outside door, hitched his head. "Hey! The wash is ready!"

The laundrymen came in, picked up the big basket between them and dumped its contents all over the floor. A lot of towels and sheets and things came spilling out. They opened one of the sheets to its full width and rolled the "drunk" into the middle of it. Then they took his legs and forced them over until they touched his head, doubling him in two. Then they tied the four corners of the sheet together, into a big lumpy bundle. They put some of the laundry back into the basket, thrust the big bundle in the middle, and wedged some more down on top of it. When they got all through it didn't look much fuller than before, maybe a little plumper in the middle, that was all.

Rosetti looked it over. Then I heard him say, "There's a little starting to come through over on the side here. Jam a couple more towels in to soak it up. And don't forget the bricks when you get to the end of your route."

Then he sat contentedly back on the edge of the girls' dressing-table, swinging one leg back and forth. He took out a little stick of sandpaper and meticulously rubbed it back and forth over one nail, and blew on it.

"D'ya think anyone saw him come in?" one of the others asked.

Rosetti went to work on a second nail. "Sure, everybody saw him come in. And nobody saw him go out again, for sure. And it still don't mean a thing. Because nobody saw this part of it, what happened to him in between. I'll be the first one to go down to headquarters to answer their questions—before they even have time to call me. That's the kind of a public-spirited citizen I am!"

The three of them laughed.

Someone tried the doorknob from the outside just then and the one blocking it called out cheerfully: "Have to wait a few minutes, girls. We're holding a stag party in here."

The laundrymen were ready to go now, with their enormous burden suspended between them, shoulder to shoulder. One of Rosetti's two men accommodatingly opened the outside door for them. "Heavy wash tonight," one of them gasped as they staggered out.

"Sure," was the grinning answer, "we're dirty people up here. Didn't you know that?"

They closed the back door after them and put up all the chains. I was fighting to stay on my feet—at least, until they got out and went back where they'd come from. My head was swimming and my eyes were blurred; I was all weak at the knees; and I was afraid I wasn't going to be able to hold out and they'd hear me go down. I knew what was doing it, and it wasn't lack of air. The city hadn't taken long to teach me things. I knew I'd just seen a man killed before my very eyes.

I kept swaying from side to side like a pendulum, and each time braking my fall by clutching at one of the dresses hanging behind me.

They were opening the door now—in another minute they'd be gone. But I keeled over first.

Maybe the noise from outside covered it, I don't know. They must have been clapping for Jean's number about then. I went down sideways into the narrow little trough I was standing in, and a lot of soft things came piling down on top of me, and everything went dark . . .

It seemed only a minute later that the sliding doors split open and light shone in on me once more. Jean was bending over me, helping me up. She had a street coat on now. She looked haggard. "I'm going to take you out with me," she whispered. "Lean on me."

The humming noise from outside had stopped now; there was a stony silence. She touched some cologne-water to my temple and it stung unexpectedly. I felt it and there was a welt there. "What happened?" I asked dazedly. "Did I do that when I fell?"

"No, I had to do that, with a slipper-heel, when you started to come to—with those three she-rats in here big as life. You'll never know what I've been through for the past half-hour or so! Luckily, I had a hunch something was wrong, and came back here just before the rest did. I couldn't get you out unconscious the way you were, and any minute I was afraid you'd come to and give yourself away. Every time one of them wanted something from back here, I'd jump and get it for her—they must have thought I was crazy. When I saw you starting to stir, I had to hit you, to keep you quiet until they got out of here. I told them I saw a bug on the closet-floor.

"Come on, the girls have gone home and the place has closed up for the night. The men are in the office counting up the take. Hurry up, before they miss me."

We staggered over to the back door together, and she started loosening the chains.

"I'm all right now," I said weakly. "I guess it was too stuffy in there."

We were out in the service passage now. She looked at me as if she didn't believe me. "What'd you see?" she asked sharply. "Are you sure it wasn't anything you saw while you were in there?"

Somehow I couldn't bring myself to talk about it, even to her. "Nothing," I said.

Riding down in the back elevator she turned aside, fumbled some more with her stocking, brought out another hundred-dollar bill.

"Jimmy," she said, handing it to the operator, "you never saw this girl come here tonight."

"What girl?" he asked, when he was able to get his breath back.

"That's it exactly," she nodded, satisfied.

She took me somewhere to get some coffee to brace me up. Mostly, I guess, she tried to talk me into going back home. But nothing she could say had any effect on me. You know how it is when you're eighteen.

"No," I said. "I'm staying. If I can't stay with you, then I'll stay on my own."

She sighed. "I was like that once, too. That's why I wish you'd listen to me and go home. I don't want what happened to me to happen to you."

"What happened to you?"

She didn't answer.

"What was that place up there?" I asked curiously.

"Forget you were ever up there. Stay if you must, but promise me one thing—that you'll never go near there again. I'll find a furnished room for you and come around to see you whenever I can. And Francie"—her hand covered mine in desperate appeal for a moment—"if you did see something you shouldn't have up there tonight, don't ever open your mouth about it, don't ever mention it to a living soul—for both our sakes, yours and mine as well. Try to forget about it, that's the best way. I've seen things too, from time to time, that I've had to forget about."

"Why don't you leave there, Jean?"

"I can't." She gave a wry smile. "I'm a little tired, and a whole lot disillusioned, but I still—want to go on living for a while."

I just sucked in my breath and looked at her when I heard that.

Late as it was, we went looking for a room then and there. I had to stay some place, and although she didn't say so, it was obvious that Jean lived right up there in that penthouse, as a sort of permanent resident-manager to look after Rosetti's interests.

We took a cab to save time on our quest, and passed Chalif-Bleekman's on our way. I looked out and thought, "There's my mascot." The lights in the shop window had gone out long ago, but you could still make out the mannequins, like ghosts in the dim shine of the street-lights. I asked her about the store.

"I used to work there when I first came here," she told me. "I'll take you in with me tomorrow; maybe I can get you a job there."

She found a room without much trouble. It was too late at night to be very choosey, and I was too dead-tired to care. Anything would have looked good to me by then.

The last thing she said was: "Now if you did see something, erase it from your mind. Always remember, there's nothing you and I can do about it. We're up against something that's too big for us."

To the end I couldn't bring myself to admit it to her. "No, I didn't see anything," I reiterated.

She knew I was lying, and I knew she knew. I heard her light step go down the stairs, and the taxi that had waited for her below drove off. Afterwards I found another hundred-dollar bill, the second one she'd given me that night, under the soap dish on the washstand.

It was only when I was half undressed that I realized I'd left the little bag with my few things in it in the back room of that place where she worked.

I was too tired to be as frightened as I should have been.

Her face paled when I first told her about it the next day. "It must have been found by now! There's a maid up there that's a stooge for Rosetti. Did anything in it have your name on it? Was there anything to show whom it belonged to?"

I tried to remember. "I don't think so—" Then my own face blanched. "Wait a minute. There was a snapshot of me in the flap under the lid, but without any name or anything on it—"

She'd got her second wind by now. "It's all right, keep cool. It's still not fatal. Here's our only out. If Rosetti asks me, I'll say some stray or other I used to know on one of my jobs showed up with a hard-luck story and tried to put the touch on me. She'd been put out of her room and she left her things with me. I slipped her something to get rid of her. As long as they don't think you were right there when—"

I knew what she meant. *When the laundry was carried out.*

"—you're safe enough," she concluded.

She was as good as her word, and got me a job at Chalif-Bleekman's modeling negligées. Then she left me. "I won't be able to see you very often, after this once," she warned me. "Rosetti doesn't take chances with any of us, and he has eyes and ears all over town. I might be followed when I least expect it, and bring them down on you."

"If you want me in a hurry," was the last thing I said, "you can always meet me by the mannequin." I explained about the window mascot of mine. "I'll make it a point to stop there a minute on my way in and out."

That was the last I saw of her for some time, but I could understand her reasons for staying away, so I wasn't particularly worried. Meanwhile, I started to get the hang of the city a little better and lose some of my greenness.

They were nice to me at the place I worked, and the job was easy, after you once got over being self-conscious about walking up and down the aisles in nothing but lace and ribbons.

I made several girl friends, who worked there with me, and I also got myself a boy friend—my first. His name was Eddie Dent. He was a salesman in an auto showroom, and it looked like I'd hit the jackpot the very first time. But more about him later.

Although I grew wiser, I didn't forget my mascot. Even Eddie couldn't take her place. They'd put a new outfit on her long ago, since the night I'd first seen her, but I still stopped before her on my way in and out each day and told her all about how things were coming, and she still smiled in that same protective, encouraging way. She made blue days bright, and bright days brighter.

I was beginning to forget that nightmare scene I'd witnessed the first night of my arrival, and in a little while more it would have faded away like something that had never happened. Then suddenly it all came back with a crash. A succession of crashes, each one worse than the one before.

I'd brought a newspaper back to my room with me after work, and when I opened it a face seemed to leap up from its pages and strike at me. Handsome, with silvery-white hair. The laundry basket must have come apart. They'd picked him up out of the river.

Well-known Sportsman, Missing Two Weeks, Found Dead, the caption said. And underneath, my eyes ran through the welter of fine print, taking in a phrase here, a phrase there. ". . . Masters was known to have made many enemies in the course of his long career . . . his only son committed suicide less than a month ago after incurring heavy gambling losses . . . Police are trying to reconstruct his movements . . . Among those who came forward to aid them was Leo Rosetti, through whose cooperation they have been able to establish that one of the last places visited by Masters before he met his death was a small private party given by

Rosetti at his own home. He was definitely absolved of all connection with the crime, however. Rosetti's first inkling of what had become of his friend of long standing was when he reported him missing after repeated attempts to communicate with him for the past two weeks had failed . . ."

They didn't guess. They didn't know. But I did. Jean and I both did. I didn't sleep so well that night.

I put it up to the mannequin on my way in to work next morning. "How can I go on keeping quiet about it? Shouldn't I tell them?"

And her rueful smile seemed to suggest: "What about Jean? It means her life if you do."

That was the first crash.

When I clocked out that night there was a man standing there by my mascot—waiting for one of the other girls in the store, I guess. It meant I had to stand right next to him for a moment or two, while I was exchanging my usual silent confidences with her, but he didn't even seem aware of me.

I had a funny feeling, on my way home, that I was being followed, but each time I looked around, there wasn't anyone in sight—so I put it down to nervousness and let it go at that. The feeling wouldn't leave me, though, right up to my own door.

I'd been home about five minutes when I thought I heard a creak on the flooring outside in the hall. I stiffened, listening. It came again, nearer the door but less distinct than the first time. But no knock or anything followed.

I realized now that my instinct had been right. There had been someone following me all the way home, even though I hadn't been able to distinguish who it was. There was almost certainly someone standing out there now, motionless, trying to listen to me just as I was trying to listen to him. I tiptoed over, bent down, and put my eye level with the keyhole. Chilling confirmation came at once. My view was blocked. Instead of the opposite side of the hall, all I could see was a blur of dark suiting, standing there perfectly still.

The voice nearly threw me back on my heels, it came through so unexpectedly. The most terrifying thing about it was the casual, matter-of-fact tone he used, as though there were no door in between, as though I had been in plain sight the whole time.

"Come on, little lady, quit playing hide and seek."

Under a sort of hypnotic compulsion, I touched the key finally, gave it a gingerly little twist as though it was red hot, and he did the rest.

He came in slowly. It was the same man who had been standing outside the store. He had a funny little cowlick down the middle of his forehead, like a fish-hook, and it wouldn't stay back. I couldn't take my eyes off it.

He closed the door after him. Then he heeled his hand at me, showing a glint of silver. He said: "You're Francine Everton, that right?"

I said it was.

He took out a newspaper and was suddenly holding Masters's picture before my eyes. "Ever see this man before?"

"No!" The sudden shock alone made my denial convincing, if nothing else.

"Are you sure of that?"

"Yes!" If I said I'd seen him, I'd have to say I'd seen him killed. If I said I'd seen him killed—

"Who's the woman got you your job at Chalif's?"

So they'd found that out. I decided to bluff it out. It was the only thing I could do. "An acquaintance of mine. Her name is Edwards, I think. I don't know her very well. I ran into her on the street and told her I had no job."

It came with treacherous glibness. "When was the last time you were up there?"

Instinct, like a fine wire running through me, jangled warningly: "Make one admission, anywhere along the line, and the whole thing'll come out." I said, "Up where? What do you mean?"

"Then how do you explain this?"

Even more suddenly than the newspaper, he had opened an envelope and was holding a charred fragment of snapshot before me. Everything that didn't matter had been burned away. The face remained, yellowed but perfectly recognizable.

Sparring for time, I asked: "How'd it get burnt?"

He flicked back: "How'd it get where it got burnt?"

"I'd been put out of my room just before I met my girl friend. I had no place to go. She—took a little bagful of my belongings with her, to keep them for me until I found a place. She was supposed to bring them back, but she never did—"

"And you've never been up where she hangs out at any time?"

"Never. She didn't seem to want me to look her up—"

"I don't doubt that," he said dryly. It was suddenly over, to my unutterable relief. I'd thought it would go on for hours yet.

He got up to go. "Well, kid, maybe you're telling the truth and maybe you're not. Maybe you're afraid to." He got as far as the door, and then added: "Don't be afraid to. We'll look after you—" He waited a minute and then went on: "Are you sure there isn't anything more you want to tell me?"

"How could there be, when I've told you everything there is?"

He closed the door. It opened again, unexpectedly. "Armour's the name," he added, "in case you should change your mind."

It closed a second time and I heard the stairs creak complainingly with his descent. I turned and flopped down by the window, peeping under the drawn shade.

I saw him come out and look up, and then he went down the street.

A figure detached itself from the shelter of a dark doorway opposite and started over toward the house I lived in. I knuckled the pane to attract his attention, threw up the lower sash, and called down guardedly: "Don't come in, Eddie. Wait for me around the corner."

It was my boy friend. I didn't want him to get mixed up in it. When I went out to meet him, I went all the way around the block in the opposite direction and approached the corner from the far side—a primitive precaution that wouldn't have fooled anybody if I was really being watched.

He said: "Who was the guy just up there to see you?"

I took his arm. "I'll tell you all about it. Let's get away from here first." I hadn't meant to say that. I only realized it after it was out. I couldn't tell him all about it. And then again—why not?

I waited until we were in a secluded booth in our usual Chinese restaurant. He said: "What's the matter, Francie? Is something on your mind? You don't seem yourself tonight."

It was so easy to get started, after that. What was more natural than to confide your troubles to your boy friend?

"He was a detective, that man you saw," I blurted out.

He wasn't as surprised as I'd expected him to be. He piled rice on my plate. "What'd he want with you?" he said.

"This man Masters they picked up from the river—he held his picture up to my eyes and asked me if I'd ever seen him before."

A forkful of chow mein halted halfway to his mouth.

"I said no, of course."

The forkful of chow mein went the rest of the way up.

"Then he asked me about—about a friend of mine named Jean Edwards, that got me my job. Asked me if I'd ever been up to her place. I said no, of course."

"Then what're you downhearted about? You gave him straight answers to straight questions. That's all there is to it. What's bothering you?"

"Nothing," I said muffledly.

He looked at me a minute or two. He scribbled something down on a scrap of paper and handed it to the Chinese waiter. I saw the waiter take it over to the bandleader. The music came around me, soft and persuasive.

All your fears are foolish fancies maybe—

Eddie stood up, held out his arms. "Come on, Francie, that's ours. You never could resist that number. It'll fix everything up."

I leaned my head against him as we glided around in the twilight dimness. "Feel better now?" he whispered.

"A little."

"Never mind, baby, it'll all come out in the wash."

I went out of step. "Oh, don't—don't use that word. I can't stand it—"

"Why?"

It got away from me so easily, like the tail of a kite, when the kite's already out of your hands. "Because it always reminds me of the way I saw him carried out that night—"

"Who, Masters?" He kept guiding me around softly in the shadowy crowd. "But I thought you said you weren't up there—"

"I told him that. But I was. I was hiding up there in a closet. I saw the whole thing happen. I can't tell you more than that about it, Eddie, because there another person involved—"

The music ended and we went back to the booth. He had to make a phone call when the kumquats came on. It took him a little while, but he was smiling the same as ever when he came back. We didn't talk about it any more after that. I'd got it off my chest and I felt a lot better.

Instead of going on to a show the way we usually did, he took me back to my room. "You're tired and you ought to get a little rest, Francie."

"Suppose he comes around again?"

"He won't." He sounded strangely confident. "He won't bother you any more." Then he said: "I'll wait across the street until I see your room light go on, so you'll feel safer." Almost as though he knew ahead of time . . .

I went in and up the stairs and unlocked my darkened room. There were two messages under my door—a telegram and a phone message from Jean, in the landlady's writing—*Jean Edwards wants you to come up to her place at once, highly important.* Then when I opened the telegram, to my surprise that was from Jean too. Just five words—*Meet me by the mannequin.*

I ran to the window first of all, threw it up, signaled down to Eddie. "Eddie, wait for me. I have to go out again."

A large black car had drawn up a few doors down, and the driver had come over to him to ask for a light or something. I saw the two of them standing there chatting casually the way men do.

Then I stood there knitting my brows over the two messages. One contradicted the other. Maybe one was fake, but if so, which one of the two? Her words that first night rang in my ears again. "Promise me you'll never go near there again." Still and all, both could be from her and both could be on the level. Maybe something had happened to change her plans. Maybe she'd found out she couldn't get away, and had sent the second message to cancel the first. The thing was, which one had preceded the other? Well, there was a way of finding that out.

I knocked on the landlady's door. "Which of these came first—can you tell me?"

"The telegram," she said unhesitatingly. "I remember I'd just finished slipping it under your door, when the phone started to ring down in the lower hall, and that was for you too."

"Thanks," I said. Jean's place had it, then. The phone message was the one to go by.

I hurried outside to Eddie. The other man was gone now, but the car was still standing there.

"That was a guy I used to know," he began. "He said I could have the use of his car until he comes out again—"

I hardly paid any attention to what he was saying. "Eddie, don't ask me any questions, but—just come along with me, will you?"

"You bet," he agreed, the way a boy friend should.

We passed Chalif's on our way up to Jean's place. I was glad now that I hadn't taken the telegram at its face value. There was no one in front of the mannequin. Jean had changed her mind after sending it.

"Stop just a minute," I said, on an impulse.

"Why here? The store was closed hours ago—"

"No, you don't understand. I have a habit whenever I'm in trouble—"

"Oh, yeah. That mascot of yours. You told me about that once." He veered accommodatingly to the curb and braked.

I jumped out and went over, while he stayed in the car. The window lights were on, the way they were every night until midnight. She was in a different gown tonight. Then I remembered it was Thursday. They changed the window displays every other Thursday. They must have just finished dressing the window before we got there.

There was something about her face—A shock went through me as I halted before the thick plate-glass. *It was Jean's face!* I must be delirious, or losing my mind. She made a swift little gesture, hidden from the street. Touched one finger to her lips to warn me to silence. Then her hand stiffened into the mannequin's rigid wrist-bent pose again. I smothered a scream.

She remained motionless after that—all but her lips. I could see them wavering slightly. She was trying to say something to me. I watched them with desperate intentness, while she repeated endlessly, until I got it: "Don't—go. Don't—go. Don't—go."

"Come on," Eddie called impatiently from the car. "I thought you were in such a hurry to get wherever it is you're heading for."

"Don't—go." The silent syllables kept pounding through the glass. She added an almost imperceptible shake of her head, invisible except to me.

"Are you coming? What's holding you up?"

"No," I said, hypnotized. I couldn't take my eyes off her face.

He got out, strode over to me, caught me roughly by the arm. "Why—what's the matter?" A sudden change had come over him—I couldn't quite identify it yet. He didn't waste a glance on the figure in the window. His back was to her. Over his shoulder I could see the warning shake of her head become frenzied.

"Then I'll give it to you right here—what's the difference where you get it, as long as we shut you up for good!"

The mask had fallen off, and I saw him now, for the first time, as he really had been all along. His face was now as repulsive as Rosetti's and those other men's. He had me trapped between two showcases, where the main store-entrance was, and there wasn't a soul in sight on the streets to help me.

He cast a quick glance over his shoulder, as though trying to decide whether to risk the sound of a gunshot. Then, instead, he brought out something stubby, and it suddenly doubled its length in his hand. A wicked blade shot out of it right while he held it.

"So you saw Masters go out with the dirty wash, did you? Well, here's an extra mouth to tell it to the cops through—a mouth in the middle of your heart!"

A terrible game of puss-in-corner began between us. As I shifted from side to side, looking for an opening, he shifted in accompaniment each time, blocking me. I didn't dare take my eyes from that vicious knife feinting at me, but I was dimly aware of a flurry of motion behind him in the store window.

Suddenly I saw an opening—or thought I did. Maybe he gave it to me purposely. He had shifted over a little too far to one side. I darted for the avenue of escape like an arrow, flashed through—almost, but not quite. He swerved quickly behind me, his free hand shot out, clamped itself on my shoulder and pinned me fast. I could feel the flirt of air as the knife swept up. It would come down over me and plunge into my heart . . .

There was a flash inside the window beside me, a hollow thud, and pieces of glass fell out, leaving a jagged hole shaped like a maple leaf. A puff of smoke misted Jean's head and shoulders for a minute, then rose and disappeared. She hardly seemed to have moved at all. One hand, that had held a tinseled evening-bag until now, now grasped a snub-nosed revolver instead. Cottony smoke still licked from it.

The knife clattered to the sidewalk before my eyes. Then, horribly, his whole weight sagged against me from behind. I stepped forward, and he fell to the ground and lay there without moving.

Jean had disappeared inside the store. I was still cowering there, staring at his body, when she unlocked the front door and came out—still in the metallic wig she'd worn in the window.

"You poor innocent. Do you know who you picked for a boy friend? Rosetti's star banker. He presides at the main roulette table up at The Place every night. They must have sicked him on you purposely, to find out if you knew enough to be dangerous to them. And the minute he found out, he reported back to Rosetti.

"Luckily, I happened to get on an extension phone in the next room while he was making his tip-off call tonight. I had to reach you fast, and I didn't know how to do it. You were already out with the very guy that had fingered you. It was a cinch he wasn't going to let you out of his sight. Something you said last time I saw you came back to me. 'If you ever want me in a hurry and don't know where to find me, you can always meet me by the mannequin.'

"I got a hold of a gun and slipped out. I sent you a telegram to your room, and then I went over to the store. They were in the midst of dressing the windows when I got there, and the entrance had been left unlocked, so the guy supervising the work could slip out front and inspect the window every once in a while. That gave me an inspiration. I couldn't just wait for you on the open sidewalk. Eddie knew me too well. He would have spotted me and whisked you off with him before I had a chance to get in my warning. He was too good a triggerman to fool around with. I had to get the drop on him in some way.

"So I sneaked inside, unnoticed, and hid behind one of the counters until the window dressers had finished and gone. Then I opened the window, took out your mascot, changed clothes with her, fixed up my face and arms with some ochre powder I found in the store, put on her metalic wig, and stood there in her place, with the gun in my little jeweled bag.

"It was taking a big chance, until I had frozen into the right pose, but the streets are pretty quiet around here and no one passing by on the outside caught me at it. Then I had to hold the pose for what seemed like hours, and I thought you'd never come."

"What'll we do now?" I asked helplessly, looking down at the still form at our feet.

She shrugged. "I'll have to stay out of course, now that I've made the break, but it's just a matter of a day or two before they get the two of us. How can we buck a machine like the one Rosetti has got?"

"A detective named Armour—he was the one who questioned me—said if I ever had anything to tell him, he'd look after me."

"That's what they all say, but how can we be sure they're not taking presents from Rosetti on the side—"

"No, he was different. He was honest. You could see it in his face. He had a funny little cowlick down the middle of his forehead, like a fishhook, and it wouldn't stay back—"

"My God!" she exclaimed.

I said: "What's the matter?"

"Then they got him too, tonight. He must have been up there looking around for evidence single-handed, the fool! That proves he was honest, if nothing else. There was a guy with a cowlick drifting around from table to table, going through the motions of playing. I noticed him before I left. I could tell by Rosetti's face that they were wise to him, were getting ready to close in on him. Trixie was getting out the blanks and sombrero, to cover it up, when I came away. I bet he's already gone out in the wash!"

The prowl-car must have sidled up with its siren muffled. The first we knew about it was when two cops jumped out with guns drawn.

Jean didn't waste any time—there wasn't any to waste. "O.K. I did this, and here's the gun. But if you've got any sense you won't stop to ask questions about this guy. He'll keep until later. Send in a call quick, for all the reserves they can spare. Do you two know a plainclothesman named Armour?"

One of them nodded. "Yeah, Danny Armour. He's attached to this precinct."

"Well, he's attached to the sky-patrol by now, but if you get up there in time you may be able to catch them red-handed with the body. Rosetti's gambling place—I'll take you in the back way."

One of them said in a low voice to the other: "He was up to something tonight. I saw him marking bills in the back room—"

The other one hitched his gun ominously. "We'll take a chance. Put in the call, Bill."

And so I got my first ride in a police radio-car.

We stopped around the corner from Jean's place. She led the way in through the delivery entrance.

What she asked the colored boy on the elevator should have been very funny. Somehow it wasn't, it was gruesome.

"Has any laundry been sent out from upstairs yet, Jimmy?"

He said: "Yes, Miss Jean. The truck just pulled away li'l while ago. Pow'ful big wash tonight, too."

"Too late," she moaned.

One of the cops with us said through his clenched teeth: "Dead or alive, he's still evidence. Hurry up, what'd that truck look like?"

"I've seen it. You can spot it a mile away," Jean snapped. "Ivory-colored, and all lacquered-up like a bandbox. It'll be a toss-up between the two rivers, though."

"Well, this is a westbound street, so we'll take the one it heads for!"

We climbed back in the patrol-car and tore off again. The cordon was beginning to form around Rosetti's place as we left.

That truck must have made marvelous time, to get all the way down where we finally caught up with it. But our ride was nothing short of maniacal. I wasn't able to draw a full breath from the time we took off.

We overtook it halfway to the lonely warehouse district along the waterfront, screeched a little too far past, nearly turned over, but managed to come up onto the sidewalk in the process. The two "laundrymen" were armed, but never had a chance to prove it. The cops were on them before they'd even finished staggering out. By the time Jean and I came up they already had the big basket of "wash" out on the ground and were ripping it open.

They kicked away the blood-spattered towels and pillow cases, and I saw his face by the pale arc-light. It was he, all right, the man who had come up to my room. The cowlick was jagged and stiff with blood now.

"He's still evidence, poor fellow," one of the cops said.

"He's better than that!" Jean explained electrically, straightening up from bending over him. "There's still life in him, I just felt his heart! They were in too much of a hurry this time. Get him to a hospital quick, and you may still be able to pull him through!"

I'd thought we'd ridden fast on the first two legs of our trip but we had practically been bogged down compared to that stretch from waterfront to hospital.

I never thought I'd see that cowlick again, but I did—three weeks later, when Jean and I were taken down to the hospital. I even heard a voice come from under it. He was weak as a rag, but they'd pulled him through. The assistant D.A. who was going to prosecute Rosetti and his whole ring for murder was present at his bedside, to make the final arrangements with us. Jean was to be granted immunity for turning State's evidence as to the operation of Rosetti's many gambling establishments that she had presided over. I didn't need immunity to agree to testify to the murder of Masters, because I hadn't done anything.

I saw that cowlick all through the trial, sticking out stubborn as ever from under a huge gauze head-bandage.

Rosetti has long since been just a blackout in a prison lighting-system, but I'm still seeing that cowlick.

I see it every Saturday night around 8, and sometimes during the week, when I answer the doorbell in the little flat that Jean and I have taken together. And it won't be long now before I'll be Mrs. Cowlick— Mrs. Armour to you!

Placebo

ANDREW VACHSS

I know how to fix things. I know how they work. When they don't work like they're supposed to, I know how to make them right.

I don't always get it right the first time, but I keep working until I do.

I've been a lot of places. Some of them pretty bad—some of them where I didn't want to be.

I did a lot of things in my life in some of those places. In the bad places, I did some bad things.

I paid a lot for what I know, but I don't talk about it. Talking doesn't get things fixed.

People call me a lot of different things now. Janitor. Custodian. Repairman. Lots of names for the same thing.

I live in the basement. I take care of the whole building. Something gets broke, they call me. I'm always here.

I live by myself. A dog lives with me. A big Doberman. I heard a noise behind my building one night—it sounded like a kid crying. I found the Doberman. He was a puppy then. Some freak was carving him up for the fun of it. Blood all over the place. I took care of the freak, then I brought the puppy down to my basement and fixed him up. I know all about knife wounds.

The freak cut his throat pretty deep. When the stitches came out, he was okay, but he can't bark. He still works, though.

I don't mix much with the people. They pay me to fix things—I fix things. I don't try and fix things for the whole world. I don't care about the whole world. Just what's mine. I just care about doing my work.

People ask me to fix all kinds of things—not just the boiler or a stopped-up toilet. One of the gangs in the neighborhood used to hang out in front of my building, give the people a hard time, scare them, break into the mailboxes, petty stuff like that. I went upstairs and talked to the gang. I had the dog with me. The gang went away. I don't know where they went. It doesn't matter.

Mrs. Barnes lives in the building. She had a kid, Tommy. He's a sweet-natured boy, maybe ten years old. Tommy's a little slow in the head, goes to a special school and all. Other kids in the building used to bother him. I fixed that.

Maybe that's why Mrs. Barnes told me about the monsters. Tommy was waking up in the night screaming. He told his mother monsters lived in the room and they came after him when he went to sleep.

I told her she should talk to someone who knows how to fix what's wrong with the kid. She told me he had somebody. A therapist at his special school—an older guy. Dr. English. Mrs. Barnes couldn't say enough about this guy. He was like a father to the boy, she said. Took him places, bought him stuff. A real distinguished-looking man. She showed me a picture of him standing next to Tommy. He had his hand on the boy's shoulder.

The boy comes down to the basement himself. Mostly after school. The dog likes him. Tommy watches me do my work. Never says much, just pats the dog and hands me a tool once in a while. One day he told me about the monsters himself. Asked me to fix it. I thought about it. Finally I told him I could do it.

I went up to his room. Nice big room, painted a pretty blue color. Faces out the back of the building. Lots of light comes in his window. There's a fire escape right off the window. Tommy tells me he likes to sit out there on nice days and watch the other kids play down below. It's only on the second floor, so he can see them good.

I checked the room for monsters. He told me they only came at night. I told him I could fix it but it would take me a few days. The boy was real happy. You could see it.

I did some reading, and I thought I had it all figured out. The monsters were in his head. I made a machine in the basement—just a metal box with a row of lights on the top and a toggle switch. I showed him how to turn it on. The lights flashed in a random sequence. The boy stared at it for a long time.

I told him this was a machine for monsters. As long as the machine was turned on, monsters couldn't come in his room. I never saw a kid smile like he did.

His mother tried to slip me a few bucks when I was leaving. I didn't take it. I never do. Fixing things is my job.

She winked at me, said she'd tell Dr. English about my machine. Maybe he'd use it for all his kids. I told her I only fixed things in my building.

I saw the boy every day after that. He stopped being scared. His mother told me she had a talk with Dr. English. He told her the machine I made was a placebo, and Tommy would always need therapy.

I go to the library a lot to learn more about how things work. I looked up "placebo" in the big dictionary they have there. It means a fake, but a fake that somebody believes in. Like giving a sugar pill to a guy in a lot of pain and telling him it's morphine. It doesn't really work by itself—it's all in your mind.

One night Tommy woke up screaming and he didn't stop. His mother rang my buzzer and I went up to the apartment. The kid was shaking all over, covered with sweat.

He saw me. He said my machine didn't work any more.

He wasn't mad at me, but he said he couldn't go back to sleep. Ever.

Some guys in white jackets came in an ambulance. They took the boy away. I saw him in the hospital the next day. They gave him something to sleep the night before and he looked dopey.

The day after that he said he wasn't afraid any more. The pills worked. No monsters came in the night. But he said he could never go home. He asked if I could build him a stronger machine.

I told him I'd work on it.

His mother said she called Dr. English at the special school, but they said he was out for a few days. Hurt himself on a ski trip or something. She couldn't wait to tell Dr. English about the special medicine they were giving the boy and ask if it was all right with him.

I called the school. Said I was with the State Disability Commission. The lady who answered told me Dr. English was at home, recuperating from a broken arm. I got her to tell me his full name, got her to talk. I know how things work.

She told me they were lucky to have Dr. English. He used to work at some school way up north—in Toronto, Canada—but he left because he hated the cold weather.

I thought about it a long time. Broken arm. Ski trip. Cold weather.

The librarian knows me. She says I'm her best customer because I never check books out. I always read them right there. I never write stuff down—I keep it in my head.

I asked the librarian some questions and she showed me how to use the newspaper index. I checked all the Toronto papers until I found it. A big scandal at a special school for slow kids. Some of the staff were indicted. Dr. English was one of the people they questioned, but he was never charged with anything. Four of the staff people went to prison. A few more were acquitted. Dr. English, he resigned.

Dr. English was listed in the phonebook. He lives in a real nice neighborhood.

I waited a couple of more days, working it all out in my head.

Mrs. Barnes told me Dr. English was coming back to the school next week. She was going to talk to him about Tommy, maybe get him to do some of his therapy in the hospital until the boy was ready to come home.

I told Tommy I knew how to stop the monsters for sure now. I told him I was building a new machine—I'd have it ready for him next week. I told him when he got home I wanted him to walk the dog for me. Out in the back where the other kids played. I told him I'd teach him how.

Tommy really liked that. He said he'd try and come home if I was sure the new machine would work. I gave him my word.

I'm working on a new machine in my basement now. I put a hard rubber ball into a vise and clamped it tight. I drilled a tiny hole right through the center. Then I threaded it with a strand of piano wire until about six inches poked through the end. I knotted it real carefully and pulled back against the knot with all my strength. It held. I did the same thing with another ball the same way. Now I have a three-foot piece of piano wire anchored with a little rubber ball at each end. The rubber balls fit perfectly, one in each hand.

I know how to fix things.

When it gets dark tonight, I'll show Dr. English a machine that works.

The Ghost of Monday

Andrew Klavan

By Friday, it was gone. Fletcher read the paper on his way home from Wall Street, and there was not a sign of it. The blackout at Grand Central Terminal had replaced it on the front page. Within, it had given way to an anti-import demonstration in the garment district and a drug-related shootout in the Heights. It amused him. After all his worry, all his wrestlings with the inner angels of conscience and fear, it had not even been news for a week. In the great tidal wave of events, it was a droplet. It had vanished without a trace.

He threw the newspaper away before he got on the elevator. He rode upstairs with his hands folded in front of him and his eyes trained on the doors. A corner of his mouth twitched upward: the suggestion of a smile. Other than that, he betrayed nothing.

He loosened his tie as he entered his apartment. He kicked off his shoes as he shut the door. He liked the feel of the shag beneath his stockings. He tossed his briefcase down by the bar and poured himself a drink.

He drank standing by the window, looking down on Fifth Avenue. He watched the string of green traffic lights running away into the crystal darkness. He watched the cabs' red taillights weaving beneath them, and beneath the golden crown atop the Crown Building, and the solemn iron cross atop the red brick steeple of the Presbyterian church, and between all the avenue's towering, concrete walls, which narrowed to the vanishing point.

The tapping annoyed him. This was the third day he had heard it. He knew it was coming from the bathroom and suspected it was in the pipes, but he wanted to make sure before he called a plumber. It was probably a steady thing, but it entered his consciousness now as if it had just begun again after a pause. He flinched and turned toward the noise just in time to see a flutter of tan skirt disappear around the hall corner.

"What the hell," Fletcher said. He put his drink down on the coffee table. He walked to the hallway.

He called: "Hello?" Then he snorted. "Good, Fletcher, talk to yourself," he said aloud.

Still, he went down the hall. There were three doors down there. The bathroom was to the right, the bedroom to the left, the closet straight ahead. He flicked on the bedroom light, glanced in. Nothing there. Of course there was nothing there. He tried the closet, feeling silly. Finally, he hit the bathroom light, and went in.

The tapping seemed to come from someplace right next to the tub. He couldn't pin it down exactly. It was a steadily repeated rap, muffled, like someone knocking on the door of a neighboring apartment. All the sounds of the building traveled through the bathrooms. You could never tell which apartment they were coming from.

He stood looking down at the tiles beside the tub, he noticed an odd smell. Faint, but thick, swampy. The tapping must be caused by something backing up in the pipes. He thought: Tan skirt. She always did dress well. But blackmail is blackmail, all the same.

The thought was unbidden. He shook it off. He turned to go. But as his eyes crept across the mirror over the sink, he had an odd sensation. It seemed to him for a moment as if his reflection had paused while he turned. Paused to stare at him and smile while he continued to turn away. He wheeled back to it. It was just as it should be. Everything was just as it should be.

Irritated, he grimaced at himself in the glass. He killed the bathroom light and stepped across the hall to the bedroom again.

He decided to get undressed. He'd get into bed, maybe give the Walker papers another onceover. There was not a thing wrong with them, he knew that, but it would put his mind at ease. It was a special trust, after all. The boss had assigned it to him personally. The boss would have handled it himself, in fact, if he hadn't been so distraught about his wife.

He went to the bedroom closet and opened the door. There was a man standing inside, waiting—a man with wild laughter in his eyes and an axe in his hands. The man stepped forward, raising the axe above his head. Fletcher had time to let out one high-pitched shriek, and then the man buried the blade in his brain.

And was gone. He seemed to pass right through Fletcher. The blade did not bite flesh or smash bone. It simply dissolved on contact and disappeared. Fletcher reeled backward. He sat down hard on the bed. His face sank into his hands. He felt sick at his stomach. The man with the axe: it had been he. It had been Fletcher himself.

Slowly, he looked up, looked around him at the empty room. Had he really had such madness in his eyes? He hadn't felt mad. He had felt very calm, very logical. Remembering the old camping axe like that. He hadn't used it in years.

The tapping began again, louder now. And drifting from the bathroom with it came that rancid smell. He tried not to take it in, but it crawled into his nostrils. It seemed to drip, viscid, down the back of his throat.

He cursed: a small, strangled noise. He stood. His fists clenched, he strode into the bathroom. He paused there in the dark, the smell thick all around him, clogging his senses, the tapping louder, clouding his mind. He held his breath. With an angry sweep of his hand, he snapped on the light.

The tub was filled with blood again.

"Damn!" He growled it now. A single step took him to the tub's edge. He reached down for the chain on the drainage plug.

Her hand rose, dripping, out of the bath and grabbed him. Her fingers wrapped tightly around his wrist. He felt the dampness of them. As he tried to pull free, he saw the diamond on her engagement ring flash in the light. Crazily, he thought: Had she been anyone but the boss's wife. Had she just not threatened to tell.

The strength of the hand was preternatural. It dragged him toward the blood-filled tub. The tapping was like thunder now inside his head. He cried out and pulled free.

The hand sank down, out of sight. The tapping ceased. Only the blood remained. He wanted to close his eyes, to make it vanish. He couldn't. He was afraid.

Instead, he stood staring as the blood began to drain away. It drained slowly, with a soft gurgle. He kept staring as the level sank lower and lower. It was low enough so that nothing could be hidden beneath, but he kept staring. Finally, the last of it spiraled down. The tub was empty.

The tub had to be empty. He had seen to it, had scrubbed it thoroughly when he was finished. The hand, the arm—all the pieces—he had loaded them into the trunk, one by one. It had made him gag to do it, but he had gotten it done. Loaded them into the trunk and thrown the trunk in. . . .

All at once, the tapping returned. It was a pounding now. It was right beside him. He spun around. The trunk had come back. It was sitting on the bathroom floor again. The pounding came from inside it. It grew louder and louder. The top of the trunk began to shudder with the force of it. The top of the trunk began to rise.

Fletcher was babbling as he ran from the apartment. He was laughing as he tore down the firestairs; out into the lobby; out into the night. He was still laughing when the cop found him. He was sitting under a streetlight, hugging his knees and laughing. When the officer leaned toward him to check him out, Fletcher looked up at him and smiled. He crooked his finger at the cop, and the cop leaned closer.

"Nothing vanishes," Fletcher said, giggling. Then he told the whole story.

The cop was spellbound.

A Good Head for Murder

CHARLES W. RUNYON

*S*he drove down the twisting Mexican road, while he dozed beside her and listened to the music from Uruapan. She struck
the brake suddenly, throwing him forward against the dash. He saw the
animal leave the glow of the headlights and slink into the thorny brush
at the side of the road.

She gasped. *"Did you see that dog?* It couldn't possibly have been
carrying—"

"It was," said Gordon Phelps, lighting his pipe. "A human head. I
wonder whose it could've been?"

"Gordon! How can you just . . . just . . ."

"Sit here? I don't know what else to do. What does one do in a
situation like this?"

"Well—follow it!"

Her shrill voice trembled on the edge of panic. Gordon felt an icy
calm weighting him down in his seat. Had he been alone he might
have given way to the sharp teeth of hysteria which nibbled at his
mind—but he always reacted contrary to Ann.

"Through a trackless waste of mesquite? Ann, they don't call this
'Little Hell' for nothing. It's totally uninhabited."

"Somebody lives here . . . or did."

"Yes, I suppose you could call the head evidence of human habitation.
And where you find one person you might find another. Which is sort
of what I'm afraid of."

"What do you mean?"

"The person who, uh, severed the head could be . . ." he waved his hand at the dust-covered bushes which bulged out into the graveled track, "lurking, you know . . ."

"Oh!" She tromped the accelerator. The car threw up its nose and jumped forward, paused, made another jackrabbit leap—and died.

"You forgot to shift into low," said Gordon.

"Oh! This darned . . . old . . . *heap.*" Keys jingled as she turned the switch. The starter groaned. The car inched forward in a series of tiny lurches.

"The clutch," Gordon said. "You didn't push your clutch in. This rental car doesn't have an automatic shift, you know."

"I *know.* Please don't talk while I'm driving."

Gordon opened his mouth, then closed it as the engine caught. Tires grated on loose gravel, the rear end skewed leftward as the car moved forward with agonizing slowness. A thorny branch clawed at the front fender, smacked the windshield, and scree-eee-eeched along the side of the car. Gordon shuddered as the sound blazed a track of fire up his spinal ganglia. After eight years of teaching he'd never gotten used to fingernails on a blackboard.

The front wheels found the packed tracks and the vehicle picked up speed, pumping fine gray dust up through the floorboards. Gordon leaned forward in the seat, his spine rigid as a steel rod. The headlights swept along the bank of thorns as the car swiveled around a right angle turn. Shattered twigs tickety-ticked against metal as she raced up the steep slope, skewed around another curve, then dipped down into a valley.

"If we hadn't had the flat back there . . ." Her voice trailed off.

"We'd have been to the coast. I know. But we had it, and we aren't . . . and if you don't stop taking those curves so fast, we never will be."

"If they'd just put up little warning signs . . ."

"They'd bankrupt the country. This road is nothing but curves. Look out for that rock!"

He held his breath as she swerved to straddle a rubber-streaked gray boulder. A metallic thump sounded from below and rumbled the length of the car. He let his eyes drift to the oil gauge. The needle held steady. At least the oil pan had survived.

But now something dragged behind, clattering against the gravel.

"Tailpipe," he muttered.

"What?"

The clatter ceased. He decided not to look back to see what had fallen off. The car still moved, so it hadn't been a vital part.

"Why don't you let me drive?"

"You said your eyes were tired."

"That was before—watch it!"

He hunched his shoulders as a stubby tree limb loomed out of the dusty foliage. It passed over the roof of the car with less than an inch to spare. With the heel of his palm he wiped the dust off the side window and looked out. The aerial bent backward at a forty-five degree angle.

"Slow down. Nobody's after us."

The car slowed slightly. "But good heavens, Gordon, a human head . . . a dog carries a human head across the road in front of us and we don't even . . . I mean, I'm beginning to feel awfully wrong about this."

"You want to go back?"

She paused. "Do you?"

"There's no place to turn around."

"You're so good at rationalizing, Gordon."

He leaned back and fingered a kitchen match out of his watch pocket, scraped his thumbnail across the head, and held the flame to his pipe. In the rear view mirror he saw nothing but a billowing fog of dust, tinted red by the taillights. It had trailed them for the last two hundred miles.

The taste of the fragrant smoke relaxed him slightly. "Call it rationalizing, if you will. The local people, I understand, are rather primitive. Used to settling quarrels in the quickest way, with machetes. Best for the local authorities to handle it, if there are any."

"And if there aren't?"

He forced down a rising annoyance. "All right, let's say we went back, and I managed to find the head. What would we do, carry it all the way to the beach? Turn it in at the hotel and say, Here's a little item we picked up along the road? We'd be hung up with the authorities for the entire vacation—maybe longer."

"I wasn't thinking about the head. I meant . . . the rest of the body."

Gordon muttered, "Wouldn't do him much good without his head."

"I don't think it was a 'him,' Gordon."

"Come now. It was all coated with dust. You couldn't have gotten any impression of gender."

"It had long hair . . ."

"That's an indication of nothing these days."

". . . and an earring, one of those jade pendants, with a loop of copper wire running through it."

"You're fantasizing, my dear."

"I *know* what I saw. I think it was a white woman."

"With how many freckles across the bridge of her nose?"

"I don't feel particularly humorous, Gordon."

"I don't either—but are we going back? We aren't, because we can't turn around, and we'd never find the spot anyway. We've crossed fifty valleys, and they're all exactly alike. Anyway, I'm not sure we've got enough gas for it. I don't know what kind of mileage we're getting in this car."

"You told me once that if I had more than one excuse I didn't have any."

"Okay, I don't have any excuse. But we're not going back!" He bit down hard on the stem of his pipe and fumbled another match out of his pocket. "When we get to the hotel, we'll make discreet inquiries. If any disappearances have been reported, we'll tell about the head. Otherwise, silence is golden. Agreed?"

"What if it just happened? There won't be any report, will there?"

"Just let me do the talking when we get to the hotel. Will you do that?"

"I don't see how I could do otherwise, since I don't speak the language."

Gordon knew it was the best he could expect. She liked to keep her options open, so that if he were proved wrong, she could always say she had reservations.

What the hell do we look like, a couple of Indians? Part of an old joke, burlesque vintage, a man and a woman go into the hotel and ask for a room, and the clerk asks if they have reservations. . . .

Thinking too much . . . too hard . . . trying to keep his mind off the horror in the road. He now wished he'd stopped—gone back and picked up the bloody thing, looked into its eyes and said, *Cynthia, who did this to you, my dear?*

Ann would never have understood. She would not even have *wanted* to understand. New to the hard line of reality, home-school-church-and-family, all life as constricted as a baseball diamond, touch all the bases and when you cross home plate God is there to shake your hand. . . .

Then he had to admit that he had chosen *her*, out of a vast pool of available females (so it seemed in retrospect) because she'd always turned in neat papers and was never late to class. Whereas he was sloppy and dilatory. Contrasts always hooked him. Black-white. Antonym-synonym. She was tall, willowy, ash blonde; he was stocky and black-haired. He'd visualized a balanced marriage, or at worst a seesaw of authority, but his aimless hedonism stood no chance against her patient logic. In all life's choices he saw a high road and a low road, but she always picked the one closest to earth. Take his degree in education: "You'll have the summers for your beachcombing and there's the sabbatical every seven years. . . ." But summers had been occupied in fixing up the house, and the first sabbatical was spent building the cabin on the lake. He began to wonder if he hadn't let the wine stand too long in the glass. . . .

A new rattle had developed somewhere in the left rear. He listened for a moment, decided it was one of the fender mountings and not something which would collapse and leave them stranded in this godforsaken country. It was hot, stuffy inside the car, but he could not open the windows because of the dust. Still it sifted in, fine as talc, around the windows and doors. He could feel it coating the inside of his nostrils, crusting his lips with the dry burning taste of alkali. He closed his eyes and tried to visualize the hotel on the beach where Norval had described the green lawns, the spacious swimming pool, the sun-drenched balconies, and the low, low rates. But he kept thinking of the head and how clean the cut had been, right below the Adam's apple. . . .

The car jolted, bounced, came down with a crunch that jarred his teeth. Dust billowed up from the floor. Looking out, he saw that they were crossing a dry wash, one of dozens they'd negotiated during the last seven hours.

"Gordon . . ."

He turned and saw her round glasses reflecting the glow of the headlights. Behind them her eyes were wide and staring.

"What's the matter?" he asked.

"I saw a foot sticking out from under a bush back there."

His heart lurched, then went on beating faster. "Where?"

"When we crossed the creek bed."

"Why didn't you stop?"

"I don't know."

"You probably saw a tree root."

"I saw a *foot*."

"Oh, hell! What's the point of arguing? Stop the car and back up."

"I *can't*. I can't even back up our own car, let alone this dilapidated wreck."

"You want me to do it?"

"I just want to get to the end of this trip, Gordon. I don't want to back up or turn around or anything. I just want to get *off . . . this . . . road!*"

Then why did you tell me about the foot? he thought, but he said nothing. She'd sounded like a little girl on the brink of a tantrum, refusing to go into the dark spooky bedroom. He wasn't too calm himself. The foliage pressed in toward the center of the road, making him feel hemmed in. Forward visibility was less than twenty yards. He held his breath as they rounded a curve, half-expecting to see an Aztec priest with a stained obsidian knife, ripping the pulsing heart out of a naked torso . . . an eerie thought. . . .

He stiffened as the engine coughed, sputtered, then settled into a strained growl as it carried them up the steep ridge. His eyes slid to the gas gauge. That settled the question of backing up. It might even settle the question of going forward, though he had a feeling there was more in the tank than the gauge showed. The steep pitch of the hill would drain everything to the rear. . . .

He breathed a sigh of relief as the car topped the ridge and tipped down into another ravine. The gas gauge edged off the peg and stopped at one-eighth full.

After a minute she spoke. "You were probably right. That was only a gnarled tree root back there."

Immediately he felt wary. "I see. And the head?"

"Oh . . . a coconut."

"Why not a pumpkin? Ichabod Crane thought he saw a head, but it was only a pumpkin."

She said nothing for several heartbeats. "Pumpkins don't grow here."

"Neither do coconuts."

"Well, they have trucks, you know. It could have fallen off a truck."

"And where did it get that hair?"

"Coconuts have hair—sort of."

"And jade earrings."

"Oh, Gordon, for heaven's sake. Are we going to spend our whole vacation chewing over this thing?"

"It might be the lesser of two evils."

"What do you mean by that?"

"Nothing." He stuck his pipe in his mouth and clamped his teeth on the bit. Her protest that she had *not* seen a foot was proof to Gordon that she had seen it—and was now so shaken that she wanted to back out of the whole reality sequence.

As for his comment about the lesser evil—he meant that he'd be only too happy to sit in a safe, comfortable hotel and mull over this intriguing mystery. The thing he dreaded most was a sudden *denouement*. He had a feeling that the head had been only a preliminary, like the first rumble of thunder which presages the downpour. . . .

Coming to another one of those miserable gullies. Beyond the scoured basalt bedrock he saw what looked like a crooked branch, off one of those slick white-barked eucalyptus trees that grew in the arroyos. He *hoped* it was that. Even as the car bounded across the wash, he ground his pipe between his teeth and silently prayed that the sharp bend in the middle was only an accident of growth and not an articulated elbow . . . that those curved appendages were only blunt-ended rootlets which happened to total five in number . . .

She had to swerve to miss the object, and in that moment he saw it clearly, coated with a white film of road dust.

Gordon drew a deep breath, then let it out slowly. He felt an odd relaxation of tension; he identified it as the end of self-deception, the closure of doubt, the presence of a certainty which could be . . . *must* be dealt with. No more speculation, no more games with reality . . .

"Stop the car, Ann."

Instead she speeded up. He glanced over and saw her sitting rigid behind the wheel, looking neither right nor left, the mouth set in a tight, downcurving line. . . .

"Ann . . ." He touched her forearm lightly, felt the hard rigidity of muscle. He reached down and turned off the switch. The engine died, but she didn't seem aware of it. She pumped the accelerator until the car shuddered to a halt in the middle of the roadway.

"Ann, we've got to go back."

"No!" She made a grab for the keys; he caught her wrist and took her hand in his, stroking it until the tight hard knot of her fist unclenched, and her hand lay trembling in his. . . .

"Ann, that was definitely a human arm. You saw it too, didn't you?"

"Yes." Her voice sounded small and weak.

"Well, then . . . ?"

"You were right the first time, Gordon. I think we'd better not get involved."

"I was *wrong* the first time. We *are* involved. I don't like it, but we are. Now, wait—before you argue, think. How many cars pass along this road? One, two, three per night? Those people back at the station, the ones who patched our tire, *they* know we came this way. There's no turning off this road. It leads straight from the crossroads to the hotel on the beach. So what if somebody comes along behind us and picks up that arm? Assuming the most elementary investigation, they'll find out we were the last ones along this road. And they'll ask us, Did you see an arm lying beside the road? Why didn't you pick it up? Why didn't you report it?"

He spoke with calm emphasis, as if he were lecturing to his class. In fact, he felt utterly detached, as if he were standing on a cool, windy mountain top and looking down upon a rolling, writhing mass of humanity.

"You could go back and kick it into the brush," she said.

"Then we'd be concealing evidence of a crime."

"How do you know it was a crime?"

"I doubt that it's legal to go around dismembering corpses in Mexico."

"So? Who would know?"

"We would know."

"My conscience can handle it."

"It's not a matter of conscience. It's . . ." His mind groped for words to explain his feeling that this was one of life's watersheds, where one stream opens into a broad green valley, and the other narrows to a canyon filled with thorns and venomous reptiles. He was determined that this time she would not force him into the low road, no matter how logical and self-preservative it might be.

"It's a question of responsibility," he said finally.

"Is it *our* responsibility?"

"I'm afraid it is."

"I don't agree. It's not our country, these aren't our people, we don't even speak the lang—"

He reached across her and punched in the light button. She gasped as sudden darkness pressed in upon them.

"Gordon, what are you doing?"

"Trust me, Ann." He opened the glove compartment and took out the flashlight. He opened the door and stepped out, pausing to let his eyes acclimate to the darkness. Above him on the ridge, a gnarled tree lifted its tufted fingers against the faint blue glow of the skyline. The stars were incredibly bright, as though a white-hot furnace leaked light through a velvet curtain. He walked to the back of the car and looked down the pale strip of gravel. Nothing moved. He listened until his body ached with the effort, but heard nothing. Was that normal? Hadn't he read somewhere that the absence of night sounds signified a lurking predator?

He lifted the trunk lid, careful to make no sound. The dim yellow beam of his flashlight revealed a dusty burlap bag and a lug wrench. He closed the trunk gently and walked around to her window. She rolled down the glass and he handed her the lug wrench.

"Keep this in your hand, just in case."

Her cold, damp fingers touched his. He took her hand and squeezed it, waited until the answering squeeze came, faint at first, then a tight, desperate clutch.

"Let's go on, Gordon."

Gently he disengaged her hand. "Roll up the window and lock the doors. I'll be right back."

His footsteps on the gravel sounded loud—obscene, like someone eating potato chips at a funeral. Strange to retrace on foot the distance covered in a car. He seemed to have walked a long time. Had he passed the arm? No, the road still sloped downward; he hadn't yet reached the dry wash. He thought of returning to the car and backing it down the road. He didn't like all this space separating him from Ann. She was already terrified, here in the midst of desolation, in a foreign land, in total darkness. . . .

You're not yodeling for joy yourself, Phelps.

The arm had a curious sheen in the red-yellow light. The hand—frozen in a grasping reflex—tripped his brain into visions of a grunting, gasping death struggle. Could there be blood and tissue under the fingernails, a shred of fabric which would lead to the murderer?

Let the police worry about that.

He reached down to pick it up, then straightened and listened. From beyond the ridge came the growl of a laboring engine. Headlight beams fanned across the sky—and his car sat blocking the road. Something had to be done.

For a second he stood wavering. Run back and leave the arm lying
there? No, have to pick it up . . .

He threw the burlap over the arm and grasped it gingerly between
his fingers. He shut off his flashlight and started at a fast trot back to
the car. He felt a vague surprise at how heavy the arm felt, but then
he'd never carried an unattached human arm before.

The truck crested the ridge. Twin lights dipped down and shone
through the car, silhouetting Ann's head behind the wheel. He broke
into a run, jerked open the car door, and tossed the burlap bundle onto
the floor behind the seat.

"Scoot over, quick!"

She slid over and he thrust himself behind the wheel. The approaching headlights dazzled him. He groped, found the switch. The
engine coughed and died. Damn rental car. Why couldn't he have
driven his own? Couldn't be sure of finding gas, better fly to Guadalajara
and hire a car, that's what Norval had said. . . .

Curse you, Norval.

The engine caught, and he jerked on the lights. The oncoming lights neither dimmed nor swerved, but came on like a pair of blinding suns. They
stopped so close he could feel the heat against his face, burning his eyes.

"They've got the road blocked," said Ann. Her tone was the same
one she used to tell him there was a raveling on his sleeve.

He shifted into reverse and twisted his head to look out the back
window. He saw nothing but two spinning green discs on a sheet of
coruscating purple. He was blind as a mole. Without backup lights he'd
surely blunder into the brush. . . .

The truck was red and riding high on heavy-duty shocks. A square
chrome grille glittered above a baby-blue bumper which carried the
words: EL TORO DEL CAMINO. Bull of the road. A sign of aggression
which seemed borne out by the man who stepped down from the cab.
He looked . . . not tall, but thick and broad as an oak stump. He wore
grease-stained khaki pants and a once-white undershirt which now bore
finger paintings of oil on dust. A dusty red bandanna hung around his
thick neck. His stubbled cheeks spread in a wide grin, and Gordon
thought of the Mexican bandit in *The Treasure of Sierra Madre*. . . .

"Hand me that lug wrench," he said, holding out his hand. He felt
the bar smack his palm and reflected that his best defense would be a
savage merciless attack. Yet he knew his civilized reflexes would make
him hesitant and clumsy. . . .

"He's got a gun," said Ann, in the same flat tone she'd used before.

Gordon saw it as the driver turned to speak to someone up in the cab—ugly blue steel death-dealer clipped to his belt above the rear pocket.

The man hitched up his pants and started toward the car.

Gordon said, "Don't talk. I'll try to bluff our way past him."

The driver stood grinning outside the window, his face only inches from the glass. Waving his hands and dipping his shoulders, he ripped off twenty seconds of rapid Spanish.

"Did you understand him?" asked Ann.

"Too fast. He's using some local dialect." Gordon pushed out the side vent and spoke through the narrow gap: "No entiendo."

"Muñeca?" The man waited, his brows lifted in question. "Muñeca?"

Gordon shook his head. "No understand. Americano."

"Ah . . . Americano!" The man bent down and pressed his nose against the window. "Sí, Americano." He stepped back, lifted his hand and waggled his fingers, then trotted around behind the truck.

"Was he waving goodbye?" asked Ann.

"I think he wants us to wait."

"He isn't giving us any choice."

Gordon watched the driver come out from behind the truck with a grotesquely truncated object under his arm. Ann gasped as he held it up in front of the headlights. Gordon saw the naked, headless, limbless female torso and thought: *This can't be real, we've driven off the world and dropped into a nightmare. . . .*

The smooth breasts had no nipples, the round tummy lacked a navel, and the space between the truncated thighs was only a smooth mound of plastic. . . .

"Gordon, is that a . . . *mannequin?*"

He couldn't speak, but let his breath out in a long sigh. Only then did he realize how tense he'd been. His muscles went limp, his spine wilted into its normal curvature.

He felt utterly ludicrous. The driver stood in the headlights' glare, demonstrating by signs how the dummy had shaken apart in his truck, and how the parts had tumbled out one by one. Gordon reached behind the seat and seized the arm wrapped in burlap. . . .

He froze as the driver came back to the window.

"Ha visto alguna parte? La cabeza? Cabeza?" He held his hands to his temples and rocked his head from side to side.

"*Cabeza*—he wants to know about the head," said Ann.

"I know. Keep quiet." Gordon put his mouth to the vent. "A dog got it. Dog. What's the word for dog? *Perro. Perro.*"

The driver tilted his head and looked puzzled.

"Rowf! Rowf!" barked Gordon.

"Ah . . . *perro, sí. Grácias. Muchísimas grácias!*"

The driver grinned and saluted, then ran back and climbed into his truck. A minute later the engine roared, and the big vehicle backed into the crackling brush. The driver waved his hand as Gordon drove past.

Neither spoke until they crested the ridge. The road stretched straight ahead, with neither hill nor curve breaking its slow descent to the coastal plain. Moonlight glittered on the crinkled sea. Off to the right he saw splotches of light which marked the hotel complex. He heard a choking sound beside him and turned to Ann.

"Are you laughing or crying?"

"Both," she said.

"You think I was silly?"

"No. You were awfully brave—even if the danger wasn't real. And you were right about stopping. Can you imagine if we'd just kept driving? All our lives we'd have been haunted . . ." She talked without stopping for breath—her way of releasing tension. ". . . And what paranoid assumptions we made! That all unexplained deaths are a result of murder, that all foreigners are hostile. There's only one thing I don't understand."

"What's that?"

"Why didn't you give the nice man back his arm?"

Gordon reached behind the seat and groped for the burlap-wrapped bundle.

"There's another assumption we make about foreigners," he said. "That even though they're shrewd, they haven't the intelligence to pull off a really cool subterfuge. Like carrying around a dummy in order to recover a lost corpse."

He gripped the arm just below the elbow, avoiding the cold, sticky end which had shocked him so much the last time.

"This one's real," he said.

Later he realized he shouldn't have laid it in her lap—but he wasn't thinking straight at the time.

Golden Tuesday

CELIA FREMLIN

*T*he tiny moment of suspense, the passing flicker of dread lest, this time, Coral would not be waiting for him at their usual table—this was all part of William's Tuesday happiness, and he wouldn't have missed it for anything. He paused in the doorway of the discotheque, savoring these moments of delicious terror (delicious because unfounded) while the pop music that Coral loved streamed out past him into the winter night, and his eyes searched the rosy dimness inside for a gleam of cool blonde hair, for a glimpse of pouting, impatient lips, fashionably metallic, and drawing, restless with waiting, on yet another cigarette.

As he stood there, bathed in the drumbeat rhythm, and with the pale glittering young people surging past him out of the night, William didn't feel 48. He didn't feel married; and least of all did he feel like the saintly, devoted paragon of a husband that his wife's illness had forced him into becoming.

Yes, forced. All through the years when Eleanor had been well and strong and like anyone else's wife, William had been like anyone else's husband—cheerfully selfish, casually loving, and full of complaints, as are a man's rights.

But Eleanor's illness had finished all that. It had silenced his complaints, pole-axed his selfishness. All that was left was the loving—casual no longer, but nursed and coddled like an overfed cat, bloated with pity and good intentions.

"What a wonderful husband!" the neighbors were beginning to say of him. "Whatever would she do without him?" "The patience of an angel," they were saying. "Never a cross word, even now that she's grown so trying, poor thing!"

Actually he had been hustled into being wonderful, inch by inch, and fighting all the way. Slowly, inexorably, Eleanor's aching back, her worsening stomach pains, had forced him back and back, blocking first one exit and then another, until at last here he was, like a man trapped by the advancing tide, finally and irrevocably at the mercy of her encroaching illness.

By attacks of nausea, by bouts of uncontrollable shivering, her sickness had got him into its power; bit by bit, day after day, it had molded him, twisting and transforming his commonplace flesh into an angel substance, the stuff of which martyrs are made. He had accepted his role of martyr because he could not fight it; he nursed Eleanor with tenderness and devotion because these seemed to be the only tools left to him; and his reward for all this was a monstrous, ever-increasing tedium, as Eleanor grew more and more boring, lapsed more and more into pain . . .

Someone had put on another record. It roared out from the russet darkness of the discotheque like a trumpet call to Youth, and William's nostrils quivered at the summons like those of an old warhorse. Youth, youth! His 48 years seemed to slide away into the night, and so did all thought of his dreary middle-aged wife, hollowed out by her dreary middle-aged operations.

He was free, free of it all, for one golden evening! Free like these bearded striplings, like these dozy half-grown girls, delicious in their ignorance of pain! Free! Free! His magic Tuesday evening had begun!

William pushed open the swinging door and marched, head held high, into the very shrine of youth, marched tall and proud because he had a girl in there of his very own. A girl as gloriously young as the rest, and as delectable, and waiting for *him.*

"Willy! *There* you are! I was beginning to think something had happened! I was afraid you'd had to stay with *her!* Oh, Willy, *darling!*"

She always welcomed him with these exclamations, reaching out her silver-tipped little fingers to draw him down beside her, into the place she had been guarding for him on the red plastic cushions. He loved the feel of her soft hands not yet touched by work; and he loved too her never-failing surprise, Tuesday after Tuesday, at his successful arrival at the rendezvous. The predictability of her every word and gesture was infinitely soothing to him; it gave to these Tuesday evenings a luminous quality, the precious minutes sliding through his fingers like a necklace of well-loved jewels. He knew already what her next words were going to be, and how he was going to answer them; he waited, joyously expectant as a child awaiting his familiar bedtime story.

"Is *she* any better?"

Coral's voice held just the note of anxious melancholy that is appropriate for asking about a hopeless invalid; but behind the sweet concern in her gray eyes William could see dancing an eagerness for morbid details that exactly matched his own aching need to confide them. Coral loved to hear of Eleanor's petulance, her sickroom fads and fancies, her endless aches and pains—loved to hear of them every bit as much as William longed to tell of them. It made them both feel so *healthy*, he and Coral, so vital, so united in the singular glory of not being ill!

And so William shook his head sadly, as he always did in answer to Coral's inquiry; he looked into her sparkling, expectant eyes, and to keep that enchanting eagerness dancing for him he raked his wearied memories for the things she most loved to hear.

She loved to hear that Eleanor had refused to take her medicine again, that she had scolded William for not responding quickly enough to her night bell, endlessly dragging him from sleep. She loved to hear that Eleanor had asked him, perhaps, for dry toast, or a glass of orange juice, and then, when he brought it to her, all daintily set out on a pretty lace cloth, had turned her face away in disgust, refusing to eat.

"Oh, dear!" Coral would say, licking her little silver lips. "Oh, dear, I *am* sorry! But the pain's better, is it—the pain in her back?"

Coral loved to hear about the pain in Eleanor's back; it made her own spine feel so straight and strong and youthful. She gave a lissome little shrug with it now, while she breathed her condolences, and William watched the small movement with delight. He leaned forward and kissed the smooth unlined cheek under the fall of gleaming hair.

"How marvelous it is to touch a woman who is *well!*" he murmured; and Coral glowed, and flaunted her well-ness before him for just the right length of time before gently prompting him—for after all, their time was short.

"She's not *worse*, though, is she?" she suggested, laying her little hand on William's with sweet concern. "The doctor doesn't think she's *worse?*"

The sweet secret zest in the young voice was to William like the forked flame of desire itself, and he responded to it like a lizard to the sun, his mind coming alive, darting this way and that among the sordid sickroom trivia for the kind of nourishment on which his and Coral's relationship flourished and grew fat.

"Not *worse*—not really," he said, with studied fairness, and whetting Coral's appetite by the tiny delay. "But it's the sickness, you see, she can't seem to keep anything down. No matter how carefully I prepare it."

Coral's silvery, knowledgeable voice broke in, right on cue.

"You know why that is, Willy, don't you? You do realize why she is doing it? Unconsciously, of course—I don't mean she'd *deliberately* do such a thing to you—but *unconsciously* she's equating food with love. By rejecting the food you offer her she's rejecting your love. Rejecting it out of jealousy, because she can't bear not to have all of it, every minute of the day. Her demands on your love have gone beyond all reason, my poor darling."

Sweet Coral! She never failed him, never! Aloud he said, "Oh, Coral, how wonderful it is to be with someone who *understands!* I couldn't talk about this to anyone else in the whole wide world, because it seems such a dreadful thing to say of one's own wife. But I *have* wondered myself, sometimes, if it isn't psychosomatic, some of it."

How the silver earrings bobbed and danced, in a sort of ecstasy of understanding!

"Yes," Coral murmured. "Yes, that's what I mean. Poor Eleanor. I'm sure she doesn't realize it herself, but after all, an illness *is* a way of keeping a husband at home, isn't it, when a woman hasn't—well, hasn't much else to hold him with, to make him want to stay with her."

She sipped her coffee delicately, watching him over the rim of the cup with gray, thoughtful eyes. The most wonderful part of the whole evening was just beginning, the moment they got to Eleanor's unconscious motivations. Like gods they soared together over the sick woman's disintegrating personality, pouncing on a complex here, a neurosis there, handing them back and forth to each other like jewels, with little cries of admiration.

"Of course, looking back, I can see that she always had these incipient hypochondriac tendencies . . ."

"She can't *help* it, of course, it's no use *blaming* her . . ."

"Lying in bed all day—it's no wonder her back hurts her."

"And it's not as if the doctor wasn't giving her plenty of pain killers . . ."

"You know, I've sometimes wondered if that pain of hers is really as bad as she fancies it is? I once read an article which said that jealousy, especially sexual jealousy . . ."

"And all that throwing up in the night—unconscious demand for attention . . ."

"Because she can't bear her husband to escape from her, even into sleep . . ."

The coffee in the two cups cooled in front of them as they talked. They needed no stimulant, for the thought of Eleanor, ugly and repellent on her bed of sickness, filled them with such a sense of their own health that it was like wine; it was like immortality itself.

But all too soon it was over. At eleven o'clock William must be home again, his weekly respite at an end. And only then did they look away from each other, a sort of shyness rising between them.

"If only—" began William, and stopped; and at the same time Coral murmured, "How long—" and checked herself. They moved out of the discotheque in silence, for they could not trust themselves to say another word.

When William got home he found that Eleanor had been sick again. As happened more and more frequently now, she had failed to get her head properly over the enamel bowl at her bedside; and as William, teeth clenched in a ghastly smile, set himself to his disgusting task, it suddenly flashed through his mind: This could be the last time; I don't *have* to go on like this.

And that night, as he tipped the allotted two sleeping pills into his wife's bony outstretched palm, the bottle shook and shuddered in his hand, and he felt the sweat springing out on his forehead, so that he had to turn his face away.

The impulse subsided almost as suddenly as it had assailed him; but it had left its mark, and during the ensuing week it would not leave him alone.

It would be so easy! Several times, as the days went by, he looked at the bottle as it stood on the bathroom shelf and had fantasies of mashing the pills and stirring the powder, all of it, into his wife's nighttime cup of gruel. He had visions of rushing into the discotheque next Tuesday, crying, "She's dead! She's dead!" and flinging himself into Coral's arms, and both of them sobbing for joy.

But he knew, really, that it was only a vision. One night he tipped a whole lot of the pills into the palm of his hand, handled them, and knew, for certain, that he would not dare. Why, the very feel of them on his bare skin set his heart pounding, and dizziness so blurred his vision that he could scarcely get the pills back into the bottle. Two— three—several of them went pitter-patter across the floor, and as he bent to retrieve them he felt the breath choking in his lungs, and his heart thudded as if it would burst through his ribs.

No, he, William, was not the sort of which murderers are made. He was the sort who would suffer, who would let Coral suffer. The weeks, the months, the years would go by, their love would wither, and still Eleanor would live on . . .

"William! William!"

The weak yet urgent voice twanged against his nerves, and he gave a guilty start.

"William, where are my pills?" the voice demanded, peevish and despairing. "Why are you being so long?"

Hastily, hands still trembling, he stuffed the last few pills back into the bottle.

"Coming, dear, coming," he called, and hurried into his wife's room. He looked into the gray sunken face in which no spark of beauty or gaiety was left; he looked at the sticklike arms that once, in their bloom, had held him close.

"If only I had the courage!" he thought.

But he reckoned without Eleanor's courage. The next morning, the Tuesday morning, the bottle of pills was empty, and Eleanor was dead. Dead on a Tuesday, dead on his glorious day. Had she known? And had she, knowing, chosen this day on which to release him?

He did not call the doctor, or indeed call anyone.

"Coral!" he kept repeating to himself. "When I see Coral . . ." And he sat all day in the silent house, waiting for the relief and the joy to wash over him, waiting for the moment when he would rush through the crowded discotheque crying, just as he had in his dreams, "She's dead! She's dead!"

The discotheque was more crowded and noisier than ever, and at first Coral did not hear what he was saying.

"She's *what?*" she asked as he leaned forward to repeat the news.

"She's—she's—" He stopped, and he knew in that instant that he could never tell her.

For where now would be that sense of united well-being, that glorious sense of their joint health in contrast to Eleanor's sickness? What would they talk about, he and Coral, now that Eleanor's symptoms, her complaints, and her unreasonableness were gone?

Where would be Coral's marvelous sympathy and understanding now that Eleanor had escaped them forever, had moved on into a realm where the barbed insights of pop psychology could not follow her? What *was* Coral, anyway, now that she was no longer a bulwark against his dying wife?

William stared across the table at the empty-faced little blonde, who was waiting so impatiently for him to speak.

"She's—she's worse."

"Oh, my poor Willy! She kept you up again last night, did she? Oh, I can see she did, you poor darling, you look so tired! But you shouldn't give in to it, Willy, you really shouldn't. After all, *we* know, don't we, that she's not really in pain. It's only her unconscious aggression and jealousy . . ."

It was all right! It was the old Coral again, just as she had always been! Nothing had been changed, nothing spoiled. Their Tuesday conversations could go on exactly as before.

But for how long? For how long can you keep your dead wife propped against the pillows, never calling a doctor, never letting the neighbors in? He, William, too much of a coward to be a murderer, was going to be transformed, as the days went by, into a creature far, far worse than a murderer. A monster, a ghoul—the horror of it would blazon across the front page of every Sunday paper—and all because he didn't dare do *anything*.

He wondered, dreamily whether any others of the ghouls and monsters of the world had attained their awful status in this way? By just doing nothing.

$\mathcal{B}$abysitter

DION HENDERSON

*T*he house sighed audibly and began to settle into deepening quiet. In the Tennessee stone fireplace, the white birch logs glowed cosily, and at one side the cat slept on the leather top of the drum table, legs and tail distributed casually among the figurines of Suzay's costume doll period. That is one of the last periods about which a father can be entirely carefree, Andrew Davidson thought wryly. It would be nice if he knew it at the time. After the costume dolls came the exotic boy singers, not dangerous perhaps but very noisy, and then the yearning after glamor, not so noisy but very trying, and after that the creative talent, dramatics, every room a proscenium stage, every parental admonition a cue, and this period was both noisy and trying. After that—Andrew Davidson sank gratefully into his chair. The house was warm and fully quiet except for the murmur of the FM and the soft sound of the presence of the fire, and he picked up the book he looked forward to reading.

The telephone rang.

The ringing was excessively shrill; probably his wife had turned up the bell while she was dressing to go out for bridge and had forgotten to turn it down. The cat's tail twitched perilously among the dolls. Andrew Davidson rose hastily, wanting to answer the phone before it rang again, rousing the house, and in his haste tipped over the ashtray to make a mess on the rug. The telephone rang again, shatteringly, before he could reach it. When he did, he spoke with unreasonable gruffness.

"Well, my goodness, Father," Suzay's voice said in his ear. "You sound so *cross*." She was babysitting for friends.

"Sorry," Andrew Davidson said, at least as gruffly as before. "I just tipped over the ashtray. Answering the phone."

"You poor dear," Suzay said brightly, "I'm *so* sorry but would you be a *lamb* and see whether I left my math book on the counter? There's just a *murderous* quiz coming up and I'm simply *stalled* without it."

"Just a minute," Andrew Davidson sighed, part of his mind occupied with speculation that a junior high school girl's ability to talk in italics probably rivaled the five inflections of Mandarin. He started walking to the kitchen, then paused scowling and returned to the telephone.

"You took your math book with you," he told his daughter. "I remember seeing it on the pile of assorted supplies you need to tide you over on a three hour safari."

Suzay said brightly, "Father, are you *sure?*"

"I'm positive," Andrew Davidson said. "You just haven't worked your way far enough down in the pile yet. It probably," he said acidly, "got shuffled in among the movie scripts."

"Well, cha *cha*," Suzay said. "Here it is after *all.*"

Then she did not say anything. The silence stretched out and Andrew Davidson felt a twinge of uneasiness. There was more to this call than the book query. He said quickly, "Suzay, is everything all right?"

"Why of *course,*" Suzay said, still brightly. Then she paused and said, "It's just that I have a silly feeling—"

"Silly feeling about what?"

There was no doubt about his uneasiness now. Andrew Davidson said, "Come on now, what is it?"

"Just noises," Suzay said carelessly. "I keep thinking I hear noises. At the back door. But when I go to see, no one is in sight."

"Well," Andrew Davidson said, and hesitated. More dramatics, of course. *Alfred Hitchcock Presents.* He said, "Tell me, what television thriller are you watching?"

There was a small pause, then Suzay said distantly, "Please forget that I mentioned it, Father."

"None of that," Andrew Davidson said, the uneasiness coming back despite the saving thought of melodrama. "If there's really anything out of line, I want to know about it. It wouldn't take me long to get over there."

"I would *much* prefer," Suzay remained frosty, "that you simply forget the whole thing. I'll *try* to cope with my *own* problems."

"All right," Andrew Davidson said. "That's a good Bergman heroine."

But he stood for a few moments, his hand on the phone and his lips pursed. The uneasiness was ridiculous. He knew his daughter. He was sure that he knew his own daughter very well. But still—

It took a few moments to organize his thoughts. First of all, is she at Al and Sally's tonight, or Stephenses'? No, definitely at Al's. He remembered, on the train Monday Al had asked whether Suzay would be busy Friday night. And he'd told Al to have Sally call Suzay herself. Suzay kept her own appointment book. He'd learned his lesson on that, shortly after Suzay turned thirteen and became a full-fledged babysitter. He'd accepted an assignment for her from Mrs. Parsons and when he told her, Suzay looked at him with tragic eyes. Father, how *could* you? They don't have a record player. . . . That dated the recollection, he thought parenthetically. The phase of the long-haired musicians.

But tonight it was definitely Al's house. In fact, he remembered hearing his wife call out when the car came for Suzay. Hi, Sally. That was what he remembered. Al and Sally's. Sure. Andrew Davidson reached for the small subdivision directory. He didn't know exactly where they lived. West, he thought. North, too. It couldn't be far. But it wouldn't hurt to see how far. Just in case. He picked up the directory and opened it and then sat there very quietly, feeling the color fade out of his face, feeling the draining away of something inside him, and the return of the first feeling.

It was preposterous, utterly preposterous. He'd been riding the train with Al a couple of years, sitting with the others in the smoker. Chipping in for the martinis on the last nights before a holiday. Al always brought the olives, anchovy olives, from a delicatessen in his building. Joe Kenneman had the bartender at the Press Club mix the martinis in a bottle and Al brought the olives and Pete Johnson picked up the cheese from the Exchange. But he didn't know Al's last name. It was utterly preposterous, but he didn't know Al's last name.

Andrew Davidson held the directory very still in his hand, knowing that his face had gone pale and knowing that the feeling in his stomach was not just uneasiness but the beginning of panic. He put the directory back on the stand and picked up the telephone and dialed a number decisively. Bob Appleby, in the next block. He rode the same train. He'd know. It was just a trick of the mind, anyway. Jarred by something a little out of the ordinary. Too soft, Andrew Davidson thought grimly. Gone flabby with routine crises. When Bob Appleby answered the phone, Andrew Davidson said firmly, "Bob, you know Al What's-his-name, on the train?"

"Al. Nice looking guy but he wears tweed suits."

"That's the one. He brings those olives."

"What's his last name?"

There was a pause. Andrew Davidson said more urgently, "I need to get hold of him and I can't for the life of me thin—"

"Isn't that funny?" Bob Appleby said. "I can't either. Wife's name is Sally. She's cute."

"I know," Andrew Davidson said impatiently. "That doesn't help, though. You know any of their friends?"

"Beats me," Bob Appleby said. "Wait a minute. We were at a party where they were once. Somebody said that Jim Connolly's wife was a sorority sister of Sally's." He gurgled at a private amusement. "You could try Jane Connolly."

"Oh, Lord."

"You might have to go over and have a drink before Jane will tell you, but she'll know."

"I know Jane," Andrew Davidson said.

The Connollys were in the subdivision directory. He dialed the number, hoping Jim would answer. But a throaty feminine voice said on a rising inflection, "Hel-lo?"

"Hi, Jane," Andrew Davidson said quickly. "My daughter is babysitting for Al and Sally tonight and I wanted to call her. What's their last name?"

"Oh," the throaty voice said throatily. "Andy. How nice of you. But I don't know exactly where they live now. They were building a new house the last I heard. West, I think. Or north."

She laughed throatily. "Sally's mother-in-law must have loosened up on the purse strings."

"Thanks," Andrew Davidson said. "But if I could just call her."

"That's right, dear. You asked me their name, not their address."

"Jane—"

"Of course. It's Smith, that's why you couldn't think of it. Are you sure you wouldn't like to stop over for a drink?"

"No," Andrew Davidson said. "But thanks anyway, Jane. Thanks."

He hung up the telephone and let his hand rest for a moment. He was sweating.

All right, he thought. We're all right now. Relax. Al Smith. He opened the subdivision directory. There were several Smiths. Two of them had "A" initials. One was Alfred and one was A.W. He called the Alfred Smith residence and a maid answered the phone. He called A.W. Smith, and the buzzer sounded interminably in his ear. No one answered, and the panic rose strongly in him again. He held the telephone against his ear with his shoulder and rechecked the listing and saw what he had not seen before. A.W. Smith's home was just through the block from him and A.W. Smith was sixty years old and they had met on the street several times and that definitely was not where Suzay was sitting. The panic subsided and Andrew Davidson smiled wryly. Soft, soft, he thought. You get out of practice for emergencies.

He dialed information and asked for Al Smith's telephone number.

The operator's remote, metallic voice said, "What is the address please?"

"I don't know."

The remote metallic voice shook a little. The operator said, "Are you kidding, mister? There are seven pages of Smiths in the book. . . ."

"Never mind," Andrew Davidson said. "I have a new directory."

That must be it, of course. The subdivision directory was a two-year-old Woman's Club project, and Al and Sally had been building a new house. He opened the metropolitan directory and looked at the seven pages of Smiths. There were two pages of Alberts and Alfreds and A.B. and A.C. and A.D. and A. Albert and A. Bruce and . . .

Andrew Davidson felt his eyes going out of focus. He was sweating again.

The telephone rang, shatteringly loud still, and he jumped and dropped the metropolitan directory on the floor. Then he seized the phone and said, "Hello."

"My goodness, Daddy," Suzay's voice said. "You don't have to shout."

He was immensely relieved. Then, as though hearing an echo, he realized that she'd called him Daddy instead of Father and that meant something. She was pretty cool about most things but that meant something. It was more than she could fabricate.

"Suzay," he said, "is everything all right?"

"I'm not sure, Daddy," her voice still was cool but he was positive now that she was frightened. "I think someone tried the back door a little while ago."

"Is it locked? You know what I've always told you."

"Yes, Daddy. Mr. Smith told me the same thing. The doors are all locked and no one can get in. But would you mind terribly, Daddy?"

"Sure," Andrew Davidson said. "I'll come over. Can you tell me how to get there?"

There was another pause. He was beginning to have a conditioned reflex about pauses. His stomach quivered.

"I don't know exactly," Suzay said. "It's not far, though. It only took ten minutes or so. It's a short street and there aren't very many houses. It's a lovely new house."

"But you don't know the address?"

"I'm sorry, Daddy. I didn't pay any attention."

"All right," Andrew Davidson said calmly. "But the telephone number is on the instrument right there in front of you. Just give it to me."

He wrote it down.

"All right, now, Suzay. Don't push the panic button. It may take a little while, but I'll find it."

"Daddy," Suzay's voice was a little thin. "There's a house down the block with lights on. Do you think it would be all right—"

"No," Andrew Davidson said. "Keep the doors locked and stay where you are."

He recovered the metropolitan directory and started over with the Smiths, checking the telephone number against the listings. He went through the two pages of "A" Smiths and it was not there. He shook his head and went back to the start, putting his finger very carefully on each listing, pressing so firmly on the cheap paper that he smeared the ink. The sweat trickled down his forehead into his eyes and stung, and he knew suddenly that he was sweating.

He found the telephone number on the third page. Al Smith's name was Elwood. Andrew Davidson kept his finger on the place and the relief flooded over him and he laughed aloud. There was the address: 900 Shady Lane. He wrote it down on the memo pad beneath the telephone number, then exchanged the metropolitan directory for the small one. He took the street map out of the pocket at the back, unfolded it, and ran down the index for the cross references. He did it twice. There was no Shady Lane.

Andrew Davidson took out his handkerchief and wiped his hands carefully, then his forehead and face. He lighted a cigarette. Well. Of course. The next subdivision west. Or perhaps north. Ten minutes? It couldn't be more than a couple of miles. There'd be maps down at the village. Of course. Meanwhile—

He called Information. Another remote metallic voice answered.

"I need to talk to someone who lives in the 900 block of Shady Lane," Andrew Davidson said firmly.

"What is the name, please?"

"It doesn't matter," he said. "Anyone who lives near the Elwood Smith residence at 900 Shady Lane."

The remote metallic voice said, "I can give you the number for the Elwood Smith residence."

"I already have that," Andrew Davidson said, "Thank you. I need someone else in the same block."

"I'm sorry," the voice said remotely, "I cannot give you that information."

"Look," Andrew Davidson said. "You've a street directory of telephone numbers right there beside you. Just give me the number of anyone who lives in that block. My daughter's babysitting in that house and I need to get hold of someone who lives nearby and ask them to go over there and give her a little help."

"I'm sorry," the metallic voice said even more remotely, "you will have to call the business office in the morning."

Andrew Davidson sat for a moment looking at the telephone. The cigarette burned his fingers and he dropped it with a flurry of ashes, picked it up hastily, and scrubbed the ashes into the carpet with his foot in one practiced motion. He was glad his wife was playing bridge. The situation was bad enough without having a hysterical woman to complicate matters. This way he could concentrate and at least try in an orderly way to straighten things out. He wiped his hands again. It was time now to call the police, he had enough information now so that they could help him. The village police force was not large but it was willing. That was one thing about the suburbs, you got exceptional service. He called the police number that was printed in black on the little sticker the Boy Scouts brought around to put on the telephones for emergency use. The volunteer fire department number was printed on the sticker too, in red.

Lieutenant Klecka answered the police phone. The village had a chief and a lieutenant and two patrolmen. The chief worked days and the lieutenant worked nights and each of them had a staff of one patrolman to drive the village's only squad car. It took quite a while to explain the situation to Lieutenant Klecka. He wrote it down at some length as Andrew Davidson explained.

"Okay, Mr. Davidson," he said. "I never heard of Shady Lane but I'll look it up and have Olson swing by there when he checks in on the radio. Nothing to it."

"Thanks," Andrew Davidson said, a little shaky with relief and gratitude. "Thanks an awful lot, lieutenant."

"Don't worry about a thing."

Andrew Davidson walked out to the kitchen, feeling the coolness of motion on his brow. Suddenly he was hungry. He opened the refrigerator inquisitively.

Back in the living room, the telephone shrilled; he still hadn't turned down the bell. It rang twice more before he could reach it.

Lieutenant Klecka said apologetically, "Gee, Mr. Davidson, we're having a little trouble. There isn't any Shady Lane in the village."

"I know."

"I went over the maps. There isn't anything like that."

"I know," Andrew Davidson felt the sweat start again. "Did you try some of the other subdivisions?"

"Yes, sir," Lieutenant Klecka said heartily. "We've got a collection of maps here, everything from Spring Valley clear out to Wedgewood. And you know, there isn't a Shady Lane in any of them?"

"Oh, Lord," Andrew Davidson said prayerfully. "I suppose it's a new one."

"Now that's a possibility, Mr. Davidson. There is quite a new development over there the other side of Briarcroft and it might be in there, all right."

"How can we find out?"

"I don't know," Lieutenant Klecka said sadly. "We ain't got any map of that yet."

Andrew Davidson did not say anything. There was a long pause on his end of the line, and it made the officer nervous.

"Tell you what, Mr. Davidson. As soon as I can get ahold of Olson in the prowl car, I'll come up and see you. Maybe we can figure something out."

"Yes," Andrew Davidson said in a strange voice. "Thank you."

When the lieutenant hung up, Andrew Davidson dialed Elwood Smith's number. Suzay's voice answered immediately.

"Hello, honey."

"Hello, Daddy."

"Are you all right?"

"Yes," she said. Then she said in a small voice, "Daddy, can't you find me?"

Something was changing in Andrew Davidson. It had changed his voice and now it was changing him otherwise.

"Yes, honey," he said. "I can find you. Just keep on being all right for a little while, and I'll find you."

There was a time to be orderly and reasonable, and then there was a time when being orderly and reasonable was not worth anything to you any more. Andrew Davidson went to the closet and got his coat. He would go out and drive up and would look at the signposts on the ungraded corners of the raw new streets, and he would find her. It might take all night, but he would find her. He put on his coat and hat and as he passed the stairs, one of his sleeping children upstairs coughed. He stopped, the grip of responsibility icy on him. But now there was a greater responsibility. The sleeping children would be all right. Timmy was five, Jean was eight. He would wake Jeannie and explain to her that he was going out. No, she would be frightened. It would be better to let her sleep. The spectres of disaster rose around him.

Andrew Davidson shook his head to steady himself. He saw terribly in his mind a vision of the house in flames, and the children sleeping. Then he shook his head again, and drew on his gloves. Soft or not, the time comes for hard decisions.

Not listening now for further sounds of the little ones, he went through the dining room and the kitchen and had his hand on the kitchen door when he remembered.

The car wasn't home. His wife had taken it to the bridge party, wherever it was. Wherever it was. He stood with his gloved hand on the doorknob. He didn't know where it was. He didn't know where she had gone. He didn't even know with whom she played bridge. Em and Jackie and Kate, sure. No more than that. He didn't know any of them.

"Lord," Andrew Davidson asked prayerfully aloud, "doesn't anyone know anyone else any more?"

But of course, he knew people. He knew a great many people. There were the Spencers, across the street. He could borrow their car. He went to the front of the house and looked across the street. The Spencer house was dark. Then there were the Morgans, next door. Certainly he could borrow their car. He was on his way to the dining room when he remembered the Morgans were on vacation. Pausing, he saw the lights in Ericksons' house. But the Ericksons had moved west in the spring. He didn't know the new people. He had never heard their name, and likely they had not heard his.

In the living room, the telephone jangled wildly. Andrew Davidson answered it, hardly recognizing his own voice.

"Daddy," Suzay said. "I just want you to know that I wasn't imagining things."

"I didn't think you were, honey."

"There were two men here." He felt the panic break in him.

"Not in the house—"

"No. But they rang the back doorbell and when I told them I wouldn't let them in they tried to push the door open."

"Honey—"

"No, listen, Daddy." Her voice was very steady. "I turned the porch light off and on and they didn't like it and after a while they ran off the porch."

"They may come back."

That hadn't been the right thing to say, he realized dumbly. But it did not frighten Suzay.

"I know. And I wanted to tell you what they looked like. In case you need to know later."

"Honey—" the panic was giving way to nausea.

"Listen, Daddy," Suzay said, almost brusquely. "One was older, with pale eyes and not very good teeth. The other one was younger, and dark, and he had kind of a mustache—"

Andrew Davidson sat fighting the sick feeling and his daughter's voice relentlessly described the two men. When she finished, she said, "I love you, Daddy. Goodbye."

Andrew Davidson felt a sob rise in his throat.

The telephone rang, deafeningly, close to him. He picked it up dully.

"Mr. Davidson," Lieutenant Klecka said cheerfully, "I just got hold of Olson. He was at the scene of a little fender bender down on the parkway, but he's coming in now. I'll be up in a few minutes and we'll see if we can locate your daughter."

"That may not be soon enough," Andrew Davidson said dully. He told Lieutenant Klecka about the descriptions.

"She must be a fine girl," Lieutenant Klecka said warmly. "I tell you what, I'll get on the radio and see if one of the county cars is in the neighborhood. The sheriff's office must have a section map that will show even the new streets."

"All right," Andrew Davidson said.

"Buck up," Lieutenant Klecka said. "You'll hear from us."

Andrew Davidson continued to sit by the telephone. It rang again. It did not even startle him any more. A man who obviously was calling from a list of names asked to speak to Mr. Davidson. He wanted to make an appointment to call. He wanted to talk about selling Mr. Davidson some aluminum siding.

"Please," Andrew Davidson said. "Not now."

"It will only take a few minutes of your time, Mr. Davidson. And the investment will pay off the rest of your life."

"I know," Andrew Davidson wondered at his own calm. Not calm. Dazed, maybe.

He said, "But I have a brick house."

The salesman subsided. Andrew Davidson did not remember hanging up the phone. He wanted to call Suzay back and talk to her. He wanted to keep her safe and unhurt by talking to her. He wanted to think of something that would keep her safe and unhurt in a single dramatic stroke. He thought suddenly of telling her to turn on all the lights in the house for a signal; to set fire to the roof. Anything. But he couldn't. He couldn't think of anything. He could only think in flickering pictures, like a faulty projector, of Suzay at other times, seeing her clearly but fleetingly in times past, in the blue Sachs dress on her way to her first day in school; the look on her face on the birthday when she had gotten the kitten; the strange new dignity the night of her first date. That wasn't so long ago.

A car came hastily up the street and tires squealed as it swung into his driveway. He caught a glimpse of a long whip aerial and the light mounted above the windshield. He got up hastily and went to the door and a deputy sheriff wearing sergeant's stripes on his uniform came into the house with a burst of orderly strength and direction.

"My name is Torrio," he said heartily. "Now let's get this little girl out of trouble. Where is she?"

Andrew Davidson explained. It was a rather difficult thing to explain to a man who did not live in the suburbs. Sergeant Torrio himself lived in the central city, and given a name and a brief description he could have found any of five million people within its confines inside twenty minutes. It was increasingly difficult for Andrew Davidson to explain things because when he tried to explain he found that he didn't really understand how it had happened himself. In fact, when he came to a lame conclusion, Sergeant Torrio was watching him with a veiled expression and considerably less heartiness.

But then another car came stealthily and swiftly up the street and squealed into the driveway, and Lieutenant Klecka came into the house. The two officers went out in the kitchen and spoke together in undertones. Andrew Davidson sat dumbly by the telephone. He was still wearing his coat, his hat, and his gloves. Presently the officers returned to the room.

Sergeant Torrio said to Lieutenant Klecka, "You get on the telephone and get those numbers. I'll get on the radio and have the dispatcher track it down on a map."

The officers moved with casual and practiced speed. Andrew Davidson sat down on the davenport. It did not take Lieutenant Klecka any time at all to get a telephone company supervisor and explain who he was and what he wanted, and to write down the telephone numbers of the other people who lived on Shady Lane.

"There are only two of them, Mr. Davidson," Lieutenant Klecka said. "It must be a short street."

Sergeant Torrio called something indistinguishable from outside and Lieutenant Klecka went out to the county squad car. Andrew Davidson felt something in him stir again at the activity; not hope, exactly, but a stubborn spark. He got up and looked at the telephone numbers Lieutenant Klecka had written down. At least he could do something. He dialed the first number. A child's voice answered.

"Let me speak to your father," Andrew Davidson said briefly.

"My father is down in the basement," the child's voice said. "He doesn't let me answer the telephone."

"Please call him," Andrew Davidson said.

"My mother doesn't let me answer the phone, either."

"Oh, Lord," Andrew Davidson said. "Call him, please."

"My mother's in the bathroom," the voice explained. The child said inflexibly, "My mother's taking a bath."

Andrew Davidson hung up the phone gently. Then he lifted it and dialed another number. The buzzer sounded a long while. His heart was sinking again when someone picked up the phone.

A man's voice said angrily, "Hello?"

"Thank heavens," Andrew Davidson said. "I'm glad you answered. I was afraid you wouldn't." He realized he was babbling and stopped himself. He started over, saying reasonably, "It's very important that I know where you live. How to get there, that is, You see—"

"Wise guy," the man's voice said angrily.

Andrew Davidson sat holding the phone in his hand after the click of the cutoff, staring at it unbelievingly. Then he reached over frantically, recovered the dial tone, and dialed the number again. It rang interminably. Finally someone picked up the phone and as Andrew Davidson tried desperately to talk, the unknown respondent put the instrument down angrily on a hard surface and walked away from it.

Out in the driveway, the idling engine of the county prowl car roared suddenly. The front door opened and Lieutenant Klecka shouted in, "We've got the place located, Mr. Davidson, and we're on our way."

He shut the door, then opened it to shout, "You just relax. Everything will be all right."

Andrew Davidson did not answer. If they're in time, he thought. If only they're in time.

He turned suddenly and dialed the original number. Answer, Suzay, he thought. Please answer, honey. Please be all right. Please.

There was no answer.

He could not think of what might be happening. He could not think at all. After a while he replaced the telephone in its cradle. He got up and walked across the living room, walking like an old man. He took off his gloves and straightened the fingers carefully and put them on the shelf in the closet. Then he put his hat on top of the gloves. Then he took off his coat and put it on a hanger and hung it on the rod in the closet. After that he walked into the dining room, walking very slowly and carefully, and took a decanter from the door in the buffet and poured from it into a glass. He was scarcely aware that a car had turned into the driveway. It did not move with the quiet urgency of a patrol car, and it went on into the garage. His wife was home. He would have to tell her something. He sat down at the dining room table, trying to think of what he would tell her, and how.

The kitchen door opened and his wife said, "Hi" breezily, the way she always did coming home, and there was the sound of heels on the kitchen floor. Heels. The sound of heels.

Andrew Davidson looked up. His wife was standing in the archway, her arms akimbo, frowning at the decanter and the glass in front of him but not saying anything because Suzay was standing right behind her. Suzay. *Suzay.*

His wife said, still breezily but with a warning undertone that hinted of something that might be brought up later about the decanter, "You look as though you had a quiet evening, dear."

"Suzay," Andrew Davidson said in a strangled voice. "Where did you find her?"

"At Smiths', of course," his wife looked at him with a measuring kind of a look. "I drove past Sally's to see how she was getting along and Sally and Al were just getting home, so I picked her up and brought her along."

Andrew Davidson started to stand up, he started to say something in an excess of relief and gratitude and love, and then he looked past his wife at his daughter, at his daughter's looking at him now as she had never looked at him before, and he realized that she was not going to say anything. Suzay was not going to say anything at all about the frantic hours. He had a frightening premonition that if he told his wife about it, Suzay would deny the whole thing.

Andrew Davidson sat down again heavily.

"Poor Father," Suzay said gently. "He looks as though he had a perfectly *frustrating* evening."

"Yes," he said. "I did. In a way."

There was nothing else he could say. Nothing he could say would help anyway. Somehow Suzay was beyond him now. He did not know whether she truly had been faced with the ultimate in adult danger and survived it alone, and surviving now could look at him with coolness and with pity because he had pitifully failed her; or whether she was only a shallow, idle child capable of unexpected viciousness in her boredom and her fantasy. He saw her through a faint mist, looking at him with the bland secret eyes of knowing, looking at him with a woman's impenetrable eyes. No, now he would never know.

In the living room the telephone rang again. The cat, which had been sleeping uninterruptedly on the drum table, leaped in alarm now, at last, and a figurine fell to the carpet and broke softly. His wife talked briefly on the phone and came back.

"Bob Appleby said to tell you that he remembered where Elwood Jones lives, if you still want to know," she said. "Do you know any Elwood Jones?"

"No," Andrew Davidson said thickly. "But then, sometimes, it seems as though I don't know a great many things."

He got up from the table and put on his coat. He had to take a walk. He had to go out and head off the prowl cars when they returned. He would have to explain to them that there had been some kind of ridiculous mistake. It would be very embarrassing, but the policemen would understand. They probably were used to people like him, people who were a little confused. They would not ask him what kind of a mistake.

When This Man Dies

LAWRENCE BLOCK

*T*he night before the first letter came, he had Speckled Band in the feature at Saratoga. The horse went off at nine-to-two from the number one pole and Edgar Kraft had two hundred dollars on him, half to win and half to place. Speckled Band went to the front and stayed there. The odds-on favorite, a four-year-old named Sheila's Kid, challenged around the clubhouse turn and got hung up on the outside. Kraft was counting his money. In the stretch, Speckled Band broke stride, galloped home madly, was summarily disqualified, and placed fourth. Kraft tore up his tickets and went home.

So he was in no mood for jokes that morning. He opened five of the six letters that came in the morning mail, and all five were bills, none of which he had any prospect of paying in the immediate future. He put them in a drawer in his desk. There were already several bills in that drawer. He opened the final letter and was at first relieved to discover that it was not a bill, not a notice of payment due, not a threat to repossess car or furniture. It was, instead, a very simple message typed in the center of a large sheet of plain typing paper.

First a name:

> *Mr. Joseph H. Neimann*

And, below that:

> *When this man dies*
> *You will receive*
> *Five hundred dollars.*

He was in no mood for jokes. Trotters that lead all the way, and then break in the stretch, do not contribute to a man's sense of humor.

He looked at the sheet of paper, turned it over to see if there was anything further on its reverse, turned it over again to read the message once more, picked up the envelope, saw nothing on it but his own name and a local postmark, said something unprintable about some idiots and their idea of a joke, and tore everything up and threw it away, message and envelope and all.

In the course of the next week he thought about the letter once, maybe twice. No more than that. He had problems of his own. He had never heard of anyone named Joseph H. Neimann and entertained no hopes of receiving five hundred dollars in the event of the man's death. He did not mention the cryptic message to his wife. When the man from Superior Finance called to ask him if he had any hopes of meeting his note on time, he did not say anything about the legacy that Mr. Neimann meant to leave him.

He went on doing his work from one day to the next, working with the quiet desperation of a man who knows his income, while better than nothing, will never quite get around to equalling his expenditures. He went to the track twice, won thirty dollars one night, lost twenty-three the next. He came quite close to forgetting entirely about Mr. Joseph H. Neimann and the mysterious correspondent.

Then the second letter came. He opened it mechanically, unfolded a large sheet of plain white paper. Ten fresh fifty dollar bills fluttered down upon the top of his desk. In the center of the sheet of paper someone had typed:

Thank You

Edgar Kraft did not make the connection immediately. He tried to think what he might have done that would merit anyone's thanks, not to mention anyone's five hundred dollars. It took him a moment, and then he recalled that other letter and rushed out of his office and down the street to a drugstore. He bought a morning paper, turned to the obituaries. Joseph Henry Neimann, 67, of 413 Park Place, he died the previous afternoon in County Hospital after an illness of several months' duration. He left a widow, three children, and four grandchildren. Funeral services would be private, flowers were please to be omitted.

He put three hundred dollars in his checking account and two hundred dollars in his wallet. He made his payment on the car, paid his rent, cleared up a handful of small bills. The mess in his desk drawer was substantially less baleful, although by no means completely cleared up. He still owed money, but he owed less now than before the timely death of Joseph Henry Neimann. The man from Superior Finance had been appeased by a partial payment; he would stop making a nuisance of himself, at least for the time being.

That night, Kraft took his wife to the track. He even let her make a couple impossible hunch bets. He lost forty dollars and it hardly bothered him at all.

When the next letter came he did not tear it up. He recognized the typing on the envelope, and he turned it over in his hands for a few moments before opening it, like a child with a wrapped present. He was somewhat more apprehensive than child with present, however; he couldn't help feeling that the mysterious benefactor would want something in return for his five hundred dollars.

He opened the letter. No demands, however. Just the usual sheet of plain paper, with another name typed in its center:

Mr. Raymond Andersen

And, below that:

When this man dies
You will receive
Seven hundred fifty dollars.

For the next few days he kept telling himself that he did not wish anything unpleasant for Mr. Raymond Andersen. He didn't know the man, he had never heard of him, and he was not the sort to wish death upon some total stranger. And yet—

Each morning he bought a paper and turned at once to the death notices, searching almost against his will for the name of Mr. Raymond Andersen, I don't wish him any harm, he would think each time. But seven hundred fifty dollars was a happy sum. If something were going to happen to Mr. Raymond Andersen, he might as well profit by it. It wasn't as though he was doing anything to cause Andersen's death. He was even unwilling to wish for it. But if something happened . . .

Something happened. Five days after the letter came, he found Andersen's obituary in the morning paper. Andersen was an old man, a very old man, and he died in his bed at a home for the aged after a long illness. His heart jumped when he read the notice with a combination of excitement and guilt. But what was there to feel guilty about? He hadn't done anything. And death, for a sick old man like Raymond Andersen, was more a cause for relief than grief, more a blessing than a tragedy.

But why would anyone want to pay him seven hundred fifty dollars? Nevertheless, someone did.

The letter came the following morning, after a wretched night during which Kraft tossed and turned and batted two possibilities back and forth—that the letter would come and that it would not. It did come, and it brought the promised seven hundred fifty dollars in fifties and hundreds. And the same message:

Thank You

For what? He had not the slightest idea. But he looked at the two-word message again before putting it carefully away.

You're welcome, he thought. *You're entirely welcome.*

For two weeks no letter came. He kept waiting for the mail, kept hoping for another windfall like the two that had come so far. There were times when he would sit at his desk for twenty or thirty minutes at a time, staring off into space and thinking about the letters and the money. He would have done better keeping his mind on his work, but this was not easy. His job brought him five thousand dollars a year, and for that sum he had to work forty to fifty hours a week. His anonymous pen pal had thus far brought him a quarter as much as he earned in a year, and he had done nothing at all for the money.

The seven fifty had helped, but he was still in hot water. On a sudden female whim his wife had had the living room recarpeted. The rent was due. There was another payment due on the car. He had one very good night at the track, but a few other visits took back his winnings and more.

And then the letter came, along with a circular inviting him to buy a dehumidifier for his basement and an appeal for funds from some dubious charity. He swept circular and appeal into his wastebasket and tore open the plain white envelope. The message was the usual sort:

Mr. Claude Pierce

And, below the name:

When this man dies
You will receive
One thousand dollars.

Kraft's hands were shaking slightly as he put the envelope and letter away in his desk. One thousand dollars—the price had gone up again, this time to a fairly staggering figure. Mr. Claude Pierce. Did he know anyone named Claude Pierce? He did not. Was Claude Pierce sick? Was he a lonely old man, dying somewhere of a terminal illness?

Kraft hoped so. He hated himself for the wish, but he could not smother it.

He hoped Claude Pierce was dying.

This time he did a little research. He thumbed through the phone book until he found a listing for a Claude Pierce on Honeydale Drive. He closed the book then and tried to put the whole business out of his mind, an enterprise foredoomed to failure. Finally he gave up, looked up the listing once more, looked at the man's name and thought this man was going to die. It was inevitable, wasn't it? They sent him some man's name in the mail, and then the man died, and then Edgar Kraft was paid. Obviously, Claude Pierce was a doomed man.

He called Pierce's number. A woman answered, and Kraft asked if Mr. Pierce was in.

"Mr. Pierce is in the hospital," the woman said. "Who's calling, please?"

"Thank you," Kraft said.

Of course, he thought. They, whoever they were, simply found people in hospitals who were about to die, and they paid money to Edgar Kraft when the inevitable occurred, and that was all. The why of it was impenetrable. But so few things made sense in Kraft's life that he did not want to question the whole affair too closely. Perhaps his unknown correspondent was like the lunatic on television who gave away a million dollars every week. If someone wanted to give Kraft money, Kraft wouldn't argue with him.

That afternoon he called the hospital. Claude Pierce had been admitted two days ago for major surgery, a nurse told Kraft. His condition was listed as *good*.

Well, he would have a relapse, Kraft thought. He was doomed—the letterwriter had ordained his death. He felt momentarily sorry for Claude Pierce, and then he turned his attention to the entries at Saratoga. There was a horse named Orange Pips which Kraft had been watching for some time. The horse had a good post now, and if he was ever going to win, this was the time.

Kraft went to the track. Orange Pips ran out of the money. In the morning Kraft failed to find Pierce's obituary. When he called the hospital, the nurse told him that Pierce was recovering very nicely.

Impossible, Kraft thought.

For three weeks Claude Pierce lay in his hospital bed, and for three weeks Edgar Kraft followed his condition with more interest than Pierce's doctor could have displayed. Once Pierce took a turn for the worse and slipped into a coma. The nurse's voice was grave over the phone, and Kraft bowed his head, resigned to the inevitable. A day later Pierce had rallied remarkably. The nurse sounded positively cheerful, and Kraft fought off a sudden wave of rage that threatened to overwhelm him.

From that point on, Pierce improved steadily. He was released, finally, a whole man again, and Kraft could not understand quite what had happened. Something had gone wrong. When Pierce died, he was to receive a thousand dollars. Pierce had been sick, Pierce had been close to death, and then, inexplicably, Pierce had been snatched from the very jaws of death, with a thousand dollars simultaneously snatched from Edgar Kraft.

He waited for another letter. No letter came.

With the rent two weeks overdue, with a payment on the car past due, with the man from Superior Finance calling him far too often, Kraft's mind began to work against him. *When this man dies*, the letter had said. There had been no strings attached, no time limit on Pierce's death. After all, Pierce could not live forever. No one did. And whenever Pierce did happen to draw his last breath, he would get that thousand dollars.

Suppose something happened to Pierce—

He thought it over against his own will. It would not be hard, he kept telling himself. No one knew that he had any interest whatsoever in Claude Pierce. If he picked his time well, if he did the dirty business and got it done with and hurried off into the night, no one would know. The police would never think of him in the same breath with Claude Pierce, if police were in the habit of thinking in breaths. He did not know Pierce, he had no obvious motive for killing Pierce, and—

He couldn't do it, he told himself. He simply could not do it. He was no killer. And something as senseless as this, something so thoroughly absurd, was unthinkable.

He would manage without the thousand dollars. Somehow, he would live without the money. True, he had already spent it a dozen times over in his mind. True, he had been counting and recounting it when

Pierce lay in a coma. But he would get along without it. What else could he do?

The next morning headlines shrieked Pierce's name at Edgar Kraft. The previous night someone had broken into the Pierce home on Honeydale Drive and had knifed Claude Pierce in his bed. The murderer had escaped unseen. No possible motive for the slaying of Pierce could be established. The police were baffled.

Kraft got slightly sick to his stomach as he read the story. His first reaction was a pure and simple onrush of unbearable guilt, as though he had been the man with the knife, as though he himself had broken in during the night to stab silently and flee promptly, mission accomplished. He could not shake this guilt away. He knew well enough that he had done nothing, that he had killed no one. But he had conceived of the act, he had willed that it be done, and he could not escape the feeling that he was a murderer, at heart if not in fact.

His blood money came on schedule. One thousand dollars, ten fresh hundreds this time. And the message. *Thank you.*

Don't thank me, he thought, holding the bills in his hand, holding them tenderly. Don't thank me!

> *Mr. Leon Dennison*
> *When this man dies*
> *You will receive*
> *Fifteen hundred dollars.*

Kraft did not keep the letter. He was breathing heavily when he read it, his heart pounding. He read it twice through, and then he took it and the envelope it had come in, and all the other letters and envelopes that he had so carefully saved, and he tore them all into little bits and flushed them down the toilet.

He had a headache. He took aspirin, but it did not help his headache at all. He sat at his desk and did no work until lunchtime. He went to the luncheonette around the corner and ate lunch without tasting his food. During the afternoon he found that, for the first time, he could not make head or tails out of the list of entries at Saratoga. He couldn't concentrate on a thing, and he left the office early and took a long walk.

Mr. Leon Dennison.

Dennison lived in an apartment on Cadbury Avenue. No one answered his phone. Dennison was an attorney, and he had an office

listing. When Kraft called it a secretary answered and told him that
Mr. Dennison was in conference. Would he care to leave his name?

When this man dies.

But Dennison would not die, he thought. Not in a hospital bed, at
any rate. Dennison was perfectly all right, he was at work, and the
person who had written all those letters knew very well that Dennison
was all right, that he was not sick.

Fifteen hundred dollars.

But how, he wondered. He did not own a gun and had not the
slightest idea how to get one. A knife? Someone had used a knife on
Claude Pierce, he remembered. And a knife would probably not be hard
to get his hands on. But a knife seemed somehow unnatural to him.

How, then? By automobile? He could do it that way, he could lie in
wait for Dennison and run him down in his car. It would not be difficult,
and it would probably be certain enough. Still, the police were supposed
to be able to find hit and run drivers fairly easily. There was something
about paint scrapings, or blood on your own bumper, or something.
He didn't know the details, but they always did seem to catch hit and
run drivers.

Forget it, he told himself. You are not a killer.

He didn't forget it. For two days he tried to think of other things
and failed miserably. He thought about Dennison, and he thought about
fifteen hundred dollars, and he thought about murder.

When this man dies—

One time he got up early in the morning and drove to Cadbury
Avenue. He watched Leon Dennison's apartment, and he saw Dennison
emerge, and when Dennison crossed the street toward his parked car
Kraft settled his own foot on the accelerator and ached to put the pedal
on the floor and send the car hurtling toward Leon Dennison. But he
didn't do it. He waited.

So clever. Suppose he were caught in the act? Nothing linked him
with the person who wrote him the letters. He hadn't even kept the
letters, but even if he had, they were untraceable.

Fifteen hundred dollars—

On a Thursday afternoon he called his wife and told her he was
going directly to Saratoga. She complained mechanically before bowing
to the inevitable. He drove to Cadbury Avenue and parked his car.
When the doorman slipped down to the corner for a cup of coffee,
Kraft ducked into the building and found Leon Dennison's apartment.

The door was locked, but he managed to spring the lock with the blade of a pen knife. He was sweating freely as he worked on the lock, expecting every moment someone to come up behind him and lay a hand on his shoulder. The lock gave, and he went inside and closed it after him.

But something happened the moment he entered the apartment. All the fear, all the anxiety, all of this suddenly left Edgar Kraft. He was mysteriously calm now. Everything was prearranged, he told himself. Joseph H. Neimann had been doomed, and Raymond Andersen had been doomed, and Claude Pierce had been doomed, and each of them had died. Now Leon Dennison was similarly doomed, and he too would die.

It seemed very simple. And Edgar Kraft himself was nothing but a part of this grand design, nothing but a cog in a gigantic machine. He would do his part without worrying about it. Everything could only go according to plan.

Everything did. He waited three hours for Leon Dennison to come home, waited in calm silence. When a key turned in the lock, he stepped swiftly and noiselessly to the side of the door, a fireplace andiron held high overhead. The door opened and Leon Dennison entered, quite alone.

The andiron descended.

Leon Dennison fell without a murmur. He collapsed, lay still. The andiron rose and fell twice more, just for insurance, and Leon Dennison never moved and never uttered a sound. Kraft had only to wipe off the andiron and a few other surfaces to eliminate any fingerprints he might have left behind. He left the building by the service entrance. No one saw him.

He waited all that night for the rush of guilt. He was surprised when it failed to come. But he had already been a murderer—by wishing for Andersen's death, by planning Pierce's murder. The simple translation of his impulses from thought to deed was no impetus for further guilt.

There was no letter the next day. The following morning the usual envelope was waiting for him. It was quite bulky; it was filled with fifteen hundred dollar bills.

The note was different. It said *Thank You,* of course. But beneath that there was another line:

How do you like your new job?

Going to Meet Terry

RICK HILLS

*I*t was August, it was Sunday morning, and it was hot. Nathan woke quickly, he had things to do. He had to get out of the house without waking anyone, and he had to go meet Terry.

Barefoot and bareback was how Nathan felt today, so he wore only the jeans his mother hated most. He crept down the carpeted stairway that led to the front door and to freedom, making sure to tiptoe on the outside of each stair. The less-traveled carpet pleased his bare feet. And Nathan knew that this was the only way to walk the steps without the old wood underneath creaking its usual creak and waking his parents. Sunday morning meant they'd sleep late which also meant there'd be no note for Nathan, no list of household chores he'd be expected to do before he could leave the house.

He made it through the heavy front door without a sound. The screen door's rusted spring groaned with reluctance as he opened it just wide enough to get through, but then it slipped from his grasp and slammed shut with a tattletale bang. Nathan stopped breathless for a second, straining his ears for any commotion inside the house. When he didn't hear anything, he turned and walked like an Indian across the wooden porch and leapt the three porch steps down to the grass. As he landed he thought to himself, "All right! I made it!"

Back in his parents' bedroom his mother stirred from her sleep and asked his father, "Did you hear something, dear?"

"Go back to sleep, his father answered. "It was just Nathan going out the front door."

*　　*　　*

Nathan's bare feet hit the front yard grass like flat stones skipping across smooth water. His nostrils filled with the smell of morning mist before the sun gets to it. The warm moist air was quite a change from the all-night coolness of the house and Nathan's skin goose-pimpled to get used to it. The feeling of getting away from something surrounded him as he kicked his way through the cool morning dew, yesterday's grass clippings clinging to his wet feet. The sidewalk was still cool in the elm shadows that covered every front yard on his block. Nathan looked back over his shoulder to watch his wet footprints gradually fade into dry as the cement soaked up each of his steps. "I'm the only one who knows where I am right now," Nathan thought to himself. The feeling of freedom that buzzed around his head found a home in his legs and he was off and running. It seemed the fastest he'd ever run, but it didn't seem to take any effort. Down the block he went, past Stimml's, past Johnson's, then Kennedy's, and finally he came to a stop in front of the big house on the corner, The-House-With-No-Men. There was a great-grandmother, a grandmother, a mother, and her daughter—but no men. The house was well-kept, spotless, and a little bit scary. Nathan glanced up the two steep terraces to the house and caught a glimpse of the old woman who constantly sat in her wheelchair, staring out across the broad front porch from behind a huge picture window. Nathan had heard from the older kids in the neighborhood that she couldn't walk, but Nathan had never even seen her move. She always sat the same way, in the same place, staring, staring all day long. But it was too nice a day and Nathan was feeling too good to waste his time thinking about the old woman. He crossed the street in front of The-House-With-No-Men.

Nathan walked on slowly, acting like he didn't know where he was going, but knowing all the time. The sidewalk stretched out in front of him a while and then was cut in two by some railroad tracks. Nathan didn't know where they came from, but he knew they ended up at Bodie's Lumberyard where his older brother worked Saturdays for all the pop he could drink and to shape up his muscles for high school football. The sidewalk picked up again on the other side of the tracks and it wasn't long before it turned into a concrete footbridge crossing over The Crick. Somewhere down below the footbridge was where he'd meet Terry. And if Terry wasn't there yet, he would be soon.

Nathan walked out onto the footbridge and looked down into the murky water below. This was the favorite place of the neighborhood, this was The Crick. Almost all its banks were steep, slippery mud, overgrown with patches of itchweed and stickerbushes. But here, the banks had been built from great chunks of stone block to keep them from caving in. On one of the blocks you could barely make out the number 1896, chiseled into it long ago but worn smooth over the years. Just below that, the cracks between the blocks made a natural ladder you could dig your bare toes into and climb down the wall to the sandbars and the water's edge. The stone walls made it feel like an open air room with a stream running through the middle. The water flowed in under a street bridge, over rocks and broken tiles, and gouged through ever-changing sandbars filled with half-buried tin cans and an old bicycle rim. Then it slipped quietly into a large washed-out pool with more tiles on the bottom. The tiles were flat and slick, nearly impossible to keep from slipping on with wet feet. But on the steeper sides of the banks, where they rose up out of the water, some of the tiles had broken off or worn away, leaving iron bars exposed. These were the only handholds across the tiles. The places where there were no handholds were the places you just couldn't go.

The cool crick air puffed up now and then, hitting Nathan in the face, bringing with it a damp, clinging smell of stagnant water and sewage. The stagnant water came from upstream, the sewage from a cement tunnel cut back like a cave into the sheer stone wall. The older kids said it ran under the street six or seven blocks up to the Municipal Hospital. There was always water running out of it and once Nathan had seen bits of blood-soaked cloth floating by—hospital bandages, he and Terry had decided—so all the younger kids took it for granted that the older kids knew what they were talking about. The smell was ripe, and it amazed Nathan how it never bothered the kids but always bothered the parents. The Crick was so much fun because it was strictly forbidden ("You're going to catch polio down there, you know that, don't you?" is what Nathan's father constantly told him), and it was the smell that always gave you away and usually got you grounded for a week. The smell was such a sure thing that if you really wanted a fight, all you had to do was splash somebody on purpose.

Nathan leaned out over the guard rail and stared at his reflection below. Then he watched a ball of white spit ease slowly from his lips. Finally it fell as he watched the spit and its reflection race towards each other, colliding with a splat on the surface of the water, sending rings

out breaking up his reflection. "Maybe that's why Terry isn't here yet,"
Nathan thought to himself. "Maybe Irv caught him yesterday and he's
grounded for a week." Nathan didn't like Terry's oldest brother Irv. Ever
since Terry's dad left, Irv had been acting like a big shot.

Nathan spit again but didn't wait for it to hit the water. "Well, either
he's coming or he's not," Nathan thought as he turned away from the
railing. "I can't wait for him all day."

Nathan sat on top of the stone wall where the crawl-way started and
dangled his legs over the edge, the dark mouth of the storm sewer
opening up and gently trickling its water out into the pool just below
him. The time didn't seem right to crawl down yet, so he picked up
some loose pebbles and killed time tossing them into the water, first
kerplunking them out in the middle of the pool and then eye-dropping
them like a bombardier straight down in the storm sewer stream. Nathan
heard something close and spun around quickly to see if it was Terry
sneaking up behind him. The Big Joke at The Crick was to pretend
like you were going to push your buddy off the wall, and sitting the
way he was, Nathan was an easy target for the fake push from behind.
But there was no sign of Terry. Nathan remembered how the fake
pushes sometimes scared you into laughing, sometimes scared you into
being mad. He searched for Terry again when he heard the noise again,
only to see a squirrel scratching his way up the bark of a gnarled oak
tree. Nathan laughed at himself for the false alarm and went back to
pebbling. Staring at the water made him daydream and as he listened
to the different gurgles and rushings of crick water, the sounds took
over his ears and seemed so loud inside his head that he was aware of
nothing else. Then he thought he heard something else from The Crick,
first very faint and very low, a far away moaning that built on itself,
getting louder and more painful, and then an all-out howl, filled with
hurt and despair, was in The Crick—and it was coming down and out
of the storm sewer! Nathan's breath quickened as the howl echoed and
died out of the opening and when it was gone he wasn't sure if he had
really heard it at all. But there it was again, a low, damp, rumbling of
a moan this time, becoming almost a growl that made Nathan instinctively pull his legs up to safety. He spun around to see if anyone passing
by might have heard it, too, but no one else was around, the streets
and sidewalks were deserted. The instant of silence after the sewer noise
was soon filled, was almost crashed in on by the rush of water noise.
Nathan saw something move about a block away and recognized a dog,

dancing excitedly in the gutter, his nose popping in and out of one of
the sewer grates. The dog's body jerked as if he were barking and then
the sound echoed down and out of the sewer opening once again.
"Lousy dog!" Nathan muttered to himself. "Probably chased a rat down
the sewer and now can't do anything but bark about it." Nathan watched
as the dog jumped back from the curb, then bounded up into The-
House-With-No-Men's yard, its nose close to the ground, stopping to
double-check some smell and then zigzagging on to the next smell until
he wandered out of sight. Nathan took a deep breath and exhaled it
slowly, feeling himself relax. He turned back to The Crick but for some
reason something seemed wrong. Nathan felt in a sudden flash that he
should leave The Crick, that he should go home. But then it passed.
"For crying out loud," he thought to himself, "it's only The Crick."

Nathan started down the crawl-way to The Crick below. Climbing
down was harder than climbing up and the hardest part of climbing
down was the first step. Nathan had to turn around so his back was to
The Crick, then lower himself over the edge until he could rest all his
weight on his stomach. He slowly let himself down, and then down
again, stretching his legs as far down as they could go. He looked off
in the distance at nothing, his mind instead watching the unseen wall
below, his bare toes searching for the first toehold big enough to hold
his weight and allow him to work his way down the crevices to The
Crick's edge. Once off the wall he sat on some rocks and picked rock-
grit off his belly. Nathan wouldn't admit it but the climb always scared
him. No matter how many times he went up or down the wall, he was
glad when the climb was over.

The climb down was short, but what a difference it made. The gentle
puffs of cool air that escaped The Crick up top were now a constant
breeze, closer to a cold damp wind. The water sounds seemed too loud
for such slow-running water and the steep walls all but cut out any
direct sunlight. The wind, the water, and the walls blotted out the real
world and left Nathan the only one in a world all his own. The only
intrusion was the rare passing of a car over the street bridge, and then
the rumbling that took place was more like captured thunder than a
car passing by. Nathan could remember spending days in a row in The
Crick without one person walking the short footbridge. A feeling of
being totally free swept over him and in its wake, a feeling of being
totally alone. "I wonder what the hell is keeping Terry?" he said to the

water. His pleasure from swearing like the older kids helped soothe his irritation at his friend.

Nathan mechanically rolled his pants legs up over his knees and started for the water. He chose a shallow spot with mostly sand on the bottom and waded a few quick steps out towards the nearest sandbar. He was careful not to stub his foot on any of the underwater rocks, both for his feet's sake and because he didn't want to disturb the rocks. He knew that if there were any crawdaddys around, that's where they'd be. Nathan wasn't exactly afraid of crawdaddys. He hunted them all the time with Terry. But when he was alone, he'd just as soon leave the crawdads alone.

When he reached the sandbar, the wet sand sponged down under his weight and then each footprint seeped full of water. Nathan was still thinking crawdaddys. He remembered the time he and Terry had caught a bunch of them and hollowed out an arena in one of the sandbars. Then they put all the crawdads in the center and watched them fight each other, pushing the ones that tried to crawl out back into the fight. For some reason, Terry decided to inch his way across the steep tiles to find some more. Just for a joke, Nathan waited until Terry reached the steepest part, the place where you had your hands full just staying in one place. Then he quickly picked up the biggest crawdad and, holding it at arm's length from his body, yelled, "Hey, Terry! Catch!" Terry looked up in time to see the crawdad leave Nathan's hand but he couldn't dodge the throw without slipping off the tiles. He stood there frozen, watching the crawdaddy arc across the pool and land squarely on his chest. Nathan was waiting for the fun but got more than he expected. Instead of bouncing off Terry's chest, the crawdad somehow hooked onto his shirt and clung there. Terry panicked at seeing the claws stuck to him, screamed, flailed at his shirt to knock the crawdad off his chest, and lost his footing. He slid down the tiles, trying to catch himself all the way and finally went into the water up to his waist, the crawdad falling harmlessly into the water in front of him. Nathan was so surprised that his first laugh came out as hard cough. Then he remembered the look on Terry's face and laughed until he laughed himself out, saying now and then, "You should have seen your face!" and "You've got to admit, Terry, it *was* funny!" But Terry wouldn't admit anything and he sure didn't laugh. Yeah, there'd almost been a big fight over that one.

*   *   *

Nathan's daydreaming vanished and his whole body jerked before he realized what was going on. There it was again, that same low, pain-filled moan, rolling down from up inside the storm sewer. "Goddamn dog!" Nathan said quickly, so as to scare away his fear. The howl started again but instead of dragging on and on, it stopped short, each echo of the stopping making the silence seem louder and louder. "That didn't scare me, just surprised me," he said, not being able to take his eyes off the black mouth of the tunnel. The harder he stared into the darkness, the more it seemed to draw him toward it. A tightness swelled up from his stomach as he started slowly toward the opening. "I don't know," Nathan thought to himself, "maybe there is something in there. Maybe—" And then the air around him exploded with thundering rumbles as a car passed over the street bridge. Nathan wanted to run everywhere at once and so couldn't move at all. "For crying out loud, what's got into you!" Nathan scolded himself. "First a dog and now a car. You big baby!" He took a couple of deep breaths. Then he glanced all around The Crick to remind himself of where he was. He even looked directly overhead, as if to make sure the lazy clouds were still drifting along in the late summer sky. But then his eyes wandered back to the black hole of the tunnel, as he had known they would eventually. And he also knew he would have to go into the storm sewer. Any reason for not going in there now would simply be a lie.

Nathan didn't hesitate at the opening, except to crouch down to keep from bumping his head as he ducked into the dark. The first thing he noticed was the cold, clammy dampness that clung to his skin like a wet T-shirt on a cold night. There was a steady wind coming down the sewer but all it brought was the smell of stale air and sewage. Nathan stopped a few steps into the tunnel to let his eyes adjust to the sudden darkness that crowded in around him. He strained to see deeper into the black, but black was all he saw. All the outside sounds had disappeared and in their place was a silence only dark places have, broken by the slow running stream and a distant dripping, echoing from somewhere deep in the blindness ahead.

Nathan worked his way farther and farther into the tunnel, and the farther he went, the darker it got. Every step took him away from the light outside and into the blackness. He began stumbling over things he couldn't see and the wind played tricks on his ears. He kept telling himself he'd get used to the staleness, but the air smelled just as bad as it had at first. Whenever he thought he heard something move, he'd stop dead, holding his breath. But all he would hear was the running water and the drip . . . drip . . . dripping up ahead. Nathan glanced over his shoulder and with the help of the faint light from the opening saw that the tunnel behind him was empty. But when he turned to look in front of him, all he saw was blackness. It was time to push on. He hadn't gone in far enough yet to be able to turn around and walk back out. "If this is all the farther I was going in, I may as well have not come in at all," he told the walls. Then he made a deal with himself. "I'll go in at least to the first sewer grate, the one where I saw the dog."

Nathan continued on, deeper into the sewer. He walked along the edge of the tunnel, partly to keep out of the water running down the middle, and partly to touch the wall every so often. The wall was damp, but it gave him a sense of security, a sense of where he was in the darkness, to touch it every few steps. With each step, the tunnel seemed to be closing in on him. The bottom was no longer dry along the edges, but had thick, cold mud all the way over to the wall. It was deep enough that as Nathan stepped on it, it held his weight momentarily and then he broke through the wet crust, the slime oozing through his toes and climbing up over his foot, to his ankle. Broken rocks embedded in the mud and along the concrete bottom sometimes slid by his feet, sometimes jabbed into them. He thought he was bent over enough but he kept bumping his head on the low ceiling. Cobwebs would suddenly land on his face and string out over his bare shoulders. When the first web hit him, he lurched upright, banging his head hard on the concrete. As he tried to rub away the pain, he felt his hair matted with dirt and web. After that, the cobwebs just made him angry and with his anger he felt more courage, he felt like attacking the sewer, he felt he had the sewer whipped.

Up ahead Nathan was finally able to see a faint light. "There's my sewer grate," he thought, glad to be headed out of the dark instead of into it. He looked back toward the opening, but it had disappeared in the darkness. The only light was up ahead, barely visible, spilling down from the street next to The-House-With-No-Men. "This sewer ain't so bad," he thought. "Piece of cake. Wait until Terry—" but his thoughts were stopped when he heard a loud splash up ahead. And before he could be sure if he heard a splash or not, another howl came rolling down the sewer, and then another right behind the first. Even before the echoes had a chance to die, Nathan knew what to do next. "I've had it with that dog," he muttered out loud. "Time someone taught him a lesson!"

What light there was from the sewer grate allowed Nathan to shuffle quickly through the mud, almost running, hunched over, the mud sucking at each foot and splashing up his legs. As he went closer and closer to the opening, the howls became louder and louder, tumbling over and over each other on down the tunnel behind him. But there was no place for fear in Nathan. All he could think about was reaching the sewer grate, screaming up at the dog on the street, and scaring the daylights out of him. "Who knows," it occurred to Nathan, "I might get lucky and he'll run in front of a car." Nathan was glad for the howling because it meant the dog would still be there where he could scare him. Nathan jumped into the light and started his scream—but it never left his throat. The grate was empty. No dog, no nothing. The echoes left the sewer. The only sounds were the running water, the dripping, and Nathan's heavy breathing. He stared up at the empty grate in disbelief. "He couldn't have run away that fast. How could he get away so fast?" he asked the grate. The water trickled by beneath his feet.

Nathan sat on his haunches, his head down, trying to catch his breath. He was still wondering about the dog so he didn't have time to look at what his eyes were already seeing. Gradually, he focused in on the spot where he'd been looking and what he saw made him instinctively slosh backwards a few steps. Footprints! Barefoot footprints in the mud, leading back even farther into the darkness. He went to them, compared them with his own, and suddenly the dog was the farthest thing from his mind. "Somebody else is in the sewer. Somebody else is back there." Nathan wanted to run, to get as far away as possible, but his legs wouldn't move. Then he heard it again, the moaning was starting all over again. He shot his eyes up to the grate, but it was still empty. The moaning came again, but this time he knew where it came from—from out of the blackness, echoing from deeper in the sewer. The moaning was softer than before, a tired, worn-out moan that trailed off almost into sobbing. Fear took a hold on his stomach and gave it a hard twist, making his entire body go tight. Suddenly there wasn't enough air in the tunnel and he had to grab the front of his jeans to keep from wetting them. The sobs came down the tunnel again at him and he felt exposed, standing in the dim light from the grate above. Anything in the darkness could see him without being seen. He thrashed through the mud, a few steps deeper into the sewer, and waited. Nothing. Thoughts flashed through Nathan like popcorn cooking over a high flame. "Should I yell? Or shouldn't I? Maybe they don't know I'm here. Maybe I could get away. If I yell, they'll find me. What if they're hurt? What if they want to hurt me?" That last one struck home and Nathan had turned to head back out of the tunnel, out of the blackness, when he was stopped by the moaning once more. "Help. Somebody. Help." The words came out slow and weak, hardly loud enough to cause an echo. Nathan squinted into the darkness, cupped a hand to his mouth and shouted. "Hello! Is anybody there . . . anybody there . . . anybody there" rolled up and down the sewer, the words banging louder and longer than Nathan had wanted. Then the silence took over what seemed forever, and finally Nathan heard weeping in the distance, some gasps, and then the long, hard howl again, slamming down the sewer walls, rushing over him, making his body shake and bringing an unexpected whimper from his lips. "Hang on, I'm coming . . . coming . . . coming . . ." and Nathan forced himself to move deeper and deeper into the sewer where he thought the cries were coming from.

Once past the street grate, the sewer returned just as stale, just as cold, and just as black as before. Nathan continued farther into the blackness, stopping now and then to listen to see how much farther he had to go. He finally heard some movement up ahead of him and stopped. It was coming toward him, out of the darkness. Closer and closer he could hear the mud and then the claws dug into his foot as a ball of wet fur grazed his leg and whatever it was squealed as it splashed its way through the muck behind him and on down the sewer. It all happened so fast that Nathan's heart didn't start pounding until the animal was already past him. "Take it easy," he told himself. "Whatever that was is just as scared as you are."

A spark of light flickered twice against the wall somewhere down in the darkness and then went out. "Do you have matches . . . matches . . . matches . . ." Nathan shouted. But no answer. A couple of steps farther and Nathan saw another flicker, only closer, and then all was black again. "I think I see you . . . see you . . . see you. . . . Light another one . . . nother one . . . nother one. . . ." But again no answer.

Nathan had never been this far back in the sewer, only the older kids. He wished his older brother were there right now. Nathan struggled on, trying to find good footing where he couldn't see a thing. He kept touching the wall for support and aiming toward where he last saw the flicker of light. He reached out for the wall again but it wasn't there. Nathan didn't think he had slipped that far out into the middle of the tunnel, but he took another step towards where the wall should be and still found nothing. He swung his arm in a slow, wide arc through the blackness and finally his hand struck cement. But it was a corner of a wall, the one he'd been touching all along, and then another one headed off to his left. "Another tunnel off this one?" Keeping his hand on the new wall, Nathan carefully took a step into the new tunnel. He waited a moment, listened, then took another step. He started his next step but kicked something large and wet lying on the tunnel floor. A bright flash of light exploded in his face and a wet slippery hand reached up and grabbed Nathan by the leg, squeezing hard, digging its nails into his flesh. He kicked out frantically, trying to break away, as his ears were filled with that same howl, roaring up from whatever had hold of him. Nathan's own scream joined the howl and he felt his head begin to spin. The howling died away, and as it did, the book of matches that had been ignited all at once burned down to a candlelike flame. Nathan's eyes adjusted to the lesser light but what he saw made him shake his head back and forth, sobbing, "No! No! It can't be!" There, lying at Nathan's feet, in a pool of filth and blood, one trembling hand holding the flickering book of matches, his other hand, caked with blood, grasping desperately at Nathan's leg, was Terry, his eyes looking helplessly up at Nathan through pain and blood and sewage.

"Terry! Aw hell, Terry. What's happened to you?"

Terry coughed and Nathan saw red spit ooze out of the corner of his mouth. "Help. Someone, please," Terry hissed through clenched teeth. "Don't let her get me. Not again."

"Terry! It's me, Nathan. What happened?"

"Nathan? You found me. Oh God, you found me. . . ." Terry gasped for breath as Nathan felt Terry's hand lose its grip on his leg. As he started to slide into the sewer water, Nathan grabbed him by the blood-stained shirt and tried to drag him into a sitting position.

"Oh God! Don't touch me!" Terry said through his pain. "I'm hurt, Nathan, she hurt me real bad."

"Who did, Terry, who hurt you?"

"The old lady. The old lady—oh God, she hurt me bad." The flickering of the matchbook dimmed. Nathan couldn't tell where the filth stopped and the blood began.

"What old lady, Terry?"

Terry ran his free hand across his face, streaking a watery red that ran down his cheeks. In between heavy breaths he spit out his words in short, choppy bursts. "The old lady . . . in the wheelchair. . . . At the House-With-No-Men. . . . She can walk, Nathan. This tunnel is a passage . . . a secret passage. . . . Oh, Nathan, she can walk!"

"Secret passage? What secret passage, Terry?"

Terry coughed again, struggling to talk. "I waited for you, Nathan. . . . I waited for you. . . . But you didn't come."

"What secret passage!"

"I found a door down here . . . into her basement. She caught me, Nathan. She outran me. . . . Hurt me real bad. Go get help . . . before she comes back."

"Come on, Terry, I'll get you out of here," and Nathan started to drag Terry to his feet. Terry's body jerked hard and another doglike howl escaped his lips, a howl starting low in his throat and then forced out hard, like trying to blow out a hundred candles at once. Then he lay quiet while the moan echoed its way down the sewer. "I can't move. But she'll be back. . . . She's coming back for me."

"Where is she now?"

"She went back to her cellar. Go before . . . before she gets you!" and the matches burned out, blackness rushed in on both of them. Nathan couldn't even see Terry, although he still had hold of his arm.

"Terry! Terry! Are you all right?"

"Go, Nathan . . . I hear something! She's coming back!" and Nathan felt Terry push him out toward the main sewer.

"I'm going, Terry," Nathan whispered back to the darkness. "I'm going but I'll be right back," and he searched frantically for the cement corner that would tell him he was in the main tunnel. As soon as he found it, he ran as fast as the mud and the dark and being hunched over would allow, one hand held out for the wall. Suddenly another howl came down the sewer stopping Nathan as if the mud had turned to glue. He heard voices and slowly looked back into the blackness to where they were coming from. Now there was only one voice, high-pitched like screeching tires or fingernails on a blackboard. Then a light appeared back where he left Terry; it looked like a flashlight, not the beam of light but the leftover light from around the edges. It glowed out of the secret tunnel, forming a dim curtain of light across the sewer. An old

lady's laugh came out from where Terry was lying and rushed down
the sewer past Nathan. "Well, well, well. How's my little intruder doing?
My little sewer rat, crawling around near my cellar, eh?"

"No! I wasn't doing anything, honest!"

"I think my little rat is lying to me, eh? I think it's time you see the
rest of my cellar. I'll show you what I do to filthy, lying, little sewer
rats, heh heh. . . . Wait a minute—what's this I see? Had a visitor while
I was gone, eh? Another little intruder?" Nathan caught his breath and
crouched even lower.

"You know what I think, little sewer rat? I think you need someone
to keep you company in my cellar." Nathan's legs ached from being
bent so long. He couldn't take his eyes off the dim glow of the light
back deep in the sewer. The light had started getting brighter and
brighter, the beam moving out toward the main sewer. "If that light
turns the corner," Nathan thought, "I'm as good as dead." But the light
moved back to the way it was before, and then the old lady's voice
came again. "Yes, yes, yes. You are a mess, my little boy." Nathan's
head was on fire. "Leave him alone, leave him alone!" his mind screamed
at her. From down the tunnel he heard, "Your little friend can't be far
away." Nathan started moving as carefully and as quietly as he could.
His foot shlucked up out of the mud, no louder than a whisper, but
Nathan felt cheated by being that careful and still making so much
noise. "It's time, it's time, eh?" came the old woman's voice. "But first,
my sweet little rat, I think I'll just—" and Terry's most bloodcurdling
scream yet roared out of the silence, the howl catching Nathan off
guard as his feet went out from under him in the slippery blackness.
Nathan fell hard on his backside in the cold slime. The tunnel was
overflowing with sound. The echo of Terry's scream was still banging
down the sewer and then "Ah heh heh heh!" surrounded Nathan and
seemed as if it would never leave. Trying to regain his feet in the
greaselike mud, Nathan saw the light bouncing down the secret tunnel,
swinging back and forth like whoever was carrying it was running, and
then it was in the middle of the main sewer shining directly at Nathan,
the instant brightness blinding him. "Neh heh heh heh," came from
behind the blindness. "Is this my other little rat? Just stay right where
you are and I'll come and get you, eh?" Nathan finally found his feet
and used them like never before. Hunched low and leaning forward,
there was no time to touch the wall now, he raced down the middle
of the sewer, the mud sucking at his feet, trying to hold him back.

"Neh heh heh heh heh" rushed up from behind him and then past him just as fast, rolling over and over, losing itself out ahead in the darkness. The light from the flashlight danced crazily on his back, the walls, and the ceiling. He looked back but all he could see was the bright ball of light jerking back and forth, getting closer and closer. But the light also helped him see a little bit in front of him, allowed him to see where to run, what to jump. And there up ahead was the dim light from the open sewer grate. He could yell, somebody would hear him! Nathan was running too fast to stop under the grate, his feet slipping out from under him as they were, and he slid through the mud under the opening above. Even before he stopped sliding, Nathan regained his balance, scrambled back into the light, put his face as close to the opening as he could, and screamed, "Help! Somebody! Help! Help!" He spun around and looked back up the tunnel, but the light was gone. He listened for footsteps but the only sound was his own echo, way off down the sewer, a faint, distant "Help . . . help . . . help . . ." Then the echo was gone, and in its place was, first, the silence, then the sound of running water, and then the drip . . . drip . . . dripping.

Nathan breathed as deeply as he could, trying to take in what fresh air the grate had to offer. Still no sounds of her. He looked down at his mudcovered body and scared himself to see how fast he was breathing. He listened hard to the silence, peering first into the blackness from where he had come, then into the blackness where he would have to go. Still no sound. "Maybe she's gone," he thought. "That's it. My yelling scared her back to her cellar. . . ." He listened again. Nothing. Then he heard it. It sounded like two words, very low, like an echo coming out of nowhere, and then again, this time louder but still soft, he could hear the words, "Nay—thon . . . Nay—thon . . ." Sounding like a sad, sad song. It was getting louder, or closer, Nathan couldn't tell. "Nay—thon . . . Nay—ay—thon," and then, "Neh heh heh heh!"

Nathan ducked low and ran back into the blackness. Without the flashlight it was like running with your eyes closed. The mud continued to tug at his feet, cobwebs clung to his mouth, choking him as he ran. His legs ached, threatened to give out with every stride. His back hurt with each jolt and his lungs felt as if they would burst, but still he pushed himself faster and faster. Something caught his foot and he went down sharply on one knee, the mud giving way so the concrete floor bit deeply into his skin. He rolled over and looked back just in time to see a hunched-over form fly through the dim light under the grate and then become a shadow, lumbering closer and closer, gaining on him all the time. He scrambled to his feet again and dived on into the darkness. "Less than a block," he kept telling himself. "I'm almost to The Crick." "Neh heh heh heh" came again and again down the sewer, the sound reaching for his neck, pulling at his mind, trying to drag him down. He couldn't hold back any more and started crying, gasping and weeping at the same time as he stumbled his way through the dark. Finally the dim light appeared in front of him—the opening! The Crick! The outside!

The shadow behind him wasn't gaining any more. By the sloshing sounds and heavy breathing it must have been as tired from the chase as Nathan. The light grew brighter and brighter, he could make out the entire opening now. He could see The Crick outside, getting closer and closer with each step. Nathan pushed even harder and then flew out of the sewer like a rock from a slingshot. He automatically shielded his eyes from the sudden daylight, straightened up, threw his head back, and sucked in the fresh air through his tears. He could hear heavy breathing and splashing footsteps coming after him, closer and closer, louder with each splash. Glancing up and down The Crick, Nathan saw the rock crawl-way and headed across the tiles toward it. Slipping but not falling, he reached the first handholds as the breathing and the foot-splashing became louder and louder. His muddied toes slipped once, twice, and finally took hold in the crack in the stone wall, but between the crying and the running and the falling, he was too weak to pull himself up any farther. The foot-splashing was out of the sewer now and directly below him. Nathan used all of his remaining strength, and started pulling himself slowly, ever so slowly upward, up out of The Crick. Upward and upward his body crept toward the next hand-hold, his fingers just inches away, clawing, clawing, when he felt a cold slimy hand clamp hard onto his bare leg from down below.

"Gotcha!"

Nathan clung to the wall, too exhausted to pull himself free, too terrified to let himself back down to what was waiting for him below. His strength was gone. He forced himself to look back down over his shoulder to see what held him so tightly. There, beneath him on the tiles, covered with mud and filth and carrying a flashlight, was Terry, with the kind of grin on his face that Nathan didn't like one bit. "Gotcha, Nathan," he laughed, "and man, did I get you!" Terry let go of Nathan's leg, set his flashlight down, and went to the water's edge.

Nathan let himself down slowly, then plopped down on a rock, staring at Terry and too numb to speak. "Whew, what a mess," Terry said, washing his arms in the pool of The Crick. "But even if Irv whips me, it was worth it. You should have seen your face," and Terry laughed a tired laugh. Nathan sat catching his breath. He looked at how muddy he was, then over at Terry's flashlight, then at Terry. The blood didn't look so much like blood in the daylight and Nathan noticed as Terry washed it off his arms, it came off clean, with no cuts or gashes on Terry at all. It was all beginning to sink in on Nathan. "Terry, you didn't—"

"I sure did," said Terry, the tired grin still there. "It was great!" Terry was excited over his victory and wanted to enjoy it a little longer. "What scared you the most, Nathan? The ketchup I poured all over myself, or my howls? I thought my howls were pretty good. Or was it the secret passageway? I was afraid you'd see it was a dead end—but you were too busy to even look."

"I knew there wasn't any secret passageway."

"Sure you did, Nathan. Sure you did." Terry laughed quietly to himself as he remembered something else. "You know, you almost kicked my flashlight when you were trying to get me to stand up. I thought for a while you weren't going to fall for it, that you'd turn chicken and go back out. But it turned out better than I ever expected. God, I'd give anything to see you screaming bloody murder out of that sewer grate again. I couldn't stop from laughing, I almost gave it away." And thinking about laughing made Terry laugh again.

Nathan felt the anger building up inside him. The thought of pushing Terry into The Crick crossed his mind, but he was too tired for a fight.

"Say something, Nathan."

"Why should I? All you'll do is laugh."

"Why not, Nathan? That's what jokes are for!" Terry went on, flicking his hands to dry the crick water off them. "It's no different from the Fake Push or when you threw the crawdad at me."

Nathan got up slowly and climbed up out of The Crick. When he reached the top he looked down at Terry. "A joke? You call that a joke? That was a *crappy* thing to do, Terry. And you're a bastard for doing it!"

"Ah, come on, Nathan, don't get mad. A joke's a joke. Remember what you always say. You got to admit, Nathan, it *was* funny."

"It was still a crappy thing to do," and Nathan turned and headed home. The last thing Nathan heard from The Crick was Terry's voice, high and squeaky, going "Neh heh heh heh" and then breaking out laughing in his own laugh.

Nathan walked home slowly, his head held down, his eyes watching his feet and the pavement. The hot asphalt didn't bother him, he didn't have the time for that. He kept going over and over in his mind what had happened in the sewer. "My little sewer rat!" he mocked and had to smile a little to himself. By the time he reached the corner he guessed he probably did look pretty funny screaming up out of a sewer. He felt his energy coming back. Nathan stopped in front of The-House-With-No-Men and there was the old lady in her wheelchair, still sitting in the same place, still staring out across the porch. He couldn't tell if she was looking at him or not. Then he decided she must be. To think that he had thought this old woman had been chasing him through the sewer made him smile and he waved up at her. She smiled back and nodded her head towards him the way old people do. He turned towards his house wondering how he would get cleaned up without his parents finding out. "That bastard probably got me grounded for a month," he thought to himself. "But I got to admit, it was *kind* of funny."

The Innocence
of Rachel Crewe

VIRGINIA MORICONI

*S*he came in answer to the "Help Wanted" notice which appeared
in the *Daily Telegraph*. The moment he saw her, he thought she
just might be made for the job. She was slight, but not dwarfed by her
lack of girth or inches, her hair was pulled tight away from her forehead
and securely held in place by an elastic band at the back of her head.
Her eyes, in hornrimmed glasses, looked dark and huge but that, he
thought, might be put down to a magnifying effect of the lenses; her
hands and feet were slim and finely shaped.

"Have you ever worked in a bookshop before?" he said.

"No," she said, "I haven't. I hoped you would give me a try because
I need the money."

"There's very little money in this business," he said.

To that she made no reply and there was an awkward pause in which
either of them might have been framing questions and discarding them
before they were uttered.

"What's your name?" he said, at last.

"Rachel Crewe," she said. "Yours, I suppose, is Jonathan Wyatt."

"No, that was my father's name," he said. "Mine is Lucas. Lucas
Wyatt."

There was no more conversation to be invented standing on the
threshold, and Lucas Wyatt gestured vaguely toward the interior, which
she took to mean that he wished her to step inside.

Inside, there were books everywhere—in the bookcases that lined the
walls, on tables, on chairs, in piles on the floor. Even the telephone
stood on a heap of them.

"I must explain," he said, "that I'm not a run-of-the-mill bookseller. Which is to say that I won't handle what doesn't interest me. But I will and do buy up whole libraries when there's been a death or a division in a family, if the library reflects—at least in part—my own taste in authors or periods or subjects.

"My father was the same. Jonathan Wyatt, Ltd., has been known for fifty years as a place where a highly selective reader is most likely to find either what he may have been looking for—usually in vain—or an agreeable surprise. But, as you can see, things have got out of hand."

"There *is* a certain amount of confusion," said Rachel.

"There's nothing but confusion," Lucas said. "However, I've leased three rooms upstairs and the bookcases are already in. So it was my plan to close for the month of August—we're almost at the end of July now—and put these books in order, fiction with fiction, poetry with poetry, et cetera. But then it occurred to me that I couldn't possibly do it alone, in such a short space of time, and futhermore that I really could use an assistant—someone to care for the shop when I'm on a buying spree, to help with the accounts, or just to be upstairs when I'm downstairs and vice versa."

"Can you read and write?"

"Oh, yes," she said. "I took a first in Greats at Oxford."

"Then your gifts will be wasted here," said Lucas.

"Perhaps not. The whole affair hangs or falls on whether you give me a chance."

When Jonathan Wyatt, Ltd., re-opened on the first of September, the shop was in perfect order and Lucas's sales quadrupled, since his "highly selective" readers could find at a glance the very book or author they had been seeking. He and Rachel had worked almost without respite from eight in the morning until well past midnight, seven days a week, for the whole of August. Rachel had bought a small hand vacuum cleaner and, for the first time in decades, the books on the shelves were not only in appropriate company, they were also clean. By the middle of September, Lucas felt he had something to celebrate and he asked her to dine with him, on the coming Saturday evening.

Sharp at seven thirty, he picked her up at the flat she shared with two other girls, and blushed when he saw her. She was wearing black, with very dark stockings, and very thin, needle-heeled black pumps. Only a broad coral bracelet and a pale turquoise shawl enlivened her costume. Her hair fell to her shoulders, where it curled softly at the ends, and she had left her glasses off, so that he might drown in the luminescent pools of her dark eyes.

As they had worked, side by side, he had come to know her as a fellow-laborer very well indeed. Her instant recognition of a truly rare book had invariably pleased him, and her suggestion that they save a large table on the first floor for books that she regarded as junk—to be offered for almost nothing, simply to clear the decks—had met with his instant approval. But her methods of attack, her stamina, her tireless application to the job in hand, her silent industry had told him nothing about her private self. By the end of that Saturday evening, he had fallen in love with her for, when she was not driving herself to the utmost in physical exertion, she was relaxed, trusting, a wonderful listener, and quick with a riposte, whenever he gave her an opening. By October, he felt that he must have her at all costs, and he asked her to marry him.

"We know so little about each other," she said. "Would you come down for a weekend and stay with my father and mother?"

"And apply to your father for your hand?" he said, half-joking. "What does he do, by the way?"

"He's an historian, *au fond*," she said, "but his best works are his biographies. You have them all."

"So he's Langdon Crewe," said Lucas. "Why didn't you tell me that?"

"You never asked me," said Rachel.

Dr. Crewe was cutting dahlias when the postman arrived. He thrust the flowers into a jug of water, put the kettle on to boil, and shortly appeared in his wife's morning room, with a tray.

"Post and elevenses," he said. "There's a letter from Rachel on the top of the pile."

"What does it say?" said Mrs. Crewe.

"I don't know," said her husband. "Since it's addressed to both of us, I thought I'd give you the pleasure of opening it."

Rachel's letters had always come straight to the point, and this one was no exception.

"My employer, Lucas Wyatt—about whom I've written—has asked me to marry him," she wrote. "May I bring him down for a short weekend on Saturday next?"

Mrs. Crewe read it and handed it to her husband. The habitual want

of color in her face had given way to an eggshell white and her fingers
trembled as she stirred her tea.

"Time out of mind we've asked ourselves how we'd feel—how we
should feel—when it came to this," said her husband. "For years we've
been agreed—"

"Up to this minute the question was hypothetical," said Mrs. Crewe.

"Estelle," said Dr. Crewe, "we can't tell Rachel's young man what we
don't know."

"But now that we must come to a decision," she said, "ought we not
to consider confiding our suspicions, give him the benefit of a choice?"

"Our suspicions have debased us for years," Dr. Crewe said. "Rachel
has distinguished herself many times over. . . ."

Mrs. Crewe, who had been on the verge of cardiac failure for a
long time, swallowed the two pills her husband had fetched from the
bathroom.

"Now," he said, "it's a lovely morning. May I carry you downstairs to
the garden? Both the roses and the dahlias will drive the old cobwebs
from your reflections."

For his sake, Mrs. Crewe exclaimed over the dahlias, delighted in the
roses, still exuberantly blooming so late, and smiled at him as she had
used to smile, years ago. But as soon as he had attacked the dahlias—for
the postman had interrupted him at the beginning of his labors—Mrs.
Crewe closed her eyes. In the dark chambers of her mind, it was a
harsh, November morning, nearly fifteen years ago.

"Mildred," she had said, "Miles is building a fort and Rachel's doing
a jigsaw puzzle. Shall we fold the sheets together, so that you can
damp them now and iron them in the afternoon?"

Once in the laundry, once the sheets were folded, Mildred had a
host of small problems. The hot water tap dripped constantly, all for
the want of a washer, Dr. Crewe's shirts were in rags but, with Mrs.
Crewe's permission, she could turn the collars, Miles's blue pullover had
a gaping rip but, since Mrs. Crewe had made it, surely she had an extra
screw of yarn for mending, somewhere about. On and on they prattled,
for Mrs. Crewe was devoted to Mildred, who had come when her heart
had first gone back on her, after Miles was born—and was profoundly
thankful for the interest she took in all the household affairs.

It was some twenty minutes or half an hour before she went back to
the nursery. Neither of the children was there. The wind was thrusting

and moaning in the bare boughs of the poplars and a fine rain was spitting on the window sills. Mrs. Crewe went from room to room, calling the children, but soon it was clear that they were not in the house. Alarmed, she went downstairs again, to find Mildred.

"They can't have gone out in this," said Mildred, looking sharply out the window.

"They're not here," said Mrs. Crewe.

"Perhaps Rachel took it into her head to visit Mrs. Reade," Mildred said. "Let's see if their outdoor things are missing."

But their outdoor things were not missing and a telephone call to Mrs. Reade assured them that Rachel and Miles had not come to call on her.

Frantic, Mrs. Crewe threw on a coat and searched the grounds. Mildred, almost as much upset since, although Rachel was seven, Miles was only three, joined her in the herb garden.

"Have you been down to the river?" she said.

It had been raining for the best part of a month and the river was ugly and swollen—risen to within an inch of its banks and tearing at the snarls of the willows.

"Miles would never have gone to the river," said Mrs. Crewe. "He's frightened to death of it. Even in July, it was all his father could do to get him to go out in the boat."

As they scanned the countryside in every direction, they suddenly caught sight of Rachel, her hair, her clothes dripping wet, running toward them in her stocking feet.

"Miles is in the river," she said, shuddering in the wicked wind. "I can't get him out."

Mrs. Crew and Mildred raced to the river's bank, but there was no sign of him.

"It's no use looking upstream," said Mildred. "If he's fallen in, he's gone downstream, with the current."

An hour later, they had abandoned the search. Mildred had stripped Mrs. Crewe, bundled her into her fleeciest dressing gown, laid her on the library sofa by the fire, given her the heart pills, and called the police. Thereafter, she gave Rachel a hot bath, dried her hair, wrapped her in warm clothes, and made her a cup of hot chocolate.

Late that afternoon, the little boy's body was found, caught in a tangle of roots, three miles downstream. Mrs. Crewe, delirious with terror until the tiny corpse was discovered, lapsed into a glazed silence more terrible than her piercing anguish. Dr. Crewe, long since notified, called the family doctor, who sent for an ambulance at once. He had meant to accompany his wife to the hospital, but a police inspector had arrived, and Dr. Jerrold followed the ambulance in his stead.

"We'll have to get to the bottom of this," said the inspector. "Your housekeeper tells me that the child was scared stiff of the water."

"He was," said Dr. Crewe. "We couldn't make it out. But he was only three. We expected he'd outgrow his panic."

"Yet on a day like today, of all days, he *chose* to go to the very edge of the river?" said the inspector, whose name was Barnes.

"It makes no sense," Dr. Crewe said.

"Your daughter," said Barnes, "insists that he ran down there of his own accord, slipped over the bank, and that, try as she might, she couldn't pull him out."

"She's the only witness," said Dr. Crewe. "My wife and my housekeeper were busy in the laundry for quite some time. My wife was certain that the children were playing happily in the nursery—Miles with a box of blocks, building a castle, and Rachel with a jigsaw puzzle. It never crossed her mind that either of them would leave the house in this weather."

"If a stranger had come by?" said the inspector.

"Rachel made no reference to a stranger," said Dr. Crewe.

"By this evening, I will have the autopsy report," the inspector said. "Tomorrow morning, I'll go over the ground with your daughter again. Possibly, shocked as she is, a tremendous trifle of sorts has slipped her mind, momentarily."

Dr. Crewe spent the night by his wife's bed in the hospital.

"She understands that Miles is dead," said Dr. Jerrold. "If she wants to talk about it, I don't think it can do her much harm, for a few minutes, here and there. It might help her a little. Nurse Patton, will be right at your side."

At home, Mildred took Rachel into her own bed and presently the little girl was asleep.

In the morning, Mrs. Crewe asked what the police had made of it. She seemed to be holding herself at a great distance from her husband and he wondered if she were still much subdued by the medication she was being given. She made it perfectly clear, however, that she wished to speak to the police officer in charge of the proceedings, and Dr. Jerrold gave his consent to that, provided the interview was short.

"Tell her the truth," he said to the inspector. "She's too highly strung not to know at once if you lie to her, and if she feels that she can't trust you, her life will be at even greater risk."

The inspector had just reached the hospital. Although he had hoped to interrogate Rachel, for the second time, shortly after her breakfast, he had had to wait until midday when her father came home to see if she was bearing up under the strain. Then, in Dr. Crewe's presence, he had questioned her intensively, trying to reconstruct the events leading up to the tragedy. At length, he was satisfied that, at least for the present, Rachel could not—or would not—shed any more light on the matter. He went down to the river, hoping to find, somewhere along the bank, a sign or a trace he had previously overlooked, while Dr. Crewe returned to his wife. By the late afternoon, the inspector had arrived at the hospital, where he had a word with Dr. Jerrold before entering the room where Mrs. Crewe lay as if she had been carved in stone, and Dr. Crewe sat beside her, holding her cold hand in his.

"The medical examiner's findings are consistent with your daughter's story," said Inspector Barnes. "The marks on your son's wrists and arms—there are several of them, with heavy bruising—were made before he drowned. They are also consistent with another possibility—namely, that he was forced into the river."

"What is my daughter's story?" said Mrs. Crewe, whose eyes rested anxiously on his face as though she were struggling to bring him into focus. "Does it differ in any way from what she said immediately after we discovered that Miles was lost?"

"I daresay it does not," said the inspector. "She says, and I can't shake her, that she was so interested in her puzzle that—for some while at least—she never noticed her brother was gone. When she did see that he was missing, she ran downstairs, saw the door open, and, in the distance, she saw him running as fast as his legs would carry him to the river's edge. She caught up with him just too late and, although she got a grip on him two or three times, the water tore him away from her. She rushed, so she said, downstream, looking for him, and she saw him being turned by the tide once or twice before she lost sight of him altogether. Then she ran back to get help and met you and the housekeeper in the garden, scanning the distance in all directions."

Dr. Crewe had nothing to say to that, but Mrs. Crewe's gaze was still fixed on the inspector, still glittering with desperate inquiry.

"I can't believe that the front door was standing open," she said. "The draft would have gone right through the house, we would have felt it everywhere. Nor can I believe that Miles opened it by himself. I'm quite sure he wasn't tall enough to reach the handle."

"If that's the case," the inspector said, "we're concerned either with Rachel or with an outsider."

Mrs. Crewe ceased to study him, abruptly turning her head away. The day nurse motioned the inspector to the door and Dr. Crewe stepped out after him.

"There's more to this than meets the eye," said the inspector. "It will have to be disclosed at the inquest. Your wife's testimony can, of course, be taken in hospital."

"What are you holding back?" said Dr. Crewe.

"The rest of the medical examiner's report," the inspector said. "In brief, he continues with a note that the child's legs are deeply scratched by briars. The same briars, he affirms, as those he encountered when he followed the trail from your house to the river. There are thorns embedded in the legs and thighs. He concludes that, beyond a doubt, your son was dragged to his death."

"Must my wife know that?" said Dr. Crewe.

"It's a question you should put to your doctor," said the inspector. "At the inquest, the whole story will come out, so surely she will hear it, one day or another. It might be better if she were to learn of it here and now, where immediate, expert care is available."

"Rachel was badly scratched, too," Dr. Crewe said.

"So she was," said the inspector. "But Rachel's injuries can be made to fit either version of the event. If she's telling the truth, if she ran, hell for leather, to catch up with Miles, she would have been heedless of the briars; all the same, she would have been torn by them. If, on the other hand, it was she who dragged him to the river, she would have been almost as scratched as he."

The coroner's jury returned a verdict of murder, by a person or persons unknown, being unable to reconcile the thorns in the child's legs with an accidental death. That evening, Dr. Crewe and Dr. Jerrold met in Mrs. Crewe's hospital room.

"What are we to make of it?" said Dr. Crewe.

"Two possibilities come to mind," Dr. Jerrold said. "The first is that Rachel was, as she says, so taken up with her puzzle that she didn't notice when Miles slipped away, and when she did appreciate that he was missing, she ran to the river—the only danger point in your terrain. Miles, hearing her running after him, may have scratched his own legs on the briars. It may have been nothing but a prank to him. But with Rachel at his heels, he may have misjudged the footing on the bank and then, just as she says, she may have grabbed him, lost him, and seen him being turned and tossed downstream.

"The second possibility is that someone whom the children knew and trusted lured them out, and Rachel is protecting him—or her—for reasons of her own."

"There's a third possibility," said Mrs. Crewe.

"Is there?" said Dr. Jerrold.

"Rachel herself might have dragged him to the river," Mrs. Crewe said. "Miles would have gone anywhere with Rachel."

"It's unthinkable," Dr. Crewe said.

"Is that your belief, Estelle?" said Dr. Jerrold, to Mrs. Crewe.

For answer, Mrs. Crew was racked with sobs, such heartsick, shaking sobs as to leave her husband and Dr. Jerrold in no doubt that such was, indeed, her reconstruction of the catastrophe.

The next day, Dr. Jerrold and Dr. Crewe came together once again around Mrs. Crewe's bed.

"I think," said Dr. Jerrold, "that no matter what any of the three of us imagines or accepts, it would be wise to put Rachel in therapy with a psychiatrist, trained to work with children. If she's protecting an unknown stranger, the burden will become increasingly heavy—too much for a child to bear. If she is, in fact, responsible for Miles's death, her only salvation may be in confession. In the meantime—"

"In the meantime?" Dr. Crewe said.

"In the meantime," said Dr. Jerrold, "Estelle will have to stay here for six weeks or two months at the very least. Now, Rachel adores her Uncle David and his wife, does she not?"

"How could she help it?" said Dr. Crewe. "They're childless and they spoil her morning, noon, and night. Somehow she caught their fancy as Miles never did. Perhaps because Rachel *does* love to be loved."

"Would they take her for a while?" Dr. Jerrold said. "Get her away from the scene of the disaster, spoil her morning, noon, and night, whilst I try to find a man in London who could make time for her?"

"Of course they would," said Dr. Crewe. "They've already offered to take her away from the house and all its reminders."

Rachel stayed for three months with her mother's brother, David, and his wife, Diana, whose cottage in the Cotswolds was not far from the Crewes' own property. They did spoil her, and comforted her much more than either of her parents, in their anguish, could have done. For David and Diana Wheaton were convinced that Rachel was shielding someone else—although they had no notion of who that someone else might be—and they took it for granted that she was heartbroken at the loss of her baby brother. In return, Rachel openly worshipped them and did, as her Aunt Diana said, more chores in a day than she herself could do in a month of Sundays.

Twice a week, Dr. Crewe drove her up to London for a visit with a psychiatrist whose name was Middleton. Often, betraying more anxiety than he wished, Dr. Crewe asked her if Dr. Middleton was an easy man to get along with.

"He's very kind," said Rachel.

"Do you talk to him?" said her father.

"I answer his questions," Rachel said. "And sometimes he talks to me."

After Dr. Middleton had seen her for a year, he requested an interview with her parents, Dr. Jerrold judged Mrs. Crewe fit for the trip to London, and she and her husband met Dr. Middleton in his office.

"I must tell you," said Dr. Middleton, "that I have got nowhere with Rachel. At the very least, after hearing a full report of the accident from Dr. Jerrold, and from reading the medical examiner's findings, I expected to be myself satisfied that either Rachel was indeed protecting some third person, or was herself the instrument of her brother's death. But during a year in which she has seemed quite open with me, I have come to no conclusion. With very young children, one cannot harp on the same question indefinitely, and many times Rachel and I have discussed all sorts of other subjects. I have learnt, in particular, that she is intensely attached to both of you and almost as intensely attached to her uncle and his wife. She is, I think, a person capable of depths of emotion rare in most of us. She also speaks tenderly of her brother, but she quickly admits that she hates to talk about him since, whenever she thinks of him, it brings back the memory of the terrible day on which he drowned.

"When I have thought the moment propitious, however, I have led her back to the events of that morning and her story has never varied, either in its components or in its affect. She missed him, she ran to look for him, she saw him making for the river, she caught him, when he had fallen in, by his arms, by his wrists, but eventually the force of the water wrenched him from her grasp. Given the evidence of the scratches and the thorns in his legs, I know she's lying. But whether to mask her own involvement or that of some other person I cannot even guess.

"My suggestion is that you discontinue these appointments with me. Possibly one of my colleagues might be more effective at getting at the truth, but I doubt it. My own feeling is that Rachel, over the last year, has hardened her story to the point where she may even have come to believe in it. If so, no one will succeed in pulling it apart. In which case, her best chance of developing into a well-rounded, responsible person lies in being accepted by her parents and by her uncle and her aunt just as she is, and encouraged to grow up as if nothing unusual had ever happened to her. It might, conceivably, be more harmful to keep the wound open—for it *is* a wound, whatever the truth behind it—than to let it heal over. Whatever *did* occur on that morning, I feel certain that nobody will ever know it from Rachel and, in every respect, bar that particular fragment of her history, I've found her a normal, uncommonly self-possessed, intelligent, loving, and responsive child."

Dr. Crewe was himself unable to believe that his beloved daughter— for Rachel had his heart as no one else had ever done—could have drowned her brother. Mrs. Crewe, on the other hand, was convinced that Rachel had done just that, and being an exceptionally sensitive woman, she easily imagined that Rachel's remorse must be unremitting—wherefore she gave her whole self to comforting and strengthening her child. But although Dr. Crewe and his wife wrestled with differing interpretations of the little boy's death, his loss was agony to both of them and, without Mildred, who constantly suggested pastimes—new curtains for Dr. Crewe's library, a delphinium border along the drive, painting lessons for Rachel—they would have been at a loss for the small talk of happy families and clumsy with the little girl, being torn by pitiful or protective sentiments. Often Rachel's uncle, David, or her aunt, Diana, drove by to "borrow" her and, without Rachel, the Crewes drew closer to themselves, finding some ease from pain, the one in the other. When Rachel was nearly nine, David and Diana Wheaton came by elated with their news. Childless for ten years, Diana was expecting a baby.

"I shall be scared to death of it when it comes," said Diana. "You must lend me Rachel for weeks on end to give me the courage to do all the frightful things that babies need. I know one's *not* supposed to drop them."

"Your Aunt Diana's quite beside herself," said Rachel's Uncle David. "You will come and steady her, won't you, ducks?"

"I'd be quite scared of a baby myself," said Rachel. "I was even scared when Tabitha had kittens. I was sure someone would step on one of them."

"There," said her Uncle David. "Rachel's just read us chapter number one. We must not put the baby on the floor."

Rachel went to see her Aunt Diana and the baby—a little boy called William—in the hospital. Often, on weekends, her father took her to call on her uncle and aunt, and Rachel seemed overawed by the infant. Gay and outgoing with the Wheatons, she regarded the baby with the greatest gravity.

"You have to be awfully, awfully careful of him, don't you?" she said.

"We don't even smile at him," said her Uncle David, who was playing cat's cradle with her. "We're afraid he'll think we're flippant."

During the summer, Mrs. Crewe took an unexpected turn for the worse, and once again she went into the hospital.

"Well," said Diana Wheaton to Dr. Crewe, "why don't you look on it as a blessing of sorts? Give Mildred a holiday—God knows she deserves one—and send Rachel to us."

One fine July morning David Wheaton had gone to work—he was a merchant banker—while Rachel was sitting on the steps outside the kitchen door, shelling the peas that she had just picked for their lunch, as her Aunt Diana wheeled William, in his pram, outdoors into the clearing in front of the house. William was nine months old and he loved to rock on his hands and knees. Mrs. Wheaton put the brake on the pram, which she had parked well back from the drive which curved up a steep hill to the entrance. Presently, the telephone rang and she went to answer it.

It was Rachel's mother, who was calling from the hospital, eager for news of her daughter and equally eager to let her sister-in-law know how very much better she was and how soon she hoped to go home. On and on they chatted until Mrs. Crewe said she must ring off, since Dr. Jerrold had just arrived.

Mrs. Wheaton went out to see if William was tolerably happy. To her horror, the pram was not where she had left it, and looking wildly about, she saw it, overturned, at the foot of the drive. Stricken, she ran to rescue the baby, and when she had brought him back indoors, she had a glimpse, through the opening into the kitchen, of Rachel sitting on the steps, shelling the last of the peas.

William lived for ten days, unconscious, with a fractured skull. Diana Wheaton almost lost her reason.

"It's all my fault," she said, over and over. "He *would* rock, he loved to rock. The brake must have given way."

Rachel wept in her Uncle David's arms. No one had yet given up hope for William and David Wheaton tried to reassure her. That evening, her father drove by and took her back home, leaving the Wheaton household to its agonizing hopes and fears. After William died, and before Mrs. Crewe was discharged from the hospital, Mrs. Reade, the Crewe's next door neighbor, asked Dr. Crewe to call on her.

"I thought perhaps it would be best if you heard the news from me," she said, seeing him comfortable with a whisky and soda. "The whole village is talking about the Wheaton tragedy and now, for the first time, people are talking openly about Rachel. They're saying that she *must* have drowned Miles and killed that poor baby. I've heard it on all sides, and it's occurred to me that there's a facet of this situation which may not have struck you, or may have been overlaid by your doubts and your own bereavement.

"Miles was a clown. He liked nothing better than to make himself ridiculous and everybody loved to laugh at him. Everybody, that is to say, but Rachel. When Miles was holding the floor, when the whole world was laughing with him, Rachel was *not* amused.

"After I'd first heard about the drowning, I couldn't believe that Rachel had had anything to do with it and most, if not all, of the village agreed with me. But now the Wheaton baby has died and people—myself included—are beginning to have second thoughts. They *count* for nothing, but they're there.

"You know I love Rachel," she said. "Everybody has found it impossible *not* to love Rachel, but I think, for Mrs. Crewe's sake, for your own sake, you ought to get her out of the village. You ought to sell the house and go away, Dr. Crewe."

Sick with disbelief, underlying a dreadful suspicion, Dr. Crewe went to visit his wife, who had had a relapse once she had heard of the baby's death.

"So," said Mrs. Crewe, faintly, "it's happened again."

Dr. Crewe said nothing. Images crowded his mind, clearly, rapidly. He could see Rachel, racing around the house, letting the brake off the pram, and giving it a vicious shove at the top of the drive. If he closed his eyes, he kept hearing Mrs. Reade's kindly voice, urging him to understand that Rachel's loves went too deep to admit any rivalry.

"She's an enormously possessive child," Mrs. Reade had said. "Kindness itself, when she knows she's loved, and racked by jealousy of the least invader. I could see that for myself when she and Miles used to come by for biscuits or fudgecake, yet I *couldn't* believe it. I should have warned Mrs. Wheaton."

Dr. Crewe moved Mildred and Mrs. Crewe and Rachel back to Oxford, where he had grown up, where he and his wife had lived after they were married, until Rachel was on the way. In Oxford, the only talk about Rachel was how brilliantly she was doing in school, and Dr. Crewe found some surcease in the senior common room at Magdalen. David Wheaton took a leave of absence and went to France with Diana. When they came home, they stopped in Oxford.

"I suppose," said Diana, after Rachel had gone to bed, "that you had to get Rachel out of there. Village tongues are long and sharp. But Rachel had nothing to do with it. It was my fault. My fault entirely."

When the Wheatons had left, Mrs. Crewe reached for her husband's hand and held it tightly.

"Now you know, don't you?" she said.

"I can't admit it," said Dr. Crewe. "Not to you, not to myself. I can't admit it."

"You have your work," said Mrs. Crewe.

"I have you, too," he said, "and I have Rachel."

"We both have Rachel," said his wife. "But when she's grown up, when we can't watch over her any more—"

"Let us just try to live from day to day," said Dr. Crewe.

At first, they did live from day to day, then from week to week, month to month and, at last, from year to year. Rachel *was* brilliant, a serious, curious, indefatigable student. She was also exceptionally thoughtful, doing—when she had the time—innumerable small errands or jobs around the house, so that Mildred and her mother were neither of them unduly pressed. The long shadows of old sins, if old sins there had been, grew shorter and shorter. When she had taken her first in Greats, both her parents were overwhelmed by love and pride.

It had not been lost on her that they were very hard up. The small inheritance her father had brought to his marriage should have set up his family comfortably, even if historians—or biographers—were not usually liberally remunerated for their efforts. But ever since Mrs. Crewe's heart had gone back on her, after Miles was born, the expenses had been crippling. Mildred was a costly necessity, and Mrs. Crewe's special nurses and special medications were by no means fully covered by her health insurance. Thus it was that Rachel wanted work, at the first opportunity, and thus it was that she answered Lucas Wyatt's advertisement for help in the bookshop.

When she had fallen deeply in love with him, she was in some haste to take him home to her father and mother, since her mother had, once again, gone into hospital and the cardiologist in Oxford had been cruelly candid with herself and with her father.

"Mrs. Crewe's heart is filling up her whole chest wall," he said. "She's living on borrowed seconds and you should both begin to look ahead to the day when you will have to do without her. The next attack will almost certainly be fatal."

Doting on her parents, Rachel wanted Lucas to have known them both, before she lost her mother, and she was eagerly anticipating the coming weekend. After they had fallen in love, Rachel had confided her history to him. Step by step, she had taken him over the morning when Miles had drowned—repeating the same version she had always re-enacted—and she told him about the extraordinary death of her baby cousin, William.

"No one," she said, "ever directly accused me of being responsible for the catastrophes, but after William died we left the Cotswolds and moved back to Oxford. Both my parents and my uncle and aunt were especially careful never to let me feel that I was involved in either disaster, but I knew that there were many people who supposed that I had done away with the children."

Lucas was horrified.

"What a childhood for a little girl," he said.

"Sometimes it was hard," said Rachel, "but with my family behind me, I outgrew it. In fact, I've never talked about it to a soul but you."

That same week, in Oxford, Rachel's parents were recalling the past, out loud, for the first time in many years.

"I think her fiancé should be told about it," said Mrs. Crewe. "Not warned, but told."

"And I think we should let the dead past bury its dead," said her husband. "Rachel couldn't have won the honors she has, had she been twisted, as once we wondered if she might be."

Mrs. Crewe could not let the matter rest and Dr. Crewe, worried sick about her illness, sent for Dr. Jerrold—a friend, as opposed to the cardiologist, who was, to the Crewes, simply a sophisticated machine—in the hope that he might be able to present to his sick wife the long ago under another light.

"Let's put the affair in a theoretical frame," Dr. Jerrold said. "Let's suppose, just for the moment, that Rachel had been formally accused of murdering Miles. No jury would have found against her. The evidence was wholly insufficient. Even the prosecuting attorney, in his heart of hearts, would have believed that she was shielding someone else. It's what I believe myself, and always have. Rachel lied, but she didn't kill."

"What about the Wheaton's baby?" said Mrs. Crewe.

"We must simply call it inexperience," Dr. Jerrold said. "Diana Wheaton herself has always taken the blame for that death."

"So you don't agree with Estelle?" said Dr. Crewe. "You wouldn't re-open these chapters so far behind us?"

"I would not," said Dr. Jerrold. "Rachel's subsequent record speaks for itself. She's a loving, dedicated, industrious young woman, and it would be wicked to risk the smallest blight on her present happiness."

The Crewes were enchanted by Lucas and warmed by the radiance that emanated from Rachel.

"I must confess," said Lucas, "that I'm rather second-hand, which is to say that I've been married and divorced. My first wife was and is a charming woman, but we just didn't hit it off. So we were divorced three years ago and she remarried almost immediately after."

Dr. Crewe was almost as pale as his wife, upon that announcement, for the next question was apparent and he fully realized that Mrs. Crewe's life might hang in the balance of the reply.

"Had you children?" he said, as evenly as he could.

"We had a son," said Lucas. "But my wife has custody of him and since she lives in Los Angeles, I never see him. His stepfather is a fine man and probably makes a far more conscientious parent than I ever would have done."

"He doesn't come to visit you?" said Mrs. Crewe.

"Oh, no," said Lucas. "We were all quite agreed that his loyalties shouldn't be strained. After all, he was barely a year old when his mother and I parted company. In Jonathan's terms—his name is Jonathan—his mother's husband is, effectively, his father. It's all worked out very well for the child and for my wife, and now that Rachel is ready to throw in her lot with me, I almost believe that everything is for the best, in this best of all possible worlds."

"As you've seen for yourself," said Dr. Crewe, putting his wife to bed, "there's no danger. Not the very least."

"Let us pray," said Mrs. Crewe, but her color was better and quite shortly her husband knew, from her steady breathing, that she had fallen peacefully asleep.

Rachel and Lucas had been married for over a year and seemed as much in love as if they were still a courting couple. Often they drove to Oxford, just for tea—in order not to put too much stress on the household, not to overtax Rachel's mother.

Then there came an afternoon when Lucas telephoned and asked if he might possibly arrive towards teatime and spend the night. There was a Victorian library for sale, and he was anxious to make some considerable purchases.

"Rachel won't be with me," he said. "She'll be holding the fort right here."

Dr. and Mrs. Crewe were delighted to see him, Mildred had made a sumptuous high tea and was preparing an elegant dinner.

"This is the greatest pleasure," said Mrs. Crewe. "But you're looking a little worn and tired, Lucas. Are you working too hard?"

"No," he said. "I am a little frayed, but Rachel has seen me through the worst of it."

"Have you struck a run of bad luck?" said Dr. Crewe.

"That remains to be seen," Lucas said. "To put the matter as briefly as possible, two weeks ago my ex-wife and her husband were killed in a highway accident in California. Three days ago, her brother brought

Jonathan, who's only five, home to me. It was the only solution, as you can imagine, but the child has lost what he thought of as his *real* parents. He's still dreadfully shocked and prone to exhausted tears, but Rachel's been a sort of fairy godmother to him and, once he gets over the tragedy, I'm sure we can see that he's a happy little boy again. He's really very taking."

"Where is he now?" said Mrs. Crewe.

"Why, he's home, of course," said Lucas. "With Rachel."

Mrs. Crewe collapsed in her chair and Lucas sprang up to help his father-in-law.

"Never mind about my wife," said Dr. Crewe, in a voice so harsh and high that Lucas was profoundly startled.

"Go home," said Dr. Crewe. "Go home on two wheels. Drive straight through every red light, put the accelerator to the floor. For God's sake go! For God's sake make haste!"

The urgency of Dr. Crewe's commands left Lucas suddenly terrified. He ran for the door, sprang into his car, shot down the drive, and turned toward London. Dr. Crewe laid his dead wife on the sofa and himself stumbled into a chair. More than an hour went by before he had the strength to call Dr. Jerrold.

During the afternoon, Jonathan and Rachel had been making ginger-bread men. Rachel allowed Jonathan to stick the raisins into the figures wherever he pleased, so that sometimes they stood for eyes or ears, noses or mouths, single or double lines of buttons. When they were baked and the kitchen was tidied up, Jonathan seemed pleased with his creations.

"And now," said Rachel, "I am going upstairs to run you a bath."

"I don't want a bath," said Jonathan.

"Wanting and having a bath are two different things entirely," Rachel said. "I'll run you a lovely deep one, and you can play at being a whale."

"I won't take a bath," said Jonathan. "I told you that."

"You'll take a bath," said Rachel, "because if you don't, when your father telephones—which he will, in about half an hour—I won't let you speak to him."

"You're horrid," said Jonathan. "I hate you."

"Don't be silly," Rachel said. "What you really mean is that you want to talk to your father."

"And if I do?" said Jonathan, on the verge of tears.

"You'll take a bath," said Rachel.

Jonathan followed her upstairs sulkily, but he began to undress as Rachel ran the bath.

"I've got a surprise for you," she said. "As soon as you're in the bathtub and I can hear you splashing, I'll bring it to you."

"What's the surprise?" said Jonathan.

"You just wait," Rachel said.

Lucas broke every law of the road, sped through red lights, overtook cars speeding around curves. By the time he reached the outskirts of London, darkness had long since fallen; well before he reached home the rain, which had been gathering all day long, was falling in sheets. Across the Thames the lamps on the opposite bank were a faint, yellow blur. Miraculously, he found a space to park directly in front of his house. There was still some traffic, but not a soul abroad on foot.

He turned the key in the latch in a furious hurry and the first sound he heard was of water running in the bathroom overhead. Then, over the rushing of the water, came Jonathan's voice.

"Do you mean I can play with it if I'm really good?" he said.

"Of course you can," said Rachel. "As soon as you're all clean and dry."

Listening to Rachel speak, her tone so sweet and caring, Lucas stopped halfway up the staircase to catch his breath. The last thing he wanted to do was to burst in on his wife and his son in such a maniacal state when, clearly, things were proceeding so happily above. Overpowered by a spasm of shame, by the certain knowledge that, in his heart, he had been guilty of a most shocking disloyalty to the wife whom he had chosen because he had loved her as he had never loved any other person, he turned and crept down to their little sitting room where—his hands, his whole body shaking—he poured himself a stiff drink. Then he heard her voice again.

"I'm going downstairs for a minute," said Rachel. "Don't forget to scrub your knees, and your elbows."

Lucas slunk soundlessly to the far corner of the room, at a painful loss to explain his presence. He could hear Rachel coming down the stairs, hear the creak as she opened the door to the coat cupboard under the stairwell, and small noises therein. Shortly thereafter he could hear her moving briskly about the kitchen. Relieved not yet to have been discovered, he took a long pull at the glass in his hand and listened to her opening and closing a drawer, opening and closing another. After a moment or so, she went rapidly back up to Jonathan.

On silent feet, Lucas moved toward the fireplace and sat in his own armchair. Upstairs, he heard the slam of the bathroom door—a most ordinary, everyday noise, since the door was slightly warped; only a good slam would shut it, only a heave would re-open it. Rachel, he thought, was taking no chances that Jonathan, dripping wet, might be caught in a draft.

He was of half a mind to go, as cautiously as he had hidden himself, to pray that she would never learn of his precipitate return. In fact, he was already standing up before he realized that his abrupt arrival was not simply perfectly explicable, it was obligatory. He had left her mother lifeless, almost surely dead; it was his duty to break the news to her himself, to be there, to be sure that she was not alone with a new and naked grief.

Still conscience-stricken, but filled with a sharp, sad tenderness, he took his glass to the kitchen, noticing without really seeing them Rachel's overshoes standing by the back door, and beside them two large stones, like the ones she had been using in her rock garden. On a chair were her mackintosh and hat, and a flashlight. He put his glass in the sink, went up the stairs quietly, and walked into their bedroom. The bathroom door was still closed and not a sound came from behind it.

He felt a touch of wonderment at the sight of it: Jonathan usually made a lot of noise. Then, irresistibly, his gaze fixed itself on the shiny, black plastic rectangle lying on one side of their big bed. That he recognized immediately, still folded though it was. Opened up, it would prove to be an enormous sack, designed for refuse. Designed, indeed, for whatsoever was no longer wanted in the house.

See How They Run

ROBERT BLOCH

April 2nd

Okay, Doc, you win.

I'll keep my promise and make regular entries, but damned if I'll start out with a heading like *Dear Diary*. Or *Dear Doctor*, either. You want me to tell it like it is? Okay, but the way it is right now, Doc, beware. If you've got any ideas about wading in my stream of consciousness, just watch out for the alligators.

I know what you're thinking. "Here's a professional writer who claims he has a writer's block. Get him to keep a diary and he'll be writing in spite of himself. Then he'll see how wrong he is." Right, Doc? Write, Doc?

Only that's not my real problem. My hangup is the exact opposite—antithetical, if you're looking for something fancy. Logorrhea. Verbosity. Two-bit words from a dime-a-dozen writer? But that's what they always say at the studio: writers are a dime a dozen.

Okay, so here's your dime. Run out and buy me a dozen writers. Let's see—I'll have two Hemingways, one Thomas Wolfe, a James Joyce, a couple of Homers if they're fresh, and six William Shakespeares.

I almost said it to Gerber when he dropped me from the show. But what's the use? Those producers have only one idea. They point at the parking lot and say, "I'm driving the Caddy and you're driving the Volks." Sure. If you're so smart, why aren't you rich?

Call it a rationalization if you like. You shrinks are great at pinning labels on everything. Pin the tail on the donkey, that's the name of the game, and the patient is always the jackass. Pardon me, it's not "patient," it's "analysand." For fifty bucks an hour you can afford to dream up a fancy word. And for fifty bucks an hour I can't afford not to word up some fancy dreams.

If that's what you want from me, forget it. There are no dreams. Not any more. Once upon a time (as we writers say) there was a dream. A dream about coming out to Hollywood and cracking the television market. Write for comedy shows, make big money in your spare time this new easy way, but a fancy pad with a big swimming pool, and live it up until you settle down with a cute little chick.

Dreams are nothing to worry about. It's only when they come true that you've got trouble. Then you find out that the comedy isn't funny any more, the big money disappears, and the swimming pool turns into a stream of consciousness. Even a cute little chick like Jean changes to something else. It's not a dream any more, it's a nightmare, and it's real.

There's a problem, for you, Doc. Cure me of reality.

April 5th

A little-known historical fact. Shortly after being wounded in Peru, Pizarro, always a master of understatement, wrote that he was Inca-pacitated.

Damn it, Doc, I say it's funny! I don't buy your theory about puns being a form of oral aggression. Because I'm not the aggressive type.

Hostile, yes. Why shouldn't I be? Fired off the show after three seasons of sweating blood for Gerber and that lousy no-talent comic of his. Lou Lane couldn't get a job as M.C. in a laundromat until I started writing his material and now he's Mr. Neilsen himself, to hear him tell it.

But that's not going to trigger me into doing anything foolish. I don't have to. One season without me and he'll be back where he belongs—a parking attendant in a Drive-In Mortuary. Curb Service. We Pick Up and Deliver. Ha, ha.

Gerber gave me the same pitch; my stuff is getting sour. We don't want black comedy. It's nasty, and this is a family-type show. Okay, so maybe it was my way of releasing tension, getting it out of my system—catharsis, isn't that the term? And it made me come on a little too strong. Which is where you get into the act. Blow my mind for me, put me back on the track, and I'll get myself another assignment and make with the family-type funnies again.

Meanwhile, no problems. Jean is bringing in the bread. I never figured it that way when we got married. At first I thought her singing was a gag and I went along with it. Let the voice coach keep her busy while I was working on the show—give her something to do for a hobby. Even when she took the first few club dates it was still Amateur Night as far as I was concerned. But then they hit her with the recording contract, and after the singles came the album, etc. My little chick turned into a canary.

Funny about Jean. Such a nothing when I met her. Very good in the looks department but aside from that, nothing. It's the singing that made the difference. Finding her voice was like finding herself. All of a sudden, confidence.

Of course I'm proud of her but it still shakes me up a little. The way she takes over, like insisting I see a psychiatrist. Not that I'm hacked about it, I know she's only doing it for my own good, but it's hard to get used to. Like last night at the Guild screening, her agent introduced us to some friends of his—"I want you to meet Jean Norman and her husband."

Second billing. That's not for me, Doc. I'm a big boy now. The last thing I need is an identity crisis, right? And as long as we're playing true confessions, I might as well admit Jean has one point—I've been hitting the bottle a little too hard lately, since I got canned.

I didn't mention it at our last session, but this is the main reason she made me come to you. She says alcohol is my security blanket. Maybe taking it away would fix things. Or would it?

One man's security blanket is another man's shroud.

April 7th

You stupid jerk. What do you mean, alcoholism is only a symptom?

First of all, I'm not an alcoholic. Sure I drink, maybe I drink a lot, everybody drinks in this business. It's either that or pot or hard drugs and I'm not going to freak out and mess up my life. But you've got to have something to keep your head together and just because I belt a few doesn't mean I'm an alcoholic.

But for the sake of argument, suppose it does? You call it a symptom. A symptom of *what?*

Suppose you tell me that little thing. Sitting back in that overstuffed chair with your hands folded on your overstuffed gut and letting me do all the talking—let's hear you spill something for a change. What is it you suspect, Mr. Judge, Mr. Jury, Mr. Prosecuting Attorney, Mr. Executioner? What's the charge—heterosexuality in the first degree?

I'm not asking for sympathy. I get plenty of that from Jean. Too much. I'm up to here on the oh-you-poor-baby routine. I don't want tolerance or understanding or any of that phony jive. Just give me a few facts for a change. I'm tired of Jean playing Mommy and I'm tired of you playing Big Daddy. What I want is some real help, you've got to help me please please help me.

April 9th

Two resolutions.

Number one, I'm not going to drink any more. I'm quitting as of now, flat-out. I was stoned when I wrote that last entry and all I had to do was read it today when I'm sober to see what I've been doing to myself. So no more drinking. Not now or ever.

Number two. From now on I'm not showing this to Dr. Moss. I'll cooperate with him completely during therapy sessions but that's it. There's such a thing as invasion of privacy. And after what happened today I'm not going to lay myself wide open again. Particularly without an anesthetic, and I've just given that up.

If I keep on writing everything down it will be for my own information, a matter of personal record. Of course I won't tell him that. He'd come up with some fancy psychiatric zinger, meaning I'm talking to myself. I've got it figured out—the shrinks are all authority figures and they use their labels as putdowns. Who needs it?

All I need is to keep track of what's happening, when things start to get confused. Like they did at the session today.

First of all, this hypnotherapy bit.

As long as this is just between me and myself I'll admit the whole idea of being hypnotized always scared me. And if I had any suspicion the old creep was trying to put me under I'd have cut out of there in two seconds flat.

But he caught me off guard. I was on the couch and supposed to say whatever came into my head. Only I drew a blank, couldn't think of anything. Emotional exhaustion, he said, and turned down the lights. Why not close my eyes and relax? Not go to sleep, just daydream a little. Daydreams are sometimes more important than those that come in sleep. In fact he didn't want me to fall asleep, so if I'd concentrate on his voice and let everything hang loose—

He got to me. I didn't feel I was losing control, no panic, I knew where I was and everything, but he got to me. He must have, because he kept talking about memory. How memory is our own personal form of time travel, a vehicle to carry us back, way back to earliest childhood, didn't I agree? And I said yes, it can carry us back, carry me back, back to old Virginny.

Then I started to hum something I hadn't thought about in years. And he said what's that, it sounds like a nursery rhyme, and I said that's right, Doc, don't you know it, *Three Blind Mice.*

Why don't you sing the words for me, he said. So I started.

Three blind mice, three blind mice,
See how they run, see how they run!
They all ran after the farmer's wife,
Did you ever see such a sight in your life
As three blind mice, three blind mice?

"Very nice," he said. "But didn't you leave out a line?"

"What line?" I said. All at once, for no reason at all, I could feel myself getting very uptight. "That's the song. My old lady sang that to me when I was a baby. I wouldn't forget a thing like that. What line?"

He started to sing it to me.

They all ran after the farmer's wife,
She cut off their heads with a carving knife,

Then it happened.

It wasn't like remembering. It was happening. Right now, all over again.

Late at night. Cold. Wind blowing. I wake up. I want a drink of water. Everyone asleep. Dark. I go into the kitchen.

Then I hear the noise. Like a tapping on the floor. It scares me. I turn on the light and I see it. In the corner behind the door. The trap. Something moving in it. All gray and furry and flopping up and down.

The mouse. Its paw is caught in the trap and it can't get loose. Maybe I can help. I pick up the trap and push the spring back. I hold the mouse. It wiggles and squeaks and that scares me more. I don't want to hurt it, just put it outside so it can run away. But it wiggles and squeaks and then it bites me.

When I see the blood on my finger I'm not scared any more. I get mad. All I want to do is help and it bites me. Dirty little thing. Squeaking at me with its eyes shut. Blind. Three Blind Mice. Farmer's wife. There. On the sink. The carving knife.

It tries to bite me again. I'll fix it. I take the knife. And I cut, I drop the knife, and I start to scream.

I was screaming again, thirty years later, and I opened my eyes and there I was in Dr. Moss's office, bawling like a kid.

"How old were you?" Dr. Moss said.

"Seven."

It just popped out. I hadn't remembered how old I was, hadn't remembered what happened—it was all blacked out of my mind, just like the line in the nursery rhyme.

But I remember now. I remember everything. My old lady finding the mouse head in the trash can and then beating the hell out of me. I think that's what made me sick, not the bite, even though the doctor who came and gave me the shot said it was infection that caused the fever. I was laid up in bed for two weeks. When I'd wake up screaming from the nightmares, my old lady used to come in and hold me and tell me how sorry she was. She always told me how sorry she was—after she did something to me.

I guess that's when I really started to hate her. No wonder I built so many of Lou Lane's routines on mother and mother-in-law gags. Oral aggression? Could be. All these years and I never knew it, never realized how I hated her. I still hate her now, hate her—

What I need is a drink.

April 23rd

Two weeks since I wrote the last entry. I told Dr. Moss I quit keeping a diary and he believed me. I told Dr. Moss a lot of things besides that, and whether he believed me or not I don't know. Not that I care one way or the other. I don't believe everything he tells *me*, either.

Hebephrenic schizophrenia. Now there's a real grabber.

Meaning certain personality types, confronted with a stress situation they can't handle, revert to childhood or infantile behavior levels.

I looked it up the other day after I got a peek at Moss's notes, but if that's what he thinks, then he's the one who's flipped.

Dr. Moss has a thing about words like flipped, nuts, crazy. Mental disturbance, that's his speed.

That and regression. He's hung up on regression. No more hypnosis—I told him that was out, absolutely—and he got the message. But he uses other techniques like free association, and they seem to work. What really happens is that I talk myself into remembering, talk my way back into the past.

I've come up with some weirdies. Like not drinking a glass of milk until I was five years old—my old lady let me drink that formula stuff out of the bottle and there was a big hassle over it when I went to kindergarten and wouldn't touch my milk any other way. Then she clouted me one and said I made her ashamed when she had to explain to the teacher, and she took the bottle away. But it was her fault in the first place. I'm beginning to understand why I hated her.

My old man wasn't any prize, either. Whenever we had company over for dinner he'd come out with things I'd said to him, all the dumb kid stuff you say when you don't know any better, and everybody would laugh. Hard to realize kids get embarrassed, too, until you remember the way it was. The old man kept needling me to make stupid cracks just so he could take bows for repeating them to his buddies. No wonder you forget things like that—it hurts too much to remember.

It still hurts.

Of course there were good memories, too. When you're a kid, most of the time you don't give a damn about anything, you don't worry about the future, you don't even understand the real meaning of things like pain and death—and that's worth remembering.

I always seem to start out that way in our sessions but then Moss steers me into the other stuff. Catharsis, he says, it's good for you. Let it all hang out. Okay, I'm cooperating, but when we finish up with one of those children's hours I'm ready to go home and have a nice, big drink.

Jean is starting to bug me about it again. We had another hassle last night when she came home from the club date. Singing, that's all she's really interested in nowadays, never has any time for me.

Okay, so that's her business, why doesn't she mind it and let me alone? So I was stoned, so what? I tried to tell her about the therapy, how I was hurting and how a drink helped. "Why don't you grow up?" she said. "A little pain never hurt anyone."

Sometimes I think they're all crazy.

April 25th

They're crazy, all right.

Jean calling Dr. Moss and telling him I was back on the bottle again.

"On the bottle," I said, when he told me about it. "What kind of talk is that? You'd think she was my mother and I was her baby."

"Isn't that what you think?" Moss said.

I just looked at him. I didn't know what to say. This was one time when he did all the talking.

He started out very quietly, about how he'd hoped therapy would help us make certain discoveries together. And over a period of time I'd begin to understand the meaning of the pattern I'd established in my life. Only it hadn't seemed to work out that way, and while as a general thing he didn't care to run the risk of inducing psychic trauma, in this case it seemed indicated that he clarify the situation for me.

That part I can remember, almost word for word, because it made sense. But what he told me after that is all mixed up.

Like saying I have an oral fixation on the bottle because it represents the formula bottle my mother took away from me when I was a kid. And the reason I got into comedy writing was to reproduce the situation where my father used to tell people all my funny remarks—because even if they laughed it meant I was getting attention, and I wanted attention. But at the same time I resented my father taking the credit for amusing them, just like I resented Lou Lane making it big because of what I wrote for him. That's why I blew the job, writing material he couldn't use. I wanted him to use it and bomb out, because I hated him. Lou Lane had become a father image and I hated my father.

I remember looking at Dr. Moss and thinking he has to be crazy. Only a crazy shrink could come up with things like that.

He was really wild. Talking about my old lady. How I hated her so much when I was a kid I had to displace my feelings—transfer them to something else so I wouldn't feel so guilty about it.

Like the time I got up for a drink of water. I really wanted my bottle back, but my mother wouldn't give it to me. And maybe the bottle was a symbol of something she gave my father. Hearing them was what really woke me up and I hated her for that most of all.

Then I went into the kitchen and saw the mouse. The mouse reminded me of the nursery rhyme and the nursery rhyme reminded me of my mother. I took the knife, but I didn't want to kill the mouse. In my mind I was really killing my mother—

That's when I hit him. Right in his dirty mouth.

Nobody talks about my mother that way.

Apr 29

Better this way. Don't need Moss. Don't need therapy. Do it myself. Been doing it. Regression. Take a little drink, take a little trip. Little trip down memory lane.

Not to the bad things. Good things. All the warm soft memories. The time I was in bed with the fever and mother came in with the ice cream on the tray. And my father bringing me that toy.

That's what's nice about remembering. Best thing in the world. There was a poem we used to read in school. I still remember it. "Backward, turn backward, O time in your flight, make me a child again just for tonight!" Well, no problem. A few drinks and away you go. Little oil for the old time machine.

When Jean found out about Dr. Moss she blew her stack. I had to call him up right away and apologize, she screamed.

"To hell with that," I said. "I don't need him any more. I can work this thing out for myself."

"Maybe you'll have to," Jean said.

Then she told me about Vegas. Lounge date, three weeks on the Strip. All excited because this means she's really made it—the big time. Lou Lane is playing the big room and he called her agent and told her it was all set.

"Wait a minute," I said. "Lou Lane set this up for you?"

"He's been a good friend," Jean told me. "All through this he's kept in touch, because he's worried about you. He'd be your friend, too, if you'd only let him."

Sure he would. With friends like that you don't need enemies. My eyes were opening fast. No wonder he squawked to Gerber and got me off the show. So he could move in on Jean. He had it set up, all right. The two of them, playing Vegas together. Jean in the lounge, him in the big room, and then, after the show—

For a moment there I was so shook up I couldn't see straight and I don't know what I would have done if I could. But I mean I really couldn't see straight because I started to cry. And then she was holding me and it was all right again. She'd cancel the Vegas date and stay here with me, we'd work this out together. But I had to promise her one thing—no more drinking.

I promised. The way she got to me I would have promised her anything.

So I watched her clean out the bar and then she went into town to see her agent.

It's a lie, of course. She could have picked up the phone and called him from here. So she's doing something else.

Like going straight to Lou Lane and spilling everything to him. I can just hear her. "Don't worry, darling, I had to beg off this time or he'd get too suspicious. But what's three weeks in Vegas when we've got a whole lifetime ahead of us?" And then the two of them get together—

No. I'm not going to think about it. I don't have to think about it, there are other things, better things.

That's why I took the bottle. The one she didn't know about when she cleaned out the bar, the one I had stashed away in the basement.

I'm not going to worry any more. She can't tell me what to do. Take a little drink, take a little trip. That's all there is to it.

I'm home free.

Later

She broke the bottle.

She came in and saw me and grabbed the bottle away from me and she broke it. I know she's mad because she ran into the kitchen and slammed the door. Why the kitchen?

Extension phone there.

Wonder if she'll try to call Dr. Moss.

Aprel 30

I was a bad boy.

The Dr. come. he sed what did you do.

I sed she took the bottel away.

He saw it on the floor the knive

I had to do it I sed.

He saw blood.

Like the mouse he sed.

No not a mouse. A canarry.

dont look in the trash can I sed

But he did.

My Son, My Son

ROBERT BARNARD

*L*eonard Parkin planned the birth of his son for the seventeenth of October. He was going down to London for a management conference on the sixteenth, and there was a social event of the usual dreary kind in the evening, which he decided to leave early so as to enjoy all the exciting terror of the beginning of labour. The main conference was in the morning, but the afternoon was free and he was not planning to take the train home to Peterborough until after the evening rush hour. John Julian would be born in the afternoon.

At the evening reception, held in an anonymous hotel on the fringes of Bloomsbury, Len was rather abstracted, but in the general atmosphere of wine fumes and grabs for the canapés nobody noticed. They didn't notice either when he first slipped away to the Gentlemen's, then left the hotel altogether. Len was liked, but he wasn't much noticed.

Back in the Great Northern, his usual hotel, Len put the chain on his door and lay happily on his bed. Bliss! He wondered whether to crack the little bottle of champagne in the room fridge, but he decided that champagne wasn't right, not for the labour. He would have a bottle of white wine later. What he wanted now was just to lie back on his bed and imagine it.

Marian, after all those months, feeling the first pains. The look she gave him, the certainty in her eyes and in his. "I think it's starting"— those time-honoured words which would grant Marian kinship with the millions of other women who had used them. What would he do? He would go over and kiss her tenderly on the forehead, then he would run to the telephone and ring the well-rehearsed number. The waiting, the waiting! Another terrible pain, just as he saw the flashing light of the ambulance drawing up outside.

He went with her, of course, the two of them silent in the back, he letting her grip his hand tighter and tighter as the agony came, receded, then came again. Then the arrival at the hospital, the stretchered rush to the maternity ward, he always by her side.

He lay there for two hours, picturing the scene, filling in small details, living through Marian's pain and her thrilled anticipation, being there with him beside her. Then he got up and poured himself some wine. It was good, but somehow as he drank the scene became less vivid. Natural, of course, but disappointing. He wouldn't have a drink tomorrow. He needed to be at his most alert tomorrow.

After the morning's business, all the representatives at the conference for people in the confectionary business were free to do what they pleased, and they all dispersed to boozy gatherings in pubs, on shopping sprees to Harrod's and Oxford Street, or on unspecified business in Soho. Leonard went to Hyde Park and lay under a tree in the sun. There his mind winged him back effortlessly to the maternity ward, and to himself sitting there by Marian, helping her through her labour. In real life, he suspected, he would have refused to be there with his wife, or been there only reluctantly, being faint-hearted about that sort of thing. But in his imagination he could make the labour terrible but short, and he could cut to the magical moment when the baby was born, to his touching it, blotchy and screaming, to his seeing it for the first time in Marian's arms—no, not it, but *him*, John Julian Parkin, his son and heir.

The day was sunny and he lay there, rapturous, ecstatic, more intensely alive than he had ever been. For hours he lay savouring the sensations: the sound, the smell, the touch of his newborn son. Then he walked all the way to the station, got his case out of Left Luggage and caught the train home. On the hour's journey he invented little embellishments, made more vivid the picture of his son's face. It had been a perfect day.

It was late when he finally got home, and Marian was preparing the supper.

"Have a good conference?" she asked.

"Very good indeed," he said, kissing her, feeling a sudden spurt of love for his practical, commonsensical, infertile wife. The strongest feeling in her down-to-earth heart was her passionate love for him, made poignant by her inability to have children. He could never share the birth of their son with her. Her incomprehension would have killed him stone dead.

John Julian grew apace in the months that followed, but no quicker than a natural child would have. Leonard was strict about that. As he grew his picture became sharper in his father's mind: how much hair he had at birth, and what colour it was; how quickly he acquired more; the precise shape of his snub nose; how he looked when he smiled. Naturally there were setbacks and worries: Len would sometimes enliven a long car journey on business by imagining bouts of colic or the worries of teething. The great landmark joys he usually kept for some business trip which would involve a night away from home. Then, as on that first occasion, he would slip away as early as he decently could from whatever function or meeting he was obliged to attend, shut himself in his hotel room and recreate his mental world around the son that had been born to him. The pictures were so vivid—of Marian breast-feeding their boy, of his first words and first tentative steps—that they became part of his existence, the most cherished part.

Sometimes it was quite difficult to make the transition from the imaginary to the real world. He would come through his front door with memories still crowding around him and expect to see Marian cradling John Julian in her arms, or playing with him on the floor by the fire. Then he would have to drag himself down to earth and enquire about her day rather than John Julian's, tell her what he'd been doing, not what he'd been imagining. For Marian remained the common-sense, slightly drab woman who reserved her greatest intensity for their lovemaking, while the Marian of his imagination had blossomed with motherhood, had become altogether more sophisticated and curious about the world. She had given up her job in the chain store to be with their boy, but Len never resented sharing him with her because certain times and certain duties were by common agreement his and his alone.

He was a healthy boy, that was a blessing. He played well with the other children in the street, and on the one morning in the week when he went to play-group, the leader commented on his nice disposition. Len started to imagine futures for him, though all the time with the proviso in his mind that of course John Julian would do exactly what he wanted to do when the time came for him to choose. He was an active, open-air child, but Len didn't want him to be a professional athlete. It was too short and too limiting a life. But he'd be a very good

amateur. Len always said when the Olympic Games were on that it was
a pity the facilities weren't used afterwards for a Games for *real* amateurs.
Perhaps by the time John Julian was a young man they would be, and
he would compete—maybe as a middle-distance runner, or perhaps a
pole-vaulter.

His real work would surely be something where he could use his
brain. There was no disputing that he had one, he was so forward. Len
didn't fancy his becoming a doctor, as so many parents hoped for their
children, and certainly he didn't want a surgeon son. Still, he would
like something that involved a degree of prestige. He finally settled on
Oxford and a science degree, with a fellowship to follow, and a succession of brilliant research projects.

But that was what he hoped for. The boy's future was for him to
decide, though he knew John Julian would want to talk it through with
both his parents before he made his decision.

Meanwhile there was a real highlight in his life coming up: his first
day at school. Marian had agreed—the Marian in his mind had agreed—
that he should take him on his first day. She would be taking him day
in, day out after that, she said: that would be her pleasure. It was
only right that Len should have the joy of the first day. One of the
firm's confectionary factories was near Scarborough, and Len usually
visited it once a year. He arranged to go in early September—
Tuesday the fourth, the day that school started for five-year-olds in
his area. He booked a good hotel in the upper part of the town,
near where Anne Brontë had died, and he went off with a head brim-
ming with happy anticipation.

He got through the inspection and consultations well enough. He
had had to train himself over the past five years not to be abstracted,
not to give only half his attention to matters of that kind: after all, it
would never do for John Julian's father to be out of a job. When he
was asked by one of the local managers to dinner with him and his
wife that evening, Len said with every appearance of genuine regret
that unfortunately he was engaged to visit "a relative of the wife's." In
fact, when the day's work was done, he went back to the hotel, then
took the funicular railway down to the sands. In a rapturous walk along
the great stretch of beach he imagined what his day would have been.

John Julian was excited, of course. Immensely excited. He had dressed
himself and was down to breakfast by half past seven, and when his
mother and father smiled at his enthusiasm he said that he had to pack

his schoolbag, though in fact he had done it the night before, and
packed and unpacked it for days before that. When they set out from
the front door Leonard was immensely touched when John Julian
reached up and took his hand, conscious that he needed guidance and
protection at this great moment of his life. At the gate he turned to
wave to Mummy at the door, then took Len's hand again for the ten
minutes' walk to school, sometimes shouting to friends of his own age
who were also with their parents on their first day of school. At the
school gate John Julian looked up at his father to say as clearly as if
he'd used words: "You *will* come in as you promised, won't you?" So
Len went in, as most of the parents did, knowing the new children's
classroom from the introductory tour the week before. Soon the children were mingling, playing, and discovering their new world, and the
parents, with conspiratorial glances at each other, could slip away. The
wind buffeted Len's face as he walked back to the funicular and thought
what a wrench it was to leave him, and what a happiness to walk home
with some of the other parents, talking parents' talk, swapping tales of
achievements and setbacks, hopes and prospects.

Back in the hotel room, Len imagined his day, going over things with
Marian, wondering what John Julian was doing, speculating whether he
was getting on well with his teacher ("She seemed such a nice woman").
As with most parents, such speculation was endless and self-feeding,
and Len decided to save the fetching of his son from school as a
delicious treat for next day.

His work at the factory, his talk in the canteen, was dispatched with
his usual efficiency. By late afternoon he was on the train to York, and
then on the Inter-City Peterborough, gazing sightlessly at the rolling
English countryside. His son had run into his arms at the school gates,
almost incoherent in his anxiety to tell his father everything about his
day. Len had sat him on the wall of the playground to give him a few
minutes to get his breath and tell him all the most vital points. Then
they had walked home hand in hand, John Julian still chattering nineteen to the dozen as he retrieved from his memory more facts and
encounters of vital interest in his young life. Marian was waiting at the
door and the whole thing was to do again—all the day's events re-
counted, all the jumble of impressions and opinions rolled out again for
her.

Marian in fact was not at home when he got in. She was still at her
night-school class in nineteenth-century history. Len made himself a

sandwich, poured a glass of milk, and sat by the kitchen table gazing out at the twilit garden, smiling to himself as he went through the excitements and joys of his day. He did not hear his wife let herself in through the front door. He did not realize she stood for some moments watching him as he sat there smiling contentedly. He was conscious only of a movement behind him as she snatched the breadknife from the table, and very conscious of pain as the knife went into his back.

Later, in the police station, her face raddled with tears of grief and guilt, Marian could only sob out over and over, "I knew he'd found another woman! I'd known it for months. He was so happy!"

The Man on the Stair

BRYCE WALTON

Richard Brocia III squirmed with fury on the couch, kicked his stumpy legs, pounded a chubby fist against the wall, and continued his familiar chant.

"—and then I'll kill him. I'll kill him. I'll kill him . . ."

The doctor curled deeper into his chair behind the head of the couch. He was touching his thinning gray hair, then his thin face, finally massaging his left temple gently with the tips of two long tapering fingers that quivered very slightly on the ends.

The old aching blood-throb was coming back. He squeezed shut his eyes and snapped them open, resisting a stupor of bored impatience the way a late-night driver desperately battles road euphoria's deadly spell.

One must hang in there, of course. Wait, listen sympathetically for clues, wait for Richie's defense to break—and it would. It always breaks if you wait patiently enough, and Richie's defense—this rigid, obsessive, repetitive account of his wife's imagined affairs with ghostly lovers—must wear itself out like the groove of a stuck record. Then the shriveled and desiccated fragments of Richie's personality could start limping out into the open.

Only we mustn't draw it out too long, Richie. Three months isn't really long, not in here. Three months is only a beginning when the path leads to the end of darkness; but you haven't moved at all, Richie. You revealed so little, then stopped there in the groove and it just goes round and round and round; Lara and her demonic fantasy lovers and your plans for sweet vengeance. That's all I know, Richie, and I must know more; a great deal more about many things.

In your case we simply cannot wait too long. Paranoia, in any form, even that of delusional jealousy and hallucinated lovers, can be dangerous. Proper clinical measures might call for a private sanitarium, but perhaps not. One must be sure—one must have sufficient information . . .

The doctor stopped writing in the spiral notebook. He stared wistfully at the oversized, prematurely balding top of Richie's head, the way it twisted like a wounded turtle's.

"Richie? Where are you?"

"Last night. I almost had him." Richie's mouth quivered in a baby's primal snarl. "I cut out early from my Wednesday bowling and caught them sneaking around at poolside. Heard them laugh as I slipped in through the garden and climbed over the patio fence. Same guy I told you about before when I nearly caught them parked in the car out at Hanson's Lake. I told you about that."

"Yes, you told me."

"Same guy. Tall, with the low voice."

Richie pounded the wall harder. The doctor rose as quietly as possible and rescued a gold-framed certificate before it jarred loose from the wall and fell to the floor. He put it carefully on the glass-topped desk, *Columbia Institute of Psychiatry, Bayne Kessler, M.D.*.

As the doctor turned to tiptoe back to the chair, Richie was elbowed up on his side, his odd, pale sheep eyes straining up with petulant accusation. "You weren't even listening!"

Dr. Kessler sighed and managed a benign smile. "Of course I was listening, Richie. I always listen." He sat down and picked up the spiral notebook and pen from the side table. "Please go on, Richie. You climbed the patio fence—"

Richie flounced over onto his back again. "I had him. See?" He breathed hard as he fumbled from under his suede jacket a strip of raveled white cloth and waved it like a banner. "I chased him. Just as he went over the fence I grabbed his sleeve. He tore loose and ran off through the trees. But I got this. It'll be his neck next time, and I won't lose my grip."

Dr. Kessler squinted uneasily. Torn from a shirt cuff, all right, but from whose shirt, and how? Richie often brought in trophies he claimed were left behind when he frightened away one of Lara's lovers. The cigarette lighter, the fountain pen, the handkerchief, the cigarette butts, the pocketknife, and the rest, like this bit of shirt cuff, never had initials or any other way of identifying their source. Never a wallet, a driver's license, a credit card, or anything that might separate substance from shadows.

Their faces or any distinguished body features were never quite clear to Richie. It was always night, always too dark, or he was too far away for them to be anything but fading outlines, fantasies of men who were never caught in flagrante delicto. They would never be caught except in wish-fulfilling dreams; and then, of course, there would be murder most foul.

But how to murder a delusion? Paranoids were clever at turning up substantiative evidence of systematized delusions.

"Know how I knew she'd be with him last night?" Richie waved the raveled snag of sleeve.

"Tell me, Richie."

"The night before last, Tuesday, I told Lara I was dead from lack of sleep and had to have a good night's rest. I pretended to take sleeping pills, only they were aspirin I'd put in the sleeping pill bottle. Then I pretended to be really knocked out on the couch. Lara hung around and shook me to be sure. Later, after she left, I lifted the phone and heard her on the extension setting it up with lover-boy for Wednesday night while I bowled. Same voice, like I told you. I felt sort of cruddy listening and spying . . . but I have to find out who he is so I can get him." He curled up on his side, fists clenched against his chest like a baby with colic.

Dr. Kessler was conscious of covering his growing irritation with a deliberately low, gentle tone. "And Lara? She, of course, denied again that there was anyone there?"

"Sure. Same old business. Maybe it's a plot. Maybe they've made Lara go along with a plot to brainwash me, to make me think I'm out of my tree and seeing little men who aren't there."

"Why would they do that?"

"Some of my daddy's bank. Nearly a million dollars in community property. Hell, don't you know? But I don't care. I know what I see and next time I'm going to get what I see."

Yesterday upon the stair, Dr. Kessler thought, *I saw a man who wasn't there. He wasn't there again, today. Oh, how I wish he'd go away.*

This really mustn't go on. Continuing treatment depended on knowing the exact nature of the disease. Persisting doubts about the original diagnosis must be settled. Either real or delusional lovers could serve

Richie's defensive needs, but his possible cure could not be served at all by insecure, unsubstantiated diagnosis.

His original, tentative diagnosis of delusional pathological jealousy still seemed right; what evidence he had been able to gather pointed to it. Richie could never identify a lover. He heard their whispers on the phone, in the dark, through walls, in his nightmares and day-dreams—but he never turned up a single supportive fact or clue, never any addresses, phone numbers, names, or descriptions. He said they used secret codes, even used telepathic extrasensory perception to frustrate him. On several occasions during sessions, Richie insisted that while Lara waited for him in the car, she was talking with some ubiquitous playmate. When Dr. Kessler looked down there, however, he saw the car, but no one in it—no Lara—no lover.

"There they go," Richie shouted. "Around the corner!"

Dr. Kessler saw no one disappearing around a corner, or into a crowd, or even into thin air. Delusional jealousy was not uncommon. Many had such a low opinion of themselves they couldn't imagine anyone not preferring someone else; but Richie's case added up to a rather extreme, dangerously paranoid form of the disorder. Dr. Kessler still believed that was his problem.

Yet what if that tentative diagnosis had been wrong—or just partly wrong? What if Richie's "delusions" were based on justified suspicion? What if Lara really cheated? Very discreet social inquiries had turned up nothing about Lara that supported Richie's claims, but those inquiries had been very limited by necessary prudence.

Dr. Kessler didn't believe he was wrong, but it was always possible. If he were, it called for a radically different approach to Richie's therapy.

On the other hand, if he were right, he couldn't allow a dangerous state of delusion and fantasy to continue; not without direct clinical action.

Irritation flared up suddenly, out of control. Dr. Kessler stood, leaned over Richie, and heard himself using a surprisingly hard and critical tone. "You're not kidding me, Richie. And you'd better stop kidding yourself. It isn't getting us anywhere, is it?"

Richie looked up and blinked incredulously. After a while he whispered, "What?"

"You don't want to find out who these guys are, Richie. And you never will, because you're a coward. You're afraid to find out. If you do, you know you'll find out something else, the final, unbearable truth—that you're too weak and helpless and afraid to face up to them."

Richie sat up slowly and slid down the couch away from Dr. Kessler's shadow. His face was a pale mixture of betrayed trust—and fear. He began shaking his head from side to side in painful denial.

"Yes, that's how it is, Richie, and in your heart you know it. In your imagination, your fantasies, you enjoy endless plans of bloody vengeance, but all the time you know that in reality you can only face the terror of your own helplessness and cowardly cringing—"

"No," Richie said. He jumped up and backed away. "You're all wrong. So wrong it's ridiculous."

"Am I?"

"Yes, yes, and when I catch him you'll find out how wrong you are, damn you!"

Dr. Kessler shrugged. "It's so easy to find out who they are, Richie. Do what anyone else would do—hire a private investigator."

Richie stared for half a minute. "Why . . . how can you—a doctor— suggest such a filthy thing? How can you even think of it?"

"The question is, Richie, why haven't *you* thought of it?"

"No! Do you think I'd really have some stranger, some outsider, sneak and spy on my—on Lara—to find out . . . to see what she . . ."

"Sorry, Richie. Your time's up."

Richie straightened, snarling. "My time's up here, period. I've had it with you, doctor. You can't do me any good. You don't even know why I came here, do you? I came here hoping to be able to help Lara. She's the one who is sick. She blames me for everything and won't admit she needs help. But you don't understand and you can't help, and I don't need your help. I know what to do."

"You may feel differently tomorrow, Richie. I hope so. Call me whenever you fell like it. And—"

Richie went out and slammed the door. His squatty shape blurred on the other side of the frosted pane and seemed to drift away through murky water.

Dr. Kessler moved a hand as if to call him back. Then he sank onto the couch while the office slowly turned gray and the aching blood-throb pulsed past his left temple. He massaged the ache ritualistically with the fingertips of his left hand, the way his mother used to do, knowing it was anger at himself—and fear. Also guilt and uncertainty, for losing his professional control, and giving in to exasperation—letting Richie have such an unprepared shocking broadside of cold truth.

Really shook Richie up, though, the doctor reflected. Shocked through his defenses a little. Really frightened him, without warning, without preparation. Suddenly switching from the role of warm, supportive, sympathetic listener to hard, uncompromising, directive coercion. Sometimes that can be effective; so can shock therapy— sometimes. Coercive, manipulative, authoritarian methods can also be dangerous. He really did not approve of the technique, especially with a patient about whom he still knew so little. It was almost like performing a surgical operation in the dark. Sometimes it seemed necessary to take risks, but he should be ready to assume responsibility for the result.

Dr. Kessler stood up heavily. He kept massaging his temple as he went to the window and opened the Venetian blind and realized that it was the first time all day that he'd looked out on the world. It had been snowing for hours, and it was nearly dark. There was no sky or earth in the falling quiet, only sifting snow. The world could end and he would never know it as he sat immersed in the debris of some wrecked personality.

He sat at his desk, switched on the green-shaded lamp, and a tatter of white caught his attention. The torn bit of shirt cuff fluttered on the rug near the door like a dead moth.

After peering at it for a moment, Dr. Kessler picked up the phone book and flopped it onto his desk. He riffled nervously through the yellow pages.

Dreams, delusions, lies—they are helpful clues to the unconscious; but first you must have a fair idea what is or is not true.

Ice Cream . . . Ignition Service . . . Illustrators . . . Incinerators . . . Insurance . . .

Investigators—Private.

"Flynn Detective Agency," he read. "Investigations made everywhere. Domestic troubles, personal relations, shadowing, tracing missing persons, locating, surveillance. Skillfully performed—low rates—quick results. Strictly confidential."

He called and told Mr. Flynn to start work at once, that same Friday night, even though it would count as a full day, at fifty dollars a day plus expenses. When Flynn found out anything—or an indisputable absence of anything—he was to phone Dr. Kessler at home or at his office.

Dr. Kessler waited with a tension of which he was conscious even while listening to other patients. Richie did not turn up for his Monday appointment, nor for his Tuesday or Thursday appointments, and he didn't call.

Mr. Flynn phoned Thursday night. "Mrs. Brocia never played around, I can assure you of that. And I'm absolutely sure she isn't playing around now. I'll have a full report for you tomorrow, but first I want to check something out. Something's weird here, doctor."

"Weird?"

"Yes, I think it's weird. I'll call you later."

Friday morning, as Dr. Kessler showed his ten fifty patient out, a heavy, solid man wearing a dark suit of uncertain vintage and a porkpie hat stood in the waiting room.

"Dr. Kessler?" he said softly. His face seemed dour and inflexible, with a permanent cleft of distrust between thick eyebrows.

"Yes," Dr. Kessler said, noticing that the man also had an odd sadness marking the corners of his eyes.

He opened a worn wallet. A golden badge glittered. "Detective Bates," he said. "Homicide."

Dr. Kessler felt a drop of sweat slide down the left side of his nose. It loosened a nervous flush down his back that rippled painfully. "Homicide?"

"We just took Richard Brocia into custody on suspicion of murder. You know him?"

Dr. Kessler realized that his mouth was open and the inside of it was dry. "He's a patient of mine."

"So Mr. Brocia has been telling us."

Dr. Kessler touched his finger to his left temple. "Can you tell me what happened? Can I see him? I'd like to see him as soon as possible."

"He said he didn't want to see you," Detective Bates said without expression. "But he wanted me to give you this." He held out a folded paper.

Dr. Kessler took it, unfolded it, and read:

Dear Dr. Kessler,
You said I was a coward, afraid, couldn't do it. Well, I got lover-boy, all right.
I got a gun and I shot him seven times, so he won't come messing around any more.
You were so wrong about me. You just never understood anything.

Richie

"I'm—I'm—" Dr. Kessler held the paper out as if he didn't know what to do with it. Detective Bates took it, folded it, and put it back into his pocket as Dr. Kessler went on, "—I'm sorry . . . very sorry to hear this. Who—"

"His wife, first of all."

"Lara?"

"Found her buried, or rather half buried, in the basement. Medical examiner says she's probably been buried there for about three months."

Something skidded slightly.

"The other victim was a guy who evidently tried to dig her out. Brocia came into the basement from the side door and surprised the intruder and started shooting. The victim ran, and died on the stairs leading up out of the basement."

He held out a card. "He had your calling card on him, Dr. Kessler. You know anything about him? A private investigator, name of Flynn?"

Things Had Gone Badly

PATRICIA HIGHSMITH

*T*his was the story in the newspapers, in the local paper and in *The New York Times,* and it merited about five lines in both:

> Robert Lottman, 25, a sculptor, confessed having killed his wife, Lee, 23, by blows about the head with a rolling pin in the kitchen of their home near Bloomington, Indiana. Their two-year-old daughter, Melinda, in the kitchen at the time, was unhurt in her crib when police arrived, after having been summoned by Lottman.

Robert Lottman went quietly into the hands of the police, then into a jail cell, his manner described by one journalist as "cool" and by another as "cold and indifferent."

The two-year-old Melinda was at once sent to her grandmother, Evelyn Watts, of Evanston, Illinois. Mrs. Watts expressed disbelief of her son-in-law's act. She had liked Robert Lottman, until now. She had been sure that he loved her daughter. She couldn't understand why the murder had happened. She had never seen Robert lose his temper. Robert didn't drink or take drugs. What had happened?

The psychiatrists—two—were asking the same questions in the Bloomington jail. They were not keenly interested, but a psychiatric questionnaire was a necessary formality.

"I don't know," Robert Lottman replied. "I loved her, yes. I loved her." He detested saying that to the officially engaged psychiatrists, but it seemed little to reveal, since why should he have married Lee if he hadn't loved her?

"You had quarrels?" said one psychiatrist. It was more a statement than a question. "Fights before?" That was a question.

"No, never," said Robert. He looked his interrogator in the eyes.

"Then why did you do this?" Long pause. "Sudden fit of temper?"

Robert remained silent, uncomfortable. He was thinking that he didn't have to answer, anyway. Since he had admitted striking the fatal blows, what did it matter if they had had a quarrel, if he had a fit of temper, or not? "I was not angry," Robert said finally, hoping this would satisfy the two and that they would go away. He had been sitting on the hard chair for twenty minutes.

Now the dark-haired psychiatrist said to Robert, "You know, if you and your wife had been having a quarrel—about anything—it could be a manslaughter charge. Lighter than premeditated murder."

"Come on, Stanley, no one's bringing up premeditated in this—as yet. It's a household affair."

Robert wanted to switch them both off. He wagged his head, tired and bored. The psychiatrists might think that movement "evasive," he thought. Robert did not feel in the least evasive. He felt contemptuous of the two men before him, questioning him. Robert had pride. He was not going to tell them why he killed Lee. These two might never understand. They didn't look the types to take the time. Maybe he would write out why he had killed Lee. But write it for whom? Not the court, certainly. Maybe for himself only. Robert was a sculptor, not a writer, but he could make himself clear in words if he wanted to.

"We're trying to do the best for you before the—the—uh—trial," said one of the men.

"Sentence. Before the sentence," said the other.

The best for him? What did it matter? Robert said nothing.

"You don't care what kind of sentence they give you?" asked the dark-haired one.

"That's correct. I don't care."

"There wasn't another man in the picture?" asked the plump, baldish one, in a tone of hoping that there had been.

"No. I've said that." How he had hoped for another man! "Isn't this enough? I don't know how I can tell you any more."

A minute later he was free, at least of those two. A prison guard came in and accompanied him back to his cell. Robert paid no attention to the guard. He had no intention of trying to escape out one of the doors, two of which gave onto a parking lot. The jail did not look grim or well-guarded, it was just a jail.

Robert's mind was on *another man*. There had not been another man. Funny, in a way, since Lee had been so fantastically popular when Robert had met her.

Back in his cell he was still thinking of that, Lee's popularity. She had been 20, going to art school in Chicago, when Robert met her. He had visited the Reinecker Art Institute in quest of a part-time job, two or three mornings a week, teaching sculpture. He had his own credentials from the Art Students' League in New York and from a Brooklyn academy, less well known, but he had a prize from that school, attested to by a certificate and a photograph of his work which had taken first prize. The Reinecker, however, had wanted a teacher for five mornings a week, and Robert had hesitated, said he would think it over. Nine to noon, five days a week. They would have taken Robert on, yes, and they hadn't thought it unusual that Robert wished to consider it for a few days. Robert had walked out of the superintendent's office and into the hall, down a short flight of stairs, and met Lee coming up the stairs.

He had not met her in the usual sense, and she had been with two young men, one on either side of her, all three talking, as Robert remembered it, but his eyes had met Lee's eyes for an instant. Robert could still see it as clearly as if it had been a color photograph that he carried with him. Lee was blonde, not very tall, and had blue eyes. She had been wearing beige trousers, like chino pants, a pale blue shirt or blouse.

Robert had turned and followed her. She had a smooth, oval face, a high forehead, round and rather bulging. The important thing were her eyes—intelligent, appraising, cool. Who wouldn't have followed those eyes, Robert wondered. As he had walked behind the trio in the corridor, Lee had looked back once at him, aware that he was following her. The two boys with her had eyes only for Lee, Robert remembered. Robert was to see plenty of this later. But Lee had stopped and turned, looking at him.

Robert had said, "Hello," like one stunned. Hadn't the other two fallen back a step, stunned also in the presence of love at first sight? Robert was not sure. He had managed to get out something, because he wanted her as a model, quite apart from the fact that he had fallen suddenly in love with her. "You're a student here?" Maybe he had said something like that. Anyway, Lee had said that she was not studying painting any longer and was intending to go to a photography school, somewhere else. Robert had whipped his little sketchbook from a back pocket, a pencil, had got Lee's name and address, and had given her his own. She had a telephone number. She lived with her mother in Evanston.

She had liked him, that was the important thing, enough to give him her name and address. And suddenly, too, she had been walking with him, back down the long cream-colored corridor with its closed doors on either side, bulletins and posters everywhere on the walls—and the other two young men had vanished, or were maybe standing in the corridor behind them, puzzled.

And then things had gone badly.

Robert was now sitting on his bed, thinking: *things had gone badly*. But he was thinking of two periods of time—just after he had met Lee and the past weeks. Between those times about three years had passed.

In the first bad or uncertain period, just after he met Lee, it had seemed to Robert that she was afraid of him. She refused to make dates with him, she wrote him an ambiguous note: did she want to see him again, or not? Robert lived just 30 miles or so from Evanston. One of the young men in whose company Robert had first seen Lee was still present and in full force. This Robert had discovered when he had his first date with Lee. She had had to ease the young man politely from her mother's house, and he had gone off with a smirk at Robert, as if to say, "You're wasting your time, fellow."

Robert and Lee had gone back to her mother's house after dinner (her mother was divorced), and Lee had shown him her drawings, some paintings that were not as good as her drawings, and her new photographic efforts. Robert was impressed. Many were portraits of people she knew, young and old. She had imagination and energy. The energy showed in Lee herself—a strong body neither slender nor sturdy but something in between, with a grace of movement. Above all, her energy showed in her enthusiasm for her work.

Robert had blurted out around midnight, "I *love* you—you know?" Then Lee had been silent, as if surprised (how could she be, when half a dozen men must be in love with her, Robert had thought), and then she had gone on putting away her photographs in their labeled folders and portfolios. He had not tried to take her hand or to kiss her.

And then silence—for two weeks, for a month. She was too busy to make dates, she said when he telephoned. And Robert recalled his friends' advice, with mingled gratefulness and annoyance: "Play it cool, Bob, and she'll come around to you." He was not the type to play it cool, but he had done his best, and Lee had come around, made dates with him, even said yes when he asked her to marry him. By then they had been to bed together several times in his studio. Robert was head over heels. He felt he had met a goddess. He did not care for the word goddess, but he didn't know what else to liken her to, because there was no other girl in the world like her.

The advice. Robert lit one of his remaining five cigarettes. *Advice* reminded him of his parents in New York. They had telephoned him yesterday, and he had been allowed to speak with both of them. "Is it true, Bobbie?" his mother had asked in a voice that pained Robert to remember. "We just can't believe it," his father had said in a heavy, hopeless tone. "We thought it was a mistake—of names, identity—" It wasn't a mistake, Robert had told him. Yes, he had done it. How could he explain on the telephone? Did it really matter if he explained it, much as he liked and loved his parents? Could they ever understand even if he wrote it out for them? "My life is finished," Robert had said at the end. The guard had beckoned to him then (even though his parents had been paying for the call), and Robert had told his father that he had to hang up.

If he were writing it—Robert was walking around his cell whose confinement and barred door did not bother him in the least now—he would say that Lee had become a different person. That was it, and Robert had realized that long ago, nearly two years ago. If he ever wrote anything about Lee and himself, he would have to say this from the start and emphatically. That was the essence, and that was what he had been unable to take, or accept, whatever you wanted to call it. *His fault.* Sure. Lee had the right to change, or maybe just to become herself.

When the baby was less than a year old, Robert had asked her if she wanted to divorce him.

"But why?" Lee had asked back. "What's wrong, Bob? Are you so unhappy?"

They hadn't made love for a month or more. Robert couldn't, and maybe Lee hadn't even noticed, absorbed as she was in Melinda. It wasn't the act or the pleasure of making love that was so important, meaning not even the absence of it was so important, but the fact that

Lee had become another person with motherhood—formidable word—
and with all the fussing around the house, which had begun early in
their marriage. Gradually she had dropped her photography. The equipment in her darkroom had begun to gather dust before Melinda's birth,
Robert remembered. They had got a mortgage on a pretty house, not
too big or too small, outside the town where Robert had had his rented
studio. There had been a period of shopping for furniture, curtains,
buying a fridge and a stove, but Lee hadn't stopped. Then it had been
slipcovers for the sofa and living-room armchairs, and Lee was good at
the sewing machine. Then she had become pregnant. Nothing wrong
with that, of course, and Robert had been as happy as she. Sunday
afternoon dinners at her mother's, a bit boring but bearable, sometimes
even cosy and reassuring.

Robert paused in front of the not very big mirror fastened to the
wall above his basin. He saw that he was frowning. He rubbed his chin
brusquely, barely met his own eyes. He was not interested in looking
at himself. Rotten shave he had given himself that morning. What had
he been thinking of then?

The magic just fell away, Robert thought. Would he write a sentence
like that, if he were writing about himself and Lee?

Robert felt suddenly puzzled. How could anyone write something
about anything, until it was clear in his own head? How could anyone
put into words or phrases how much he had loved Lee? The clumsiness,
the bluntness of certain pop-song lyrics came now to Robert . . . *the
catch in my throat when we meet . . . when I look in your eyes, I want to die . . . the
places we yee-eewst to go together . . .* Lee had liked pop music as background
sometimes when she sewed, changed the baby, or gave her a bath. If
only Lee had stopped doing little things, let him change the baby (he
could), just dropped everything and got back to her own work!

Robert was working himself into a torment again. Absurd. Lee was dead
and forever dead. What good did tension, even analysis, do now, really?

In the next seconds he was back to the present. His parents were
coming to see him tomorrow. Lee's mother evidently did not wish to
see him, and she had gone with Melinda to a sister's house somewhere
in Illinois. Rather, she was going, after the funeral. The funeral was
today. Robert realized that with only a mild shock; he had an impulse
to look at his wristwatch, and didn't. He knew it was still before noon,
because the guard had not brought his lunch tray. Funerals were always
in the morning, weren't they?

Then for another few seconds Robert felt that he couldn't realize what he had done. That was almost comforting, like a pill he might have taken. He did realize that his life and his work, whatever he had wanted to do in life, was over, finished. He might as well be dead now, like Lee. But they weren't going to kill him, just sentence him and imprison him. That was worse. Think about that later. He was pushing his tongue against his left eyetooth, which was nicked from a football game, way back, when Robert had been 14 or 15. A vision of little white houses, blue sea behind them, came into his eyes. Greece. Robert had been to Greece when he was 20, pack on his back, sleeping on beaches and in pine woods, getting to know the land and the people. He had hoped to have enough money one day to buy a house on a Greek island, and to live there with Lee at least half of the year, the other half in America. He had never forgotten Greece or his dream of a house there. He and Lee had used to talk about it, now and then. Greek music.

Lee's music. Lee hadn't always played pop, either on the radio or on the record player. She had liked Mahler, oddly. Depressing sometimes to Robert, fear-making, unfathomable sometimes to him. Yet now the memory of the Mahler Sixth steadied him. He had come to a big decision about Lee while Mahler's Sixth Symphony played one afternoon. He had been working on a clay model of what he called "A Dreaming Woman," the woman not reclining but on her knees with arms raised as if half ambulant in her dream. He had gone to speak with Lee about his idea.

And what had she been doing? Putting adhesive paper down on some kitchen shelves, standing on a low formica stool. Robert proposed that she divorce him and marry Tony, the bachelor architect-carpenter who lived about eight miles away, the same fellow who had hung the shelf Lee was now busy with.

"Tony?"

Robert could still hear her voice and the astonishment in it. "He's in love with you," Robert had said. "Just too polite to do anything about it. You must know it yourself."

"Are you out of your mind, Bob?"

Robert remembered her eyes then, the same straight clear gaze at him, but what a different mind or brain behind those eyes!

The difference in her was affecting his work, at least affecting his sketches of Lee. He could not see her the same way as before, because she wasn't the same. His nearly life-size nudes of her, a couple of years old by then, thumbtacked to the walls of his workroom, had seemed to mock him: you can't do it again, they seemed to say. The drawings had spirit, enthusiasm, even genius. Whose genius, his or Lee's? Robert wasn't vain, it could be his or hers, and he preferred to think it both his and hers.

So Robert had turned himself to other themes, other women's figures, if he needed them, abstracts, nature forms. Lee had become "any woman," ordinary, pretty, but uninspired and uninspiring. Robert had managed a teaching job for three mornings a week in Chicago. They could have afforded a baby-sitter, a woman to do the housecleaning once or twice a week, but Lee seemed to enjoy these chores, and she said she didn't want anyone else in the house.

If Lee began to be the cliché, the woman-next-door, Tony Wagener was the archetype of the man-next-door (formerly the nice-boy-next-door) whom the average girl would be lucky to marry. He was healthy, attractive, good-futured, aged 25, and he couldn't take his eyes off Lee. Was it any wonder that a happy idea had crossed Robert's mind? Robert had thought it might work. He still loved Lee, even in a physical way, in fact, but the letdown—of his dream? No, because Lee *had* been the way he remembered her when he met her and when they had married, for a while. Witness his drawings! Witness his three statues of her, two small and one life-size! They were good, really good!

Therefore, Tony.

"Don't you like Tony?" Robert had asked on another occasion.

"Like him? I never think about him. Why should I? He brings us wood for the fireplace—because he doesn't need it." She had shrugged.

"It might be better. You might be happier. Tony would." Robert remembered he had laughed here.

Lee had still been puzzled. "*I* don't want Tony!" And what else had she said? Had she asked him if he was miserable with her, if he didn't love her any longer?

What would he have answered in that case?

It had crossed Robert's mind to run away, simply abandon Lee and the baby. He loved the baby, was rather in awe of it as his and Lee's creation, but he had still been able to envisage disappearing rather than—something worse. The something worse hadn't been definite in Robert's mind then, he had merely feared it.

If he disappeared, Robert remembered thinking, mightn't things be better? Lee would land on her feet, if she fell at all. Tony would dance attendance and step in as soon as Lee let him, and why shouldn't she? Tony was serious about his architecture, had a degree from somewhere, and was going to climb in his profession. Robert could not imagine a more ardent suitor than Tony, if Tony were only given a chance. Tony had had a girl friend when Lee and Robert had moved into their house, but after three months or so (Tony had been doing some carpentry work for them, and had brought the girl once or twice), Tony had dropped her. Tony had fallen in love with Lee, that had been plain. Robert remembered mentioning it, early on, to Lee, and Lee had shrugged, uninterested.

Robert had been doing portraits, heads as he called them, for two people or clients in Bloomington, and for one in Chicago. They brought in money. Only middle-aged and well-to-do people could afford the luxury of having themselves or their wives cast in bronze at $3000 each. Robert had had to work in rather conventional style to get a likeness that pleased the client. He tried to be as free as he could in style, but still it bored him.

Lee had begun to bore him. Incredible realization! One day he had driven back from a sitting in Chicago, nervous, unhappy, and he had said to Lee, "What if I just disappeared?"

She had turned from the stove where she was cooking something. "What do you mean?" Her smile was almost her former smile, amused, cool, showing rather pointed white teeth between her rouged lips. She wore white sneakers, a pair of girls' maroon corduroy jeans. She couldn't wear boys' trousers, because she had a waistline and hips, though she was not plump.

What had he replied? Robert tried to remember now, because it was important, because he had really been trying to make the right sugges-tion. "I don't see that you need me any more." Robert was sure he had said that. What else could he have said? "If I went away, I'd send you money to live on, you can be sure of that." Then he had blurted out the truth: "You're not the same girl as before. It's not your fault, I think. It's *my* fault. I should never have asked you to marry me. Somehow I'm destroying *you*. And this situation or whatever it is is bothering my work. It depresses me."

"But I *am* the same person. Sure I have to spend a lot of time now with Melinda, but I don't mind that. It's normal." And at that moment hadn't she run across the kitchen to stop Melinda from poking a finger into an electric outlet? Melinda crawled around a lot, because Lee was against confining her too much in her crib. "When she's really tired, she'll sleep better," Lee often said. What else had she said? Maybe "I thought you were working rather well. Aren't you?"

And her dressing table, its top covered with little boxes of pins, lipsticks, perfume bottles, lotions, cologne. Robert had used to look at all that with a smile—mystifying objects, but Lee knew what to do with them. She made herself prettier, different. She amused herself, she amused other people. Boys and men looked at her when they went to restaurants. But Lee didn't invite attention, never had, didn't need to. Maybe men took as flirting one glance from her, but Lee could hardly go around with her eyes shut all the time. No, she hadn't flirted, and once she had decided she liked him, Robert had been the only man for her, he knew that.

One Friday morning, one of the mornings when he had to get up at seven at the latest for the Chicago art school, Robert had quit the house. He had left Lee a note saying that he was going to telephone Tony. *Try it*, Robert had written. *See if you can't love Tony as much as he loves you. You know where to reach me, at the art school. Try it for maybe a month, please? You might find yourself happier.* Robert had taken a furnished room not far from the school. If Tony didn't work out, Robert had thought of acquiring a second-hand car for himself and giving Lee the car he had taken, their car. She was able to drive. Robert envisaged a divorce, of course. He felt a divorce would be better for both of them. Some other Tony would come along. Meanwhile he missed his workroom at home, his clay, a couple of works in progress.

Tony had said on the telephone, "But what happened, Bob? A big quarrel? You sound serious?"

"Just look after her. We didn't quarrel, no. It's like a trial. I want to try it." Shocked silence at Tony's end. "She may like you better."

"Oh, no." Tony defensive now. "You've got me wrong, Bob."

"Try it. I invite you." Robert had hung up.

The following Sunday evening around eight, Robert got a telegram from Lee: CANNOT UNDERSTAND YOU. PLEASE COME HOME. I AM SO UN-HAPPY. LEE.

Robert had sent his furnished-room address to Lee on Friday, so she would have got his note Saturday morning. He had not sent the name or telephone number of his landlady, so maybe it had been easier for

THINGS HAD GONE BADLY

Lee to send a telegram straight to the address. Robert had found it under his door, when he got back from supper.

And that had been that. After a minute's debate Robert had driven back home. He had not been able to bear the thought of Lee *unhappy*— either because of being alone, or because of not liking Tony, or of being bored or annoyed by him. Robert had been willing to leave his week's rent with Mrs. Kleber, but she gave it back to him except for a charge of one extra day.

Lee's first words to him had been, "What is the matter, Bob? And Tony! What're you trying to do? I never said I liked Tony."

Tony had not been there when Robert got home. Tony had been polite, helpful, it seemed, but Lee did not want him.

Robert fell on his cell cot exhausted, and had to be awakened for his early supper. Hours ago they must have poked lunch at him. He couldn't remember, he must have been daydreaming then.

"God, I wish I had a radio," he murmured to himself. He would have switched on anything just to take his mind off Lee and himself. It grew dark early, because it was December. He walked and walked around his cell, deliberately tiring himself so he could sleep.

The next day at 1:30 P.M. his parents came. Robert was allowed to go into a side room with table and chairs and to talk with them. There were no other prisoners in the room, and only two other cells in the place, as far as Robert could see.

His mother was nervous and looked as if she had been weeping. She was blondish, wore a green tweed dress and a sheepskin coat. His father was as tall as Robert, six feet, a man of 50, a logical man. Robert recognized the downturning of his father's strong mouth. His father was displeased, he didn't understand, was going to be stubborn. Robert remembered that look from his childhood, for his minor misdemeanors. His father now had reason to be grim.

"Bobbie, you must tell us what happened," said his mother.

"What they said happened," Robert replied. "It's the truth."

"Who's they?" asked his father.

"The police, I suppose. I called the police," said Robert.

"We know that," said his mother. "But what happened at home?"

"Nothing." He stopped, having been about to say that he must have had a moment of irrationality, of anger. But that wasn't it.

"You had a quarrel? You'd had a few drinks?" asked his father. "You

can tell us the truth Bob. We're in a state of shock, I can tell you that."
His father was making an effort to get his words out; he glanced at
Robert's mother, then looked back at Robert. He said quietly and earnestly, "It's not you, Bob. You worshipped Lee, that we know.—Can't
you talk to us?"

"Was there another man in the picture?" asked his mother. "We
thought of that. This Tony you mentioned in your letters—"

"No, no." Robert shook his head. "Tony is a very polite fellow."

"Polite, well," said his father tolerantly, hoping for a lead here.

"No, it's got nothing to do with Tony," Robert said.

His mother asked gently, "What did Lee do?"

"Nothing," Robert answered. "She just changed."

"Changed how?" asked his father.

"She turned into a different person from the one I married. She didn't
do anything.—Maybe she was just herself, after all. Why not?" He tried
to sound reasonable. What they were talking about was perhaps not
susceptible to reason, not to be understood in logical terms. Also Robert
had never been intimate with his parents, or tried to talk with either
of them about his moods, his crushes and loves in his adolescence.
They had been sympathetic about his wanting to go to art school,
though Robert knew his father had considered it impractical, somehow
"easy," undemanding and unrewarding. He was an artist, therefore more
sensitive, Robert supposed they thought, so what he had done must be
all the more unbelievable to them.

"Changed how?" his father repeated. "Neglecting you maybe, paying
more attention to the baby. I've heard of that happening, but—"

"It was not that." Robert was suddenly impatient, wanted to end the
useless conversation. "I've been absolutely unreasonable," Robert said,
"and I deserve everything they're going to give me or do to me."

His mother's hand shook as she reached in her pocketbook for a
tissue, but she was not weeping now. She gave her a nose a pinch.
"Bobbie, we've talked to a lawyer by telephone, one who knows the
state laws here, and we'll see him this afternoon. He says if there had
been a quarrel about anything, if you'd been angry about something, it
would help you when—"

"I refuse that," Robert interrupted, "because it's not true."

His parents exchanged a glance, then his father said calmly, "We'll
see you again, Bob, after we talk with the lawyer. When is it, Mary,
four, isn't it?"

"Between four and four thirty, he said."

"He's coming to see us at our hotel, and I know he'll want to talk with you tomorrow morning. His name is McIver. Good man, I'm told." It was all less important to Robert than a stage play taking place at a distance from him. Lawyers, rules, putting everything into abstract phrases, more abstract than himself and Lee—which was difficult enough for Robert.

His parents got up from their chairs. Robert thanked them. They left, and Robert with them, walking quietly out of the room, into the hall where a guard stood up to escort Robert to his cell. His mother pressed Robert's hand. The guard looked at Robert's hand afterward, as if to see if his mother had put anything into it.

Before the guard closed his cell door, Robert asked for some paper and a pen. The guard brought him three sheets of ruled paper (Robert disliked ruled paper) and a ballpoint pen. When he sat down at the little table, he realized that a pack of cigarettes was bulging his back pocket. His mother had produced the pack from her handbag, Robert remembered, saying something about having had to use a machine to buy them in a hurry or she would have bought a carton.

Robert closed his eyes, deliberately tried to make his mind go blank, and at the same time think about his theme, as he did with sculpture, but now his theme was Lee as a person. When he tried to think of Lee as a piece of sculpture, he often thought of the words grace, strength, sometimes one or the other, sometimes combined. Grace was easy to combine with Lee. She had never made a clumsy gesture that he could recall. She walked gracefully, as if she weighed nothing. But the strength? She had had it, all her own, a strength that he didn't understand.

Finally he wrote (it seemed to him a fragment, but he could go back or forward from here):

To see her wilt before my eyes like that was frightening to me, like a slow death in itself. People speak of blossoming with child-birth, love, all that. It was not true in Lee's case. But what I write here is by no means an effort on my part to excuse what I did.

Did he have to add that awful last sentence? Well, he could cross it out later. For whom was he writing this, anyway?

She gave up her photography, except for some mediocre pictures of the baby. What can one do with a baby? At least in regard to Lee's former bent of character, intellect, tragedy in the human face— nothing. Instead of her good cameras, she might as well have been using a cheap pocket camera. She had stopped talking about the photography exhibitions in Indianapolis and Chicago. We used to go quite a lot. We knew some of the photographers who lived in those cities. They had gradually stopped visiting us.

All this was so unnecessary! I can look back now on the work Lee did just before we married, just after. Terrific! And easy for her! Powerful! I thought I was the cause of all this downslide, this collapse really, so I offered to go away, support her from afar, as it might be, until she found maybe another man to share her life with. She declined this and

Here Robert stopped, seeing suddenly the living room that last evening, Lee's photographs gracing the walls, blown-up, her old good stuff, people, buildings. There hadn't been a quarrel, no. Lee had been on her feet, talking about ordinary things—that there had been a telephone call from Fred Muldaven, a friend of Robert's who lived in Chicago, a painter. Melinda had been in her crib in the kitchen then. It was around six or seven in the evening. Robert had been in a strange mood, he had realized, staring at Lee without listening much to what she said. He had just driven back from Chicago, and maybe he had been drinking a cold beer straight from the can.

"Beecham's has a sale of desert boots," Lee had said, "and you could use a new pair. Those look awful."

That had been merely unimportant, boring. A couple of years before, Lee would have paid no attention whether his desert boots were worn out, or if his shoes needed a shine. Old falling-apart clothes had their place, and it was nice to dress up sometimes too, but why talk about it? Why bother trying to please the public, or whoever might look at his sloppy desert boots?

Yet nothing that evening had been what Robert could call the last straw. Rather the atmosphere had been one of quiet gloom, hopelessness, a slowing up as if something were coming to an end, like a train losing momentum because the engine has been shut off. They had gone into the kitchen. Melinda, symbol of the future, had for once been sleeping quietly. And had any vision of Lee at the Chicago art school danced before his eyes as he watched her fussing at the stove?

Had any of her enchanting air of "I don't care if I ever see you again, or not," as in the days before they married, come back into his head? Whatever, it was all gone now. He had picked up the rolling pin, floury from something Lee had just made, and that had been it.

Robert got up from the chair and walked around the cell. He moved back to the table, his hand reached out for the cigarette pack, and drew slowly back. He was thinking of something else—Lee dead, the baby at Lee's mother's, himself dead too. It was all abstract somehow. There had been no word from Lee's mother, or from Fred Muldaven (that was a new friendship and Robert supposed that Fred was now afraid of him), only from his parents, natural appurtenances, calling on him, because by blood they were linked, like a triple star floating around in space. And to be just a little more concrete, though the fact as such did not matter, Robert was going to spend the next 15 years (with the lightest sentence) in prison, working if he worked at all in a prison art department, being told when to get up and when to go to bed, being reminded of Lee day after day by barred window and door, being reminded of the way she had been, which was even worse.

He wrote one more sentence: What a terrible shame I once loved her so much. I do think that ruined everything.

Then he did light a cigarette, and stood looking at the gray and rather rough wall across from his cot. And Melinda. Should he write one *more* sentence to that young creature of whose personality he knew nothing at all? He knew something, of course: she seemed to be cheerful by nature, but that could change by the time she was 12 or so.

He decided not to write a word to Melinda. She was in good hands. She would grow up to hate him. She would look at all the pretty, the beautiful photographs of her mother, and hate him. And his statues of Lee? Would Lee's mother have those thrown away, broken up?

Robert sat on his cot for a couple of minutes, finishing his cigarette. Then he put it out in the metal ashtray on his table. For no reason he lifted his left hand and looked at his watch. 4:37 in the afternoon.

Robert stooped by his cot, facing the wall opposite in the position of a runner about to take off. Then he ran forward with all the force he had, all the force, he felt, that he had ever put into his work, and very briefly with a vision of a statue of Lee, better than any he had ever made. His head hit the wall.

Killer in the House

JAS. R. PETRIN

*Y*ou *will* be all right, won't you, Nanny?"
        'Course I will. Go out, and have fun, and leave me at home with a killer!

Nanny sat in her wheelchair, silent, angry, swathed in her blanket, watching her granddaughter Gwen fuss in and out of the bathroom, the bedroom, putting on her clothes, her scent, and her face, while her husband Will leaned his head in at the door and called with annoyance, "The car's warmed up and running, the Arabs are getting rich, are we going to the damn restaurant or not?"

"I'm *coming,* can't you give me a minute's peace? I've only got to put on my coat and see if Nanny needs anything."

Gwen came stumping across the living room, shaking the floor, and bent over Nanny. She smelled like a harlot's picnic. She was a good girl, though, Gwen was, more considerate of Nanny than her sister Liz had ever been. Considerate and caring, but none too bright. She was a stupid, and so was her husband. They were both stupids.

"Nanny," Gwen whispered, "we're leaving now. You know I'll worry about you the whole time we're gone. We may go to a movie after din-din, we may not. I don't know. But if we're late, you mustn't worry. Louie will be along. I made him promise to skip the bar at the Red Lantern tonight, to come home early and fix your dinner. So you'll only be alone for an hour or so. Now tell me, darling, if there's anything you want before we go."

She was studying Nanny's lips, and Nanny's eyes swam from the scent of her perfume.

There's lots I want, Nanny thought. *I want you to stay right here and not charge off and leave me alone with that murdering Louie, and I want Will to go on out to that freezer Louie brought here with him when he moved in and crowbar that lock open and get your frozen-stiff sister Liz out of it and thaw her out and bury her proper and Christian, and I want Louie dragged out of here by a policeman, kicking, and a rope got around him, and him hung up high until he's dead, dead, dead!*

But when a stroke comes along and hits you like a runaway wagon the way it had Nanny last fall, you were lucky if you could still draw breath.

She could feel Gwen's eyes on her face. Out in the driveway Will was revving up the Dodge like he was part of a getaway. Which maybe he was. A getaway from Nanny.

Nanny struggled to shape the words on her lips.

Killer, she mouthed, *in the house! Look . . . the freezer!*

Gwen straightened, puffing out her fat cheeks and laughing.

"Oh, Nanny, don't start up with *that* again."

"Don't start up with what?" It was Will poking his head in on a blast of winter air.

"I think she's going on about Louie's freezer again. You know how it upsets her. She thinks he's got Lizzie Mae's body inside it. I wish you'd make him open it and give Nanny a look inside so as to set her mind at rest."

Will sighed a long weary breath and rolled his eyes in his best God-give-me-strength expression.

"Look. You know I talked to Louie, and you know I explained it all to Nanny a dozen times. He keeps the freezer locked so those kids you babysit don't go trapping themselves in it and suffocating; he keeps it running so it doesn't get to smelling all skunky inside; and she doesn't need to look in it anyways because, like I told her another dozen times, me and Louie seen Liz at the mall. I seen her myself with my own two eyes, walking large as life through the Easton Mall. Now if all that don't satisfy her, nothing will. Can we go now?"

Gwen's eyes flashed with sudden annoyance.

"I wish you'd stop talking in front of Nanny like she wasn't even here. It wouldn't hurt Louie to let her have a little peek. It wouldn't hurt anybody one bit." She bent over Nanny again, with a look of concern. "There's nothing for you to worry about, darling, everything's fine. You'll see."

She kissed Nanny's forehead—lightly, so as not to smear her lipstick. Then the big door banged and they were gone.

Nanny would have stamped her foot in frustration if it were possible. Nothing to worry about!

Everything's fine, is it? But you haven't seen Louie kneeling by his freezer, reaching down into it and speaking softly and crying. No you haven't, have you?

Leaving her alone with a killer! Did they think Nanny shouldn't have fears, simply because her welfare was entirely in their hands? Neither of them had ever awakened in the night with eyes stretched wide as sealer rings, sweating, wanting to scream, run, turn over and cry out to someone, but only able to lie there with one's body wrapped around one like a steel clamp and silently shriek into the dark.

A killer in the house!

Being paralyzed, she'd learned fear, all right. Fear such as she'd never known before in her life. Fear of fire. Fear of being at the mercy of some cruel person—like a killer.

And even, because it was always present, the fear of falling.

Except for the killer, that was the worst. Even sitting quietly here at home in her chair held a terror that made her head reel. Falling out of her chair was a horrifying notion. The nightmare of it woke her every night. The slow weightless launch into space and the floor hurtling up to smash her. It was the old childhood dream of falling, falling, falling, and not being able to raise an arm to save yourself. She shuddered.

And now they'd invited a killer to stay.

Louie.

With his freezer.

The cold they'd let in was making the oil stove groan; it whirred its fan in the corner and creaked its joints at her. She wished she had thought to ask Gwen to turn it up a notch or two; she wished she could just reach out herself and give the dial a damn good twist.

But she'd have to lift her arm to do that, and it was all she could do to lift her fingers. She lifted a finger now to the little control wand on her chair, and the motor hummed and crept her across the kitchen. It hesitated before it went; the switch wanted cleaning again. She stopped a few feet from the stove and let the heat soak into her.

Her eyes were still bleary from that horrid perfume Gwen had been wafting around. She blinked once, twice to clear them; it was an awful thing to be unable to rub your eyes when you wanted to. Her eyesight had always been good. She could read the chrome letters on the stove that spelled CHAMPION, she could read the spine of the telephone book on the stand by the back doorway, she could read the name ARCTIC through the partly opened door on the . . .

FREEZER!

It was visible there in the open doorway, hulking, one hard angular white shoulder in the dark.

Louie's freezer.

The one with Lizzie Mae's body locked inside it like a frozen pork roast.

Damn it, Gwen, you could at least have thought to close that door before you went off to enjoy yourself. Nanny moved her finger to hum the motor to turn the wheelchair away and not look.

And Louie saying he had seen Liz at the mall. What rubbish. Did he think he could fool Nanny with a comment like that? Liz couldn't be in two places at the same time and she sure as heck hadn't clambered out of that freezer, what with its being locked and all, and her lying at the bottom of it stabbed or shot or strangled, with a glaze of ice over her and her lips all blue. And Will, who had backed Louie up, had only caught a glimpse from the barbershop window where he had sat breathing with the rest of the men, all of them lathered up like mad dogs, watching the women's legs go by. It wasn't as if he'd actually *spoken* to her.

But Will, listening to Louie, thought he'd seen Liz, and so neither he nor Gwen would consider the real truth. They weren't surprised at Liz's staying away; it was just like her to cut them out. They assigned no blame for the marriage breakup, and they let Louie go smiling on. They liked him. Thought he was the cat's whiskers. It was only Nanny who had seen him, when Gwen and Will were gone for groceries and he thought she was asleep, kneeling over that open freezer like a monk, bowing and talking into the frost and sobbing.

Louie was a clothing salesman, or had been. Best in the business, he liked to brag. He'd made his managers jealous, on account of, with his commissions, he made more money than they did. Or so he said.

Nanny had never warmed to him.

She hadn't liked him from the day three years ago when Liz had waltzed him in the door, hanging all over him, announcing to a shocked silence that she was marrying him the very next day. Liz had always been impulsive like that. Taking up with any half-cracked lunatic that came smiling out of the sun. She'd found three husbands that way before Louie came along, and though all three of them had been stupids, Louie had been the only one who had struck Nanny as being totally . . .

BAD!

So Nanny had done some phoning—she wasn't all seized up then—and found out some very curious things from her friend Emma Parker in Youngerville. *They'd* had a fellow just like Louie working in their clothing store—Casey's on Third Street—and he had been simply the *strangest* man! Folks had seen him on warm evenings, parked on Lover's Lookout—which was the hill over the river where the young folks liked to go—and he had a different girl with him every single time. One night a blonde, next night a redhead—always somebody different. The gossip had gone round about it, and the next thing anybody knew, he'd got the sack from Casey's and had left town. Folks had pried away at Casey with crowbars for weeks, but he wouldn't say a word about it. Said he wouldn't bring disgrace on his store.

That same night, after the phone call, Nanny had waked up screaming because she had looked on death in a dream. And the next few times she saw Louie, she saw death following one step behind him, or peeking around him, or standing next to him and holding his arm like a bride. That dream was prophetic.

He'd killed Liz, all right. Nanny had seen it coming from the first. And now here was the proof, if anybody would bother to look. In the back room. Under lock and key. In the freezer.

Of course she'd tried to warn Liz, but Liz had only turned all huffy and cold and gone for her coat, wanting to leave right away. Then she'd begun staying away altogether, which was that Louie's doing for sure, whispering evil in her ear.

Right about then the stroke had hit Nanny, and that had been Louie's doing, too, just as sure as sheep dip. He'd hexed her. Who else had the evil to do it, after all?

Oh, Louie was trouble, all right, and nothing but. In the end, Nanny had been proved right.

Just take that night Liz had phoned. She must have been crying up a storm, Gwen was so sympathetic with her. And later Nanny had overheard Gwen telling Will about it:

". . . lost his job at the store."

"How come?"

"She wouldn't say exactly. But they caught him redhanded at something . . . something pretty bad. Louie wouldn't talk about it, so she phoned the manager and he told her what it was. She was ashamed to tell me too much, but I think it was because he wouldn't leave the female customers alone. Liz said she'd always had her suspicions about that, and now she was going to leave him . . ."

So things hadn't worked out too well down at the clothing store. And after Louie's bragging how he'd been too good for all those other stores, too—he'd worked in half a dozen. It told Nanny a lot. He hadn't been victimized by jealous managers at all. It was just the old wandering fingers problem.

And suddenly Liz had stopped phoning. Just like that, no more calls. Very suspicious. Nobody saw hide nor hair of either one of them until Louie showed up at the door with his battered suitcase and his freezer. And wasn't *that* just the darnedest thing? A freezer! Most men would have brought their TV or their liquor cabinet, but here comes Louie with a freezer.

He'd explained with his easy smile that he and Liz had broken up, that Liz didn't want to be bothered with it, and he'd brought it because it was the only thing in the house they owned free and clear. And if anybody believed *that* story, they'd buy a raffle ticket with the World Trade Center as first prize.

He hadn't fooled Nanny. Not one bit.

And now here they were. All of them under the same roof. Liz in her frozen sleep; Gwen, foolish Gwen, suspecting nothing; Will, who liked having a man in the house to talk sports with; and Nanny in her chair.

And Louie.

Hating her. No, *despising* her!

He made no secret of *that*, either.

Only a week ago there had been just the two of them in the living room, watching TV, Louie seated on the end of the couch, cursing her under his breath. Oh, he was quiet and cute about it, speaking feather soft so that Gwen shouldn't hear in the kitchen, keeping his murdering hands in his lap, his murderous eyes on the television, barely moving his lips.

"Nanny, Nanny, Nanny, hard old Nanny, mean old Nanny, Nanny the witch." He'd gone on like that for twenty minutes. Oh, he was confident with her so seized up from the stroke he'd hexed on her.

Nanny closed her eyes, tried not to think of the freezer in the dark in the room behind the wall. After a while she rested.

What woke her was a thump at the door.

Somebody cursing, fumbling, laughing.

Louie was home, and tight as a tick. So he had stopped at the Lantern, after all. Nanny felt her pulse pick up a beat from somewhere, then settle itself again.

Louie was home.

Louie the killer.

And no Gwen.

Nanny waited in her chair by the stove, and at that moment the blower shut off, sighing to a stop and impressing her with the silence of the house when Louie wasn't around. Sober or drunk, he had a loud way about him. Too friendly when sober, laughing too harshly and smiling too broadly and always standing one step too close to you; and too stupid when drunk, playing the clown, telling rude jokes and mimicking famous people to turn those around him purple with laughter.

There was a crash from the steps outside, and a loud groan. A tinkle of broken glass.

He didn't fool Nanny, though.

Nanny could see the real Louie behind the smokescreen of jokes and laughter. She had known a lot of Louies in her time. He was a type. The sort you got a glimpse of sometimes when a fresh wind gusted the smoke away, and you were always strangely shocked to see just what you'd expected, like a glimpse of hard white bone in a deep red wound.

You learned a thing or two in eighty-two years.

Now she heard the jangle of keys at the lock. Louie seemed in awful shape. He was fumbling around out there badly. Despite what Gwen had said, he must have started earlier than usual today down at the Lantern, and run into some generous friends, too.

Then the door crashed open, and there stood Louie, smiling.

"Hello—Nanny!"

He swayed in the doorway, more concerned with holding himself up than in shutting out winter with the door. He had brought two cases of beer home with him, one tucked up high under his arm, the other clutched tight in his fingers and now just a boxful of broken glass, dribbling suds and amber stains over Gwen's polished linoleum.

He made one false attempt, then another, and finally managed to set the two cases down, handling even the broken one gently, as if he hoped it held something that might yet be salvaged. He fumbled his parka off, dropped it by the fridge, and, finally sensing the chill from the open door, closed it hard by falling backwards against it.

"I said *hello*, Nanny!"

He rattled a chrome chair out from the table, arranged it with extraordinary precision, and then dropped into it, letting out one of the loudest belches Nanny had ever heard.

You wouldn't dare act like this if Gwen and Will were here. You're like every other drunk I've ever seen, with a kind of radar that lets you go on fooling certain people. All the rest, you don't want to fool. Them you want to impress with how nasty you can be. But I can see through you like a glass coffin lid, mister, see your grinning death's head face getting ready to pop out at me. Oh, I know you!

Nanny was feeling the heat of the stove now. She wanted to back away a little but was afraid to draw attention to herself. If she could somehow remain inconspicuous for the next while, maybe Gwen and Will would come crunching in out of the snow, shaking off the night and filling the room with loud talk about the movie. As Gwen had promised earlier, everything would be all right.

Louie fumbled in his shirt for cigarettes. He didn't notice that he'd already put them on the table. He gave up with a flourish of disgust, leaned forward and hooked the undamaged beer case with his finger, dragged it to him across the floor. He popped the case open with one hand—even in his drunkenness it was a polished motion—opened a bottle, took a long swallow, then groped again and finally found a cigarette.

He looked at Nanny.

"S'how the hell are ya?"

Nanny found herself wondering how she could appease him, knowing in her heart at the same time that appeasement was not possible. And even if it was, there was little she could do in her condition.

"Come here, Nanny, an' have a beer."

Her fingers fluttered at the controller. She was afraid to try it, afraid not to.

"Come *on*, Nanny!"

He swayed up out of his seat, leaning towards her with a list to one

side. Then he was at the back of her chair, gripping the handles, pushing her up to the table. He was not gentle; he collided her with a table
leg.

He giggled.

"Sorrysorrysorry! I'm sorry, Nanny. Don't tell Gwen on me, Nanny."

He sat down and faced her. She could smell the stink on him now,
the acrid smoky bar, the heavy overripe scent of beer. He had mussed
his hair somehow and it jutted from one side of his head like a wig
that had slipped. He sucked on his bottle, then his cigarette, and put
his head on one side, questioningly.

"You like tellin' Gwen things about me, don't you, Nanny? Why
d'you do it? Ain't I always been friendly to you, Nanny? Don't I try to
ch—cheer you up? Huh?"

He studied her down the length of his cigarette with his careful
drunken eyes. She didn't like it. There was a menace in his tone, a
hardening towards her with those last few words.

"Tellin' Gwen madeup stories about me. Not nice, Nanny, not nice."

And I'll have even more to tell her after tonight, you pig.

"You never liked me, Nanny."

*Darn right, I never liked you. I saw you for what you were the day Liz dragged
you in here out of some barroom garbage can.*

"You worked real hard, Nanny, turnin' Liz against me. Got what you
wanted, too. Bust us up. Did a good job on us, Nanny, a real good
wrecking job."

*Not as good as I should have done. Or it'd be you out there in that freezer, and
her in here talking to me.*

Louie went to suck at his bottle, found it empty, and rapped it down
hard on the table. He probed into the case at his feet and fished out
two more bottles.

"Le's have a drink together, Nanny. An' a long talk. You and me
should've had a long talk years ago. Here, this is for you—you like
beer, dontcha?"

He pushed the bottle across the table. She wondered if in his drunkenness he had forgotten that she didn't have the use of her hands. He
was watching her and smiling as if he were the most agreeable man
God had ever put breath into. His head was propped up with the hand
that held his cigarette clipped between two nicotine-stained fingers. He
smoked steadily, taking a lungful, then regurgitating the smoke and
dribbling it out of his mouth in curds of solid white, which he then

swallowed up again. It was a wonder to Nanny that it didn't make him sick. Maybe it would yet.

"How come you doan like me, Nanny?"

Because you're evil.

"What's so wrong with me, anyway?"

You're a destroyer, a breaker-down of things, you're a killer.

"I tried t'make you like me, Nanny. Tried real hard for Liz. But you wouldn' let me, wouldn' give me a chance. An' Liz blamed *me* for that, Nanny. Me. S'at fair?"

Suddenly his heavy hand crashed down to make the table jump.

"You answer me!"

She flinched. He must have noticed.

Then he was calm again. Almost wheedling.

"Le's be friends, Nanny, okay? Le's be *good* friends. Bottoms up!" He drank, then watched her, waiting, blinking. He giggled. "Oops! Forgot, Nanny. Forgot your bum arm. Ole war wound, right? Here, lemme help you."

He picked up her bottle, loomed in at her, reaching, pressed it to her lips, tipped it forward. She took some of the bitter fluid into her mouth, gagged, and felt the rest of it splash down her chin, onto her blouse and her blanket.

Louie pulled the bottle away.

"Sorry, Nanny, sorrysorrysorry. *Sorry!* You doan drink fast, do you? You're a lady. A real lady." He frowned. "Liz was a real lady, too, jus' like her Nanny. Oh, I could have my pick of any girls, take 'em out any time I want. But Liz was special. Better than the others. I loved her. Yup. You doan b'lieve that, do you?" His face clouded. "You *never* believe me, Nanny. Liz tole me once you said I was—a *liar!*"

Again he gave the table a heavy smack.

Nanny cringed inside at his Jekyll and Hyde transformations. From calm discussion to sudden rage. She found herself hating him with every atom of her being. She had always despised drunks, and she despised this one with a special passion. This was the drunk who had ruined the life of her granddaughter Liz. The drunk who had finally killed Liz in some intoxicated rage and sealed her up in a freezer. The hate made her paralysis even more intolerable. She wished she were once again a healthy woman who could leap up and strike at this disgusting brute; or a man, a strong man, who could take him by the neck and squeeze and squeeze . . .

I hate you oh how I hate you, you drunken pig. I'd do anything to punish you for what you did to my Liz. I hope there's ghosts, and I hope I'm one real soon because even ghosts can do more in this world than a paralyzed old woman, and I'll come back to you then, cold and cadaverous and moldering, and I'll put my rotting hands on you and—

"Wanna see Liz, Nanny?"

She blinked.

He was gulping curds of smoke again and watching her with a brewing anticipation. She wondered if she had heard him right.

"Wanna see her, Nanny, or not?" He cackled. "You're pleased t'hear that, arncha? *I* know what you been tellin' Gwen. Proves you were right, doan it? Proves they should've listened to you, Nanny. You knew best. You knew nobody could walk out on ole Louie." He emptied his beer down his throat, opened another one and scowled. "But later, Nanny. Yes, I think later. Then you can see her. Okay? Drink first. You'll need it. She ain't as pretty as she used to be."

He laughed. Again he pushed the bottle at her, forcing open her mouth, pouring in the beer until she choked. He yanked it away so roughly this time that he pulled her false teeth askew. "Ooops," he said, giggling. "Sorry!" And stuck his fingers into her mouth to set them right again.

Nanny sat and glared at him. How terrible impotence was. It gripped you like a constricting snake and crushed the dignity out of you.

"You know," Louie said, "I was dancin' down at the Lantern tonight. I like dancin'. So did Liz. How 'bout you? Wanna dance, Nanny? Cut the old rug? Shake a tail feather?"

He was halfway to his feet when he fell back with a simpering grin.

"I fergot, Nanny. You doan dance so good now. Your legs doan work so hot." He took some beer, began laughing in the middle of a swallow, snorted it up his nose and coughed horribly.

He put his cigarette back in his mouth; it waggled as he spoke.

"An' your arms, too, huh, Nanny? An' your neck, an' your back, an' your feet, an' your hands—oh, you're in *awful* shape, aincha? Your whole damn bod is shot. If only you could wheel on down to the graveyard and dig yourself up a few spare parts, eh, Nanny?"

He collapsed in his chair, convulsed with laughter.

Go ahead. Laugh away. Laugh till you choke on your own rotten tongue. Then I'll do the laughing. In my mind. At your funeral while they're wheeling you down to the graveyard.

He tossed his head as if to shake the laughter away.

"I wanna dance. I'm a dancin' fool, Nanny! Me an' Liz use to dance alla time. You can do it, Nanny. I'll lead."

He pulled himself up by the edge of the table. Two bottles went crashing against the wall, scattering dark brown splinters of glass. He chortled. "Dead soldiers, Nanny." Then he had caught hold of the wheelchair from behind and was rolling her back and forth and around the room, and singing his own accompaniment.

It was a heavy chair, what with the battery and motor; he used it partly as a support for his lurching, unsteady body. Around and around he trundled her, hooting. She felt giddy. She closed her eyes; that was worse; she opened them again. The room ran liquidly around her in watercolors. The stove came and went, came and went. Louie howled in her ear. "ROUN' AN' ROUN' AN' ROUN' SHE GOES. WHERE SHE STOPS, NOBODY *KNOWS* . . ."

And he threw Nanny away.

The chair shot out and across, flying, soaring over the floor, through the room, and fetched slam-*bang!* into the stove.

The chimney pipes shuddered and dropped a dusting of soot. The stove jerked back three inches. Nanny felt herself lifted up, floating on and outward, the hot metal stove looming, halting, then receding again as she fell back into her chair, her nostrils filled with the stink of scorching steel.

She thanked God for Gwen's care in tucking her feet well back under the blanket. If not for that her toes would surely have been crushed.

She could not see Louie with her chair facing the stove. The heat beat against her face and trembled the little gray hairs that stuck out over her eyes. Behind her Louie groaned with laughter, creaked with it. In a moment or two his grunting subsided and she heard the snap of another beer being opened. The heat was terrible, she could scarcely breathe. She yanked the chair control lever angrily back and, to her surprise, the chair responded instantly and rolled her backwards.

She stopped in the center of the room. She tried to get the chair to turn but the control lever had gone dead on her again. She sighed with frustration, and a nervous convulsion shook her violently.

She could only sit.

Hoping for Gwen.

Hating Louie.

Behind her, the sound of a cigarette pack being opened, the soft pop of the breaking seal, a crinkle of paper, a whisper of foil. The hiss and flare of a match.

"By God, you're a damn good dancer, Nanny."

Go to hell, Louie. Light another match. Set yourself on fire.

An acrid scent of sulphur reached her nose.

"A *damn* good dancer, Nanny. You mus've taught Liz everythin' she knew. Oh, she was a dancer. We had a good time, Nanny, till you bust us up. Real mean of you. You turned her against me an' I never done nothin' to you. Mean. Mean as winter. Tha's you, Nanny. It's your fault me an' her had to go our ways."

Liz didn't go anywhere. You killed her.

"Now she's got nothin'. I got nothin' . . ."

Oh yes you have. You've still got her. You've got her poor dead body out there in the back room, all frost and freezer burn and snowflakes on her eyes. Wrapped up in towels, maybe, or sheets. Like an Egyptian.

"You're hard, Nanny, hard."

Yes. I'm hard. I've had to be. But I'm not like you. Not a killer.

"You're like all those mean people I used to work for. You got no compassion for a man. You got a heart of . . . of *ice.* Black ice."

Louie was beginning to wander in his thoughts. Beginning to mumble. Nanny was having trouble understanding him.

"You're old, Nanny. Used up. Got only dust in you now. Dust and ice. Ever seen dust and ice mixed together, Nanny? Like a frozen chunk of midnight. Tha's what meanness looks like, Nanny. If we opened you up now with a knife an' looked inside you, tha's what we'd see. Old black ice." She heard him scraping at his cartons for more beer. A clink of glass. "Old things, Nanny, ought to be thrown away. Heaved down the basement an' tossed on a shelf to keep the dust off it. S'all you're good for now, Nanny. That an' breakin up families."

There were more scuffling cardboard sounds, the chinking of tumbled glass.

Then a roar.

"NANNY!"

She shut her eyes. *Oh, God, what's got at him now, don't let him start flinging me round again, I'll throw up if he does, I'll faint, I'll die, oh please don't let him start in on me again!*

"NANNY, WHY'D YOU GO AN' BUST MY BEER?"

A chair crashed to the floor. Louie came around from the side into her view, breathing raggedly, and towered over her, enormous, dark, full of hurt and poison.

"WHY'D YOU DO IT, NANNY?"

I didn't break it, you stupid, stupid, stupid! Aren't I sitting paralyzed in a wheelchair? Didn't you drop it yourself when you came in? Think, you stupid, think, think!

He leaned even closer, wrinkling his face with disgust and hatred. He was only inches away now, as if he were trying to peer, not just into her eyes, but to something in behind them, her most secret thoughts.

He said, very coldly, his voice like a long sliver of ice that sank into her slowly. "I doan wanna drink with you no more, Nanny. No. I don't. You get mean when you drink, Nanny."

He pulled away then, trying to find his balance.

"An' you're even meaner when you *don't* drink, Nanny."

Leave me alone. Get your horrid stinking face away from me. Don't you dare preach to me about meanness!

"I can be mean, too, Nanny. Real mean. S'at what you want? S'at why you bust up me and Liz? To make me mean—like you?"

Go away!

"Why don't you say something, Nanny?"

BECAUSE I CAN'T! I CAN'T! I WANT TO, BUT I CAN'T!

He put on an expression of mock concern.

"Your eyes, Nanny. They're gettin' all red. You're cryin' inside of that old head, arncha, Nanny?—just the way Liz used to cry after you'd tell her some mean thing about me. Show me some tears now, Nanny. Show me some tears for what you done to me an Liz."

LEAVE ME ALONE! OH, PLEASE, PLEASE, GWEN, COME HOME AND HELP ME NOW . . . !

"*I'll* get tears out of you, Nanny. Tears for me and Liz." He straightened up, overbalanced and staggered to one side a step. "Soon as I find somethin' in this house to drink." He tottered away, opening drawers, cabinets, peering into corners bleary-eyed. "Mus' be somethin' here. Will, he'll unnerstan' when I tell him how you broke my beer. 'Cause of your meanness." He chortled. "I'm gonna have one more drink an' then I'm gonna *fix* you, Nanny."

You can't drink anything more. You mustn't. Oh dear God in heaven, don't let him find anything more to drink!

He swung her chair rudely to face the wall.

"Doan peek, Nanny."

Nanny looked down at her body, inert and immovable, something separate from herself, remote as a carving. Oh! the things this same body had done years before: like winning the sack race at the Sunday school picnic; and outclimbing the boys on the tree behind Mason's store. And even now she felt the tremendous churning life within it, the rushing and the hurrying of blood in her veins, the quivering nerves that screamed at her *run, run, run*, the terrors exploding in her brain like flash cards, visions of Louie beating her, holding lit cigarettes against her flesh, tipping her out of her chair—

Falling!

Oh, that was the worst!

The falling dream come to life. Full color and immediate. The floor starting toward her slowly, now lifting, now rising, faster, faster, now speeding, hurtling, rocketing at her while her arms planed useless at her sides.

Bang!

It was Louie slamming a cupboard door. He'd found something. A bottle. A quick new thrust of fear stabbed through her.

"Gin, Nanny. Only gin. I hate gin, Nanny, but it's better'n aftershave—better'n Aqua Velva." He cackled at his own wit like some evil warlock; she heard him guzzle a large gulp of gin straight from the bottle, then cough. "And now I'm gonna fix you up a surprise."

Nanny closed her eyes, squeezed them lock-shut tight against the world. The worst had happened. She had prayed he would not find anything to drink, not find anything more to fuel the hatred and violence in him. Gin—straight gin. It was like dashing raw alcohol over naked flame. Surely God had deserted her.

There were muffled thumps behind her, and the creaking of floorboards. She heard him grunt, then let out a long low chortle of wicked mirth.

"Just goin' to the sandbox, Nanny. Doan go away."

He shambled away down the hall, past the living room, to the back of the house. A pause. Silence followed by a harsh scrape. A door opening, closing. The flush of the toilet. Then footsteps returning.

He was coming back towards her, staggering. She kept her eyes screwed shut. He was coming, he was here! He turned her chair out into the room so that she could see what he was about. He winked, then moved off again in his uneven drunken tread. She peeked out of herself to see what he was about.

He had crossed the kitchen towards the back room doorway, the entrance to the room where he kept his freezer locked tight. But he didn't enter. He stopped. He bent over, down on one knee, reaching. *What in heaven's name—?*

He was lifting the cellar trapdoor. He was throwing back the lid. It yawned like a mouth.

Now he was up and teetering over the black cavern in the floor, swaying dangerously, doing a breath-catching float out over the opening, then lurching safely back to Nanny's side, fumbling in his pocket, clutching, withdrawing.

He dropped a flat steel key into her lap.

"You been wantin' a look into my freezer, Nanny. Well, there it is, waitin'. All you got to do is get to it." He laughed. " 'Course, I din want to make it too easy. No fun then, Nanny. So all you got to do is get over to that trap an' drop it down somehow an' roll on in there an' have yourself a look. Simple." He bent crookedly like a kindly uncle offering a gift, and gusted his sour breath into her face. "If you make it past the trap," he whispered, "I'll even help you with the padlock."

He giggled away, pleased with himself, and fell into a chair.

The cellar trap opened sideways and to the right, like the cover of an enormous book. A chain held it upright, almost vertical. It only needed a nudge to send it crashing shut again. She wanted so badly to look into that freezer; already Nanny found herself wondering if there wasn't some way she could manage it. And there was! The way she closed her own bedroom door. She could hook one front wheel behind the door, and turn sharp left to bring the door slamming down. It was dangerous. She could easily fall—fall into the cellar. But here was the freezer key, here, right in her lap. And out there was the freezer, with Liz beckoning, Liz waiting, Liz calling silently out to her . . . She had to *try*.

She thrust out her fingers to tilt the control switch to roll her forward. Nothing. She flicked at the switch again and again. Dead.

Louie cackled. He drank some more gin.

"S'matter? Outta gas? Dead batt'ry?" He squeaked with laughter, then arched his eyebrows. "Wanna boost?"

That sent a chill of terror through her. The idea of this stumbling

drunk wheeling her toward that hole in the floor was too horrifying to imagine. Her fingers danced at the switch. She had to move. Had to—
The motor whirred, rolling her forward.
Louie, already halfway to his feet, collapsed again. He clapped his hands. "Go, Nanny, go! Yeehah!"
The chair hummed Nanny across the kitchen, toward the yawning gulf in the floor. Three feet from the edge of the hole it stopped. Without even wanting to she had let go of the switch. Her nerve had given out. She wanted to continue, wanted to get out to the back room and see her Liz, her Liz, her lonely Liz, but she was brought up sharp by her own fear. Her fear of falling. That fear kept her from Liz as surely as Louie's padlock had done before. In her mind, she wept.
"Nanny! What's wrong now? Damn batt'ry again? I'll help you, Nanny, I'll help . . ."
He was standing now, grinning broadly, holding the gin bottle, swaying forward, catching himself, leaning back again, like a monstrous puppet worked by an uncertain hand on loose strings. A puppet baby taking its first steps.—Look, Ma, no hands!
Stay away, Nanny screamed in her mind, *stay away from me! Don't touch me, don't push me into that hole. Oh, Gwen, come home! come home!*
Louie took a step towards her, then another, and another.
Gwen, HELP ME!
Louie stretched out his hand for her, and stretching, lost his balance completely, tried to correct for it, leaned back, twirled around and crashed to the floor on his skinny rear end. He sat there a moment, looking back at her stunned. *Maybe he won't get up. Maybe he—*
But he *was* getting up, struggling to his feet and laughing, holding out the gin bottle. "I d'in break it, Nanny. I di'n break it!"
He began rolling her forward.
"Here we go loop-de-loop, Nanny, here we go loop-de-lie . . ."
The cellar door gaped under her wheels like a hungry maw. Two more feet, one . . .
Over the edge!
She closed her eyes. She was falling. It was just the way it had been in her dream. A slow haunting terrifying plunge into a black nothingness. A long trip through forever before the final stunning blow. An age . . .
Nothing.
She opened her eyes.

Louie was reeling around the room like an airplane out of control, laughing fit to bust. The chair was grounded above the hole. Her right front wheel was dangling magically over the abyss. Her left front wheel was caught on the side lip of the hole. If she trembled, breathed, anything, she was going to fall straight in.

"Whooo!" Louie crowed, staggering, going down, kneeling, the bottle swinging out in his hand, catching and reflecting the light. "Whooo!" Then he caught himself up, gasped, and hooted. "Nanny. What happened? Got a flat? Wanna shove?" He came at her again, this time on his knees, his face beet-red with the humor of it all.

NO! Nanny shrieked silently, *GET BACK! STAY—AWAY—FROM—ME!*

She willed him to stop, flung all the strength of her mind at him. And it worked.

He did stop.

And then he fell.

He didn't have far to go, being on his knees already, and he passed out cleanly as he came knee-boning up to her, his face diving by her in a perfect blurred pink arc, his head booming off the sheet metal corner of the stove and hitting the floor with a dull vegetable sound.

This time he didn't move.

First, Nanny told herself, *got to get away from this hole.*

She feathered the control switch timidly, trembling it back and to the left. Once, three times, five times. Then it caught. The motor hummed. It reversed her clear of the hole.

Louie lay still, his head projecting out past the stove.

His thrusting Adam's apple only a foot from her rear wheel.

A surge of triumph flashed through Nanny and carried her away. Here was her enemy at her mercy! *Not so helpless now, am I?* she gloated. She touched the control switch. The motor hummed. She stopped, and from the corner of her eye she saw Louie's neck under her big rear wheel, his larynx bulging like a rope, his throat pulsing with each surge of his heart. All she had to do now was . . .

She hesitated. It was too easy. He was so vulnerable lying there.

But what about Liz? Didn't my Liz have a right to enjoy her life, too? It hadn't been too difficult to kill her, had it? Not for a big, strong man like you. Hadn't she been vulnerable? And an execution was something different from a murder, oh yes, something quite different.

Her fingers toyed with the control lever. She watched them in amazement. Her right hand, the only part of her body she'd had any real control over for months, now seemed to have taken on a will of its own. Like a spectator, she watched, as if from a great distance, the fingers having their own way, tightening, tightening . . .

Then Louie's hand closed powerfully on the spokes of her wheel, his one eye flew open, and he grinned.

"Boo!" he said.

She shrieked in silent terror.

Louie clambered to his feet, kicked the trapdoor shut with a crash and a musty wind, and rolled her into the back room. Softly cackling he undid the lock, then paused with his hand on the lid of the freezer. He whispered:

"You ready for this, Nanny? Hope so! It's a horrible sight. A killer."

The lid flew back.

Nanny looked in.

Gentle vapors. Icy crusts. The freezer was empty.

The room spun crazily around her, grew larger, shrank away, went black, then blindingly bright. Louie went tramping away, whooping laughter, panting and wheezing with it, crashing into things. He dragged his parka around his shoulders, fumbled at the doorknob and staggered out into the night. She heard his car start, the crunch of tires on snow as he rolled away.

When Will and Gwen got home, they found Nanny parked inches away from the old stove, which was roaring away against the gale that had got its start at the North Pole, gathered power and speed on a journey to bring it leaping in at Nanny through the door Louie hadn't bothered to close. They shut the door with a huge slam, stood for a moment blinking stupidly at the broken glass, spilled beer, overturned chairs, stove knocked askew on its fireproof pad. Will ran his fingers through his hair; his face was the color of ashes. Then Gwen was at Nanny's side in a rush, kneeling, clasping Nanny's hand, fussing and full of quick, questioning words, gripping Nanny's fingers tight, her gaze darting from Nanny to the mess in the room and back again.

"Oh, I'm so sorry, so sorry, Nanny, I'll never go off and leave you like that again, never." She looked at Will toeing a sodden beer case with the tip of his shoe. "It was Louie, wasn't it? Oh, God! And he *promised* he'd take care of you." Her voice went suddenly vicious. "I'll never let him set foot in this house again! I won't! I'll throw him out—

Will, *you'll* throw him out!" She was starting to cry. "Nanny, I don't know what to say, I'm just—"

She stopped. Swallowed. Stared.

Will was mumbling away to himself: "Must've been in one of his moods. Nothing *she* could do. She must've just sat here, scared out of her wits . . ."

But Gwen stared past him. Stared into the back room with a feeling of numb bewilderment. Will turned to gaze with her into the back room shadows, at the long white waiting freezer with its lid thrown back. They then went slowly together to stand with linked hands and peer into the frosted emptiness. They turned then and looked at Nanny. Put their heads together, buzzed.

Gwen said sternly, "This freezer is empty, Nanny!"

Will stooped over her.

"Nanny, tell the truth, did you start in on him? That's it, isn't it? You made him understand your . . . your accusations. He got angry and raged around. Broke things. Then he gave you what you wanted—let you see into the freezer. That's what happened, isn't it, Nanny?" His voice was as firm and stern as his face. "I guess when he cools down and comes back, you'll owe him an apology, won't you?"

Gwen was glancing around the room, eyes angry with tears.

"Oh, this *mess!* This awful *mess!*"

Gwen and Will both shook their heads. They'd had enough.

And so had Nanny. Her trembling fingers clutched at her control lever, and the chair obediently responded, whispered her off to her room with a silk swiftness of rubber tires on linoleum. She whirred past the living room where the shadows sat slumped in the chairs, along the twilight hall to the back of the house, turned into her room, spun expertly, and caught the door with her right footrest to send it slamming shut.

The drapes were still undrawn, the night pushing in through the glass and filling the room with itself. An otherwise empty room. Like Nanny's heart. Empty yet tidy, with all the emptiness in its place.

You're too old. Too old and too foolish. A stupid. There's no place for you here any more. You caused trouble tonight. You drove Louie and Liz apart with your whisperings. You're a misery, you leave trails of miserableness behind you, it rubs off you onto other people. . . .

You're responsible for everything that's happened between those two young people.

Gwen came into the room so briskly the edge of the door clunked into Nanny's chair. She swooped in on a flood of dim electric light from the hall. She put firm hands on Nanny, hands that Nanny knew had been cleaning up the mess, impatient, sudden hands. Hands that said by their movements that they'd be better occupied somewhere else. Gwen lifted Nanny in a brisk Victorian Nurse dead lift, stretched her on the bed, tumbled her quickly out of her clothes and into her nightie, rolled her under the quilt, kissed her with hard, dry lips.

"Now you just go right to sleep. We'll have a good talk about this in the morning." She paused at the door. "I hope you're satisfied. I don't know *how* I'm going to deal with Will and Louie after this."

The door closed.

All right, then. Be in a snit. Don't even ask me if I have to go to the bathroom. Blame me for everything. I don't mind. I know it's my fault. You can punish me, dump me into this old cold bed.

And it was a cold bed. Colder than it ought to be . . .

That's what guilt does to a person. Stops their circulation. Bed, get colder. I deserve it.

And it did. A numbing cold was creeping out of the bedding in waves. Also a frosty, cloying damp which gradually became a long slim bulk under the quilt only inches away. And then she knew she was not alone in her bed.

Not alone at all.

She remembered those few moments earlier when she had sat in the corner and listened to Louie's heavy footsteps in the hall.

There was, after all, something much worse than falling.

She began her silent screams.

The Wide and Starry Sky

MICHAEL SHAARA

*H*emminge sighted the Cessna from an altitude of nine thousand feet. It was rising slowly up toward him, coming in from the west, lifting to cross the bare rock mountains between Dawson and Cedar Creek.

When Hemminge saw it, it was still so far as to be only a faint winged speck against the white ground haze, but Hemminge had very good eyes, and Hemminge had been watching for it, for any plane. He circled with great care, his heart pounding. He did not think the Cessna could see him, but he was going to make certain. He circled slowly to the east, making sure that he would come down on the Cessna from out of the sun.

It was a magnificent day for flying. The air was clear in all directions over the black hills, clear and still. The ground haze was thick and white, but that was all the better; it drowned the land in a soft steamy ocean, blotting out everything but Hemminge and the Cessna and the mountains that rose up out of the mist in great black wedges. Hemminge went into his dive, his heart beating violently, but his hands steady and his mind clear. Nerves of iron, Hemminge thought, you must keep nerves of iron. The hand mustn't tremble now like it did the other time, when you nearly botched the job and missed and almost let him get away. No. This time you must be clear, and calm, Hemminge thought, as Sunday morning, Easter Sunday. He was picking up speed now, swiftly, easily, gliding down the sky in one long silent swoop, boring down on the Cessna like a sleek, silent arrow. Remember, Hemminge told himself, keep the mind clear and the hand steady, remember the plane will kick to the right when you fire and correct for that, remember that you are faster than he is and must guard against overshooting, and remember to recover quickly, because he must not have time to use his radio—but now the Cessna was rising up toward him with exploding suddenness, and he centered it in his sights in the last instant and began firing from a long way off. The bullets reached out in gleaming streams and went into the Cessna, exactly into the cabin, exactly between the wings where he had aimed them. And then they had time to stitch forward quickly across the motor cowling and chew at the propeller before he had to lift his own plane slightly to keep from collision, diving on past the Cessna in a roaring split second, but even so he could see it beginning to wobble.

He pulled out of his own dive in time to see the Cessna begin to fall. It was smoking, but not yet really burning. It fell, leaving a long slow smudge in the sky, and Hemminge swung to follow it down, his heart beating even more wildly now with the joy, the exultant joy of the kill. He did not think that there was anybody alive in the plane, but decided to make sure. He bored in once more on the Cessna and gave it a long burst, the coup de grace. He pulled up then and circled and watched it fall, beginning to burn at last. And when it went in, he circled sadly and gave a grave, proud, tender salute, the victorious airman to his fallen enemy. He turned off at last and opened his plane up wide, heading for home. He felt very fine. It had been a good clean kill.

"At least they were dead before it hit the ground," Harry Ball said.

Captain Lockwood had nothing to say.

"Isn't it about time they got the bodies out?" Ball asked.

Lockwood shook his head. "Need a torch for that. Have to wait until tomorrow."

Ball stared up into the sky. Night was coming, but more than that, there was wind and heavy rain. Off in the west, black clouds were rising; he could see lightning flashing and heard the rolling growl of thunder. He looked down again into the mangled cabin and said, "One of them was a woman."

Captain Lockwood looked at him. There was no expression on Ball's face. He was a young man. He had been a state trooper for less than five years; but he had long since learned the law officer's quiet, calm, silent look, and nothing showed on his face but what he wanted there. Yet Lockwood could tell that he was moved.

"They must have been just going off on a vacation," Ball said.

The plane had come down in a box canyon about thirty miles due east of Cedar Creek. It had been sighted early that afternoon, but there was no road into the canyon. Army helicopters had to be flown down from the air base upstate. There had been a doctor in the first copter, but he turned out not to be necessary. The other copters had carried men from the sheriff's department and the state police, and a man from the Civil Aeronautics Authority. They were gathered now on the floor of the canyon in the growing dark. Nobody was saying much and two of the army men had made a fire out of brushwood, and the light of it flickered weirdly across the jagged wreckage of the plane. The army men wanted to get out of there before the approaching storm came down, but nobody else was in a hurry. They were all looking at the plane.

The plane was no longer a plane, but only big ripped shards of silver metal spread all over the canyon floor. The Cessna had been entirely metal; it had not burned very much, but had come down into the rocks like a bomb. There was nothing recognizable except here and there the flat surface of a piece of wing, or tail, and it was these that bore the bullet holes. An army man had been the first to notice the bullet holes. Nobody else quite believed him until they saw the holes themselves. The main evidence was one door of the plane, the right door, which had been hurled away from the wreck only slightly damaged. There was no doubt that the holes in the door were bullet holes.

The door was lying now at the feet of Harry Ball. He was staring at it rather than into the crushed bloody mass of the cabin. Ball had seen many an auto wreck and some even worse than this, but still, this one jarred him. He did not yet know why. Afterwards he would figure that it was probably because he was a pilot himself, in his spare time. He was a tall man with a slightly bent nose in a rugged, patient face. There was that about him, the tall, blue-eyed look, that had made some of his buddies give him the nickname "High Noon." He towered over Captain Lockwood. He stood without saying anything, feeling a weird, peculiar disgust. Lockwood did not say anything either, and after a while they were joined by Jack Biancoli of the CAA. "They're bullet holes all right," Biancoli muttered, still stunned.

"What are you going to do?" Lockwood said quietly.

Biancoli shook his head. "Listen," he said earnestly, "you think it was murder? Or do you think somebody's just gone nuts?"

Lockwood shrugged. "Can't tell yet. We're checking on the two in the plane. But I don't think we'll come up with anything. It figures to be a nut. It has the feel of a nut. You know what I mean?"

"It sure does," Ball said.

"Well," Biancoli gestured vaguely with his hands. "What can you do for me?"

Lockwood remained silent. He was a slow, thorough man and he had not yet had time to focus on the problem. After a moment he said:

"You ground everybody in the state. We'll get help from the air force, help search for the guy."

"Can't do that," Biancoli insisted grimly. "Can't ground everybody; businessmen would raise hell. And how do we even know he's from this state? Might be registered anywhere, even Canada. I can't even guess what make plane he's flying. Could be anything from a Cub to a converted pursuit—"

"No," Harry Ball interrupted. "The killer must have been flying a light plane."

"Why?" Lockwood said.

"Well, trying to shoot down a little plane like this from a real fast plane like a converted army job is harder than it looks. A regular fighter's much too fast, it couldn't turn with a real small plane. It'd have one sweet time trying to get a shot at any little plane if the little plane had warning—"

"If the little plane had warning," Biancoli muttered.

"It still figures to be another light plane," Ball said, "for other reasons. First, those were thirty caliber bullet holes—"

"You fly, Harry, don't you?" Lockwood said suddenly.

Ball nodded.

"Got your own plane?"

Ball shook his head.

Lockwood went on looking at him thoughtfully, then said, unexpectedly, "Good," and turned to Biancoli.

"First we check the mental hospitals," Lockwood said. His voice was firm; he had studied the problem and was beginning to shift into high gear now. "Find out if there's a record of anybody anywhere who had delusions about being a war ace. Next we alert the air force and ask them to post a couple of squadrons high up over this whole area. Then we try to blanket the area with radar, radioing the air force to come on down and look if any plane starts making suspicious moves. In the meantime, we start checking planes for evidence of weapons. Another thing, if this guy has a gun in his plane he's flying from a private strip. That ought to be easy."

"How about checking the gun itself?" Biancoli said. "There must be a record . . ."

"No dice. There must be thousands of unregistered machine guns in this country. No way of checking. But there aren't too many private strips."

"I hope to God you're right."

"There's one thing. You'll have to figure whether or not you want to issue a warning to all pilots."

Biancoli started. "What?"

"If this is a nut, he'll be up again, looking for somebody else. If we can pass this off to the papers as just another wreck, not let anybody know we found the bullet holes, the killer'll be maybe a little less cautious about coming out again."

Biancoli blew a breath, rubbed his face nervously.

"Otherwise," Lockwood went on, "the nut might just possibly pack up and leave for somewhere else. Take the gun out of his plane and ship it to another state, and start all over. And we lose him."

"Sam," Biancoli said, his face turned suddenly strange in the dim light of the fire, "listen—"

"It's your choice."

"No. Listen. This has been nagging me. I didn't—last week two planes crashed in these mountains." Harry Ball felt a sudden chill. "They were both little Cubs," Biancoli said. "They both burned. The weather was perfect; we couldn't figure why they went in. We inspected the wrecks, but we couldn't do much out here, in the hills. But listen, we weren't looking for bullet holes."

Lockwood nodded.

"All the fabric was burned," Biancoli said. "We never saw any bullet holes."

"I think you better check again."

"It could be that this one nut got all three of them."

"It could be," Lockwood said.

"My God."

"A nut is a nut," Lockwood said. "With a nut, you never know. But he'll be up again looking for somebody else, that I guarantee you. You check on those other two wrecks. In the meantime we'll—" he stopped abruptly, turning to glance at Ball. He thought for a moment, then swung back on Biancoli.

"We can try a trap," he said. "We'll get some private planes and have them fly back and forth over these mountains. If this joker comes out again our boys will have radios and the air force will be waiting up high, in jets." He swung back to Ball. "Harry," he said, a very faint smile in his eyes, "you seem interested. Want to volunteer to fly?"

"Yes," Harry Ball said.

Under the wide and starry sky, dig the grave and let me lie. The phrase was running through Hemminge's mind over and over and over again, the silent peaceful beautiful words soothing and smoothing the mighty pain in his head. He was lying on a cot on the screened porch in the darkness of night. It was raining heavily, blowing down through the screen on him, and he was soaked through, but he did not mind it. The cool water on his face dulled the pain, the pain, which was all he could think about. All through the rain there was wild white lightning, but Hemminge could not see it. His eyes, whether open or closed, saw only the strange, glowing, jagged lines that were a part of the headaches, had come with the headaches for as far back as Hemminge could remember. The pain was always bad, but the pain of this one was enough to drive a man out of his mind. I'll go mad, Hemminge thought, I'll go mad. Under the wide and starry sky, under the wide and starry sky . . .

Yet the headache was going away. In the midst of the pain he could sense the slight lessening, the nerves quieting, dulled now before the awful pain they could no longer feel, and Hemminge began to be dazedly grateful. Earlier, the pain had been so bad he had been sick to his stomach. Under the wide and starry sky, he thought, remembering at the same time the misery of that sickness. But the headache was definitely going away. The fact that he could think proved it was going away. But under the wide and starry sky, dig the grave—there, now even his vision was coming back. He had just seen a flash of lightning.

He lay for another hour on the couch. The pain was not gone, but it was bearable; compared to what it had been, the pain now was nothing. But he was exhausted. He lay on the couch until he had some energy; then he stumbled on into the kitchen and made himself coffee. On the way into the kitchen he had to go through the living room, and there almost tripped over the body of his wife. Looking down at her, suddenly the vision of her bloodied head hit him with a shuddering knife blow in the chest. The memory of what he had done to her blossomed stark and murderous before he could shut it out. But he did not want to think of it. Toodle-oo, toodle-oo, he thought, and that was the end of it. He made his coffee and went wet and dripping back out to the porch.

The rain was letting up. In one of the last flashes of lightning, he saw his plane perched blue and lovely, alive, on the strip by the house. A wave of love for the plane came over him, a proud, gentle love. He raised his coffee cup toward the plane. Thee and me, he thought lovingly, we are one flesh. He drank the coffee and lay down.

But the trouble with lying down was that you always thought too much. You are pretty far gone, aren't you? he told himself, in a burst of brutal clarity, but mercifully that faded away and his mind went back to the muddied fragments of poems and dreams and sweet violent visions that were all that was left of him now, Arthur Hemminge, a small fat man with graying hair, not yet fifty years old.

Now he could no longer stop himself from thinking. Visions passed through his mind like black flak bursting around a dying plane. My father was a proud and virtuous man—vision of his father in a fine flying uniform—and now I'm a pilot, too, Hemminge thought, and wouldn't he be proud now—but *hate, hate,* Hemminge shuddered with hate for his father. And he could admit it now, what a wonderful feeling to roll and revel in the hate for his father—who did not want me or anything or anybody, but the fine proud talk about flying, and, and . . . Before other memories of his father Hemminge's mind halted, and swung off down the dark halls of his life, passing the mother he had loved who was dead, and the son he had loved who was dead, and now even the wife, and my God, Hemminge thought, what I love is all dead. And visions now arose of great planes sweeping through the sky like black vultures and Hemminge began to cry.

I had a father, Hemminge thought, and I had a son, and . . . and now I've gone mad.

He knew that, from time to time. The most horrible moments of all were when he could see himself clearly, when he could no longer blot himself out and bury his mind in visions. It was peculiarly horrible the way it had happened—things seemed to reverse themselves, not like you expected it to happen at all. First the pain and the visions and the weird flowing feeling, especially at night. During those you knew you were going insane, but did not know what to do about it. Then the electric pinging sensations that came and went, and periods of total blackness, from which you awoke with sweating horror wondering what of all those things you had dreamed was real, and what wasn't.

And then gradually, but with increasing swiftness, the true break-down, the orgy in the mind, and the last muffled cry for help, and after that nothing, nothing, the shadow world and the red figures all around you and death, from which you rose in brief bright flashes of clarity and saw yourself as you had become, the clear tragic moments which were the most horrible of all not only because of what you had become, but because there was no longer any possibility of help, of cure, you were this mad thing here and would be this mad thing until you died. Under the wide and starry sky . . .

In psychiatric clinics you can find many beautifully written, clear and clinical reports of just what things it took to drive a certain person mad. In the case of Arthur Hemminge, the prime mover would have been, of course, the father, the tall proud war pilot whom Arthur loved and whom the father not only never loved, but never hated either, just simply ignored. Hemminge's mother, who would have loved him, died too young. That was a contributing factor. The father forced Arthur to fly too early, after filling him with wild, terrible stories of how planes crashed, and so embedded in the boy a fear of airplanes, and of heights. That was also a contributing factor. Arthur's only son became a pilot, and was one of the few American airmen to be killed in the Korean War. That was probably the final factor. The report would say of Arthur Hemminge that he had fixed on airplanes as the cause and solution of all his life's pain.

And so when Arthur Hemminge took his father's inheritance and bought himself a lonely place in the mountains and learned, finally, to fly, the fear of heights now suddenly, oddly gone, and built himself a private landing strip and began his weird path of murder, the reasons were obvious: by becoming a pilot himself he could take his place at last with his father, his son, a man among men, a fighter pilot among pilots, and yet at the same time he would be destroying the things that had taken the loves of his life from him—airplanes.

All this a report would say simply, and with truth, and yet—Arthur Hemminge was forty-three years old before he broke. It took him forty-three years of bitter building to bring him to the moment when his mind fragmented like pulverized glass and he became the odd horrible thing that he became, but it took forty-three years to do it. Forty long years of memories and events entered one after the other in endless succession, day after day, a tiny moment here, a gesture there, words overheard and words spoken directly to him, memories of his small son, brutal memories like the telegram from the War Department, sweet contrasting memories of his mother. All added together brought the moment when he went, finally and for good, insane.

To understand what Arthur Hemminge was is to understand all of those moments, to enter into Arthur Hemminge's mind. And a clinical report is not enough for that, whole books are not enough for that, there is a mystery to insanity which remains a mystery, even to the insane. Most of all, perhaps, to the insane, who sometimes have, like Arthur Hemminge, those terrible moments of clarity, rising like islands in a boiling sea.

So Arthur Hemminge lay on his couch in the desolate midst of nowhere, his mind filled with the roiled visions of madness. He had killed his wife the day before, when she found out what he was doing and wanted him to go to a doctor. He could not help thinking about her, and from her he thought suddenly—women and children. Women and children must die in a war, because that is one of the things that makes war so terrible. And he thought: a pilot not only shoots down planes. He strafes. He bombs. Visions of bombs bursting among crowds of civilians swarmed in his brain.

I have to do that, he said aloud. All pilots have strafing missions. So I must bomb crowds. He sat up on the couch. He tried to think. Now where could I find a big crowd?

When Harry Ball got to Pat's house, it was very late and she was not in a good humor. She was standing in her doorway, tapping her foot, looking very small, soft, blue-eyed, and delightful. Looking at her, he began to hunger for her, gently, dangerously, and he pulled himself back. Remembering, he told himself, she's got a backbone of steel. Don't be fooled by the softness, or you'll be in trouble.

"Hey," he said happily.

"Well," Pat glowered, "have a nice vacation?"

"Honey," Ball murmured, soothing, reaching for her.

"Now, none of that," Pat fended him off, "you *promised* me you'd be here by eight o'clock—"

Ball kissed her. She was stiff and unbending and then suddenly she melted, coming to him, and he held her close for a moment silently.

He had driven a long way that night and he was tired and maybe that was part of it, but he suddenly wanted only to hold her and feel the warmth of her all the rest of the night. I'm in love with you, he thought, the words rising in his mind, shocking and warming him. But he said nothing. When he released her she looked up at him, her eyes searching, and then she said: "You. Oh, you," and then turned and went away from him, going for his coffee.

He went to her father's favorite chair and sat down. He looked after her, shaken. Pat was the one and only girl he had been dating for the past six months. She was a nurse in the hospital at Dawson. He had known he was in love with her for several weeks, but he had not said anything about it. He did not know what to do about it. Pat was possibly too much for him. When he was with her, he was never quite sure just who was in command, under that fluffy exterior lurked a girl with a mind of her own. Harry Ball was old fashioned enough to want to be the boss in his own house. And honest enough to realize that with Pat he might not be. She was more than strong-willed; she had "education." Because Ball had not gone to college himself, it was a barrier between them.

It was not Pat's barrier; it was his own. He knew that, but he could not seem to help it. There was a certain poise in Pat, the way she used words, the words she used, the ease with which she could carry on conversations about things Ball did not know. Education and intelligence are two different things, and Ball knew that and knew also that he was no fool, but . . . he had a deep inviolable belief that a man should not feel inferior to his wife. He had a need in him to father, to protect. So he said nothing. And went on falling in love with her, falling slowly, helplessly, like a man sliding down a long, long glacier.

She came back with coffee and plunked it down by him, and plunked herself down on his lap. He reached up and turned out the light and there were a few lovely seconds in the dark, and then she reached up with determination and turned the light on again.

"Coward," he said.

"Uh-uh," she shook her head teasingly, then slyly tapped her temple. "Brains. Part of my foxy campaign." Which brought it up all over again. Ball frowned. "What's the matter?"

"Nothing." Ball turned away. "A hard day."

He began to tell her about it and soon he even forgot that she was still on his lap.

"They're giving *you* a plane?" Pat said, startled.

"Yep. A Navion. Lockwood borrowed it from some big wheel in the state government. There're about six more volunteers. We'll all be flying back and forth in shifts. We'll catch the bugger. But boy, isn't that something?" He chuckled. "To be paid for flying?"

"The poor man," Pat murmured.

"Poor man?"

"The man you're looking for."

"Poor man?" Ball repeated, astonished.

"Well, he's insane, obviously."

Ball stared at her. Pat looked down at him coldly.

"He's a sick man," she said. "Most policemen just don't seem to realize . . . well, you shouldn't talk about him as if he were just another . . . purse snatcher."

Ball dropped his eyes. After a moment he said:

"I get it. Time for a lesson in psychology. All right," he reached out for his coffee. "Go ahead."

She looked at him for a moment. Then got up off his lap.

"Well, let's have the lecture," Ball said.

"If you're going to act like that—"

"I know I don't know anything about psychology," Ball said. "I know I'm just a dumb insensitive clod. But honey," he leaned forward brutally, "this here poor man you're talking about has killed, altogether, six people, six real live human people. Two of them women. Killed them for no damned reason in the world that makes a difference to me. If we don't get to him very quickly, somebody else who is alive right at this moment, walking around healthy and full of beans right now, will be spread all over the county maybe this time tomorrow."

Pat sighed. "Harry, I wish you wouldn't—"

But Ball went on relentlessly. "You say he's sick. Yeah. Well. The people he killed are just as dead as if he was healthy as a pink hog. I don't want to know his temperature or his pulse or any of that. I leave that to people like you. My job is to get him. If I run across him, I'll kill him."

Ball had not meant to be that brutal, but all of this had jarred him.

"What an awful thing to say." Pat rose, flushed.

"Listen, now, this is my job. I don't mind you passing judgment on Cezanne or how to do a hysterectomy or any of that, okay. But this is my job, and I am not bad at it. My job is to see that this joker does not kill anybody else, and if I have to kill him to do it, then that's my job, and this poor man stuff is not for me."

"So that's what it is," Pat said softly, staring at him. "Your pride has been hurt. It's your pride."

"Pride, hell!" Ball said. Now he stood up. "I've seen it too many times. We're always the villains, guys like me, the brutal cops. Every day we get the sociologists, the psychologists, coming down and telling us what we do wrong. You've got to treat poor Ferd gently, he's not a common criminal, he's sick! And so we give them poor Ferd and they treat him in some understaffed hospital and have to let him go too soon and then we only have to get him again, and again . . ."

"I'm sorry," Pat said, still staring at him. "But you know, I don't think you'd kill him."

"You don't think I would, huh?"

"You couldn't anyway. You won't have a gun."

"They're arming the planes," Ball grinned. "Old Lockwood's having them install guns in the planes, just in case. He said he wouldn't send his boys looking for any killer without a chance to fight back."

"Now you're being melodramatic," Pat said, stiffening.

"Another four-barrelled word," Ball said. "Where's my hat?"

"Harry," Pat said. He stopped.

"It's the college, isn't it? That's what holding you back."

"Holding me back from what?"

"From loving me."

It was the first time the word "love" had ever come out between them. Ball said nothing. He stared at her, tortured by the sweet sight of her, by the proud rage within himself.

"Harry," she said, pleading.

"No," Ball said. "It's no good. You won't even leave my job alone. What am I if you take over my job?"

He went on out the door. He did not look back. Something inside was telling him that all this was ridiculous, that he would probably never even see the killer, that some of what she had said was right, was true, but . . . he did not turn back. He drove home through the same rain that was falling, at that moment, on Arthur Hemminge.

The next day Hemminge did not fly. He was busy preparing bombs. He wasted a lot of time trying to be complicated and exact, but in the end he decided on simple gasoline. He puttered away most of the afternoon, humming with delight. But just before sundown, he went back into the house and stumbled again across the body of his wife.

After that he had a very difficult time. He could not seem to think clearly. Almost immediately the headache began coming back. The glowing lights began again in the corners of his eyes; he could feel the pressure building as if black water was being pumped into his head. He was tremendously depressed; he became violently angry. Usually the headaches gave him a few days' peace in between, but now he had hardly gotten over one when another one began. He raged around the yard while he still had his sight, kicking, destroying, emptying gasoline and burning it. Then he blacked out.

When he came to, it was dark and the stars were out. He could not move. He lay on the ground in the cool grass, staring upward. The pain in his head had come and gone; looking upward into the cool heaven, the mighty black, he felt a moment of enormous peace. He slept.

He awoke some time later, just before the sun came up. He was still in the grip of a deadly paralysis; he had to fight himself to move, get up. He staggered back to the house, but did not go in. He sat on the porch. He had not shaved in several days; his beard was thick and dark. He lifted his face to the morning, remembering last night's brief moment of peace. He prayed. What he said did not make any sense, but there was no one to hear him. He prayed for a long while, tears streaming down his cheeks. Eventually he stopped.

It's time to fly, he thought. In the red glow of the horizon he could sense men moving about him—pilots! Man your planes! He could see long lines of great black planes outlined against the sky, flames winking on in the exhausts one by one. I'm coming, he said aloud.

He rose and ran out to his plane, hearing the squadron thump by around him in heavy flight boots. He started to sing. He gassed the plane and loaded the gun. Planes roared all around him. He took his place in the line, answering commands over the radio from the tower. When it was his turn, he took off and climbed high up into the sun, along with the rest of the Dawn Patrol. When the squadron broke off, Hemminge waved them all goodbye. He settled down alone, the hunter, searching for game in the clear vaulted sky.

Just before he took off that morning, Harry Ball was handed a letter from Pat. One of the boys had gone up to the hospital where she worked, and she had given it to him to deliver. Ball stuffed the letter into his shirt pocket, unopened, and took off. Once out of the traffic pattern, he pulled back on the stick and began the long slow climb to the west, toward the mountains. The letter was heavy in his pocket, but he did not open it. There was a force in him urging him to open the window and let the letter slip out into swift empty air.

Harry Ball was a hard man, and he had not broken with Pat lightly; for two days now he had been making it clear to himself that he would not call her again, he would not see her again. He admitted to himself that he loved her, but that made no difference. He had come very close to kneeling to her, but his pride had held him back. And he knew that because of his pride he had lost her, and he also knew that there was nothing else he could have done. Because there was that same proud thing in Pat which also could not kneel to him. And what kind of marriage would that make? Ball thought, two people forever fighting each other for control. And after all, Ball thought, I'm thirty years old. Maybe I am not a man for marriage.

So it was all done. Ball looked around at the sky and made an effort to push Pat out of his mind. He flew on over the mountains, high in the morning sun, forcing himself to think about the killer—whom he could begin now to really and truly hate, a startling feeling, a new and murderous feeling. But now Ball had something personal in this, and so scanned the sky intently, searching for any other plane in the dark blue above, forgetting Pat enough to feel a stomach-tightening thrill as he approached a high bank of clouds, thinking that the killer could be waiting just ahead, hanging swift and hidden in among the soft white folds.

But the killer did not come, and abruptly the murderous feeling in Ball died. The sky was wide and white and empty. Ball flew on toward the west with the letter in his pocket, soothed by the drone of his engine, and gradually the fact of the letter in his pocket no longer jarred him. I can handle it, he thought. I can say that I won't call her again and I won't. And he knew that to be true. Then he took the letter out calmly, coldly, and opened it.

My darling—Ball read—*I love you. I have been sitting here all night trying to think of the right words, but all that matters is that I love you. I cannot get over the feeling that I have really and truly lost you, that you will never come back. My darling, I have been terribly wrong. You are all I want in the world.*

Because you mean so much to me, I have tried to mean something to you, but I had never tried to make anyone love me before and I did not know how. I had to be something special to you, but all I had to give were a few long words and theories I learned in school, and I only wanted to impress you, but more than anything else now I want you, and no theories, no words. I accused you of pride, but it was my own pride that hurt us. Darling. I do not care about pride. I love you. I will love you whether or not you have to kill, whether or not you come back to me. I love you. I can't seem to say that enough. I only wish I had said it before, that it is not too late. But it is all stored up in me, waiting to come out. I will come to you, if you will only call. I love you. Pat.

Ball put the letter down. He was shaken. Well, he thought. He studied the letter for a long moment, trying to get his mind into focus. She went a long way, he thought. Somebody had to give and she saw that and so she gave. And it was her place to give in, wasn't it?

Wasn't it?

In the midst of all his emotion, in the midst of the absolute certainty that he had been right all along, Ball felt a sudden stab of doubt. There was something wrong. He did not know what it was, but it was jarring him. It began to occur to him that he had humbled her, had forced her to come to him. But . . . was that bad? He had needed her to come to him. He did not know why that was so but it was so. He flew on a straight line, thinking about it, trying to discover the thing that still bothered him. He flew on without looking around him, or behind, up at the sun, and in the end the letter nearly cost him his life.

Hemminge came down on him from directly above, out of the sun.

The first Ball knew of it was a pluck, plucking sound at his right wing. He turned and stared stupefied at black holes being stitched with astounding speed across metal. What saved him was instinct. He rammed the left wing hard down, dropping the nose; the bullets meant for his cabin zipped by him through the air. He did not see the other plane coming, but he heard it go by, felt the blast of air from it going by. He dropped far down to the left before pulling up and he had no idea what to do. At the top of his climb he saw the other plane for the first time and stared at it across the open air, losing precious time just to see it, still stunned, and realized that it was a Comanche, a trim new Comanche, blue and silver and glittering in the sun.

It came at him again, nose on and shooting. He swung hard to get away and made a very bad mistake; the Comanche slipped lethally in on his tail and bullets plucked again at the Navion, at the fuselage behind him. He thought of the radio, for a call for help, but there was no time. He needed both hands to fly the plane. He dropped the nose again, gathering speed, rocking wildly back and forth, but the Comanche stayed with him. A bullet smashed through the canopy above him, spattering pieces into his hair. He had an enormous urge to pull up, but once again instinct saved him, telling him that if he pulled up now the Comanche would have him broadside, a lovely shot right into the cockpit. He did the only thing he had left to do—he let down flaps and hauled back on the throttle. The Navion slowed drastically; the Comanche overshot and brushed him going by, picking up speed.

Ball fought for altitude, but it was impossible to keep the Comanche below him. It was much faster than he was; it gave him no time for the radio. As it came at him again he turned to face it; in desperation he pushed the little button on the dash that fired his gun. The Navion kicked back as the gun went off; he could see the bullets sliding away, missing, but the Comanche veered crazily and Ball heard incredible sounds begin on the radio receiver. It was a long eerie second before Ball understood. The killer was speaking to him. The Comanche had swung off high above him in a confused circle, and was speaking, yelling. In German.

Ball did not know any German, but there was no mistaking the guttural sounds. The killer probably thought he was fighting a real war, against a German ace. But there was no mistaking the other thing, the weird, jittery, unnatural thing in the voice that came down from the other plane. Dribbling, spattering sounds. The killer was shouting at him, and coming down.

Ball had time for a quick cry into the radio—Harry Ball, Mayday, Mayday, near Bear Creek, over Bear Creek—before he had to fight again to keep the Comanche off. He wanted to get one more message across, at least one, that the killer was flying a blue and white Comanche, but bullets came into the canopy again and the killer would not stop talking, and the voice rattled Harry Ball's mind so that he could not speak, but had to go down again in a dive, with the Comanche following. He pulled the same trick, and it worked again, and as the Comanche slid by him Ball raised his nose slowly and the killer was dead ahead, and Harry Ball's hand was on the machine gun button, and time froze as Ball looked down and saw the black helmet in the cockpit, the wild green scarf around the neck, no sound coming over the radio, and Harry Ball didn't shoot.

He pulled up slowly; the Comanche went down and away. Harry Ball felt sick in the pit of his stomach. He felt that he had almost done a dirty thing. It would have been like running over a dog that comes out in front of you on the highway. It struck him now that Pat had known that he would not be capable of doing this thing, just as he had known it but had been too perverse to admit. And then a new sound came over the radio, a strange deep voice, puzzled, plaintive, in English:

"But why didn't you shoot?"

Harry Ball did not answer. He radioed another quick Mayday, giving the Comanche's serial number. But the Comanche broke in, coming back at him, saying, "You should have shot. You had me fair and square."

But now Ball was in control. The Comanche seemed no longer as fast and sure, and Ball, watching it, sensed that the Comanche was through, and knew at the same time that if he had to kill the Comanche he would do it, as soon as it became really necessary, because regardless of the sickness in this man he had his job to do—but thank God it was not going to be necessary. He said into the radio: "Give up, Comanche. I'll follow you down."

At the moment something caught the corner of his eye. Glancing up quickly, he saw the jets coming, two of them, trailing thin smoke down the sky. Ball said something else into the radio, but the Comanche did not answer. It swung quickly to meet the jets, a lovely little plane gleaming a burning blue in the afternoon sun. It rose up toward them and the jets broke apart, swung out in a wide pincer, and the Comanche went up between them, climbing.

Ball tried to follow, but the Navion was too slow. The Comanche went on rising, higher, higher, and now again Ball could hear sound on his radio, an even stranger sound, *singing*. The man was singing now, a broken unintelligible song in that eerie unnatural voice, and even the jets were silent, but swung easily around the little plane like huge fast fish around a slow blue minnow. They would follow him wherever he went. It was all done and they knew it, and as Ball watched he saw the Comanche suddenly roll over on its back, and it began to go down.

The man was still singing, humming. Ball listened to him and watched the plane go down, picking up speed, falling faster and faster with the engine wide open, boring straight down, the watching jets sweeping grandly down after it. For a moment Ball thought that the Comanche was making one last effort to get away, but then the singing stopped and there was a dead silence in the radio, and the Comanche kept going down, moving so fast now that Ball knew he would never pull it out any more, not even if he wanted to. And so the Comanche went straight down, falling out of the sunlight into the rising dark, and the man in the plane began to speak, praying, and he was still praying when the Comanche blew up in the rocks.

The three planes circled above aimlessly, silently. Ball could not think of much to say to the other men. They did not say much to him. After a moment he heard one of the jet pilots give the position of the wreck. He turned off then and started the long flight home.

When he got home, he called Pat and told her that he loved her.

The Anderson Boy

JOSEPH HANSEN

*P*rothero, fastening the pegs of his car coat, pushed out through the heavy doors of the Liberal Arts Building, and saw the Anderson boy. The boy loped along in an Army surplus jacket and Army surplus combat boots, a satchel of books on his back. His hair, as white and shaggy as when he was five, blew in the cold wind.

He was a long way off. Crowds of students hurried along the paths under the naked trees between lawns brown and patched with last week's snow. But Prothero picked out the Anderson boy at once and with sickening certainty.

Prothero almost ran for his car. When he reached it, in the gray-cement vastness of Parking Building B, his hands shook so that he couldn't at first fit the key into the door. Seated inside, he shuddered. His sheepskin collar was icy with sweat crystals. He shut his eyes, gripped the wheel, leaned his head against it.

This was not possible. The trip to promote his book—those staring airport waiting rooms, this plane at midnight, that at four A.M., snatches of sleep in this and that hotel room, this bookseller luncheon, that radio call-in program, dawns for the *Today Show* and *Good Morning, America,* yawns for Johnny Carson. Los Angeles in ninety-degree heat, Denver in snow, Chicago in wind, New York in rain; pills to make him sleep, pills to wake him up; martinis, wine, and Scotch poured down him like water. Three weeks of it had been too much. His nerves were frayed. He was seeing things. The very worst things.

He drove off campus. By the shopping center, he halted for a red light. He thought about his lecture. It had gone well, which was surprising, tired as he was. But he'd been happy to be back where he belonged, earning an honest living, doing what he loved. Promotion tours? Never again. His publisher was pleased. The book was selling well. But Donald Prothero was a wreck.

The Anderson boy loped across in front of him. He shut his eyes, drew a deep breath, opened his eyes, and looked again. He was still sure. Yet how could it be? It was thirteen years since he'd last seen him, and more than a thousand miles from here. On that night, the boy had been a pale little figure in pajamas, standing wide-eyed in the dark breezeway outside the sliding glass wall of his bedroom, hugging a stuffed toy kangaroo. Prothero, in his panicked flight, naked, clutching his clothes, had almost run him over.

The boy had to have recognized him. Prothero was always around. He'd taught the boy to catch a ball, to name birds, lizards, cacti, to swim in the bright-blue pool just beyond that breezeway. Prothero had given him the toy kangaroo. He should have stopped. Instead, he'd kept running. He was only eighteen. Nothing bad had ever happened to him. Sick and sweating, he'd driven far into the desert. On some lost, moonlit road, half overgrown by chaparral, he'd jerked into his clothes, hating his body.

He'd known what he had to do—go to the sheriff. He'd started the car again, but he couldn't make himself do it. He couldn't accept what had happened. Things like that took place in cheap books and bad movies, or they happened to sleazy people on the TV news. Not to people like the Andersons. Not to people like him. It could wreck his whole life. He went home. To his room. As always. But he couldn't sleep. All he could do was vomit. His father, bathrobe, hair rumpled, peered at him in the dusky hall when Prothero came out of the bathroom for the third time.

"Have you been drinking?"

"You know better than that."

"Shall we call the doctor?"

"No, I'm all right now."

But he would never be all right again. Next morning, when he stripped to shower, he nearly fainted. His skin was caked with dried blood. He nearly scalded himself, washing it off. He trembled and felt weak, dressing, but he dressed neat and fresh as always. He kissed his mother and sat on his stool at the breakfast bar, smiling as always. He was a boy who smiled. He'd been senior class president in high school, captain of the basketball team, editor of the yearbook. These things had been handed him, and he'd accepted them without question. As he'd accepted scholarships to University for the coming fall. As he'd accepted his role as Jean Anderson's lover.

His mother set orange juice in front of him, and his mug with his initial on it, filled with creamy coffee. He knew what she would do next. He wanted to shout at her not to do it. He didn't shout. They would think he was crazy. She snapped on the little red-shelled TV set that hung where she could watch it as she cooked at the burner-deck, where his father and he could watch it while they ate. He wanted to get off the stool and go hide. But they would ask questions. He stayed.

And there on the screen, in black and white, was the Anderson house with its rock roof and handsome plantings, its glass slide doors, the pool with outdoor furniture beside it, the white rail fence. There in some ugly office sat the Anderson boy in his pajamas on a moulded plastic chair under a bulletin-board tacked with papers. The toy kangaroo lay on a floor of vinyl tile among cigarette butts. A pimply faced deputy bent over the boy, trying to get him to drink from a striped waxpaper cup. The boy didn't cry. He didn't even blink. He sat still and stared at nothing. There were dim, tilted pictures, for a few seconds, of a bedroom, dark blotches on crumpled sheets, dark blotches on pale carpeting. Bodies strapped down under the blankets were wheeled on gurneys to an ambulance whose rear doors gaped. The Sheriff's face filled the screen—thick, wrinkled eyelids, nose with big pores, cracked lips. He spoke. Then a cartoon tiger ate cereal from a spoon.

"People shouldn't isolate themselves miles from town." Prothero's father buttered toast. "Husband away traveling half the time. Wife and child alone. Asking for trouble."

"He came home." Prothero's mother set plates of scrambled eggs and bacon on the counter. "It didn't help."

"All sorts of maniacs running loose these days," Prothero's father said. "Evidently no motive. They'll probably never find who did it."

His father went to his office. His mother went to a meeting of the Episcopal Church altar guild. He drove to the Sheriff's station. He parked on a side street, but he couldn't get out of the car. He sat and stared at the flat-roofed, sand-colored building with the flagpole in front. He ran the radio. At noon, it said the Sheriff had ruled out the possibility of an intruder. The gun had belonged to Anderson. His were the only fingerprints on it. Plainly, there had been a quarrel and Anderson had shot first his wife and then himself. The Anderson boy appeared to be in a state of shock and had said nothing. A grandmother had flown in from San Diego to look after him. Prothero went home to the empty house and cried.

Now, at the intersection, he watched from his car as the boy pushed through glass doors into McDonald's. He had to be mistaken. This wasn't rational. Horns blared behind him. The light had turned green. He pressed the throttle. The engine coughed and died. Damn. He twisted the key, the engine started, the car bucked ahead half its length and quit again. The light turned orange. On the third try, he made it across the intersection, but the cars he'd kept from crossing honked angrily after him.

The Anderson boy? What made him think that? He'd known a runty little kid. This boy was over six feet tall. A towhead, yes, but how uncommon was that? He swung the car into the street that would take him home beneath an over-arch of bare tree limbs. The boy looked like his father—but that skull shape, those big long bones, were simply North European characteristics. Millions of people shared those. The odds were out of the question. It was his nerves. It couldn't be the Anderson boy.

He went from the garage straight to the den, shed the car coat, and poured himself a drink. He gulped down half of it and shivered. The den was cold and smelled shut up. He hadn't come into it yesterday when he got home from the airport. The curtains were drawn. He touched a switch that opened them. Outside, dead leaves stuck to flagging. Winter-brown lawn with neat plantings of birches sloped to a little stream. Woods were gray beyond the stream.

"Ah," Barbara said, "it is you."

"Who else would it be?" He didn't turn to her.

"How did the lecture go?"

"Who built the footbridge?" he said.

"The nicest boy," she said. "A friend of yours from California. Wayne Anderson. Do you remember him?"

"I was going to build it," he said.

"I thought it would be a pleasant surprise for you when you got home. I was saving it." She stepped around stacks of books on the floor and touched him. "You all right?"

"It would have been good therapy for me. Outdoors. Physical labor. Sense of accomplishment."

"He said you'd been so nice to him when he was a little boy. When he saw the lumber piled up down there, and I told him what you had in mind, he said he'd like to do it. And he meant it. He was very quick and handy. Came faithfully every day for a whole week. He's an absolute darling."

Prothero finished his drink. "How much did you have to pay him?"

"He wouldn't let me pay him," she said. "So I fed him. That seemed acceptable. He eats with gusto."

Flakes of snow began to fall. Prothero said, "It's hard to believe."

"He saw you on television in San Diego, but it was tape, and when he phoned the station, you'd gone. He thought you'd come back here. He got on a plane that night." She laughed. "Isn't it wonderful how these children just leap a thousand miles on impulse? Could we even have imagined it at his age? He got our address from Administration and came here without even stopping to unpack. Not that he brought much luggage. A dufflebag is all."

"You didn't invite him to stay."

"I thought of it," she said.

He worked the switch to close the curtains. He didn't want to see the bridge. It was dim in the den and she switched on the desk lamp. He was pouring more whiskey into his glass. He said, "I didn't ask you about Cora last night. How's she doing?"

"It's a miracle. You'd never know she'd had a stroke." He knew from her voice that she was watching him and worried. His hands shook. He spilled whiskey. "You're not all right," she said. "I've never seen you so pale. Don, don't let them talk you into any more book peddling. Please?"

"Is he coming here again?"

"Yes. This afternoon." She frowned. "What's wrong? Don't you want to see him? He's very keen to see you. I'd say he worships you—exactly as if he were still five years old."

"They don't mature evenly," Prothero said.

"He hasn't forgotten a thing," she said.

In thickly falling snow, the Anderson boy jumped up and down on the little bridge and showed his teeth. He was still in the floppy Army surplus jacket. The clumsy Army surplus boots thudded on the planks. He took hold of the raw two-by-fours that were the railings of the bridge and tried to shake them with his big, clean hands. They didn't shake. Clumps of snow drifted under the bridge on the cold slow surface of the stream. Prothero stood on the bank, hands pushed into the pockets of the car coat. His ears were cold.

"It would hold a car." The Anderson boy came off the bridge. "If it was that wide. Not a nail in it. Only bolts and screws. No props in the stream-bed to wash out. Cantilevered."

Prothero nodded. "Good job," he said. "Your major will be engineering, then, right?"

"No." Half a head taller than Prothero, and very strong, the boy took Prothero's arm as if Prothero were old and frail, or as if he were a woman, and walked him back up the slope. "No, my grandfather's a contractor. I started working for him summers when I was fourteen. I got my growth early." He stopped on the flags and pawed at his hair to get the snow out of it. His hair was so white it looked as if he were shedding.

"So you learned carpentry by doing?" Prothero reached for the latch of the sliding door to the den.

But the Anderson boy's arm was longer. He rolled the door back and with a hand between Prothero's shoulderblades pushed the man inside ahead of him. "It's like breathing or walking to me." He shut the door and helped Prothero off with his coat. "And just about as interesting." He took the coat to the bathroom off the den. He knew right where it was. Prothero watched him shed his own jacket there and hang both coats over the bathtub to drip. He sat on the edge of the tub to take off his boots. "I wouldn't do it for a living."

"What about coffee?" Barbara came into the den. Prothero thought she looked younger. Maybe it was the new way she'd had her hair done. "It will be half an hour till dinner."

"I'll have coffee." The Anderson boy set his boots in the tub. He came out in a very white sweater and very white gym socks. His blue jeans were damp from the snow. He lifted bottles off the liquor cabinet and waved them at Barbara while he looked at Prothero with eyes clear as water, empty of intent as water. "Don will have a stiff drink."

"I'll have coffee," Prothero said, "thanks."

The Anderson boy raised his eyebrows, shrugged, and set the bottles down. Barbara went away. The Anderson boy dropped into Prothero's leather easy chair, stretched out his long legs, clasped his hands behind his head, and said, "No, my major will be psychology."

"That's a contrast," Prothero said. "Why?"

"I had a strange childhood," the Anderson boy said. "My parents were murdered when I was five. But you knew that, right?"

Prothero knelt to set a match to crumpled newspaper and kindling in the fireplace. "Yes," he said.

"I didn't. Not till I was sixteen. My grandparents always claimed they'd been killed in a highway accident. Finally they thought I was old enough to be told what really happened. They were murdered. Somebody broke in at night. Into their bedroom. I was there—in the house, I mean. I must have heard it. Shouts. Screams. Gunshots. Only I blacked it all out."

"They said you went into shock." The kindling flared up. Prothero reached for a log and dropped it. His fingers had no strength. The Anderson boy jumped out of the chair, picked up the log, laid it on the fire. Sparks went up the chimney. He rattled the firescreen into place and brushed his hands.

"I stayed in shock," he said. "I couldn't remember it even after they told me. They showed me old snapshots—the house, my parents, myself. It still didn't mean anything. It was as if it was somebody else, not me."

"You wouldn't even talk." Prothero wanted not to have said that. He went to the liquor cabinet and poured himself a stiff drink. "It was on television. On the radio."

"Oh," Barbara said, coming in with mugs of coffee.

"I told you, didn't I?" the Anderson boy asked her.

"He's going to be a psychologist," Prothero said.

"I should think so," Barbara said, and took one of the mugs back to the kitchen with her.

The Anderson boy clutched the other one in both hands and blew steam off it. He was in the easy chair again. "I didn't utter a sound for weeks. Then they took me to a swim school. I was afraid of the water. I screamed. They had to call a doctor with a needle to make me stop."

Prothero blurted, "You could swim. I taught you."

The Anderson boy frowned. Cautiously he tried the coffee. He sucked in air with it, making a noise. He said, "Hey, that's true. Yeah, I remember now."

Prothero felt hollow. He drank. "Just like that?"

"Really. The pool—one of those little oval-shape ones. How the sun beat down out there—it made you squint." He closed his eyes. "I can see you. What were you then—seventeen? Bright-red swim trunks, no?"

Jean had given them to him. He'd been wearing floppy Hawaiian ones. The red ones were tight and skimpy. They'd made him shy but she teased him into wearing them. He felt her trembling hands on him now, peeling them off him in that glass-walled bedroom where the sun stung speckled through the loose weave of the curtains, and her son napped across the breezeway. Prothero finished his drink.

The Anderson boy said, "And there was a big striped beach ball. Yeah." He opened his eyes. "It's really fantastic, man. I mean, I can feel myself bobbing around in that water. I can taste the chlorine. And I won't go near a pool. They scare me to death."

"Every pool has chlorine and a beach ball." Prothero poured more whiskey on ice cubes that hadn't even begun to melt. "My trunks had to be some color."

"No, I swear, I remember. And that's why I came. When I saw you on TV, it began to happen. I began to remember—the house, the desert, my parents."

"The shouts?" Prothero asked numbly. "The screams? The gunshots?"

"Not that." The Anderson boy set down his mug. "I've read enough to know I'll probably never remember that." He pushed out of the chair and went to stand at the window. The light had gone murky. Only the snow fell white. "You can help me with the rest but you can't help me with that." He turned with a wan smile. "I mean, you weren't there. Were you?"

A shiny red moped stood under the thrust of roof above the front door. With the sunlight on the snow, it made the house look like a scene on Christmas morning. When the motor that let down the garage door stopped whining, Prothero heard the whine of a power saw from inside the house. The saw was missing from its hangers on the garage wall. He went indoors and smelled sawdust.

The Anderson boy was working in the den. He wasn't wearing a shirt. Barbara was watching him from the hall doorway. She smiled at Prothero. The noise of the saw was loud and she mouthed words to him and went off, probably to the kitchen. The Anderson boy switched off the saw, laid it on the carpet, rubbed a hand along the end of the eight-inch board he'd cut, and carried it to the paneled wall where pictures had hung this morning. He leaned it there with others of its kind and turned back and saw Prothero and smiled.

"Don't you ever have classes?" Prothero asked.

"I didn't get here in time to register," the Anderson boy said. "I'm auditing a little. I'll enroll for fall. He nudged one of the stacks of books on the floor. He was barefoot. "You need more shelves."

"I work in here, you know." The pictures were piled on the desk. He lifted one and laid it down. "I have lectures to prepare, papers to read, critiques to write."

"And books?" the Anderson boy said.

"No," Prothero said, "no more books."

"It was your book that led me to you," the Anderson boy said. "I owe a lot to that book."

Prothero looked at a photo of himself on a horse.

"I won't get in your way," the Anderson boy said. "I'll only be here when you're not." He looked over Prothero's shoulder "Hey, you took me riding once, held me in front of you on the saddle. Remember?"

Barbara called something from the kitchen.

"That's lunch," the Anderson boy said, and flapped into his shirt. "Come on. Grilled ham-and-cheese on Swedish rye." He went down the hall on his big clean bare feet. He called back over his shoulder, "Guess whose favorite that is."

In the dark, Prothero said, "I'm sorry."

"You're still exhausted from that wretched tour." Barbara kissed him tenderly, stroked his face. "It's all right, darling. Don't brood. You need rest, that's all." She slipped out of bed and in the snow-lit room there was the ghostly flutter of a white nightgown. She came to him and laid folded pajamas in his hands. They were soft and smelled of some laundry product. "Sleep and don't worry. Worry's the worst thing for it."

He sat up and got into the pajamas. Buttoning them, he stared at the vague shape of the window. He was listening for the sound of the moped. It seemed always to be arriving or departing. The bed moved as Barbara slipped into it again. He lay down beside her softness and warmth and stared up into the darkness.

She said, "It's what all the magazine articles say."

"Who paid for the shelving?" he asked.

"You did," she said. "Naturally."
He said, "It's you I'm worried about."
"I'll be all right," she said. "I'll be fine."

The sound of the moped woke him. The red numerals of the clock read 5:18. It would be the man delivering the newspaper. He went back to sleep. But when he went out in his robe and pajamas to pick up the newspaper, he walked to the garage door. The moped had sheltered there, the new one, the Anderson boy's—the marks of the tire treads were crisp in the snow. There were the tracks of boots. He followed them along the side of the house. At the corner he stopped. He was terribly cold. The tracks went out to and came back from one of the clumps of birches on the lawn. Prothero went there, snow leaking into his slippers, numbing his feet. The snow was trampled under the birches. He stood on the trampled snow and looked at the house. Up there was the bedroom window.

In the new University Medical Center, he spent three hours naked in a paper garment that kept slipping off one shoulder and did nothing to keep from him the cold of the plastic chairs on which he spent so much of the time waiting. They were the same chairs in all the shiny rooms, bright-colored, ruthlessly cheerful, hard and sterile like the walls, counters, cabinets, tables.

Needles fed from the veins in his arms. He urinated into rows of bottles. A bald man sat in front of him on a stool and handled his genitals while he gazed out the wide and staring tenth-floor window at the city under snow. The paper of his garment whispered to and mated with the paper on the examination table while his rectum was probed with indifferent ferocity. The X-ray table was high and hard, a steel catafalque. He feared the blocky baby-blue machine above it would snap the thick armatures that held it and drop it on him. The nurse need not have asked him to lie rigid. When he breathed in at her request, the sterilized air hissed at his clenched teeth. They told him there was nothing wrong with him.

"Do you remember the rattlesnake?" the Anderson boy asked. He had cut channels in the uprights and fitted the shelves into them. The workmanship was neat. Horizontals and verticals were perfect. He was staining the shelves dark walnut to match the others already in the den. The stain had a peculiar smell. Prothero thought it was hateful. The big blond boy squatted to tilt up the can of stain and soak the rag he was using. "We were always out there taking hikes, weren't we? And one day there was this little fat snake."

"Sidewinder," Prothero said. "I thought you weren't going to be here when I was here."

"Sorry," the Anderson boy said. "I loused up the timing on this. Can't stop it in the middle. I'll be as fast about it as I can." He stood up and made the white of the raw fir plank vanish in darkness. "If you want to work, let me finish this half and I'll clear out."

"I was trying to teach you the names of the wildflowers. It would have been February. That's when they come out. Sidewinders don't grow big."

"It's a rattlesnake, though. Poisonous. I mean, you let me handle a non-poisonous snake once. I can still feel how dry it was. Yellow and brown."

"Boyle's king snake." Prothero took off his coat.

"You remember what you did?" the Anderson boy said.

"About the sidewinder?" Prothero poured a drink.

"Caught it. Pinned it down with a forked stick back of its head. It was mad. It thrashed around. I can shut my eyes and see that. Like a film."

"I didn't want it sliding around with you out there. You could stumble on it again. If I'd been alone or with grownups I'd have just waited for it to go away."

The Anderson boy knelt again to soak the rag. "You had me empty your knapsack. You got it behind the head with your fist and dropped it in the sack. We took it to the little desert museum in town."

"There was nothing else to do," Prothero said.

"You could have killed it," the Anderson boy said.

"I can't kill anything," Prothero said.

"That's no longer accepted," the Anderson boy said. "Anybody can kill. We know that now. It just depends on the circumstances."

Kessler was on the University faculty, but he had a private practice. His office, in a new one-story medical center built around an atrium, smelled of leather. It was paneled in dark woods. A Monet hung on one wall. Outside a window of diamond-shaped panes, pine branches held snow. From beyond a broad, glossy desk, Kessler studied Prothero with large, pained eyes in the face of a starved child.

"Has it ever happened to you before? I don't mean isolated instances—every man has those—I mean for prolonged periods, months, years."

"From the summer I turned eighteen until nearly the end of my senior year in college."

Kessler's eyebrows moved. "Those are normally the years of permanent erection. What happened?"

"I was having a crazy affair with, well, an older woman. In my home town. Older? What am I saying? She was probably about the age I am now."

"Married?" Kessler asked.

"Her husband traveled all the time."

"Except that once, when you thought he was traveling, he wasn't—right?"

"He caught us," Prothero said. "In bed together."

"Did you have a lot of girls before her?"

"None. Sexually, you mean? None."

There were *netsuke* on the desk, little ivory carvings of deer, monkeys, dwarfish humans. Prothero thought that if it were his desk he'd be fingering them while he listened, while he talked. Kessler sat still. He said:

"Then she did the seducing, right?"

"We were on a charity fund-raising committee." Prothero made a face. "I mean, I was a token member, the high-school's fair-haired boy. The rest were adults. She kept arranging for her and me to work together."

"And after her husband caught you, you were impotent?"

"For a long while I didn't know it. I didn't care. I didn't want to think about sex." He smiled thinly. "To put it in today's parlance—I was turned off."

"Did the man beat you? Did he beat her?"

Prothero asked, "Why has it started again?"

"It's never happened in your married life?"

Prothero shook his head.

"How did you come to marry your wife? Let me guess—she was the seducer, right?"

"That's quite a word," Prothero said.

"Never mind the word," Kessler said. "You know what I mean. The aggressor, sexually. She took the initiative, she made the advances." His smile reminded Prothero of the high suicide rate among psychiatrists. Kessler said, "What do you want from me?"

"Yes," Prothero said. "She was the seducer."

"Has she lost interest in you sexually?"

"There's nothing to be interested in," Prothero said.

"Do you get letters from the woman?"

"What woman? Oh. No. No, she's—she's dead."

"On this book-promotion tour of yours," Kessler said, "did you see the man somewhere?"

Prothero said, "I wonder if I could have a drink."

"Certainly." Kessler opened a cabinet under the Monet. Bottles glinted. He poured fingers of whiskey into squat glasses and handed one to Prothero. "Been drinking more than usual over this?"

Prothero nodded and swallowed the whiskey. It was expensive and strong. He thought that in a minute it would make him stop trembling. "They had a child," he said, "a little boy. I liked him. We spent a lot of time together. Lately, he saw me on television. And now he's here."

Kessler didn't drink. He held his glass. "What's your sexual drive like?" he asked. "How often do you and your wife have sexual relations?"

"Four times a week, five." Prothero stood up, looking at the cabinet. "Did."

"Help yourself," Kessler said. "How old is he?"

The trembling hadn't stopped. The bottle neck rattled on the glass. "Eighteen, I suppose. With his father away most of the time, he took to me."

"Does he look like his father?"

"It's not just that." Prothero drank. "He keeps hanging around. He's always at the house." He told Kessler about the footbridge, about the bookshelves. "But there's more. Now he comes at night on that damn motor bike and stands in the dark, staring up at our bedroom. While we're asleep."

"Maybe he's homosexual," Kessler said.

"No." Prothero poured whiskey into his glass again.

"How can you be sure?" Kessler gently took the bottle from him, capped it, set it back in place, and closed the cabinet. "It fits a common pattern."

"He's too easy with women—Barbara, anyway, my wife." Prothero stared gloomily into his whiskey. "Like it was her he'd known forever. They've even developed private jokes."

"Why not just tell him to go away?" Kessler asked.

"How can I?" Prothero swallowed the third drink. "What excuse can I give? I mean, he keeps doing me these kindnesses." Kessler didn't answer. He waited. Prothero felt his face grow hot. "Well, hell, I told him to keep out from under my feet. So what happens? He's there all the time I'm not. He's got changes of clothes in my closet. His shaving stuff is there. My bathroom stinks of his deodorant."

Kessler said. "Are they sleeping together?"

"Barbara and that child?"

"Why so appalled?" Kessler said mildly. "Weren't you a child when you slept with his mother?"

Prothero stood up.

"Don't go away mad," Kessler said, "You're going to get a bill for this visit, so you may as well listen to me. You're afraid of this boy. Now, why? Because he looks like his father—right? So what happened in that bedroom?"

"That was a long time ago." Prothero read his watch.

"Not so long ago it can't still make you impotent," Kessler said. "Thirty years old, perfect health, better than average sexual drive. It wasn't a beating, was it? It was something worse."

"It was embarrassing," Prothero said. "It was comic. Isn't that what those scenes always are? Funny?"

"You tell me," Kessler said.

Prothero set down the glass. "I have to go," he said.

When he stepped into the courtyard with its big Japanese pine, the Anderson boy was walking ahead of him out to the street. Prothero ran after him, caught his shoulder, turned him. "What are you doing here? Following me?"

The boy blinked, started to smile, then didn't. "I dropped a paper off on Dr. Lawrence. I've been sitting in on his lectures. He said he'd like to read what I've written about my case—the memory-loss."

Prothero drew breath. "Do you want a cup of coffee?"

"Why would you think I was following you?" The Anderson boy frowned at the hollow square of offices, the doors lettered with the names of specialists. "Are you feeling okay?"

"Nothing serious." Prothero smiled and clapped the boy's shoulder. "Come on. Coffee will warm us up."

"I have to get home. My grandparents will be phoning from California." He eyed the icy street. "I sure do miss that sunshine." His red moped was at the curb. He straddled it. Prothero couldn't seem to move. The boy called, "The shelves are finished. I'm going to lay down insulation in your attic next." He began to move off, rowing with his feet in clumsy boots. "You're losing expensive heat, wasting energy." The moped sputtered. If Prothero had been able to answer, he wouldn't have been heard. The Anderson boy lifted a goodbye hand, and the little machine wobbled off with him.

Prothero ran to his car and followed. The boy drove to the edge of town away from the campus and turned in at an old motel, blue paint flaking off white stucco. Prothero circled the block and drove into an abandoned filling station opposite. The boy was awkwardly pushing the moped into a unit of the motel. The door closed. On it was the number nine. Prothero checked his watch and waited. It grew cold in the car, but it was past noon. The boy liked his meals. He would come out in search of food. He did. He drove off on the moped.

The woman behind the motel office counter was heavy-breasted, middle-aged, wore rimless glasses, and reminded Prothero of his own mother. He showed the woman his University I.D. and said that an emergency had arisen: he needed to get from Wayne Anderson's room telephone numbers for his family on the West Coast. The woman got a key and moved to come with him. But a gray, rumpled-faced man in a gray, rumpled suit arrived, wanting a room, and she put into Prothero's hand the key to unit nine.

It needed new wallpaper, carpet, and curtains, but the boy kept it neat. Except for the desk. The desk was strewn with notebook pages, scrawled with loose handwriting in ballpoint pen, with type-written pages, with Xerox copies of newspaper clippings.

Dry-mouthed, he went through the clippings. They all reported the shootings and the aftermath of the shootings. The Anderson boy's mother had lain naked in the bed. The man had lain clothed on the floor beside the bed, gun in his hand. Both shot dead. The child had wandered dazedly in and out of the desert house in sleepers, clutching a stuffed toy kangaroo and unable to speak. Prothero shivered and pushed the clippings into a manila envelope on which the boy had printed CLIPPINGS. He picked up the notebook pages and tried to read. It wasn't clear to him what the boy had tried to do here. Events were broken down under headings with numbers and letters. It looked intricate and mad.

Prothero tried the typewritten pages. Neater, easier to read, they still seemed to go over and over the same obsessive points. No page was complete. These must be drafts of the pages the boy had taken to Dr. Lawrence. A red-plastic wastebasket overflowed with crumpled pages. He took some of these out, flattened them, tried to read them, looking again and again at his watch. For an instant, the room darkened. He looked in alarm at the window. The woman from the motel office passed. Not the boy. Prothero would hear the moped. Anyway, he had plenty of time. But the crumpled pages told him nothing. He pushed them back into the wastebasket. Then he noticed the page sticking out of the typewriter. It read:

Don Prothero seems to have been a good friend to me, even though he was much older. My interviews with him have revealed that we spent much time together. He taught me to swim, though I afterward forgot how. He took me on nature walks in the desert, which I also had forgotten until meeting him again. He bought me gifts. The shock of my parents' death made me forget what I witnessed that night—if I witnessed anything. But why didn't Don come to see me or try to help me when he learned what had happened? He admits he didn't. And this isn't consistent with his previous behavior. My grandmother says he didn't attend the funeral. A friendship between a small boy and a teenage boy is uncommon. Perhaps there never was such a friendship. Maybe it wasn't me Don came to see at all. Maybe he came—

Prothero turned the typewriter platen, but the rest of the page was blank. He laid the key with a clatter on the motel-office counter, muttered thanks to the woman, and fled. His hands shook and were slippery with sweat as he drove. He had a lecture at two. How he would manage to deliver it, he didn't know, but he drove to the campus. Habit got him there. Habit would get him through the lecture.

Barbara's car was in the garage. He parked beside it, closed the garage, went into the den, poured a drink, and called her name. He wondered at the stillness of the house. Snow began to fall outside.

"Barbara?" He searched for her downstairs. Nowhere. She was never away at this hour. She would have left a note. In the kitchen. Why, when she was gone, did the kitchen always seem the emptiest of rooms? He peered at the cross-stitched flowers of the bulletin board by the kitchen door. There was no note. He frowned. He used the yellow kitchen wall-phone. Cora answered, sounding perky.

He said, "Are you all right? Is Barbara there?"

"I'm fine. No—did she say she was coming here?"

"I thought there might have been an emergency."

"No emergency, Don. Every day, in every way, I'm—"

"I wonder where the hell she is," he said and hung up. Of course she wouldn't have been at her mother's. Her car was still here, and Cora wouldn't have picked her up—Cora no longer drove.

Had Barbara been taken ill herself? He ran up the stairs. She wasn't in the bathroom. She wasn't in the bedroom. What was in the bedroom was a toy kangaroo. The bedclothes were neatly folded back and the toy kangaroo sat propped against a pillow, looking at him with empty glass eyes. Its gray cloth was soiled and faded, its stitching had come loose, one of the eyes hung by a thread. But it was the same one. He would know it anywhere. As he had known the boy.

He set the drink on the dresser and rolled open the closet. It echoed hollowly. Her clothes were gone. A set of matched luggage she had bought for their trip to Europe two years ago had stood on the shelf above. It didn't stand there now. Involuntarily, he sat on the bed. "But it wasn't my fault," he said. He fumbled with the bedside phone, whimpering, "It wasn't my fault, it wasn't my fault." From directory assistance he got the number of the motel. He had to dial twice before he got it right.

The motherly woman said, "He checked out. When I told him you'd been here, going through his papers, he packed up, paid his bill, asked where the nearest place was he could rent a car, and cleared right off."

"Car?" Prothero felt stupid. "What about his moped?"

"He asked me to hold it. He'll arrange for a college friend to sell it for him—some boy. Goldberg?"

"Where's the nearest place to rent a car?"

"Econo. On Locust Street. It's only two blocks."

The directory-assistance operator didn't answer this time. Prothero ran down to the den. He used the phonebook. The snow fell thicker outside the glass doors. He longed for it to cover the footbridge. Econo Car Rentals was slow in answering, too. And when at last a dim female voice came on, he could not get it to tell him what he wanted to know.

"This is the college calling, don't you understand? He wasn't supposed to leave. His family are going to be very upset. There's been a little confusion, that's all. He can't be allowed to go off this way. Now, please—"

A man spoke. "What's this about Wayne Anderson?"

"He's just a student," Prothero said. "Do you realize he'll take that car clear out to California?"

"That information goes on the form. Routinely," the man said. "Are you a relative of this Wayne Anderson?"

"Ah," Prothero said, "you did rent him a car, then?"

"I never said that. I can't give out that kind of information. On the phone? What kind of company policy would that be?"

"If this turns out to be a kidnaping," Prothero said recklessly, "your company policy is going to get you into a lot of trouble. Now—what kind of car was it? What's the license number?"

"If it's a kidnaping," the man said, "the people to call are the police." His mouth left the phone. In an echoing room, he said to somebody, "It's some stupid college-kid joker. Hang it up." And the phone hummed in Prothero's hand.

He was backing the car down the driveway when Helen Moore's new blue Subaru hatchback pulled into the driveway next door. He stopped and honked. She stopped, too. The door of her garage opened. She didn't drive in. She got out of the car, wearing boots and a Russian fur hat. Before she closed the door behind her, Prothero glimpsed supermarket sacks on the seat. With a gloved hand, she held the dark fur collar of her coat closed at the throat. The door of her garage closed again. She came toward the snow-covered hedge. Snowflakes were on her lashes. "Something wrong?"

"I'm missing one wife. Any suggestions?"

"Are you serious?" She tilted her head, worry lines between her brows. "You are. Don, dear—she left for the airport." Helen struggled to read her wristwatch, muffled in a fur coat cuff, the fur lining of a glove. "Oh, when? An hour ago? You mean you didn't know? What have we here? Scandal in academe?"

Prothero felt his face redden. "No, no, of course not. I forgot, that's all. Wayne Anderson came for her, right?"

"Yes. Brought her luggage out, put it in the trunk. Nice boy, that."

Prothero felt sick. "Did you talk with Barbara?"

"She looked preoccupied. She was already in the car." She winced upward. "Can they really fly in this weather?"

"There'll be a delay," Prothero said. "So maybe I can catch them. She's taking this trip for me. There are things I forgot to tell her. Did you notice the car?"

"Japanese. Like mine. Darling, I'm freezing." She hurried back to the Subaru and opened the door. "Only not blue, of course—I've got an exclusive on blue." Her voice came back to him, cheerful as a child's at play in the falling snow. "White. White as a bridal gown." She got into the car and slammed the door. Her garage yawned again, and she drove inside.

Defroster and windshield wipers were no match for the snow. The snowplows hadn't got out here yet. He hadn't put on chains, and the car kept slurring. So did others. Not many. Few drivers had been fool-hardy enough to venture out of town. Those who had must have had life or death reasons. But life and death were no match for the snow, either. Their cars rested at angles in ditches, nosed in, backed in. The snow was so dense in its falling that it made blurs of the drivers' bundled shapes. They moved about their stranded machines like discoverers from some future ice age come upon the wreckage of our own.

A giant eighteen-wheeler loomed through the whiteness. Prothero was on the wrong side of the road. He hadn't realized this. The truck came directly at him. He twisted the wheel, slammed down on the brake pedal. The car spun out of control—but also out of the path of the truck. He ended up, joltingly, against the trunk of a winter-stripped tree. He tried for a while to make the car back up, but the wheels only spun.

He turned off the engine and leaned on the horn. Its sound was frail in the falling snow. He doubted anyone would hear it up on the empty road. And if the crews didn't find him before dark they would stop searching. By morning, when they came out again, he might be frozen to death. There was a heater in the car, but it wouldn't run forever. He left the car, waded up to the road. He saw nothing—not the road itself, now, let alone a car, a human being. He shouted, but the thickly falling

snow seemed to swallow up the sound. It was too far to try to walk
back to town. Too cold. No visibility. He returned to the car. If he
froze to death, did he care?

They found him before dark and delivered him, though not his car,
back home. For a long time he sat dumbly in the den, staring at his
reflection in the glass doors. Night fell. The doors became black mirrors.
He switched on the desk lamp, reached for the telephone, drew his
hand back. He couldn't call the police. Not now, any more than on
that desert night twelve years ago. He got up and poured himself a
drink. And remembered Goldberg. He got Goldberg's telephone number
from Admissions, rang it, left a message. He sat drinking, waiting for
Goldberg to call. *Barbara*, he kept thinking, *Barbara*.

He heard the Anderson boy's moped. He had been asleep and the
sound confused him. He got up stiffly and stumbled to the front door.
The snow had stopped falling. The crystalline look of the night made
him think it must be late. He read his watch. Eleven. He'd slept, all
right. Even the snowplow passing hadn't wakened him. The street, in
its spaced circles of lamplight, was cleared. He switched on the front
door lamp. Goldberg came wading up the walk in a bulky windbreaker
with a fake-fur hood, his round, steel-rimmed glasses frosted over. He
took them off when he stepped into the house. He had a round, innocent, freckled face. Prothero shut the door.

"Why didn't you phone?" he said.

The boy cast him a wretched purblind look and shook his head. "I
couldn't tell you like that."

"Where is Anderson? Where did he tell you to send the money when
you sold his moped?"

"Home. San Diego," Goldberg said. "Is that whiskey? Could I have
some, please? I'm frozen stiff."

"Here," Prothero thrust out the glass. Goldberg pulled off a tattered
driving glove and took the glass. His teeth chattered on the rim. Prothero said, "What was his reason for leaving? Did he tell you?"

Miserably, Goldberg nodded. He gulped the whiskey, shut his eyes,
shuddered. "Oh, God," he said softly, and rubbed the fragile-looking
spectacles awkwardly on a jacket sleeve, and hooked them in place. He
looked at the door, the floor, the staircase—everywhere but at Prothero.
Then he gulped the rest of the whiskey and blurted, "He ran off with

your wife. Didn't he? I laughed when he said it, but it's true, isn't it? That's why you phoned me."

Prothero said, "My wife is in Mankato. Celebrating the birthday of an ancient aunt. I called you because I'm worried about Anderson."

"Oh, wow. What a relief." Goldberg's face cleared of its worry and guilt. "I knew he was a flake. I mean—I'm sorry, sir, but I mean, a little weird, right? I was a wimp to believe him. Forgive me?"

"Anything's possible," Prothero said.

"He really sold me." Goldberg set the empty whiskey glass on one of a pair of little gilt Venetian chairs beside the door. "See, I said if he did it I'd have to tell you. And he said I didn't need to bother—you'd already know." Goldberg pushed the freckled fat hand into its glove again. His child's face pursed in puzzlement. "That was kinky enough, but then he said something really spacey, okay? He said you wouldn't do anything about it. You wouldn't dare. What did he mean by that?"

"Some complicated private fantasy. Don't worry about it." Prothero opened the door, laid a hand on the boy's shoulder. "As you say, he's a little weird. Disturbed. And my wife's been kind to him."

"Right. He had a traumatic childhood. His parents were murdered. He told you, right?" Goldberg stepped out onto the snowy doorstep. "He said he liked coming here." Halfway down the path, Goldberg turned back. "You know, I read your book. It helped me. I mean, this is a killer world. Sometimes you don't think there's any future for it. Your book made me feel better." And he trudged bulkily away through the snow toward the moped that twinkled dimly in the lamplight at the curb.

Prothero shut the door and the telephone rang. He ran for the den, snatched up the receiver, shouted hello. For a moment, the sounds from the other end of the wire made no sense. Had some drunk at a party dialed a wrong number? No. He recognized Barbara's voice.

"Don't come!" she shouted. "Don't come, Don!"

And the Anderson boy's voice. "Apple Creek," he said. "You know where that is? The Restwell Motel." Prothero knew where Apple Creek was. West and south, maybe a hundred miles—surely no more. Why had he stopped there? The snow? But the roads would have been cleared by now. "We'll expect you in two hours."

"Let her go, Wayne. She had nothing to do with it."

"She has now. Don't worry. She's all right."

She didn't sound all right. In the background, she was screaming. Most of her words got lost. But some Prothero was able to make out. "He's got a gun! Don't come, Don! He'll kill you if you come!"

"I'll be there, Wayne," Prothero said. "We'll talk. You've got it wrong. I'll explain everything. Don't hurt Barbara. She was always good to you."

"Not the way my mother was good to you."

Prothero felt cold. "You keep your hands off her."

"We're going to bed now, Don," the Anderson boy said. "But it's all right. You just knock when you get here. Room eighteen. We won't be sleeping."

"Don't do this!" Prothero shouted. "It was an accident, Wayne—I didn't kill them! I was only a kid!"

But the Anderson boy had hung up.

The keys to Barbara's car ordinarily hung from a cup hook on the underside of a kitchen cupboard, but they weren't there now. He ran upstairs. He was the professor, but she was the absent-minded one in the family. She sometimes locked the keys inside her car—so she kept an extra set of keys. He fumbled through drawers with shaking hands, tossing flimsy garments out onto the floor in his panic.

He found the keys, started out of the bedroom, and saw the tattered toy kangaroo staring at him from the bed with its lopsided glass eyes that had seen everything. He snatched it up and flung it into a corner. He ran to it and drew back his foot to kick it. Instead, he dropped to his knees, picked it up, and hugged it hard against his chest and began to cry, inconsolably. *Dear God, dear God!*

Blind with tears, he stumbled from the room, down the stairs, blundered into his warm coat, burst into the garage. When he backed down the drive, the car hard to control in the snow, twice wheeling stupidly backward into the hedge, the kangaroo lay face down on the seat beside him.

He passed the town square where the old courthouse loomed up dark beyond its tall, reaching, leafless trees, the cannon on the snow-covered lawn hunching like some shadow beast in a child's nightmare. No—the building wasn't entirely dark. Lights shone beyond windows at a corner where narrow stone steps went up to glass-paned doors gold-lettered POLICE. He halted the car at the night-empty intersection and stared long at those doors—as he had sat in his car, staring at the sunny desert police station on that long-ago morning. *I was only a kid!* He gave a shudder, wiped his nose on his sleeve, and drove on.

The little towns were out there in the frozen night that curved over the snowy miles and miles of sleeping prairie, curved like a black ice dome in which the stars were frozen. Only the neon embroidery on their margins showed that the towns were there. At their hearts they were darkly asleep, except for here and there a streetlight, now and then a traffic signal winking orange. He had never felt so lonely in his life. He drove fast. The reflector signs bearing the names of the little lost towns went past in flickers too brief to read.

But there was no mistaking Apple Creek, no mistaking that this was the place he had headed for in the icy night, the end of his errand, the end of Don Prothero, the end so long postponed. The Restwell Motel stretched along the side of the highway behind a neat white rail fence and snow-covered shrubs, the eaves of its snow-heaped roof outlined in red neon tubing.

And on its blacktop drive, not parked neatly on the bias in the painted slots provided by the management but jammed in at random angles, stood cars with official seals on their doors and amber lights that winked and swiveled on their rooftops. Uniformed men in bulky leather coats, crash helmets, stetsons, and boots stood around, guns on their thighs in holsters, rifles in their gloved hands.

Prothero left his car and ran toward the men. The one he chose to speak to had a paunch. His face was red under a ten-gallon hat. He was holding brown sheepskin gauntlets over his ears. He lowered them when he saw Prothero, but his expression was not welcoming.

Prothero asked, "What's happening here?"

"You want a room? Ask in the office." The officer pointed at a faroff door, red neon spelling out OFFICE. But at that instant a clutch of officers on the far side of the bunched cars moved apart and Prothero saw another door, the door they all seemed interested in. Without needing to, he read the numbers on the door. 18.

"My wife's in there!" he said.

The heavy man had turned away, hands to his cold ears again. But the brown wool hadn't deafened him. He turned back, saying, "What!" It was not a question.

"Barbara Prothero." He dug out his wallet to show identification cards. "I'm Donald Prothero."

"Hasenbein!" It was a name. The bulky man shouted it. "Hasenbein!" And Hasenbein separated himself from the other officers. He was at least twenty years younger than the bulky man. "This here's Lieutenant Hasenbein. You better tell him. He's in charge."

Hasenbein, blue-eyed, rosy-cheeked, looked too young to be in charge of anything. Prothero told him what seemed safe to tell. "He became a friend. He's disturbed."

"You better believe it," Hasenbein said. He dug from a jacket pocket a small black-and-white tube, uncapped it, rubbed it on his mouth like lipstick. "See that broken window?" He capped the tube and pushed it back into the pocket. "He fired a gun through that window." Hasenbein studied him. "Why did he stop here? Why did he telephone you? What does he want? Money?"

"There's something wrong with his mind," Prothero said. "He's got it into his head that I harmed him. He's trying to avenge himself. He phoned to tell me to come here. No, he doesn't want money. I don't know what he wants. To kill me, I guess. What brought you here?"

"The manager. He came out to turn off the signs. The switch box is down at this end. And he heard this woman screaming in unit eighteen—your wife, right? He banged on the window and told them to quiet down or he'd call the Sheriff. And the kid shot at him. Luckily, he missed."

Prothero's knees gave. Hasenbein steadied him. "Is my wife all right?"

"There was only the one shot."

"There are so many of you," Prothero said. "Can't you go in there and get her out?" He waved his arms. "What's the good of standing around like this?"

"It's a question of nobody getting hurt needlessly."

"Needlessly! He could be doing anything in there—he could be doing anything to her!" Hasenbein didn't respond. He was too young. He was in way over his head.

Prothero ran forward between the cars. "Barbara!" he shouted. "Barbara? It's Don. I'm here! Wayne? Wayne!" Two officers jumped him, held his arms. He struggled, shouting at the broken window, "Let her go, now! I'll come in and we'll talk—I said I'd come, and I came!"

No light showed beyond the broken window, but in the eerie, darting beams of the amber lights atop the patrol cars Prothero saw for a moment what he took to be a face peering out. The Anderson boy said, "Tell them to let you go." Prothero looked at the officers holding him. They didn't loosen their grip on his arms. Hasenbein appeared. He twitched the corners of his boyish mouth in what was meant for a reassuring smile and turned away.

"Anderson?" he shouted, "we can't do that! We can't let him come in there—we can't take a chance on what will happen to him! Why don't you calm down now, and just toss that gun out here and come out the door nice and quiet with your hands in the air? We're not going to hurt you—that's a promise! It's a cold night, Anderson, let's get this over with!"

"Where's Barbara?" Prothero shouted. "What have you done with her? If you've hurt her, I'll kill you!"

"Sure!" the Anderson boy shouted. Now his face was plain to see at the window. Prothero wondered why nobody shot him. "You killed my father and my mother, why not me? Why not finish off the whole family? Why didn't you kill *me* that night? Then there wouldn't have been any witnesses!"

"I didn't kill them!" Prothero gave his body a sudden twist. It surprised the men holding him. It surprised him too. He fell forward. The cold blacktop stung his hands. He scrambled to his feet and lunged at the broken window. He put his hands on the window frame and leaned into the dark room.

"Your father came in from the breezeway—he was supposed to be out of town." Prothero heard his own voice as if it were someone else's voice. He had cut his hands on the splinters of glass in the window frame and could feel the warm blood. "He had a gun, and he stood there in the doorway and shot at us." Prothero wondered why the boy didn't shoot him now. He wondered what had happened to the officers. But the words kept coming.

"It was dark, but he knew where to shoot. I heard the bullet hit her. I've heard it in my nightmares for years. I rolled off the bed. He came at me, and I kicked him. He bent over and I tried to get past him, but he grabbed me. I fought to get away and the gun went off. You hear me, Wayne? He had the gun—not me. He shot himself! His blood got all over me, but I didn't kill him, I didn't kill him, I—"

"All right, sir." Hasenbein spoke almost tenderly. He took Prothero gently and turned him. He frowned at Prothero's hands and swung toward the officers standing by the cars, the vapor of their breath gold in the flickering lights. "We need a first-aid kit here." Hasenbein bent slightly toward the window. "Okay, Thomas—you can bring him out now."

"My wife," Prothero said. "Where's my wife?"

"Down at the substation where it's warm," Hasenbein said. "She's all right."

A frail-looking officer with a mustache brought a white metal box with a red cross pasted to it. He knelt on the drive and opened the box.

Carefully, he took Prothero's bleeding hands. Prothero scarcely noticed. He stared at the door of unit eighteen. It opened and a police officer stepped out, followed by the Anderson boy in his shapeless Army fatigues and combat boots. He was handcuffed. Under his arm, a worn manila envelope trailed untidy strips of Xeroxed newspaper clippings. He looked peacefully at Prothero.

"What did you do to Barbara?" Prothero said.

"Nothing. You put her through this—not me. You could have told me any time." With his big, clean, carpenter's hands made awkward by the manacles, he gestured at the officers and cars. "Look at all the trouble you caused."